Night of the Dark Dragons

"Turn back! Turn back! It's no use. It's death for you all up there. They're woken up now in the tower, and you'll just make Them angry if you go there."

"*Them?*" called Jim. "You mean the Dark Powers?"

"Them—Them!" wailed the mere-dragon despairingly. "Them that built and live in the Loathly Tower, that sent the blight on us five hundred years ago. Can't you feel Them waiting for you? They that never die, they who hate us all. They who draw to Them all terrible evil things."

Jim knew the mere-dragon spoke the truth, but there was no turning back. Angie was in the Loathly Tower—and somehow, some way, though it might cost more lives than his own, he would set her free . . .

Also by Gordon R. Dickson
now available from Ballantine Books:

MISSION TO UNIVERSE

THE
Dragon
AND THE
George

Gordon R. Dickson

A Del Rey Book

BALLANTINE BOOKS • NEW YORK

A Del Rey Book
Published by Ballantine Books

Library of Congress Catalog Card Number: 76-18074

ISBN 0-345-27201-3

Manufactured in the United States of America

Book Club Edition: July 1976

First Printing: October 1976
Fifth Printing: January 1980

First Canadian Printing: November 1976

Cover art by Boris Vallejo

Thys boke ys for
Bela of Eastmarch,
Who hath in hys own time
known a dragon or two

Chapter 1

At 10:30 a.m., sharp, James Eckert pulled up in front of Stoddard Hall on the Riveroak College campus, where Grottwold Weinar Hansen had his lab. Angie Farrell was not, however, ready and waiting at the curb. Of course.

It was a warm, bright September morning.

Jim sat in the car and tried to keep his temper under control. It would not be Angie's fault. That idiot of a Grottwold undoubtedly had dreamed up something to keep her working overtime in spite of—or perhaps because of—the fact he knew she and Jim were supposed to go home-hunting this morning. It was hard not to lose his temper with someone like Grottwold, who was not only one of the world's nonprizes but who had been very patently trying to take Angie away from Jim and get her for himself.

One of the two big doors on the front of the Stoddard Hall opened and a figure came out. But it was not Angie. It was a stocky young man with bushy reddish hair and mustache, carrying an overstuffed briefcase. Seeing Jim in the car, he came down the steps over to the car and leaned on the edge of the opened window on the curb side of the front seat.

"Waiting for Angie?" he asked.

"That's right, Danny," said Jim. "She was supposed to be out here to meet me, but evidently Grottwold's still hanging on to her."

"That's his style." Danny Cerdak was a teaching assistant in the Physics Department. He was the only other Class AA volleyball player on campus. "You're going out to see Cheryl's trailer?"

1

"If Angie ever gets loose in time," said Jim.

"Oh, she'll probably be along any second now. Say, do the two of you want to drop over to my place after we play tomorrow night? Nothing special, just pizza and beer and a few other people from the team with their wives and so forth."

"Sounds fine," said Jim, glumly, "if I'm not stuck with some extra work for Shorles. Thanks, in any case, though; and we'll certainly be there if we can make it."

"Right." Danny straightened up. "See you tomorrow for the game, then."

He went off. Jim returned to his own thoughts.

At the same time, he told himself, maturity dictated that he should not lose his emotional control over something like this—even though they only had two hours to get to the trailer court and return and have lunch before getting Angie back to her part-time job as Grottwold's lab assistant. He must remember that frustration was a part of life. He had to learn to live with the whole business of selfish department heads, inadequate salaries and an economy that was pinching Riveroak College here, like all other educational institutions, to the point where it seemed that about all you could do with a doctorate in medieval history was use the diploma to shine your shoes, before going to apply for a job as a grain shoveler—

Jim hauled himself up in his thoughts at this point, having noticed that, far from calming him down, this rehearsing of things to be endured had his fists white-knuckled and beginning to bend the ancient steering wheel of the Gorp. Nothing about the Gorp was strong enough to ignore that kind of treatment. For a ten-year-old Fiat, it was still a faithful little car, but no honest person could call it in good shape. On the other hand, Jim himself—like many Class AA volleyball players—was in shape with a vengeance. He stood a shade under six feet, but even professional weight-guessers usually underestimated by twenty or more his two hundred and ten pounds, which he carried mostly in bone and hard muscle. Unfortunately, that sort of physical engine, matched with an instinct for taking direct action when challenged—which was useful on the volleyball courts with the caliber of opponents Jim had been facing in tournament play for some years now, but not perhaps the best thing socially—gave Jim reason to consider that he had cause for concern about himself.

Thank heaven for Angie. The beautiful thing about her was that she could get results from people without becoming at all annoyed with them, in situations when Jim would have sworn that the other persons were deliberately looking for a fight. How she managed it, Jim had never been able to figure out. As far as he could see, all she did was to explain matters in a level, friendly voice. Whereupon, for some reason, the other people immediately stopped doing whatever they had been doing that was antagonistic and became friendly and helpful. Angie was really rather special; particularly for someone hardly bigger than a minute. Look at the way she handled Grottwold . . .

Jim woke to the fact that time had been sliding away as he had been sitting here thinking. He looked at his watch and scowled. Nearly a quarter to eleven. This was too much. If Grottwold didn't have the sense to let her go, Angie herself ought to have broken away by this time.

He pushed open the car door on his side, and was just getting out, when one of the two big front doors swung open again and Angie came running down the steps to the car, pulling on her light beige topcoat as she ran. Her brown eyes were bright and her cheeks pink with her hurry.

"Oh, there you are," said Jim, getting back in.

"I'm sorry." Angie got into the Gorp on her side and slammed the door behind her. "Grottwold's all excited. He thinks he's right on the verge of proving astral projection is possible—"

"Whichjection?"

Jim keyed the Gorp to life and pulled away from the curb.

"Astral projection. Setting the spirit free to wander

3

outside the body. What with the results he's been getting using advanced input on biofeedback circuitry to duplicate certain forms of sleep states—"

"You aren't letting him experiment on you, are you? I thought we got that settled."

"Don't get all worked up, now," Angie said. "I'm not letting him experiment *on* me, I'm helping him with his experiments. Don't worry, he's not going to hypnotize me, or anything like that."

"He tried it once."

Jim pulled the Gorp out of the college grounds onto West Street and turned down on the ramp leading to Highway Five.

"He only tried. *You* were the one who hypnotized me, if you'll remember—after Grottwold taught you how."

"Anyway, you're not to let anyone hypnotize you again. Me or Hansen, or anybody."

"Of course," said Angie, softly.

There she went, doing it again—just what he had been thinking about, Jim told himself. Now *he* was the one she'd just handled. All of a sudden there was no more argument and he was wondering what he had gotten excited about in the first place. He was also feeling half guilty for making a fuss over something that probably had not been that important to begin with.

"Anyway," he said, heading out along Highway Five toward the trailer court Danny Cerdak had told him about, "if this trailer for rent turns out to be the deal Danny said it was, we can get married and maybe, living together, we can get by cheaply enough so you won't have to work for Grottwold as well as holding down your assistantship in English."

"Jim," said Angie, "you know better."

"We could."

"We could not. The only reason the co-op can get by charging us a hundred twenty apiece per month for food and board is that it makes slop food in quantity and beds us all down in double-decker bunks in dormitories. Any place we find for ourselves is going to

4

put our living costs up, not down. I can't manage meals for us as cheaply as the co-op can. No, I can't quit my work with Grottwold. But at least having a place of our own will make it seem worth while to go on. We've got to have a place of our own—but let's not fool ourselves about the expense."

"We could sort of camp out in the new place, the first few months."

"How could we? To cook and eat, we've got to have utensils, and a table to eat on. We need another table so we can each have one to correct tests on and so forth for our jobs at the college. And chairs. We need at least a mattress to sleep on, and something like a dresser for the clothes that can't be hung up—"

"All right. I'll get an extra job, then."

"No, you won't. I had to stop work on *my* thesis. You're going to stick with writing papers for the academic journals until you publish something. Then see Shorles keep you out of that instructorship!"

"Oh, hell," said Jim. "I'll probably never get anything published anyway."

"You better not mean that!" For once Angie sounded almost angry.

"Well, actually, no," Jim said, a little shamefacedly. "Actually, this last paper was going pretty well this morning before I headed off for class."

Professor Thibault Shorles, head of the History Department, liked his assistants to sit in on all of his classes, in addition to doing the usual work of correcting tests, reserving reference books for the students in the course, and so forth. It was a neat little whim that added eight hours a week to the time Jim otherwise required to put in to earn his hundred and seventy-five dollars a month.

"How was he?" Angie asked. "Did you ask him about the instructorship again?"

"He wasn't in the mood."

"He wasn't? Or you weren't?"

Jim winced internally. Shorles had interviewed Jim at the History Association meeting last year in Chicago; and as good as promised him a recently created instructorship just added to the history department Shorles headed at Riveroak. With this prospect, Angie had tried for, and to the happiness of both of them, got, a teaching assistantship in the English Department. She was still working for her doctorate in English literature, Jim having been three years ahead of her at Michigan State, where they met as graduate students. With both of them set for jobs at the same academic institution, it had looked as if they had the future taped. But then when they had gotten here, Shorles broke the news that because of last-minute budget problems, Jim could not be given his instructorship until the spring quarter at the earliest. Meanwhile, Shorles had a teaching assistantship open . . .

It had taken Jim less than a month to find out the real nature of the "budget problem." Like academic departments in many colleges and universities, the staff teaching history at Riveroak College was riddled with internal politics. Two established factions in the department opposed each other on almost every point. Shorles, independent of both, had gotten by for years by playing them against each other. But an additional instructor added at this time could cause a reshuffling of allegiances and a resultant upset in the neat balance of power. On the other hand, Professor Theodore N. Jellamine, the outspoken, motorcycle-riding vice-chairman of the department, was thinking of retiring this coming spring. His leaving would mean promotions for those under him; and by controlling these, Shorles could then absorb a new instructor into a fresh balance of power hand-tailored by himself.

"I'm sorry, Angie," said Jim, contritely. "I had to sit through that class for a hour with nothing to do but look interested and think of what he's done to us; and by the time the bell rang, I didn't dare talk to him for fear I'd put one in his teeth when he turned me down again."

There was a moment's stark silence in the car as they drove along; then Jim, staring straight ahead out the windshield, felt his arm squeezed gently.

"That's all right," Angie told him. "If you felt like

that, you did the right thing. You'll catch him sometime when you're able to talk calmly about it."

They drove on for a little while longer without talking.

"There it is," said Jim, nodding to the right, off the highway.

Chapter 2

The Bellevue Trailer Court had not been laid out with an eye to attractiveness and none of its owners in the past twenty years had done anything to amend the oversight. Its present proprietor, in his fifties, was as tall and heavy as Jim Eckert, but his skin was now too large for his long face. The flesh had fallen into folds and creases, and the Prussian blue shirt he wore ballooned loosely about him. His faded maroon pants were drawn into deep puckers at his waist by a thin black belt. His breath smelled as if he had just been snacking on overripe cheese, and in the sun-hot interior of the empty mobile home he showed Jim and Angie this aspect of him was hard to ignore.

"Well," he said, waving at the mobile home walls about them, "this is it. I'll leave you to look it over. Just come back to the office when you're ready."

He took his breath outside, leaving the door open behind him. Jim looked at Angie, but she was running her fingers over the cracked varnish on one of the cupboard doors above the sink.

"It's pretty bad, isn't it?" Jim remarked.

It was. Obviously the mobile home was in the last stages of its life. The floor canted visibly behind Jim and as visibly canted toward the trailer's other end, where Angie now stood. The sink was stained and gritty, the dusty windows sat loosely in their framing, and the walls were too thin to give anything but minimum insulation.

"It'd be like camping out in the snow when winter comes," Jim said.

He thought of the ice-hard January of a Minnesota winter, both of them twenty-three miles from Riveroak College and the Gorp running on threadbare tires plus a worn-out motor. He thought of summer sessions at the college and the baking heat of a Minnesota July as they both sat in here with endless test papers to correct. But Angie did not answer.

She was opening and shutting the door to the trailer's shower-and-toilet stall. Or, trying to shut it. The door did not seem to latch very well. Her shoulders in the blue jacket were small and square. He thought of suggesting they give up, go back and check the listings at the Student Housing Bureau once more for an apartment around the college. But Angie would not admit defeat that easily. He knew her. Besides, she knew he knew it was hopeless, their trying to find anything the two of them could pay for close in.

Some of the dreary grittiness of the mobile home seemed to blow through his soul on a bleak wind of despair. For a moment he felt a sort of desperate hunger for the kind of life that had existed in the European Middle Ages of his medievalist studies. A time in which problems took the shapes of flesh-and-blood opponents, instead of impalpable situations arising out of academic cloak-and-dagger politics. A time when, if you ran across a Shorles, you could deal with him with a sword, instead of with words. It was unreal that they should be in this situation simply because of an economic situation and because Shorles did not want to disturb the political balance of his department.

"Come on, Angie," Jim said. "We can find something better than this."

She wheeled around. Under her dark hair, her brown eyes were grim.

8

"You said you'd leave it up to me, this last week."

"I know . . ."

"For two months we hunted around the campus, the way you wanted. Staff meetings for the fall semester start tomorrow. There isn't any more time."

"We could still look, nights."

"Not anymore. And I'm not going back to that co-op. We're going to have a place of our own."

"But . . . look at this place, Angie!" he said. "And it's twenty-three miles from the campus. The Gorp could throw a rod tomorrow!"

"If he does, we'll fix him. And we'll fix up this place. You know we can do it if we want to!"

He yielded. They went back to the trailer park office and the manager.

"We'll take it," Angie told him.

"Thought you'd like it," said the manager, getting papers out of a drawer in his littered desk. "How'd you happen to hear about it, anyway? I haven't even advertised it yet."

"Your former tenant was the sister-in-law of a friend of mine," Jim answered, "guy I play volleyball with. When she had to move to Missouri, he told us her mobile home was available."

The manager nodded.

"Well, you can count yourself lucky." He pushed the papers across to them. "I think you told me you both teach at the college?"

"That's right," said Angie.

"Then, if you'll just fill in a few lines on these forms and sign them. You married?"

"We're going to be," said Jim, "by the time we move in here."

"Well, if you aren't married yet, you've either got to both sign or one of you has to be listed as subrenting. It's easier if you both sign. Then that'll be two months rent, the first and the last, as a deposit against damage. Two hundred and eighty dollars."

Angie and Jim both stopped handling the papers.

"Two-eighty?" Angie asked. "Danny Cerdak's

9

sister-in-law was paying a hundred and ten a month. We happen to know."

"Right. I had to raise it."

"Thirty dollars more a month?" said Jim. "For that?"

"You don't like it," said the manager, straightening up, "you don't have to rent it."

"Of course," Angie said, "we can understand you might have to raise the rent a bit, the way prices are going up everywhere. But we just can't pay a hundred and forty a month."

"That's too bad. Sorry. But that's what it costs now. I'm not the owner, you know. I just follow orders."

Well, that was that. Back in the Gorp once more, they rolled down the windows and Jim turned the key in the ignition. The Gorp gorped rustily to life. They headed back down the highway toward the college.

They did not talk much on the way back in.

"It's all right, though," Angie said as Jim pulled into the parking lot next to their co-op and they went in together to lunch. "We'll find something. This chance opened up all of a sudden. Something else is bound to. We'll just keep looking until it does."

"Uh-huh," said Jim.

They cheered up a little over lunch.

"In a way," Angie explained, "it was our own fault. We got to counting on that mobile home too much, just because we'd been the first ones to hear about it being vacant. From now on, I'm not going to count on anything until we've moved into it."

"You and me both."

By the time they had eaten, little time was left. Jim drove back to Stoddard Hall and let Angie out.

"You'll be through at three?" he asked. "You won't let him keep you overtime?"

"No," she said, closing the car door and talking to him through the open window. Her voice softened. "Not today. I'll be out here when you pull up."

"Good," he said; and watched her go up the steps and vanish through one of the big doors.

Putting the Gorp in gear, he pulled away and around to the other side of the campus to park in his usual space behind the History Building. He had said nothing to Angie, but over lunch a decision had crystalized inside him. He was going to confront Shorles with the demand that he give him his instructorship without any further delay—by the end of spring quarter and the beginning of the first summer session at latest. He ran up the three flights of the back set of stairs and came out into the long, marble floor corridor where most of the top staff members in the department had their offices.

Shorles was one step above anyone else in the department. He had a secretary in his outer office, who doubled as secretary to the department itself. Jim came through the door now and found her retyping something that looked suspiciously like the manuscript of Shorles' latest paper on the Etruscan roots of modern civilization.

"Hi, Marge," Jim said. "Is he in?"

Jim glanced toward the door leading to Shorles' separate office as he spoke, and saw it closed. So he knew Marge's answer almost before she gave it.

"Not just now," said Marge, a tall, sandy-haired girl in her mid-thirties. "Ted Jellamine's with him. They shouldn't be more than a little while, though. Do you want to wait?"

"Yes."

He took one of the hard seats for visitors in the outer office; and, at her desk, Marge resumed typing.

The minutes crawled slowly by. Another half-hour passed and another quarter-hour on top of that. Suddenly the door burst open and out came Shorles, carrying his ample belly energetically before him and closely followed by Ted Jellamine in cowboy boots and a checkered houndstooth jacket. As they headed for the outer door without pausing, Shorles spoke to his secretary.

"Marge, I won't be back this afternoon. We're headed for the Faculty Club. If my wife calls, she can find me there."

Jim had got to his feet automatically as the door opened and taken half a step in pursuit of the two men as they snailed through the room. Noticing him now, Shorles gave him a cheerful wave of a hand.

"Marvelous news, Jim!" he said. "Ted, here, is going to stay on another year!"

The door slammed behind both men. Jim stared at it, stunned, then turned to Marge, who looked back at him with sympathy.

"He just wasn't thinking. That's why he broke the news to you that way," she said.

"Ha!" said Jim. "He was gloating and you know it!"

"No," Marge shook her head. "No, really, you're wrong. He and Ted have been close friends for years; and Ted's been under pressure to retire early. But we're a private college with no automatic cost-of-living increases in the pensions, and with this inflation Ted wants to hang on to his job for the present if he still can. He really was just happy for Ted, when it turned out Ted could stay on; and he just didn't think of what that meant to you."

"Mmph!" said Jim, and stalked out.

He was all the way back to his parking spot before he calmed down long enough to check his watch. It was almost two-thirty. He had to pick up Angie again in half an hour. He had no time to do much of anything before then, either on his essay, or in the way of his duties as assistant to Shorles—not that he felt overwhelmingly like doing work for Shorles right now. He got into the Gorp, slammed the door and drove off, hardly caring where he went as long as it was away from the campus.

He turned left on High Street, turned left again on Wallace Drive, and emerged a few minutes later on the Old River Road alongside the Ealing River: two-lane asphalt strip that had been the old route to the neighboring town of Bixley, before Highway Five had been laid over the rolling farmland on a parallel route.

The old road was normally free of traffic and today was no exception. It was even relatively free from

12

houses and plowed fields, since most of the ground was low-lying and inclined to be marshy. Jim drove along with no particular destination in sight or mind, and gradually the peace of the riverside area through which he was passing began to bring him back to some coolness of mind.

Gradually he brought himself to consider that possibly Marge had been right and that Ted Jellamine might in his own way have been as concerned about *his* future and *his* livelihood as Jim was himself. It was a relief to come around to this point of view, because Ted Jellamine was the one other member of the History Department whom Jim liked personally. Like Jim, he was an individualist. It was only the factors of their situation that made them competitors.

But, outside of this crumb of comfort, Jim gleaned little happiness out of this new development. Perhaps it was not Ted who was to blame, but the tight economic situation which squeezed them all. Nonetheless, once again Jim caught himself wishing that life and the problems it produced were more concrete and in a position to be attacked more directly.

He glanced at his watch. It was fifteen minutes till three. Time to head back to Angie. He found a crossroad, turned the Gorp around and drove back toward the campus. Luckily, he had been driving slowly along the river road and was not that far from town. It would not do to have her standing and waiting for him, after all his insistence that she not let Grottwold keep her overtime and make him wait outside.

He pulled up in front of Stoddard Hall, actually with a couple of minutes to spare. Turning off the motor, he waited. As he sat, he put his mind to work to decide on the best way of breaking the news of his latest blow to Angie. To come up with news of this kind on the same day their hopes of renting the mobile home had been dashed was the worst possible timing. For a short while he played with the notion of simply not saying anything about it today at all. But of course that would never work. She would want to know why he had not told her immediately; and she would be quite right in asking. They would get nowhere if they fell into the habit of hiding bad news from each other out of a mistaken idea of kindness.

Jim glanced at his watch and was startled to see that while he had been sitting thinking, nearly ten minutes had gone by. Angie was staying overtime, after all.

Something popped inside Jim. Suddenly he was completely angry—cold angry. Grottwold had pulled his delaying tactics once too often. Jim got out of the Gorp, closed the door and headed up the front steps to the Hall. Inside the big double doors was the main staircase, its shallow stair treads capped with gray granite which had been worn into hollows by student's feet over a number of years. Jim went up them two at a time.

Three stories up and thirty feet down the hall on the right was the frosted-glass door to the laboratory section in which Grottwold had a ten-foot-square cubicle. Jim went through, saw the door to the cubicle was closed and strode in without knocking.

Grottwold was standing before what looked like some sort of control panel to Jim's right; and he looked around startledly as Jim burst in. Angie was seated against the far wall in what looked like a dentist's chair, facing Jim, but with her head and the upper part of her face completely covered by what looked like the helmet of the hair dryer in a beauty shop.

"Angie!" Jim snapped.

She disappeared.

Jim stood for a timeless moment, staring at the empty chair and the empty helmet. She could not be gone. She could not have just winked out like that! What he had just seen was impossible. He stood there waiting for his eyes to disavow what he had just seen and return him sight of Angie, still before him.

"*Apportation!*"

The strangled yell from Grottwold jarred Jim out of his half-stunned condition. He swung about to face the tall, shock-haired psychology graduate, who was

14

himself staring at the empty chair and helmet with a bloodless face. Life and purpose came back to Jim.

"What is it? What happened?" he shouted at Grottwold. "Where's Angie?"

"She apported!" stammered Grottwold, still staring at the place where Angie had been. "She really apported! And I was just trying for astral projection—"

"What?" Jim snarled, turning on him. "What were you trying?"

"Astral projection! Just astral projection, that's all!" Grottwold yelped. "Just projecting her astral self out of her body. I wasn't even trying to get her to experience an actual projection. All I was hoping for was just enough astral movement to register on the microammeters connected to the plant ganglia I'm using as response indicator. But she *apported* instead. She—"

"Where is she?" roared Jim.

"I don't know! I don't, I swear I don't!" the tall young man's voice climbed the scale. "There's no way I can tell—"

"You better know!"

"I don't! I know what the settings on my instruments are; but—"

Jim took three steps across the room, picked the taller man up by the lapels of his lab jacket and slammed him back against the wall to the left of the instrument panel.

"GET HER BACK!"

"I tell you I can't!" yelled Grottwold. "She wasn't supposed to do this; so I wasn't prepared for it! To get her back I'd first have to spend days or even weeks figuring out what happened. Then I'd have to figure out some way of reversing the process. And even if I did, by that time it might turn out to be too late because she'd have moved out of the physical area she's apported to!

Jim's head was whirling. It was unbelievable that he should be standing here listening to this nonsense and shoving Grottwold against the wall—but far more believable, at that, than that Angie should really have disappeared. Even now, he could not really believe what had happened.

But he had seen her disappear.

He increased his grip on Grottwold's lapels.

"All right, turkey!" he said. "You get her back here, or I'll start taking you apart right now."

"I tell you I can't! Stop—" Grottwold cried as Jim pulled him forward from the wall preparatory to slamming him back against it—or through it, if that was possible. "Wait! I've got an idea."

Jim hesitated, but kept his grip.

"What is it?" he demanded.

"There's just a chance. A long chance," Grottwold babbled. "You'd have to help. But it might work. Yes, it might just work."

"All right!" Jim snapped. "Talk fast. What is it?"

"I could send you after her—" Grottwold broke off at something that was almost a shriek of terror. "Wait! I'm serious. I tell you this might work."

"You're trying to get rid of me, too," said Jim between his teeth. "You want to get rid of the only witness that could testify against you!"

"No, no!" said Grottwold. "This will work. I know it will work. The more I think about it, the more I know it'll work. And if it does, I'll be famous."

Some of the panic seemed to go out of him. He straightened up and made an effort—an unsuccessful one—to push Jim away from him.

"Let me go!" he said. "I have to get my instruments, or I can't do Angie or anyone else any good. What do you think I am, anyway?"

"A murderer!" said Jim, grimly.

"All right. Think what you want! I don't care what you think. But you know how I felt about Angie. I don't want anything to happen to her, either. I want to get her back safely here as much as you do!"

Cautiously, Jim let go of the other man but kept his hands ready to grab him again.

"Go ahead, then," he said. "But move fast."

"I'm moving as fast as I can." Grottwold turned about to his control panel, muttering to himself. "Yes, that's the way I thought I set it. Yes . . . Yes, there's no other way . . ."

"What are you talking about?" Jim demanded.

Hansen looked back at him over one boney shoulder.

"We can't do anything about getting her back until we know where she's gone," he said. "Now, all I know is I asked her to concentrate on anything she liked and she said she'd concentrate on dragons."

"What dragons? Where?"

"I don't know where, I tell you! It could be dragons in a museum, or anyplace! That's why we have to locate her; and why you've got to help or we can't do it."

"Well, tell me what to do, then," said Jim.

"Just sit down in the chair there——" Grottwold broke off as Jim took a menacing step toward him. "All right, then, don't do it! Take away our last chance to bring her back!"

Jim hesitated. Then, slowly, reluctantly, he turned back to the empty dentist's chair at which Grottwold had been pointing.

"You'd better be right about this," he said.

He walked over and seated himself gingerly.

"What are you going to do, anyway?" he asked.

"There's nothing to worry about!" said Grottwold. "I'm going to leave the control settings just the way they were when she apported. But I'll lower the voltage. That must have been what made her apport in the first place. There was just too much power behind her. I'll reduce the power and that way you'll project, not apport."

"What does that mean?"

"It means you won't go anywhere. You'll stay right there in the chair. Only your mind'll reach out and project in the same direction Angie went."

"You're sure about that?"

"Of course I'm sure. Your body will stay right in the chair. Just your astral self will go to join Angie. That's the way it should have worked for her in the

17

first place. Maybe she was concentrating too hard—"

"Don't try to blame it on her!"

"I'm not. I just— Anyway, don't you forget to concentrate, too. Angie was experienced in this sort of concentration. You aren't. So you'll have to make an effort. Think of Angie. Concentrate on her. Concentrate on her in some place with dragons."

"All right," Jim growled. "Then what?"

"If you do it right, you'll end up wherever she apported to. You won't really be there, of course," said Grottwold. "It'll all be subjective. But you'll feel as if you're there, and since Angie's on the same instrument setting, she ought to be aware of your astral self being there, even if no one else there is."

"All right, all right!" said Jim. "But how do I get her back?"

"You'll have to get her to concentrate on returning," Grottwold answered. "You remembered how I taught you to hypnotize her—?"

"I remember, all right!"

"Well, try to hypnotize her again. She's got to become completely oblivious to wherever her present surroundings are before she'll be able to apport back here. Just put her under and keep telling her to concentrate on the lab, here. When she disappears, you'll know she's come back."

"And what," said Jim, "about me?"

"Oh, it's nothing for you," Grottwold said. "You just close your eyes and will yourself back here. Since your body never left here to begin with, you'll automatically return the minute you don't want to be someplace else."

"You're sure about that?"

"Of course I'm sure. Now, close your eyes— No, no, you've got to pull the hood down over your head . . ."

Grottwold stepped over and pulled the hood down himself. Jim was suddenly in a near-darkness faintly scented with the perfume of Angie's hair spray.

"Remember now," Grottwold's voice came distantly to him through the open bottom of the helmet, "con-

18

centrate. Angie—dragons. Dragons—Angie. Close your eyes and keep thinking those two things . . ."

Jim closed his eyes and thought.

Nothing seemed to be happening. There was no sound from outside the helmet, and with the thing over his head he could see nothing but darkness. The scent of Angie's hair spray was overwhelming. Concentrate on Angie, he told himself. Concentrate on Angie . . . and dragons . . .

Nothing was happening, except that the hair-spray odor was making him dizzy. His head swam. He felt huge and clumsy, sitting under the hair dryer with his eyes closed this way. He experienced a thudding in his ears that was the sound of his heart, beating along the veins and arteries of his body. A slow, heavy thudding. His head began to swim in earnest. He felt as if he were sliding sideways through nothingness and in the process expanding until he bulked like a giant.

A sort of savagery stirred in him. He had a fleeting desire to get up from where he was and tear something or someone apart. Preferably Grottwold. It would be sheerly soul-satisfying to take hold of that turkey and rip him limb from limb. Some large voice was booming, calling to him, but he ignored it, lost in his own thoughts. Just to sink his claws into that george—

Claws? George?

What was he thinking about? This nonsense was not working at all.

He opened his eyes.

Chapter 3

The helmet was gone. Instead of into hair-spray-scented darkness, he stared at rock walls leading up to a ceiling also of rock, high above his head and flickeringly lit by reddish light from a torch blazing in a wall sconce.

"Blast it, Gorbash!" roared the voice he had been trying to ignore. "Wake up! Come on, boy, we've got to get down to the main cave. They've just captured one!"

"One . . . ?" Jim stammered. "One what?"

"A george! *A george!* WAKE UP, GORBASH!"

An enormous head with crocodile-sized jaws equipped with larger-than-crocodile-sized fangs thrust itself between Jim's eyes and the ceiling.

"I'm awake. I—" What he was seeing suddenly registered on Jim's stunned mind and he burst out involuntarily, "A dragon!"

"And just what would you expect your maternal grand-uncle to be, a sea lizard? Or are you having nightmares again? Wake up. It's Smrgol talking to you, boy. Smrgol! Come on, shake a wing and get flapping. They'll be expecting us in the main cave. Isn't every day we capture a george. Come on, now."

The fanged mouth whirled away. Blinking, Jim dropped his eyes from the vanishing apparition and caught sight of a huge tail, an armored tail with a row of sharp, bony plates running along its upper surface. It swelled larger as it approached him—

It was his tail.

He held up his arms in front of him. They were enormous. Also, they were thickly scaled with bony plates like those on his tail but much smaller—and his claws needed manicuring. Squinting at the claws, Jim became aware of a long muzzle stretching down and out from where his formerly "invisible" nose had been. He licked dry lips and a long, red, forked tongue darted out briefly in the smoky air.

"Gorbash!" thundered the voice once more; and Jim looked to see the other dragon face glaring at him from a stone doorway. It was in fact, he saw, the entrance to the cave he was in. "I'm on my way. Catch up or not—it's up to you."

The other disappeared and Jim shook his head, bewildered. What was going on here? According to Grottwold, no one else was supposed to be able to see him, let alone—

Dragons?

Dragons who talked . . . ?

To say nothing of his being—he, Jim Eckert—himself a dragon . . .

That was the absolutely ridiculous part. He, a dragon? How could he be a dragon? Why would he be a dragon, even if there *were* such things as dragons? The whole thing must be some sort of hallucination.

Of course! He remembered, now. Grottwold had mentioned that what he would seem to be experiencing would be entirely subjective. What he was apparently seeing and hearing must be nothing more than a sort of nightmare, overlying whatever real place and people he had reached. A dream. He pinched himself.

—And jumped.

He had forgotten noticing that his "fingers" had claws on them. Large claws, and very sharp ones. If what he was experiencing was a dream, the elements of that dream were damned real!

But, dream or not, all he wanted was to find Angie and get out of here, back to the ordinary world. Only, where should he look for her? He had probably better find someone he could describe her to, and ask if she'd been seen. He should have asked whoever it was he had been "seeing" as the "dragon" trying to wake him up. What was it the other had been saying? Something about "capturing a george . . . ?"

What could a george be? Or was it George with a capital G? Maybe if some people here appeared as dragons, then others would appear as St. George, the dragon-slayer. But then, the other dragon had referred to "a" george. Perhaps the dragons called all ordinary, human-looking people by that name, which would mean that what they had really captured was probably—

"Angie!" Jim erupted, suddenly putting two and two together.

He rolled to all four feet and lumbered across the cave. Emerging through its entrance, he found himself in a long torchlit corridor, down which a further dragon shape was rapidly receding. Concluding this must be the—what it had called itself—grand-uncle of the body Jim was in, Jim took after him, digging in his memory to turn up the name the other had used for himself.

"Wait for me, uh—Smrgol!" he called.

But the other dragon shape turned a corner and disappeared.

Coming up rapidly in pursuit, Jim noticed that the ceiling of the corridor was low, too low for his twitching wings, which he could now see out of the corners of his eyes evidently trying to spread themselves in reflexive response to his speed. He turned the corner himself and emerged through a large entrance into a huge, vaulted chamber that seemed jammed to overflowing with dragons, gray and massive under the light of a number of wall torches that cast large shadows on the high granite walls. Not watching where he was going, Jim ran squarely into the back of another dragon.

"Gorbash!" thundered this individual, jerking his head around and identifying himself by this cry as the maternal grand-uncle again. "A little respect, blast you, boy!"

"Sorry!" boomed Jim. He was still not used to his dragon-voice and the apology came out like the explosion of a signal cannon.

But apparently Smrgol was not offended.

"That's all right, that's all right. No harm done," he thundered back. "Sit down here, lad." He leaned over to rear in the ear of the dragon next to him. "Make room for my grand-nephew, here."

"What? Oh, it's you, Smrgol!" bellowed the other dragon, turning his head to look. He shifted over about eight feet. "All right, Gorbash, squeeze in. We're just getting down to discussion on the george, now."

Jim pushed his way between the two of them, sat down and began to try to make sense of what was going on around him. Apparently the dragons in this world all spoke modern English . . . Or did they? Now that he listened closely to the verbal tumult around him, the words that his ear was hearing seemed to disagree with the sense that his mind was making out of it. Maybe he was talking "dragon" and didn't know it? He decided to file that question for examination at a more leisurely moment.

He looked about. The great sculptured cave in which he found himself had seemed at first to be aswarm with literally thousands of dragons. On closer look, the idea of thousands gave way to hundreds, and this in turn resolved itself to a saner estimate of perhaps fifty dragons of all sizes. Size-wise, Jim was pleased to note, he was not among the smallest there. In fact, no dragon close to him at the moment, with the single exception of Smrgol, could compare to him in size. There was, however, a monster across the room, one of those who seemed to be doing most of the talking, gesturing now and then to a box-like shape of about dragon size, placed beside him on the stone floor and covered with a richly worked piece of tapestry that looked far beyond the capability of dragon claws to produce.

As for the discussion—verbal brawl was perhaps a better description of it. A discussion among dragons appeared to consist of all of them talking at once. Their voices were tremendous in volume and the stone walls and ceiling seemed to shiver under the resonances of the titanic bellowing. Smrgol lost no time in getting into it.

"Shut up, you—Bryagh!" he exploded at the oversize dragon beside the tapestry-covered object. "Let someone get a word in edgewise who's had more experience with georges and the rest of the upper world than everyone else of you put together. When I slew the ogre of Gormely Keep there wasn't a dragon here that was out of the shell yet."

"Do we have to listen to your battle with that ogre one more time?" roared the oversize Bryagh. "This is important!"

"Listen, you inchworm!" Smrgol thundered. "It takes brains to beat an ogre—something you haven't got. Brains run in my family. If another ogre cropped up nowadays, me and Gorbash here'd be the only two tails seen above ground for the next eighty years!"

The argument between the two gradually dominated the lesser bellowings that were going on. One by one, Jim noticed, the other dragons shut up and sat back to listen, until only his grand-uncle and Bryagh were left shouting at each other.

". . . Well, what do you want to do about it, then?" Bryagh was demanding. "I caught it right above the main cave entrance. It's a spy, that's what it is."

"Spy? What makes you think it's a spy? Georges don't go spying on dragons, they come looking for a fight. Fought a good many in my time that way." Smrgol expanded his chest.

"Fight!" sneered Bryagh. "Ever hear of a george nowadays out to fight without its shell? Ever since the first george we've known, when they were looking for a fight they had their shells on. This one was practically peeled!"

Smrgol winked ponderously at the dragons near him.

"Sure you didn't peel it yourself?" he boomed.

"Does it look like it? Look!"

And, reaching down, Bryagh twitched off the tapestry from the box-like shape, revealing an iron cage. In the cage, crouching miserably behind its rough bars, was—

"ANGIE!" Jim cried.

He had forgotten the tremendous capabilities of the dragon-voice. Or, rather, he had not yet had a real chance to test them out. He had instinctively called Angie's name at the top of his lungs, and a shout at the top of a dragon's lungs was something to hear— provided you had earplugs and were safely over the horizon.

Even that oversize assembly in the cave was shaken. As for Angie, she was either blasted flat on her back or fainted.

Gorbash's grand-uncle was the first to recover from the shock.

"Blast it, boy!" he bellowed, in what Jim now unhappily realized were normal dragon conversational tones, "you don't have to burst our eardrums! What do you mean—'hanchee'?"

Jim had been thinking fast.

"I sneezed," he said.

A dead silence greeted this remark. Finally Bryagh retorted.

"Who ever heard of a dragon sneezing?"

"Who? *Who?*" snorted Smrgol. "*I* heard of a dragon sneezing. Before your time, of course. Old Malgu, my mother's sister's third cousin, once removed, sneezed twice on one day a hundred and eighty-three years ago. Don't tell me you never heard of a dragon sneezing. Sneezing runs in our family. It's a sign of brains."

"That's right," put in Jim hastily. "A sign my brains are working. Busy brains make your nose itch."

"You tell 'em, boy!" Smrgol rumbled, in the second dubious silence following this remark.

"I'll bet!" roared Bryagh. He turned to the rest of the assembly. "You all know Gorbash. Mooning around aboveground half the time, making friends with hedgehogs and wolves and what all! Smrgol here's been talking up his grand-nephew for years, but Gorbash's never showed anything yet that I know of —least of all, brains! Shut up, Gorbash!"

"Why should I?" Jim shouted, hastily. "I've got as good a right to talk as anyone else here. About this—uh—george, here—"

"Kill it!" "Burn it alive!" "Hold a raffle, and the winning diamond gets to eat it," a roar of suggestions interrupted him.

"No!" he thundered. "Listen to me—"

"*No*, is right," trumpeted Bryagh. "*I* found this george. If anybody gets to eat it, it'll be me." He glared around the cave. "But I got a better use for this george. I say, let's stake it out where the other georges can see it. Then, when some of them come to get it back, we'll jump them when they aren't expecting it and grab the lot of them. Then we'll sell them all back to the rest of the georges for a lot of gold."

When Bryagh said the word "gold," Jim saw all the dragon eyes around him light up and glitter; and he also felt a hot bite of avarice warming his own veins. The thought of gold rang in his head like the thought of a fountain of water to a man dying of thirst in the desert. Gold . . . A slow, swelling murmur of approval, like the surf of a distant sea storm, rose up in the cave.

Jim fought down the gold hunger in his own dragon-breast, and felt panic rising in its stead. Somehow he had to turn them all from this plan of Bryagh's. For a moment he toyed with the wild idea of snatching up Angie, cage and all, and making a run for it. Even as he thought this, it came to him that it was not such a wild idea after all. Until he was able to see Angie close to Bryagh—and Bryagh was about his own size—he had not realized how big he was. Even squatting on his haunches, as he was not, his head was in the neighborhood of nine feet off the floor of the cave. Standing upright on all four feet, he would probably measure six feet or better at a front shoulder, with as much as half that length again of powerful, limber tail. If he could catch the other dragons all looking the other way for a moment . . .

But then it sank in on him that he did not know the way out of this underground place. He had to assume that a further opening dimly seen at the cave's far end led to a passage which would take him to the surface. Some faint, Gorbash-memory seemed to assure him this was so. But he could not count on the subconscious memories of this body he was inhabiting. If he should lose his way—be trapped with his back against some wall, or in some blind passage—the other dragons might well tear him apart; and Angie, even if she survived that battle, would lose her only possible rescuer. There had to be another way.

"Wait a minute," he called out. "Hold on!"

"Shut up, Gorbash!" thundered Bryagh.

"Shut up, yourself!" Jim bellowed back. "I told you my brains were busy. They just came up with the best idea yet."

Out of the corner of his eyes he saw Angie sitting up in her cage with a dazed expression, and felt relief. The sight gave him courage and he doubled the volume of his voice.

"This is a female george you've got here. Maybe that didn't strike any of you as something important; but I've been aboveground often enough to learn a thing or two. Sometimes female georges are especially valuable—"

At Jim's shoulder, Smrgol cleared his throat with a sound like an airhammer biting into particularly stubborn concrete.

"Absolutely correct!" he boomed. "It might even be a princess we've got. Looks to me something like a princess. Now, a lot of you nowadays don't know what princesses are; but in the old days many a dragon found a whole pack of georges after him because the george he picked up turned out to be a princess. When I fought the ogre of Gormely Keep, he had a princess locked up along with his pack of other female georges. And you ought to have seen the georges when they got that princess back. Now, if we stake this one out, they might send a regular army against us to try and get it back . . . No, staking it out's too risky. Might as well just cut our losses and eat—"

"On the other hand," shouted Jim, quickly, "if we treat her well and hold her—'it,' I mean—for a hostage, then we can make the georges do anything we want—"

"No!" roared Bryagh. "It's my george. I won't stand for—"

"By my tail and wings!" The tremendous lung power of Smrgol cut the other dragon off. "Are we a community, or a tribe of mere-dragons? If this george is actually a princess and can be used to stop these shelled georges from hunting us all over the landscape, then it's a community property. Oh yes, I see some of you with the gold-lust still in your eyes; but just stop and think that the life-lust is maybe something just a little bit more important. How many of you here would like to face just a single george in his shell, with his horn aimed at you? Eh? We've had enough of this nonsense. The boy here's got a real idea—surprised I didn't think of it myself. But then my nose wasn't itching; his was. I vote we hold the george here hostage until young Gorbash can go find out what it's worth to the other ones. How about it?"

Slowly at first, and then with mounting enthusiasms, the dragon community voted to do as Smrgol had suggested. Bryagh completely lost his temper, swore for forty straight seconds at near full dragon-volume, and stamped out of the meeting. Seeing the excitement was over, other members of the community began to drift off.

"Come, my boy," Smrgol puffed, leading the way to the cage, and covering it once more with the tapestry. "Pick up the whole thing, there. Careful! Not too quickly. You don't want to shake the george around too much. Now, follow me. We'll take it up to one of the topside caves opening on the cliff face. Georges can't fly, so it'll be safe enough there. We can even let it out of the cage and it'll get some light and air. Georges need that."

Jim, carrying the cage, followed the older dragon up a number of winding passages until they came out into a small cave with a narrow—by dragon standards—opening on thin air. Jim set the cage down, Smrgol rolled a boulder into place to block the entrance by which they had come, and Jim stepped to the edge of the outer opening to look around at the countryside. He caught his breath at the sight: one-hundred-plus feet of sheer cliffside drop to the jagged rocks below.

"Well, Gorbash," said Smrgol, coming up beside him and draping a friendly tail over the younger dragon's armor-plated shoulders. "You've talked yourself into a job. Now, my boy, I don't want you to be offended at what I'm going to say."

He cleared his throat.

"The truth is," he went on, "just between the two of us, you really aren't too bright, you know. All that running around on the surface you used to do and consorting with that fox, wolf, or whatever-it-was friend of yours was not the right sort of education at all for a growing dragon. Probably I should have put my foot down; but you're the last of our family, and I . . . well, I thought there wouldn't be any harm in letting you have a little fun and freedom when you were young. I've always backed you up before the other dragons, of course, because blood's thicker than water, and all that. But brains really aren't your strength—"

"I may be brighter than you think," Jim said, grimly.

"Now, now, don't be touchy. This is just between you and me, in private. It's no disgrace for a dragon to be thick-headed. It *is* a disadvantage in this modern world, though, now that georges have learned how to grow shells and long, sharp horns and stings. But the point I want to impress on you is something I wouldn't admit to any other dragon. If we're to survive, sooner or later we're going to have to come to some kind of terms with these georges. This constant warfare doesn't seem to be cutting down *their* numbers much, but it's decimating *our* ranks. Oh, you don't know what that word means—"

"Of course I do."

"You surprise me, my boy." Smrgol looked at him, startled. "What's it mean, then? Tell me!"

" 'The destruction of a considerable part of'—that's what it means."

"By the primal egg! Maybe there's hope for you after all. Well, well. What I wanted to do was impress you with the importance of your mission, and also with its dangers. Don't take chances, Grand-nephew. You're my only surviving relative; and, in all kindness I say it—in spite of all that muscle of yours—any shelled george with a bit of experience would chop you up in an hour or so."

"You think so? Maybe I'd better make it a point to keep well out of sight—"

"Tut-tut! No need to get touchy. Now, what I want to do is try and find out from this george here where it came from. I'll leave, myself, so as not to frighten it unduly. If it won't talk, leave it here where it's safe and fly up to that magician who lives by the Tinkling Water. You know where that is, of course. Due northwest of here. Start negotiations through him. Just tell him we've got this george, what it looks like, and that we want to discuss terms for a truce with the georges. Leave it up to him to make arrangements. And whatever you do"—Smrgol paused to look Jim sternly in the eyes—"don't come back downcave to me for more advice before you leave. Just go. I'm having trouble enough holding control here with what prestige I have. I want to give the impression you're capable of handling this all by yourself. Understand?"

"I understand," said Jim.

"Good." Smrgol waddled to the open-air entrance of the cave. "Good luck, boy!" he said, and dived off.

Jim heard the beating of his great, leathery wings descending and dying out in the distance. Then he turned back to the cage, pulled the tapestry off it once more, and discovered Angie huddled in the back of it, as far away from him as she could get.

"It's all right," he told her, hastily. "It's just me, Jim . . ."

He was hunting about for some part of the cage that would open up. After a second, he found a door with a heavy padlock on it, but there was no key. Experimentally, he took hold of the door with one large, clawed paw, grasped a cage bar with another, and pulled. The padlock twanged and disintegrated, the cage bar broke into pieces, the door flew open. Angie screamed.

"It's just me, I tell you, Angie!" he said, annoyed. "Come out, now."

Angie did not come out. She scooped up one of the broken pieces of bar and held it like a dagger, underhanded, with its sharply splintered end toward him.

"Stay away from me, dragon!" she said. "I'll blind you if you come close!"

"Are you crazy, Angie?" cried Jim. "I tell you it's *me!* Do I look like a dragon to you?"

"You certainly do," said Angie, fiercely.

"I do? But Grottwold said—"

At that moment the ceiling seemed to come down and hit him on the head.

. . . He swam back to consciousness to find Angie's concerned face hovering over him.

"What happened?" he said, shakily.

"I don't know," she said. "You just suddenly collapsed. Jim—it really is you, Jim?"

"Yes," he said, stupidly.

". . ." said Angie.

He did not catch exactly what she said. Something peculiar was going on in his head, like a mental equivalent of the sort of double vision that sometimes follows a concussion. He seemed to be thinking with two minds at once. He made an effort to settle down with one set of thoughts; and succeeded in focusing in, mind-wise, after a fashion. Apparently with an effort he could keep his mind undivided.

"I feel like somebody hit me over the head with a club," he said.

"You do? But, really, nothing happened!" Angie was sounding distressed. "You just went down as if you'd fainted, or something like that. How are you feeling now?"

31

"Sort of mixed up in the head," Jim answered.

He had pretty well conquered the impulse to think on two tracks at once; but he was still aware of something like a separate part of his mind sitting, contained but apart, in the back of his consciousness. He made an effort to forget it. Maybe, if he ignored it, the feeling would go away. He concentrated on Angie.

"Why is it you believe it's me, now, and you didn't before?" he demanded, sitting up on his dragon-haunches.

"I was too upset to notice you were calling me by my name," she said. "But when you kept using yours, and then when you mentioned Grottwold, I suddenly realized it could be you, after all, and he'd thought of sending you to rescue me."

"Thought! Hah! I told him to get you back or else! But he told me I was only supposed to project, and other people probably wouldn't even see me. Only you would."

"What I see is one of the dragons they have here. You've projected, all right. But you've projected your identity into a dragon-body."

"But I still don't see— Wait a minute," said Jim. "I thought earlier I must be speaking dragon. But if I'm speaking dragon, how come you can understand me? You ought to still be speaking English."

"I don't know," said Angie. "But I could understand the other dragons, too. Maybe they all speak English."

"They don't—I don't. Listen to what I'm saying. For that matter, listen to the sounds *you're* making."

"But I'm speaking ordinary, colloquial—" Angie broke off, with an odd look on her face. "No, you're right. I'm not. I'm making the same sort of sounds you're making, I think. Say 'I think.' "

"I think."

"Yes," Angie said, thoughtfully, "it's the same sounds; only your voice is about four octaves or so deeper than mine. We must both be speaking whatever language they have here. And it's the same language for people and dragons. That's wild!"

" 'Wild' is the word for it," said Jim. "It can't be! How would we learn a complete new language, just like that?"

"Oh, I don't know," said Angie. "It *could* be, in the case of a subjective transfer, such as we both had in order to get here. Maybe the universal laws are different here and there's only one language possible, so that when you talk in this world, or wherever this is, your thoughts automatically come out in this one language."

Jim frowned.

"I don't understand that," he said.

"I guess I don't either. Anyway, it doesn't matter. The main thing is, we can understand each other. What did he call you—that other dragon?"

" 'Gorbash.' It seems that's the name of his grand-nephew, the one whose body I'm in. *His* name's Smrgol. Evidently he's almost two hundred years old and he's got a lot of authority with the other dragons. But never mind that. I've got to send you back; and that means I've got to hypnotize you first."

"You made me promise never to let anyone hypnotize me."

"That was different. This is an emergency. Now, where's something to rest your arm on? There, that rock will do. Step over here."

He pointed to a loose boulder, one of several in the cave. This particular one was about waist high on Angie. She went over to it.

"Now," said Jim. "Lay your forearm down on top of it as if it was a table. That's right. Now concentrate on being back in Grottwold's lab. Your forearm is getting lighter. It's rising, rising—"

"Why hypnotize me?"

"Angie, please concentrate. Your forearm is get-ting lighter. It's rising. It's lighter, it's rising, rising. It's getting lighter. It's rising—"

"No," said Angie, decisively, taking her arm off the boulder. "It's not! And I'm not about to be hypnotized until I know what's going on. What happens if you hypnotize me?"

"You become able to concentrate completely on being back in Grottwold's lab and so you reappear there."

"And what happens to you?"

"Oh, my body's there, so any time I don't want to be someplace else, like here, I return to it automatically."

"But that's supposing you're just a disembodied spirit. Are you sure you can go back that easily if you're in another body, like this dragon one?"

"Well . . ." Jim hesitated. "Of course I am."

"Of course you're not!" said Angie. She looked upset. "This is all my fault."

"Your fault? This? Of course not. It's Grottwold's—"

"No," said Angie, "it's mine."

"It isn't, I tell you! Maybe it isn't even Grottwold's fault. His equipment could have just had some kind of a breakdown that sent you out, body and all, and made me end up in this Gorbash-body instead of completely apporting."

"His equipment didn't break down," Angie insisted. "He just went ahead the way he always does and experimented without knowing what he was doing. That's why it's all my fault. I knew he was like that, but I didn't tell you because we needed the extra income; and you know how you are."

"How I am? No," said Jim, grimly. "How am I?"

"You'd have fussed at me; and worried about something happening—and you'd have been right. Grottwold's just like a baby with a shiny toy, playing with that equipment of his, in spite of the degrees he has. Anyway, it's settled."

"Good," said Jim, relieved. "Now, just put your arm back on the top of that rock and relax—"

"I didn't mean that!" said Angie. "I mean there's no way I'm going to go back without you."

"But I can go back just by not wanting to be someplace else!"

"Try it."

Jim tried it. He closed his eyes and told himself that he no longer wanted to be anyplace else but back in his own body. He opened his eyes again, and Angie was standing watching him with the walls of the cave all around them.

"You see?" said Angie.

"How can I want to be someplace else while you're still here?" Jim demanded. "You've got to go back safely to our own world, before I can want to be back there, too."

"And leave you here alone, not knowing whether you'll ever make it or not, and Grottwold without the slightest idea of how he sent me here in the first place, so he'd never be able to send me back again? Oh, no!"

"All right! *You* tell *me,* then. What else is there to do?"

"I've been thinking," said Angie, thoughtfully.

"About what?"

"That magician the other dragon was talking to you about. The magician you were going to open negotiations with, on me."

"Oh, him," Jim said.

"That's right. Now, you know that these georges —these people they apparently have around here —are never going to have heard of me. The first thing they'll do when the magician carries word to them about me is look around to see who they know who's missing; and they're going to find no one is. Then, if I'm not one of their own people, why should they get into any negotiations to get me back from the dragons—let alone give the kind of concessions your grand-uncle seems to want—"

"Angie," Jim explained, "he's not my grand-uncle. He's the grand-uncle of this body I'm in."

"Whatever. The point is, once the georges figure out I don't belong to them, they won't have any interest in saving me. So, when you go to the magician—"

"Wait a minute! Who said I was leaving you, to go anywhere?"

"You know as well as I do that that's what you have to do," Angie answered. "You know we don't have a chance any other way. But it might be, it just barely might be, that this magician can help us both get back. If nothing else, you could teach him to hypnotize both of us at once, so that we'd go back together, or something— Oh, I don't know! It's the only chance we've got, and you know it as well as I do. We've got to take it!"

Jim opened his mouth to contest this point and then closed it again. As usual, she had exercised that verbal judo of hers to leave them both on her side of the argument.

"But what if the magician doesn't want to help?" he protested feebly. "After all, why should he help us, anyway?"

"I don't know; but maybe we can find some reason," said Angie. "We have to."

Jim opened his mouth and once more closed it again.

"So off you go and find him. And when you do, be honest with him. Simply tell him about our situation with Grottwold. Ask him if there's any way he can help us get back, and any way we can make it worth his while. We've got nothing to lose by being open and straightforward with him."

To Jim's mind this did not ring like the foregone conclusion it apparently was to Angie. But she was winning.

"And leave you here, meanwhile?" was all he could manage to say.

"And leave me here. I'll be just fine," Angie answered. "I heard what you said at the end, down in the big cave. I'm a hostage. I'm too valuable to hurt. Besides, the way that old dragon was talking to you, the Tinkling Water must be close. You can probably go there, talk to that magician and get back in an hour or two. It's just about the middle of the day here—hadn't you noticed? You can learn what to do and get back here safely before night."

"No." Jim shook his head. "If I hypnotize you, at

36

least you'll get home. We start playing games like this magician business and maybe neither one of us will. I won't do it."

"Well, I won't let you hypnotize me," said Angie. "I'm not going to leave you here with maybe no way to get back, or something worse, even. So what are you going to do?"

She had, Jim thought, a neat way of sealing up all the exits except the one she wanted him to use.

"All right," he said finally and unhappily.

He walked to the edge of the sheer drop, then caught himself and teetered there.

"What's wrong?" demanded Angie.

"I just thought," Jim said, a little thickly. "Gorbash obviously knew how to fly. But do I?"

"You could try it," she suggested. "It'll probably just come to you. I'd think it would, instinctively, once you were in the air."

Jim looked down at the jagged rocks far below.

"I don't think so," he said. "I really don't think so. I think I'd better move the boulder there and go back down the inside route."

"Didn't the old dragon— What's his name . . . ?"

"Smrgol."

"Didn't old Smrgol warn you not to come downcave again? What if you meet him on the way and he says you're not to go, after all? Besides, the Tinkling Water may be far enough away so you'll *need* to fly to get there."

"True," said Jim, hollowly. He thought it over. There seemed to be no alternative. He shuddered and closed his eyes. "Well . . . here goes nothing."

He jumped outward and began to flail his wings wildly. The air whistled about him as it might if he was either flying or falling like a stone. He was sure he was falling. There was something like a sudden soundless explosion in the back of his head, and his wings stretched, slowed and began to encounter resistance. He could feel air against their undersurfaces in the same way the back pressure of the water on an oar can be felt by somebody rowing.

Hope flickered faintly alight in him. If he were going to smash on the ground, he certainly should have done it by this time? On the other hand, maybe he was just managing to delay his descent, sliding down at a steep angle toward a collision with the rocks some distance from the base of the cliff?

He could stand the suspense no longer. He opened his eyes and looked.

Chapter 4

Once more, as when he cried out on seeing Angie, he had underestimated dragon capabilities. The ground was not rushing up to meet him. To the contrary, it was far, far, below him, odd little patches of wood alternating with open country. He was at least a couple of thousand feet up and climbing rapidly.

He paused for a moment and his wings stiffened out automatically in glide position. Still, he did not descend. He woke abruptly to the fact that he was soaring—instinctively riding a thermal, an uprising current of warm air, after the fashion of balloonists, sailplaners and the large birds of his own remembered world. Of course! He kicked himself mentally for not thinking of it before. The larger birds were mainly soaring birds because of the effort required for them to fly. He remembered now hearing that most of the heavier hawks and eagles would refuse to fly on days that were completely windless.

The same thing had to be true—or more so—for dragons, with their enormous weight. Evidently, like the lion, who could make a very fast charge but maintain it for only a small distance, a dragon's great muscle power could lift him quickly to soaring heights. But from then on it must be a matter of his riding the available winds and thermals.

Apparently, such riding was instinctive stuff to his Gorbash-body. Without conscious thought he found he had lined himself up with the sun above his right shoulder and was sailing northwestwardly away from the cliff face where he had taken off. In fact, the cliff itself was now dwindling into inconspicuousness behind and below him. Far away on the rim of the horizon before him was the dark-green belt of a wide-stretching forest. It moved steadily toward him, and he toward it without effort; and almost without his being aware of it, he began to enjoy himself.

It was hardly the time for such self-indulgence, particularly with Angie held prisoner behind him in a cave; but Jim found it so difficult not to feel good that he finally relaxed and allowed himself to do so. For one thing, it was just past noon of a thoroughly superb day sometime in late spring or early autumn. The sky was a lucent blue, touched here and there by just that small number of little, fleecy clouds that would serve as grace notes to set off the beauty of the day as a whole. Even from a couple of thousand feet up (dragons apparently shared the telescopic vision of the large birds of prey as well as their soaring inclinations) the gorse-fuzzed open moors, the pines and oak tree clumps he saw below him had a sort of dewy freshness about their appearance. With Gorbash's acute sense of smell, Jim could even catch the faint medley of green odors rising from the countryside; and the scent slightly intoxicated him.

He felt powerful, capable and a little reckless. In fact, for two cents he would go back and face down the whole rest of the dragon community, if necessary, to free Angie. The double-thinking back part of his mind even seemed strangely sure none of the others could match him at flying. He puzzled over that impression, then remembered that Smrgol and even Bryagh had referred to Gorbash spending more of his time aboveground than was usual for dragons. Perhaps because he had been out of the caves more and had

had to fly more frequently, Gorbash was in better training than the others?

An unanswerable question. But it reminded him of all the other questions that his incredible adventure raised. This world had more unreal elements in it than a sane mind could imagine. Dragons—let alone dragons that talked—were incredible. Somehow this world must have a set of physical and biological laws that made this possible; and someone with a doctorate in history, with a fair number of science courses along the way, ought to be able to figure those laws out—and, having figured them out, make use of them to his and Angie's advantage.

He would have thought that language would be the main problem in this other world. Only, it wasn't. The more he thought of it the surer Jim was that he, in this Gorbash-body, was not talking modern English —or any other form of English. Apparently he was talking dragon with no trouble at all; although the mental channels that seemed to translate this into modern English—colloquial modern English at that— in his head, were puzzling, to say the least. As a medievalist, Jim could both speak and read Middle and Old English, and with a doctorate he could also read and make himself understood in modern French and German. In addition to these languages, he had a smattering of modern Spanish, a few words of modern Italian, and a good knowledge of all the Romance languages in their medieval forms. Finally, he could read both classical and church Latin with facility, and work his way through classical Greek with the help of a dictionary in that language.

All in all, a pretty fair set of qualifications for any-one adventuring into any period of the European Middle Ages. Only, it seemed, none of these were useful. It was not his major areas of interest that he would find useful here but his minor ones. Still, there had to be a system of logic behind any operating environment; and if he kept his eyes open and put two and two together . . .

He soared on steadily through the air, thinking intensely. But his thoughts eventually went in a circle and ended up getting nowhere. He simply did not have enough data yet to come to conclusions. He gave up and looked around below him once more.

The wood had evidently not been as close as he had first thought. Although he was making very good time indeed—Jim estimated his air speed as somewhere in the area of fifty to seventy miles an hour— the green band of trees was still the same small distance off. On the other hand, he did not seem to be tiring at all. In fact, he felt as if he could soar like this indefinitely.

He did feel the first, slight tickling of an appetite, however. He wondered what, as a dragon, he ate. Not —he winced away from a thought—no, definitely not human beings. If that was ordinary dragon fare, he'd just have to go hungry. Perhaps the magician could help him out in the foot department as well as with the means of getting Angie and himself home again.

He was finally beginning to get close to the wood now. He could make out separate trees. They were all pine, spruce and balsam, growing close together. For the first time a doubt crossed his mind. If he had to search through that forest on foot . . . But then he reassured himself. He could not have been expected to know exactly where this Tinkling Water place was, or Smrgol would not have reminded him that it lay to the northwest. On the other hand, if it had been a hard place to find, the older dragon, with the low opinion he had of Gorbash's mentality, would have given more explicit directions and double-checked to make sure his grand-nephew had them straight.

Possibly there would be something he could see from the air, Jim thought, as he began to swoop down on a long arc that would bring him in close above the treetops.

Suddenly, he saw it: a tiny clearing among the trees with a stream running through it and cascading over a small waterfall at its upper end. Beside the stream was a pool with a fountain, and a small, oddly narrow, peaked-roof house surrounded by grass and

41

flower beds, except where a gravel path led from the edge of the dense woods up to the house's front door. A signpost of some sort stood to one side of the path just before the door.

Jim set down on the path with a thump.

In the silence that followed his rather heavy landing, he distinctly heard the sound of the water of the fountain falling and splashing in the pool. It did, indeed, tinkle—not like the sound of small bells, but with the very distant, fragile notes of glass wind chimes, clashing in the light breeze. The sound was somehow inexpressibly lulling to the nerves, and the rich and mingled odors rising from the blossoming flowers in the flower beds reinforced the effect; so that all at once Jim felt as if he had been plunged into a dream place where nothing was quite real and certainly nothing was overly important.

He moved slowly up the path and paused to read the signpost before the house. The sign itself was a plain, white-painted board with black lettering on it. The post on which it was set rose from among a riot of asters, tulips, zinnias, roses and lilies-of-the-valley, all blooming in complete disregard for their normal seasons. Printed on the board in black, angular letters was the name S. Carolinus. Jim went on up to the front door, which was green and sat above a single red-painted stone step.

He knocked.

There was no answer.

In spite of the soothing effect of the fountain and the flowers, Jim felt a sinking sensation inside him. It would be just his luck and Angie's to arrive at the residence of S. Carolinus when S. Carolinus was not within it.

He knocked again—harder, this time.

The sound came of a hasty step inside the house. The door was snatched inward and a thin-faced old man with a red robe, black skullcap and a thin, rather dingy-looking white beard stuck his head out to glare at Jim.

"Sorry, not my day for dragons!" he snapped. "Come back next Tuesday."

He pulled his head back in and slammed the door.

For a moment Jim merely stared. Then comprehension leaked through to him.

"Hey!" he shouted; and pounded on the door with some of his dragon-muscle.

It was snatched open furiously once more.

"Dragon!" said the magician, ominously. "How would you like to be a beetle?"

"You've got to listen to me," said Jim.

"I told you," Carolinus explained, "this is not my day for dragons. Besides, I've got a stomach ache. Do you understand? This-is-not-my-day-for-dragons!"

"But I'm not a dragon."

Carolinus stared at Jim for a long moment, then threw up his beard with both hands in a gesture of despair, caught some of it in his teeth as it fell down again, and began to chew on it fiercely.

"Now where," he demanded, "did a dragon acquire the brains to develop the imagination to entertain the illusion that he is *not* a dragon? Answer me, O Ye Powers!"

"The information is psychically, though not physiologically, correct," replied a deep bass voice out of thin air beside them and about five feet off the ground —causing Jim, who had regarded the question as rhetorical, to start.

"Is that a fact?" said Carolinus, peering at Jim with new interest. He spat out the hair or two still remaining in his mouth and stepped back, opening the door. "Come in, Anomaly—or do you have a better name for yourself?"

Jim squeezed through the door and found himself in a single cluttered room which evidently took up the full first floor of the house. It contained pieces of furniture and odd bits of alchemical equipment indiscriminately arranged about it. S. Carolinus closed the door behind him and walked around to face Jim again. Jim sat down on his haunches, ducking his head to avoid hitting the ceiling.

"Well, my real name is James—Jim Eckert," he said. "But I seem to be in the body of a dragon named Gorbash."

"And this," said S. Carolinus, wincing and massaging his stomach, "disturbs you, I gather." He closed his eyes and added faintly, "Do you know anything that's good for an unending stomach ache? Of course not. Go on."

"I'm afraid not. Well, the thing is— Wait a minute. Are you talking dragon, or am I talking whatever language you're talking?"

"If there's a language called 'dragon,'" said S. Carolinus, grumpily, "naturally, you're talking it. If you were talking it, I'd be talking it with you—naturally. Actually we're simply talking. Will you stick to the point? Go on about yourself."

"But, I mean, do dragons and humans here— I mean georges—speak the same language? I mean, I seem to be speaking your language, not mine—"

"Why not?" Carolinus said, closing his eyes. "In the domain of the Powers there is only one language possible—by definition. And if you're not talking to the point in five seconds, you're a beetle, on general principles."

"Oh. All right. Well," Jim explained, "the thing is, I'm not so interested in getting out of this dragon-body as I am in getting back to where I came from. My—uh—Angie, the girl I'm going to marry—"

"Yes, yes, on October thirteenth," said Carolinus impatiently. "Get on with it."

"October thirteenth? This October? You mean in just three weeks?"

"You heard me."

"But, I mean—so soon? We didn't hope—"

Carolinus opened his eyes. He did not mention beetles, but Jim understood immediately.

"Angie—" he began hurriedly.

"Who is where?" Carolinus interrupted. "You're here. Where's this Angie?"

"At the dragon cave."

"She's a dragon, too, then?"

"No, she's human."

"I see the difficulty."

"Well, yes— No," said Jim. "I don't think you do. The difficulty is, I can send her back, but possibly I can't get back myself; and she won't go without me. Look, maybe I better tell you the whole story from the beginning."

"Brilliant suggestion," said Carolinus, wincing and closing his eyes again.

"You see," said Jim, "I'm a teaching assistant at a place called Riveroak College. Actually, I ought to be an instructor in the English Department . . ." He ran rapidly over the whole situation.

"I see," Carolinus replied, opening his eyes finally. "You're sure about all this, now? You wouldn't prefer to change your story to something simpler and more reasonable—like being a prince ensorceled into a dragon by a rival with access to one of those Inner Kingdom charlatans? No?" He sighed heavily and winced again. "What do you want me to do about it?"

"We thought you might be able to send both Angie and myself back where we belong."

"Possible. Difficult, of course. But I suppose I could manage, given time and a proper balance between Chance and History. All right. That'll be five hundred pounds of gold or five pounds of rubies, payable in advance."

"What?"

"Why not?" Carolinus inquired, frostily. "It's a fair fee."

"But—" Jim almost stammered. "I don't have any gold—or rubies."

"Let's not waste time!" snapped Carolinus. "Of course you have. What kind of a dragon would you be without a hoard?"

"But I don't!" Jim protested. "Maybe this Gorbash has a hoard someplace. But if so, I don't know where it is."

"Nonsense. I'm willing to be reasonable, though. Four hundred and sixty pounds of gold."

"I tell you I don't have a hoard!"

"All right. Four twenty-five. But I warn you, that's my rock-bottom price. I can't work for less than that and still keep house and goods together."

"I don't have a hoard!"

"Four hundred, then, and may a magician's curse— Just a second. You mean you really don't know where this Gorbash-hoard is?"

"That's what I've been trying to tell you."

"*Another* charity patient!" exploded Carolinus, flinging skinny fists in the air, furiously. "What's wrong with the Auditing Department? Answer me!"

"Sorry," came the invisible bass voice.

"Well," said Carolinus, calming, "see that it doesn't happen again—for another ten days at least." He turned once more to Jim. "Haven't you any means of payment at all?"

"Well," Jim said, cautiously, "about this stomach ache of yours. I've just been thinking . . . Does it go away after you eat something?"

"Yes," said Carolinus, "as a matter of fact it does, temporarily."

"I was just thinking you might have what people where I come from call a stomach ulcer. People who live and work under a good deal of nervous pressure often get them."

"People?" Carolinus looked at him suspiciously. "Or dragons?"

"There aren't any dragons where I come from."

"All right, all right," said Carolinus, testily. "You don't have to stretch the truth like that. I believe you about this stomach devil. I was just making sure you knew what you were talking about. Nervous pressure —exactly! These ulcers, how do you exorcise them?"

"Milk," said Jim. "A glass of cow's milk six or eight times a day until the symptoms disappear."

"Ha!"

Carolinus turned about, darted over to a shelf on the wall and took down a tall black bottle. Uncorking it, he poured what looked like red wine into a dusty glass goblet from one of the nearby tables, and held the goblet up to the light.

"Milk," he said.

The red liquid turned white. He drank it off.

"Hmm!" he said, with his head on side, waiting. "Hmm . . ."

Slowly a smile parted his beard.

"Why, I do believe," he said, almost gently, "it's helping. Yes, by the Powers! It is!"

He turned to Jim, beaming.

"Excellent! The bovine nature of the milk has a remarkably placating effect on the anger of the ulcer, which must, by-the-bye, be a member of the family of Fire Demons, now I come to think of it. Congratulations Gorbash, or Jim, or whatever your name is. I'll be frank with you. When you mentioned earlier you'd been a teaching assistant at a college, I didn't believe you. But I do now. As fine a small bit of sympathetic magic as I've seen for weeks. Well, now" —he rubbed bony hands together—"to work on your problem."

"Possibly . . ." said Jim, "if you could get us together and start out by hypnotizing us both at once—"

Carolinus' white eyebrows shot up on his forehead like startled rabbits.

"Teach your grandmother to suck eggs!" he snapped. "By the Powers! That's what's wrong with the world today! Ignorance and anarchy!"

He shook a long and not-too-clean forefinger under Jim's muzzle.

"Dragons galumphing hither and yon—knights galumphing yon and hither—naturals, giants, ogres, sandmirks and other sports and freaks each doing their billy-be-exorcised best to terrorize his own little part of the landscape. Every jackanapes and teaching assistant in his blindness setting himself up to be the equal of a Master of the Arts. It's not endurable!"

His eyes lit up exactly like live coals and glowed fiercely at Jim.

"I say it's not! And I don't intend to endure it, either! We'll have order and peace and Art and Science, if I have to turn the moon inside out!"

"But you said for five hundred—I mean, four hundred pounds of gold—"

"That was business. This is ethics!" Carolinus snatched up some more of his beard and gnawed on it for a moment before spitting it out again. "I thought we'd chaffer a bit about price and see what you were worth. But now that you've paid me with this ulcer spell . . ." His tone became thoughtful suddenly; his eyes dimmed, unfocused, and seemed to look elsewhere. "Yes. Yes, indeed . . . very interesting . . ."

"I just thought," Jim said, humbly, "that hypnotism might work, because—"

"Work!" cried Carolinus, returning abruptly to the here and now. "Of course it'd *work*. Fire will work to cure a bad case of the dropsy. But a dead-and-cindered patient's no success! No, no, Gorbash (I can't remember that other name of yours), recall the First Law of Magic!"

"The what?"

"The First Law—the *First Law!* Didn't they teach you anything at that college?"

"Well, actually, my field was—"

"Forgotten it already, I see," sneered Carolinus. "Oh, this younger generation! The Law of Payment, you idiot! For every use of Art of Science, there is a required or corresponding price. Why do you think I live by my fees instead of running through the aleph tables? Just because a number is transfinite doesn't mean you can use it to get something for nothing! Why use hawks and owls and cats and mice and familiars instead of a viewing crystal? Why does a magic potion have a bad taste? Everything must be paid for, in *proportion!* Why, I wouldn't have done what this wooden-headed Hansen amateur of yours did without having built up ten years' credit with the Auditing Department first; and I'm a Master of the Arts. He's pushed his debit right to the breaking point—it can't go any further."

"How do you know?" asked Jim.

"Why, my good teaching assistant," said Carolinus,

"isn't it obvious? He was able to send this maiden of yours—I assume she is a maiden?"

"Well—"

"Well, well, call her a maiden for form's sake. Academic question, anyway," Carolinus snapped. "The point I'm making is that he was able to send her back completely, body and all; but he only had enough credit with the Auditing Department after that to transport your spirit, leaving your body behind. Result, you're an Imbalance in the here and now—and the Dark Powers love something like that. Result, we have a nice, touchy situation—now that I look a little deeper into it—ready to turn things here very much for the worst. Hah! If you'd only been a little more clever and learned, you'd have realized you could have had my help without paying for it with that ulcer exorcism. I'd have helped you anyway, just in order to help myself and all of us here."

Jim stared at him.

"I don't understand," he said, finally.

"Naturally not—a mere teaching assistant like yourself. All right, I'll spell it out. The fact of your appearance here—yours and this Angie's—has upset the balance between Chance and History. Upset it badly. Imagine a teeter-totter, Chance sitting on one end, History on the other, swinging back and forth—Chance up one moment, then Chance down and History up. The Dark Powers love that. They throw their weight at the right moment on a side that's already headed down, and either Chance or History ends permanently up. One way we get Chaos. The other we get Predictability and an end to Romance, Art, Magic and everything else interesting."

"But . . ." Jim found himself drowning in a sea of words, "if that's the case, what can we do about it?"

"Do? Push up when the Dark Powers push down. Push down when the Dark Powers push up! Force a temporary balance and then hit them head on—our strength against their strength. Then, if we win that final battle, we can set your situation to rights

49

and be back on permanent balance again. But there'll be trouble, first."

"Look here, though—" Jim was beginning.

He was about to protest that Carolinus seemed to be making the situation out to be far more complicated than was necessary. But he had no chance to finish his sentence. Just then a loud thud outside the house shook it to its foundations; and a dragon voice thundered.

"Gorbash!"

"I knew it," said Carolinus. "It's already started."

Chapter 5

He led the way to the door, threw it open and strode out. Jim followed. Sitting on the path about a dozen feet from the door was Smrgol.

"Greetings, Mage!" boomed the old dragon, dipping his head briefly. "You may not remember me. Name's Smrgol. You remember that business about the ogre of Gormely Keep? I see my grand-nephew got to you, all right."

"Ah, Smrgol. I remember," said Carolinus. "That was a good job you did."

"He had a habit of dropping his clubhead after a swing," Smrgol explained. "I noticed it along about the fourth hour of the battle. Left himself wide open for just a second. The next time he tried it, I went in over his guard and tore up the biceps of his right arm. After that it was just a matter of finishing."

"I remember. Eighty-three years ago. So this is your grand-nephew?"

"I know," said Smrgol. "A little thick-headed and

all that—but my own flesh and blood, you know. How've you been getting along with him, Mage?"

"Well enough," said Carolinus, dryly. "In fact, I'll venture to promise this grand-nephew of yours will never be the same again."

"I hope so," Smrgol said, brightening. "Any change is a change for the better. But I've bad news, Mage."

"Don't tell me!"

"Don't . . . ?" Smrgol stared.

"I was being sarcastic. Go on, go on," said Carolinus. "What's happened now?"

"Why, just that that young inchworm of a Bryagh's run off with our george."

"WHAT?" cried Jim.

The flowers and grass lay down as if in a hurricane. Carolinus tottered, and Smrgol winced.

"My boy," he said, reproachfully. "How many times must I tell you not to shout? I said Bryagh's taken the george."

"WHERE?" Jim yelped.

"Gorbash!" said Smrgol severely. "If you can't talk about this in a polite tone, we won't include you in the discussions after this. I don't know why you get so excited whenever we mention this george."

"Listen—" said Jim. "It's time you found out something about me. This george, as you call her, is the woman I—"

His vocal cords seemed to become paralyzed suddenly. He was unable to say another word.

"—and to be sure," Carolinus interrupted quickly, shoving into the gap caused by Jim's sudden and unexpected silence, "this is a matter of concern to all of us. As I was telling Gorbash, the situation is bad enough already without our making it worse. Eh, Gorbash?"

He bent a penetrating eye on Jim.

"We want to be careful and not make it any worse than it is already, don't we? We don't want to disturb the already disturbed fabric of things any more than it already is. Otherwise, I might not be able to be of any help."

Jim found his vocal cords suddenly free to operate again.

"Oh? Oh . . . yes," he said, a trifle hoarsely.

"And to be sure," repeated Carolinus, smoothly, "Gorbash has asked the right question. Where has Bryagh taken this so-called george?"

"Nobody knows," Smrgol answered. "I thought maybe you could find out for us, Mage."

"Certainly. Fifteen pounds of gold, please."

"Fifteen pounds?" The old dragon visibly staggered. "But, Mage, I thought you'd want to help us. I thought you'd— I don't have fifteen pounds of gold. I lived up my hoard a long time ago."

Shakily, he turned to Jim.

"Come, Gorbash, it's no use. We'll have to give up our hope of finding the george—"

"No!" cried Jim. "Listen, Carolinus! *I'll* pay you. I'll get the fifteen pounds somewhere—!"

"Boy, are you sick or what?" Smrgol was aghast. "That's only his asking price. Don't be in such a sulphurous hurry!"

He turned back to the magician.

"I might be able to scrape together a couple of pounds, maybe, Mage," he said.

They dickered like fishwives for several minutes while Jim sat quivering with impatience; and finally closed on a price of four pounds of gold, one pound of silver and a large flawed emerald.

"Done!" said Carolinus.

He produced a small vial from his robes and walked across to the pool at the base of the fountain, where he filled the vial about half full. Then he came back and searched among the soft grass around the edge of one flower bed until he found a small, sandy, open spot between the soft green blades. He bent over and the two dragons craned their necks down on either side of him to watch.

"Quiet now," Carolinus warned. "I'm going to try a watchbeetle—and they're easily alarmed. Don't breathe."

Jim held his breath. Carolinus tilted the vial in his

hand and a drop fell on the little sandy open spot with a single glass-chime musical note. *Tink!* Jim could see the bright sand darken as the moisture sank into it.

For a second nothing happened; then the wet sand cracked, opened, and a fine spray of lighter-colored, drier sand from underneath spouted into the air. A small amount of this under sand grew about a depression that sank and became a widening hole, like the entrance to an anthill. An occasional flicker of small black insect limbs could be seen, rapidly at work. After a second the work ceased, there was a moment of silence, and then an odd-looking black beetle popped halfway out of the hole and paused, facing up to them. Its forelimbs waved in the air and a little, squeaky voice like a cracked phonograph record repeating itself far off over a bad telephone connection came to Jim's ears.

"Gone to the Loathly Tower. Gone to the Loathly Tower. Gone to the Loathly Tower."

The watchbeetle stopped abruptly, popped back out of sight and began churning away inside the hole, filling it in.

"Not so fast!" Carolinus snapped. "Did I give you leave to go? There're other things than being a watchbeetle, you know. There're blindworms. Come back at once, sir!"

The sand spouted into the air once more. The watchbeetle reappeared, its front limbs waving agitatedly.

"Well, well—speak up!" said Carolinus. "What about our young friend here?"

"Companions!" creaked the watchbeetle. *"Companions! Companions!"*

It ducked out of sight again. The sand began to work itself smooth once more; and in a couple of seconds the ground looked as if it had never been disturbed.

"Hmm," Carolinus murmured thoughtfully. "It's the Loathly Tower then, that this Bryagh of yours has taken the maiden to."

Smrgol cleared his throat noisily.

"That's that ruined tower to the west, in the fens, isn't it, Mage?" he asked. "Why, that's the place the mother of my Gormely Keep ogre came from, as the stories go. The same place that loosed the blight on the mere-dragons nearly five hundred years ago."

Carolinus nodded, his eyes hooded under his thick white brows.

"It's a place of old magic," he answered. "Dark magic. These places are like ancient sores on the land, scabbed over for a while but always breaking out with new evil whenever the balance of Chance and History becomes upset."

He went on musingly, speaking almost more to himself than to Jim and the older dragon.

"Just as I feared," he said, "the Dark Powers haven't been slow to move. Your Bryagh belongs to them, now—even if he didn't, before. It'll be they who caused him to take the maiden there, to become a hostage and weapon against Gorbash here. It's a good thing I took a stern line with that watchbeetle just now and got the full message."

"Full message?" Jim echoed, puzzled.

"That's right—the full message." Carolinus turned commandingly upon him. "Now that you know your lady's been taken there, no doubt you're all ready to go to her rescue, aren't you?"

"Of course," said Jim.

"Of course *not!*" snapped Carolinus. "Didn't you hear the second part of the watchbeetle's message? 'Companions!' You'll have to have companions before you dare venture close to the tower. Otherwise your Angela and you are both doomed."

"Who is this Angela?" Smrgol asked, puzzled.

"The Lady Angela, dragon," said Carolinus. "The female george Bryagh took to the tower."

"Ah," said Smrgol, a little sadly. "Not a princess then, after all. Well, you can't have everything. But why does Gorbash here want to rescue her? Let the other georges do whatever rescuing there has to be—"

"I love her," said Jim, fiercely.

"Love her? My boy," Smrgol scowled, aghast, "I've put up with a good deal of your strange associates in the past—that wolf and so forth. But falling in love with a george! There's a limit to what any decent dragon—"

"Come, come, Smrgol," said Carolinus, impatiently. "There are wheels within wheels in this matter."

"Wheels . . . ? I don't understand, Mage."

"It's a complex situation, derivative from a great many factors, unobvious as well as obvious. Just as in any concatenation of events, no matter how immediate, the apparent is not always the real. In short, your grand-nephew Gorbash is also, in another sense, a gentleman named Sir James of Riveroak, obligated to rescue his lady from the Dark Powers now controlling Bryagh, the Loathly Tower, and the Powers-know-what-else. In words of one syllable, therefore, he whom you know as Gorbash must now embark on a quest to restore the balance between Chance and History; and it is not for you to criticize or object."

"Or understand either, I suppose," Smrgol said, humbly.

"One might say that," barked Carolinus. "In fact, I do!" His voice softened somewhat. "We're all caught up in a new battle for freedom from domination by the Dark Powers, Smrgol. And it's going to be a battle that makes your set-to with the ogre of Gormely Keep seem unimportant. You can stand aside if you want, but you can do nothing to change what's coming."

"Stand aside? Me?" Smrgol huffed. "What kind of dragon do you take me for? I'm with Gorbash—and with you too, Mage, if you're on the same side he is. Just tell me what to do!"

"I am," said Carolinus, dryly. "Very well, Smrgol. In that case, you'd better get back to the other dragons and start making them understand what's at stake here and just where Bryagh, you, and Gorbash stand on matters. As for you—" he turned on Jim.

"I'm headed for that tower, like it or not," said Jim.

"Do, and you'll never see your lady again!" Carolinus' voice cracked like a gunshot. His eyes were burning once more. "Do it, and I wash my hands of you; and if I wash my hands of you, you've no hope! Now—will you listen?"

Jim swallowed his immediate impulse to take off then and there. There might be something in what Carolinus was about to say. In any case, he and Angie would still need the magician's help to get home again, even after Angie was rescued. It would hardly be wise to make an opponent of Carolinus now.

"I'll listen," he answered.

"Very well, then. The Dark Powers have taken your lady to their tower for the very reason that they hope to draw you into their territory before you've gathered the strength to oppose them. They want you to come immediately to the rescue of the Lady Angela; because if you do, you'll be easy to defeat. But if you hold off until you've gathered the companions the watchbeetle indicated, it's they who can be defeated. Therefore, you're foolish if you go now."

"But what'll they do to Angela—I mean, Angie—" said Jim, "when they see I'm not coming right after her? They'll figure she's no good as a means to stop me, and do something terrible to her—"

"They cannot!" Carolinus snapped. "By taking the lady they've over-extended themselves, made themselves vulnerable. If they treat her any way but well, all who might oppose them—man, dragon and beast —will form a solid front against them. There're rules at work here; and just as if you go now to her rescue you will certainly lose, so if they harm their hostage *they* will certainly lose!"

Jim found himself wavering in his firm intention to go after Angie at once. He remembered his earlier determination to figure out the system by which this world operated. If Carolinus was correct . . . and the magician was a very convincing arguer . . .

"But you're sure she'll be all right if I don't get to that tower right away?" Jim asked.

"She'll only be other than all right if you do go now."

Jim gave in with a deep sigh.

"All right," he said. "What do I do, then? Where should I go?"

"Away!" said Carolinus. "That is, in exactly the opposite direction which you would use in returning to the dragon cave from which you came."

"But, Mage," put in Smrgol, puzzled, "away from the cave is exactly toward the fens and the Loathly Tower. And you just finished saying he shouldn't go to the tower—"

"Dragon," cried Carolinus, wheeling on Smrgol. "Have I got to argue with *you,* now? I said 'away!' I didn't say 'to the tower.' The Powers give me patience! Have I got to explain the intricacies of Advanced Magics to every dumbwit and numbskull who flies in here, or don't I? I ask you?"

"No!" said the deep bass voice out of thin air.

"There," Carolinus said in a relieved tone, mopping his brow. "You heard the Auditing Department. Now, no more talk. I've got my hands too full as it is. Off with you to the dragon cave, Smrgol. And away with you, Gorbash, in the opposite direction!"

He turned around and stamped into his house, slamming the door shut behind him.

"Come, Gorbash," boomed Smrgol. "The Mage's right. Let me get you started in the right direction, then I'll leave you on your own. My, my, who'd have thought we'd run into such interesting times in my old age?"

Wagging his head thoughtfully, the elderly dragon sprang into the air, leathery wings opening out with a thunderous clap, and mounted skyward.

After a second's hesitation, Jim followed him.

Chapter 6

"You can just see the beginning of the fens, there—that misty, bluish line beyond that bit of forest coming in from the north and stretching out like a finger across your way."

Smrgol, soaring alongside Jim, broke off as they left the thermal they had been rising upon and had to use their wings to get to another. The prevailing breezes seemed to be blowing against them.

Jim noticed that the older dragon had a tendency to fall silent when he had to exert himself flying. It gave the information Smrgol seemed determined to impart something of a fragmentary feeling.

"Nothing important comes out on the fens nowadays to concern our people, of course. Except, that is," Smrgol went on abruptly as they caught another thermal and started on a long, buoyant glide toward the dimly seen fens, "for the mere-dragons. Relatives of ours, as you know, Gorbash. Distant, naturally. You'll have some fifteenth or sixteenth cousins among them without a doubt, though probably they won't remember the connection. Never were a very solid branch of the family to start with; and then when this blight hit them—well, they generally fell apart."

Smrgol paused to clear his throat.

"Took to living separately, even from each other. There are no good caves out there among all that bog and water, of course. They must be feeding themselves mostly on fish from the sea, nowadays, I don't wonder. Only an occasional sandmirk, sea lizard or stray chicken is to be found in that sort of territory. Oh, there are a few small holdings and impoverished farms on the borders of the fens, and occasionally they can be raided. But even those'll have suffered from the blight; and everything they own'll be stunted or hardly worth the eating to a healthy dragon like you or me, boy. Why, I've even heard some of our mere-dragon relatives have fallen so low as to try and exist on garden truck. Heard of one even eating cabbages. Cabbages! Unbelievable . . ."

Once more they had to use their wings to reach another thermal; and by the time they got to it and Smrgol took up talking again, it was obvious to Jim's ears that the older dragon was definitely winded.

"Well, there you have it . . . Gorbash . . ." he said. "I guess that covers it, pretty well. Keep . . . your head, my boy. Don't let your natural . . . dragon fury run away with you; and you can't help . . . But do well. Well, I guess I'd better be turning back."

"Yes," said Jim. "Maybe you'd better. Thanks for the advice."

"Don't thank me . . . boy. Least I can do for you. Well . . . good-bye, then . . ."

"Good-bye."

Jim watched Smrgol fall off in a sloping dive, turning a hundred and eighty degrees as he swung to catch a lower thermal and the wind from the seacoast, which was now behind him. Smrgol dwindled quickly and Jim turned his attention back to what lay ahead of him, personally.

Below him at the moment, the forest and open ground over which Jim had approached the woods holding Carolinus' house had given way to a wide landscape of desolate moors, interrupted by strands of just a few trees, and some poverty-stricken huts made of what looked like fallen branches tied together in bundles, the roofs thatched with hay or grass. The inhabitants of these, when surprised outside their dwelling, invariably scurried for shelter at the sight of Jim winging overhead. They were dressed in furs rather than in more conventional clothes and did not appear to be a very attractive people.

However, as Jim continued on his flight, these habitations became more and more occasional and finally disappeared altogether. The moors were ending now and the forest Smrgol had pointed out was close. Unlike the coniferous woods around the Tinkling Water, this other growth was apparently of deciduous trees such as oaks and willows. They all seemed curiously leafless for this time of year and their branches, seen from above, had a gnarled and tangled look that gave the forest a particularly forbidding look; as if it was the kind of place that would not easily let out again anyone who wandered into it on foot. Jim felt a twinge of smugness at being able to soar safely above it.

In fact, once again the intoxication of being airborne was making him feel better than conditions justified. He had no real idea of what he was headed into; but that did not seem to disturb his cheerful feeling. He had wanted to go to the Loathly Tower and Carolinus had argued against it. But here he was, at Carolinus' direction, going toward it anyway. Whatever the reason was for his being headed in this direction, what he was doing at the moment felt to him particularly *right* . . .

Now, the far edge of the forest was almost underneath him. Beyond, there was nothing but the green fenland, stretching to a misty deeper-blue line which must be the open sea. The fens was a good-sized area, he saw, a greenly lush, low-lying wilderness of land and water. It filled the landscape before him to the skyline in all directions except straight ahead, where the sea blue showed.

He searched about it with the telescopic vision of his dragon-eyes for some sight of a structure which could be the Loathly Tower, but he could pick out nothing. The breeze that had been blowing against him dropped abruptly, and a new, light wind began to push from behind him. He stretched his wings to it, and let it carry him, gliding at a small angle down the invisible air surface as if it was some miles-long, magic slide. The fenland rose to meet him: spongy, grass-thick earth, broken into causeways and islands by the blue water, thick-choked itself in the shallower bays and inlets with tall seagrass and club rushes.

Flocks of water fowl rose here and there like eddying smoke from one mere, drifted over and settled on the surface of another, a few hundred yards away. Their cries, thinned by the distance, came faintly to Jim's hypersensitive ears.

Ahead, heavy clouds were piling up above the coastline to the west.

Jim soared on, above the still water and the soft grass, smelling the distant saltwater. He looked worriedly at the declining sun which was just now beginning to slip down behind the thick cloudbank he had just noticed. It would be nightfall before long. He was hungry and he had absolutely no notion of what he should do once it was dark. Certainly, he could not continue in the air. It would not be pleasant to fly full-tilt into the ground because he could not see where he was going. It would not be pleasant, in fact, to fly full-tilt into one of the bays or meres. He could land and travel onward on foot—but there would probably be bogs.

The sensible thing once the sun set, he thought, would be to spend the night on one of the small land patches below him. Not that such a prospect sounded very comfortable. Also, he would be completely exposed down there if anything decided to creep up on him.

Jim was brought up short in his thoughts at this point by the sudden remembrance of what he was. He had, he realized, been thinking like a human, not like a dragon. What, in its right mind, would want to creep up on a dragon? Outside of a knight in armor. And what would a knight in armor be doing prowling around in the dark? Or another dragon, for that matter? The only other dragon he had any reason to fear around here, if Smrgol's report on the mere-dragons had been correct, was Bryagh; and Bryagh would be making a mistake if he came anywhere near, in the mood possessing Jim right now.

In fact, thought Jim, he would like nothing better

than to get his jaws and claws on Bryagh right now. He felt a grim and sullen anger begin to kindle in him like a hot coal fanned to life just beneath his breastbone. The feeling was rather enjoyable. He let it kindle and grow until it suddenly occurred to him that it was a dragonly, rather than a human, anger he was feeling. Perhaps this was what Smrgol had been talking about when he had advised Gorbash not to let his dragon-fury run away with him.

Jim made a determined effort to put the emotion aside, but the inward fire he had kindled did not seem disposed to go out that easily. He struggled with it, alarmed now, and—as luck would have it—just at that moment he caught sight of another dragon shape, down on one of the spits of land directly in front of him.

The other dragon was concerned with something lying in the grass. What it was, Jim could not make out from this height and angle; but in any case, its identity was academic. The sight of the other dragon had been all that was needed to bring to full flame the fury now within him.

"Bryagh!" The word snarled, unbidden in his throat.

Reflexively, he nosed over and went into a dive like a fighter plane, his sights locked on the target below.

It was a dive sudden enough to take the dragon underneath utterly by surprise. Unfortunately, it had one natural drawback. Even a small flivver airplane with its motor cut off makes a noticeable amount of noise descending in a steep dive; and a large dragon such as Gorbash had no less air resistance than the average two-seater light airplane. Moreover, the dragon below had evidently had some experience with such a noise; for without looking upward he made one frantic leap and went tumbling head over tail out of the way as Jim slammed down onto the ground at the spot where a second before the other had been.

The attacked dragon came to the end of his tumbling, sat up, took a look at Jim and began to wail.

"It's not fair! It's not fair!" he cried in a—for a

dragon—remarkably high-pitched voice. "Just because you're bigger than I am! And I had to fight two hours for it. It almost got away half a dozen times. Besides, it's the first good-sized one to wander out onto the fens in months, and now you're going to take it away from me. And you don't need it, not at all. You're big and fat, and I'm weak and hungry . . ."

Jim blinked and stared. He glanced from the dragon down to the thing in the grass before him and saw that it was the carcass of a rather old and stringy-looking cow, badly bitten up and with a broken neck. Looking back at the other dragon again, he realized for the first time that the other was little better than half his own size, and so emaciated that he appeared on the verge of collapse from starvation.

". . . Just my luck!" the other dragon was whimpering. "Every time I get something good, someone comes along and takes it away from me. All I ever get is fish—"

"Hold on!" said Jim.

"—Fish, fish, fish! Cold fish, without any warm blood in them to put strength in my bones—"

"Hold on, I say! SHUT UP!" Jim bellowed, in Gorbash's best voice.

The other dragon stopped his complaining as abruptly as if he was a record player whose plug had been pulled.

"Yes, sir," he said, timidly.

"What're you talking about?" demanded Jim. "I'm not going to take your cow away from you."

"Oh no, sir," said the other dragon; and tittered as if to show that nobody could accuse him of not knowing a good joke when he heard it.

"I'm not."

"He-he-he!" chuckled the smaller dragon. "You certainly are a card, your honor."

"Dammit, I'm serious!" snapped Jim, backing away from the carcass. "Go ahead, eat! I just thought you were someone else."

"Oh, I don't want it. Really, I don't! I was just joking about being starved. Really, I was!"

"Look," said Jim, taking a tight rein on his dragon-temper, which was beginning to rekindle, "what's your name?"

"Oh, well," said the other. "Oh, well—you know—"

"WHAT'S YOUR NAME?"

"Secoh, your worship!" yelped the dragon, fearfully. "Just Secoh, that's all. I'm nobody important, your highness. Just a little, unimportant mere-dragon."

"You don't have to swear it to me," said Jim. "I believe you. All right, Secoh"—he waved at the dead cow—"dig in. I don't want any myself, but maybe you can give me some directions and information about this territory and what lives here."

"Well . . ." Secoh hedged. He had been sidling forward in fawning fashion while the conversation was going on, until he was once more almost next to the cow. "If you'll excuse my table manners, sir. I'm just a mere-dragon—" And he tore into the meat before him in sudden, ravenous fashion.

Jim watched. His first impulse was the compassionate one of letting the other get some food inside him before making him talk. But, as he sat and observed, Jim began to feel the stirrings of a not inconsiderable hunger himself. His belly rumbled, suddenly and audibly. He stared at the torn carcass of the cow and tried to tell himself it was not the sort of thing any civilized person would want to eat. Raw meat—off a dead animal—flesh, bones, hide and all . . .

"Say," said Jim, drawing closer to Secoh and the cow, and clearing his throat, "that does look rather good, after all."

His stomach rumbled again. Apparently his dragon-body had none of his human scruples about the eatability of what he was looking at.

"Secoh?"

Secoh reluctantly lifted his head from the cow and rolled his eyes warily to Jim, although he continued to chew and gulp frantically.

"Er, Secoh—I'm a stranger around these parts," said Jim. "I suppose you know your way around pretty well. I— Say, how does that cow taste?"

"Oh, terrible— Mumpf—" said Secoh with his mouth full. "Stringy, old—awful, really. Good enough for a mere-dragon like me, but not for—"

"Well, about those directions I wanted . . ."

"Yes, your worship?"

"I think— Oh, well, it's your cow."

"That's what your honor promised," replied Secoh, cautiously.

"But you know, I wonder," Jim grinned confidingly at him, "I just wonder how a cow like that would taste. You know I've never tasted anything quite like that before?"

"No, sir." A large tear welled up in Secoh's near eye and splashed down upon the grass.

"I actually haven't. I wonder—it's up to you, now— would you mind if I just tasted it?"

Another large tear rolled down Secoh's cheek.

"If—if your honor wishes," he choked. "Won't you —won't you help yourself, please?"

"Well, thanks," said Jim.

He walked up and sank his teeth experimentally into a shoulder of the carcass. The rich juices of the warm meat trickled over his tongue. He tore the shoulder loose . . .

Some little time later, he and Secoh sat back, polishing bones with the rough upper surfaces of their forked tongues, which were abrasive as the coarsest sandpaper.

"Did you get enough to eat, Secoh?" Jim asked.

"More than enough, sir," replied the mere-dragon, staring at the denuded skeleton with a wild and famished eye. "Although if you don't mind, your honor, I've got a weakness for marrow—"

He picked up a thighbone and began to crunch it like a stick of candy.

"Tomorrow we'll hunt up another cow and I'll kill it for you," said Jim. "You can have it all to yourself."

"Oh, thank you, your honor," said Secoh, with polite lack of conviction.

"I mean it—now, about this Loathly Tower, where is it?"

"The wh-what?" stammered Secoh.

"The Loathly Tower. The Loathly Tower! You know where it is, don't you?"

"Oh yes, sir. But your honor wouldn't want to go there, would your worship? Not that I'm presuming to give your lordship advice—" Secoh cried suddenly, in a high and terrified voice.

"No, no. Go on," said Jim.

"—but of course I'm only a little, timid mere-dragon, your honor. Not like you. But the Loathly Tower, it's a terrible place, your highness."

"How terrible?"

"Well . . . it just is." Secoh cast an unhappy look about him. "It's what spoiled all of us, you know, five hundred years ago. We used to be just like you other dragons— Oh, not so big and fierce as you, of course, sir. But then, after that, they say the Dark Powers got pushed back again and sealed up, and the tower itself broken and ruined—not that it helped us mere-dragons any. Everybody else just went home and left us the way we'd become. So, it's supposed to be all right, now. But all the same I wouldn't go near there if I was your worthiness, I really wouldn't."

"But what's there that's so bad?" demanded Jim. "What sort of thing, specifically, is it?"

"Well, I wouldn't say there was any *thing* there," replied Secoh, cautiously. "It's nothing your worship could exactly put a claw on. It's just that whatever or whoever goes near it—without belonging to it, I mean —it does something to them, sir. Of course, it's the evil sorts that head for it in the first place. But sometimes things just as strange seem to come from it, and lately—"

Secoh caught himself and became very busy searching among the bones of the cow.

"Lately, what?"

"Nothing—really, nothing, your excellency!" cried Secoh, a little shrilly, starting up. "Your illustriousness shouldn't catch a worthless little mere-dragon up like that. We're not too bright, you know. I only meant . . . lately the tower's been a more fearful place than ever. No one knows why. And we all keep well away from it!"

"Probably just your imagination," said Jim, shortly.

He had always been a skeptic by nature; and although this strange world was clearly full of all sorts of variances with the normal pattern of things as he knew them, his mind instinctively revolted against too much credit in the supernatural—particularly, he thought, the old B-movie horror type of supernatural.

"We know what we know," said the mere-dragon with unusual stubbornness. He stretched out a scrawny and withered forelimb. "Is *that* imagination?"

Jim grunted. The meal he had just gulped down had made him drowsy. The gray last light of day was leaden in its effect upon his nerves. He felt torpid and dull.

"I think I'll grab some sleep," he said. "Anyway, how do I find the Loathly Tower from here?"

"Just go due west. You won't be able to miss it."

A shiver was to be heard in the last words of the mere-dragon, but Jim was becoming too sleepy to care. Dimly, he heard the rest of what Secoh was telling him.

"It's out along the Great Causeway. That's a wide lane of solid land running due east and west through the fens for about five miles, right to the sea. You just follow it until you come to the tower. It stands on a rise of rock overlooking the edge of the ocean."

"Five miles . . ." Jim muttered.

He would have to wait until morning, which was not an unpleasant prospect. His armored body seemed undisturbed by the evening temperature, whatever it was, and the grassy ground beneath him was soft.

"Yes, I think I'll get some sleep," he murmured. He settled down on the grass and yielded to an impulse of his dragon-body to curl his long neck back and tuck his head bird-fashion under one wing. "See you in the morning, Secoh."

"Whatever your excellency desires," replied the

mere-dragon in his timid voice. "I'll just settle down over here, and if your worship wants me, your worship has only to call and I'll be right here . . . "

The words faded out on Jim's ear as he dropped into sleep like an overladen ship foundering in deep saltwater.

Chapter 7

When he opened his eyes, the sun was well above the horizon. The bright, transparent, cool light of early morning lit up the clear blue arch of sky overhead. The seagrass and the club rushes swayed slightly in the early breeze that was sending a series of light ripples over the stretch of shallow lake near where Jim lay. He sat up, yawned expansively and blinked.

Secoh was gone. So were the leftover bones.

For a second Jim felt a twinge of annoyance. He had been unconsciously counting on tapping the mere-dragon for more information about the fens. But then the annoyance faded into amusement. The picture of Secoh stealthily collecting the denuded bones in careful silence and sneaking away before daybreak tickled Jim's sense of humor.

He walked down to the edge of the lake and drank, lapping like some enormous cat and flipping several pints of water into his throat with each flick of his long tongue. Satisfied at last, he looked westward toward the misty line of the ocean and spread his wings—

"Ouch!" he said.

Hastily he folded the wings again, cursing himself mentally. He should, of course, have expected this from the way Smrgol had run out of breath while flying yesterday. The first attempt to stretch Gorbash's wings had sent what felt like several keen-edged knives stabbing into muscles he had seldom used before. Like anyone else who has suddenly overexercised a body out of shape for such activity, he was stiff as a board in that portion of his body he had most need of at the moment.

The irony of it did not escape him. For twenty-six years he had gotten along quite nicely without wings. Now, after one day's use of them, he was decidedly miffed to have to proceed on foot. His amusement gone, he turned his head toward the ocean and set about following a land route.

Unfortunately, it could not be a direct route. Instinctively, he tried to travel on land as much as possible, but often he had to jump small ditches—which caused his wings to spread instinctively and sent fresh stabs of pain into his stiff flying muscles—and once or twice he had to actually swim a ditch or small lake too wide to jump. This taught him why dragons preferred to walk or fly. Unlike humans, they apparently had a slightly higher specific gravity than water. In other words, unless he swam furiously, he had a tendency to sink. And his dragon-body, Jim found, had a near-hysterical fear of getting any water up its nose.

However, proceeding by these methods, he finally gained a rather wide tongue of land which he assumed to be the Great Causeway that Secoh had spoken about. He had seen nothing else to compare with it in the fens and, if further proof were needed, it seemed to run westward as far as he could see, as straight as a Roman road. It could almost, in fact, have been built there: it was several feet higher than most of the surrounding bits of land, covered with bushes and even an occasional tree.

Jim rolled on the grass—he had just finished swimming one of the stretches of water too wide to jump—and flopped, belly-down, in the sun. A tree nearby kept the sun out of his eyes, the heat of the daystar's rays were soothing to his stiff muscles and the grass was soft. He had walked and swum away most of the

69

morning and the midday hush was relaxing. He felt comfortable. Dropping his head on his foreclaws, he dozed a bit ...

He was awakened by the sound of someone singing. Lifting his head, he looked about. Someone was coming out along the causeway. Jim could now hear the dry clopping of a horse's hooves on the firm earth, the jingle of metal, the creak of leather, and over all this a fine, baritone voice carolling cheerfully to itself. Whatever the earlier verses of the song had been, Jim had no idea. But the chorus he heard now came clearly to his ear.

> "... A right good spear, a constant mind—
> A trusty sword and true!
> The dragons of the mere shall find
> What Neville-Smythe can do!"

The tune was one of the sort that Jim may have heard somewhere before. He was still trying to decide if he really knew it or not, when there was a crackling of branches. A screen of bushes some twenty feet away parted to disgorge a man in full plate armor, with his visor up and a single strip of scarlet pennon afloat just below the head of his upright lance; he was seated on a large, somewhat clumsy-looking white horse.

Jim, interested, sat up for a better look.

It was, as things turned out, not the best possible move. Immediately, the man on horseback saw him and the visor came down with a clang, the long lance seemed to leap into one steel-gauntleted hand, there came a flash of golden spurs, and the white horse broke into a heavy-hooved gallop, directly for Jim.

"A Neville-Smythe! A Neville-Smythe!" roared the man, muffledly, within his helmet.

Jim's reflexes took over. He went straight up into the air, stiff wing muscles forgotten, and was just about to hurl himself forward and down on the approaching figure when a cold finger of sanity touched his mind for a fraction of a second and he flung him-

70

self instead into the upper branches of the tree that had shaded his eyes.

The knight—as Jim took him to be—pulled his horse to a skidding stop on its haunches directly under the tree; and looked up through the branches at Jim. Jim looked back down. The tree had seemed fairly good-sized when he was under it. Now that he was up in it, with all his dragon-weight, its branches creaked alarmingly under him and he was not as far above his attacker's head as he would have preferred to be.

The knight tilted back his visor and canted his head back in order to see upward. In the shadow of the helm Jim made out a square-boned, rather lean face with burning blue eyes over a large, hooked nose. The chin was jutting and generous.

"Come down," said the knight.

"No thanks," replied Jim, holding firmly to the tree trunk with tail and claws.

A slight pause followed in the conversation as they both digested the situation.

"Damned catiff mere-dragon!" said the knight, finally.

"I'm not a mere-dragon."

"Don't talk bloody nonsense!"

"I'm not."

"Course you are."

"I tell you, I'm not!" said Jim, feeling a preliminary stirring of his dragonly temper. He got it back under control, and spoke reasonably. "In fact, I'll bet you can't guess who I really am."

The knight did not seem interested in guessing who Jim really was. He stood upright in his stirrups and probed upward with his lance through the branches, but the point came a good four feet short of Jim.

"Damn!" said the knight, disappointedly. He lowered the lance and appeared to think for a moment. "If I take off my armor," he said, apparently to himself, "I can climb that goddam tree. But then what if he flies down and I have to fight him on the bloody turf, after all?"

"Look," called Jim, "I'm willing to come down"—

the knight looked up eagerly—"provided you're willing to listen with an open mind to what I have to say, first."

The knight thought it over.

"All right," he said, at last. He shook the lance at Jim, warningly. "No pleas for mercy, though!"

"Of course not."

"Because I shan't grant them, dammit! It's not in my vows. Widows and orphans, men and women of the Church and honorable enemies surrendering on the field of combat. But not dragons!"

"No," said Jim, "nothing like that. I just want to convince you of who I really am."

"I don't care who you really are."

"You will," Jim said. "Because I'm not really a dragon at all. I've been put under an . . . ensorcelment to make me look like a dragon."

"A likely story."

"Really!" Jim was digging his claws into the tree trunk, but the bark was flaking away under his grasp. "I'm as human as you are. Do you know S. Carolinus, the magician?"

"I've heard of him," grunted the knight. "Who hasn't? I suppose you'll claim he's the one who ensorceled you?"

"Not at all. He's the one who's going to change me back as soon as I can find the lady I—to whom I'm affianced. A real dragon ran off with her. That's what I'm doing so far from home. Look at me. Do I look like one of your ordinary mere-dragons?"

The knight considered him.

"Hmm," he said, rubbing his hooked nose thoughtfully. "Come to think of it, you are a size and half on what I usually run into."

"Carolinus found my lady had been taken to the Loathly Tower. He sent me out to find some Companions, so I could go and rescue her."

The knight stared.

"The Loathly Tower?" he echoed.

"That's right."

"Never heard of a dragon—or anyone else in his

right mind, for that matter—wanting to go to the Loathly Tower. Shouldn't care to go there myself. By heaven, if you *are* a dragon, you've got nerve!"

"But I'm not," said Jim. "That's why I've got—er—nerve. I'm a gentleman like yourself, bent on the rescue of the lady I love."

"Love?" The knight reached into a saddlebag, produced a piece of white cloth and blew his nose. "I say, that's touching. You love this demoiselle of yours?"

"Doesn't every knight love his lady?"

"Well . . ." The other put his handkerchief away again. "Some do, some don't, politics being what it is these days. But it *is* a coincidence. You see, I love my lady also."

"Well, then," said Jim, "that's all the more reason you shouldn't interfere with me in my efforts to rescue mine."

The knight went into one of his moments of obvious thought.

"How do I know you're telling the truth?" he said, at last. "Bloody dragons could say anything!"

Jim had a sudden inspiration.

"I'll tell you what," he said. "Hold your sword up, point down. I'll swear on the cross of the hilt that what I say is true."

"But if you're a dragon what good will that do? Dragons don't have souls, dammit!"

"Of course not," retorted Jim. "But a Christian gentleman does; and as a Christian gentleman, I wouldn't dare forswear myself, now would I?"

Jim could see the knight visibly struggling with the inverted logic of this for several moments. Finally he gave up.

"Oh, well," he said, held up his sword by the blade and let Jim swear on it.

He put the sword back in its sheath. Jim let go the trees and half jumped, half flapped down to ground.

"It might be . . ." said the knight, moodily, staring at Jim as Jim stood up on his hind legs to dust the bark and twigs from his foreclaws. "There was a

73

palmer in gray friar's-cloth came to the castle last Michaelmas and spoke a rhyme to me before he left:

> *"Betyde thee weale yn any fyght*
> *When'ere thou kenst thy cause ys right."*

But I don't see how it applies."

"Don't you?" said Jim, thinking rapidly. "I'd say it was obvious. Because I'm bent on rescuing my lady, if you tried to kill me, your cause would be wrong. Therefore weale wouldn't have betyded you."

"By St. John!" said the knight, admiringly. "Of course! And here I thought I was just out after some mere mere-dragon today! What luck! You're sure this cause of yours is right? No doubt about that, I suppose?"

"Of course not," said Jim, frostily.

"Well, then, I *am* in luck. Naturally, I'll have to demand permission of my lady, since there's another demoiselle involved. But I can't see her objecting to an opportunity like this. I suppose we'd better introduce ourselves, since there's no one around to do it for us. I take it you know my arms?"

He swung his shield around for Jim's inspection. It showed, on a red background, a wide X of silver, like a cross lying over sideways, above a rather fanciful-looking animal in black, which Jim made out to be lying down in the triangular space under the lower legs of the X.

"The gules, a saltire silver, of course," went on the knight, "are the Neville of Raby arms. My great-grandfather, as a cadet of the house, differenced with a hart lodged sable—and, of course, I'm in the direct line of descent."

"Neville-Smythe," said Jim, remembering the name in the song he had just heard and any memories he could dig up on the subject of heraldry. "I bear—in my proper body, that is—"

"Assuredly, sir," Neville-Smythe agreed.

"An—gules, typewriter silver on a desk sable. Sir James Eckert, Knight Bachelor." Jim suddenly remembered something Carolinus had mentioned in explaining him to Smrgol and took a chance on gaining a little authority. "Baron of Riveroak. Honored to make your acquaintance, Sir Brian."

Neville-Smythe lifted off his helm, hung it on the pommel of his saddle and scratched his head puzzledly. He had light brown hair, rather compressed by the helm; and now that his face was out in the sunlight, it could be seen that he was no older than Jim. What had given the impression of a greater maturity in the shadow of the visor was a very deep tan and little sun wrinkles around the outer corners of Neville-Smythe's blue eyes. Also, a white scar seamed his lower right cheek down to the jawline, adding a veteran-like touch to his appearance.

"Typewriter . . ." Sir Brian was muttering to himself. "Typewriter . . ."

"A—local beast, rather like a griffin," said Jim, hurriedly. "We have a lot of them in Riveroak— That's in America, a land over the sea to the west. You may not have heard of it."

"Damme if I have," replied Sir Brian, candidly. "Was it there that you were ensorceled?"

"Well, yes and no," said Jim, cautiously. "I was transported to this land of yours by magic, as was the lady—Angela. Then when I woke, I found myself bedragoned."

"Were you, now?" Sir Brian had bright-blue eyes, amazingly innocent-looking in comparison to his tanned and scarred face. "Angela, eh? Fair name, that."

"As she herself is fair," answered Jim, gravely.

"You don't say, Sir James! Perhaps we ought to have a bit of a go on behalf of our respective ladies while we've got the chance, before we get to know each other too well for it."

Jim swallowed.

"On the other hand," he said, quickly, "you were telling me about your lady. What was her name?"

"The Lady Geronde." Sir Brian began to fumble about his saddlebags. "I've got her favor here, someplace. Wear it on my arm when I expect to run into someone, of course, but when one's out hunting dragons— Half a moment. It must be right here under my hand . . ."

"Why don't you just tell me what it's like?" Jim suggested.

"Oh, well." Sir Brian gave up his search. "It's a kerchief, you know. Monogrammed. 'G.d'C.' The Lady Geronde Isabel de Chaney, presently chatelaine of the Castle Malvern. Her father, Sir Orrin, went off to the wars against the Eastern heathen three years ago Whitsuntide, less five days; and there's been no word of him since. If it weren't for that and the fact that I have to do all this scurrying around the countryside, winning worship and so forth, we'd have been married by this time."

"Why do you do it, then? Go riding around the countryside, I mean?" Jim asked, curiously.

"Good Lord, Geronde insists on it! Once we're married, she wants me to come home safe, you know."

Jim did not follow this argumental development in the conversation. He said so.

"Why, how do you people manage things, overseas?" demanded Sir Brian. "Once I'm married, with my own lands, I've got to produce my own levy of men if my lord or the King calls on me for service in war. If I don't have a name, I'll be forced to march out with a raggedy-breeched bunch of bumpkins and clodpoles out of my own fields, who'll like as not take to their heels at the first sight of trained men-at-arms, and probably leave me no choice but to die on the spot for honor's sake, if not for other reasons. On the other hand, if I'm known about as a warrior of some worth, I'll have good, experienced men coming and wanting to serve under my banner, because they know, do you see, that I'll take good care of them. And, by the same token, they'll take good care of me."

"Oh," said Jim.

"And besides," went on Sir Brian, ruminatively, "this chasing about does keep one in shape. Though I must say the mere-dragons we have around here don't give you much of a workout. That's why I had high hopes of you there for a moment. Doesn't do to practice with the neighbors, you know. Too much chance of a lost temper and a feud resulting."

"I see," said Jim.

"However," said Sir Brian, brightening, "all's well that ends well. And this quest of yours to rescue your lady can certainly be worth a dozen mere-dragons to my reputation. Though, as I say, I'll have to get permission from Geronde, first. Happily, Castle Malvern's only a day and a half's ride from here. *Long* days, though; so hadn't we better be moving?"

"Moving?"

"Traveling. Covering distance, Sir James!" Brian squinted up at the sun. "We've only about a half-day's light left to us now, and that means noon or better of the second day before we can see the gates of Castle Malvern. So, shall we?"

"Hold on a minute," said Jim. "You're talking about both of us going to this Castle Malvern. Why?"

"My good sir, I explained why," said Sir Brian with a touch of impatience, reining his horse about so that it faced to the east. "The Lady Geronde must give her permission, first. After all, my first duty's to her."

Jim stared.

"I still don't follow you," he said, at last. "Permission for what?"

But Brian was already walking his horse away from the ocean. Jim hurried to catch up with him.

"Permission for what?" he repeated.

"Sir James," said Brian, severely, turning his head to look Jim squarely in the eyes—on horseback, his head was just about level with Jim's as Jim walked on all fours. "If this continued questioning is a jest of some sort, it is in sorry taste. What else could I seek my lady's permission for, than to accompany you on your quest and make one of the Companions you told me you were seeking?"

Chapter 8

They went along silently, side by side. Brian stared straight ahead as he rode, looking somewhat stiff-faced and offended. Jim was busy adjusting to the idea of the knight as a Companion.

He had not really paid that much attention when Carolinus had echoed the watchbeetle in saying that Jim would gather Companions to aid him in rescuing Angie and facing up to the Dark Powers. But as far as he had thought about it, he had assumed he would be selecting those who would join him. He had not really envisioned them thrusting themselves upon him.

Obviously, Brian was not likely to be a liability as a Companion. Plainly, he had no lack of courage and his appearance testified to some experience in combat. But beyond these things, what did Jim really know about the man? Nothing, in fact, except for the meager facts of his name, arms, and the identity of his lady.

On the other hand, was it wise to look a gift horse in the mouth? Carolinus had spoken of forces at work and given the impression that inhabitants of this world were about to be divided by them into two camps—that of the Dark Powers and that of those who, like Jim, were in opposition to them. If that was the case, then it ought to be possible to identify the camp to which any particular individual belonged by watching to see who and what he lined up with.

Brian had lined up with Jim. Therefore, he ought to be in the camp of those opposing the Dark Powers, by definition . . .

Jim came up out of his thoughts to realize that the knight was still riding alongside him stiffly, with a very obvious, if invisible, chip on his shoulder. A small apology might be in order.

"Sir Brian," said Jim, a little awkwardly. "Excuse me for not understanding that you were offering yourself as a Companion. The truth of the matter is, things are different where I come from."

"Doubtless," said Brian, unsmilingly.

"Believe me," said Jim, "there was no jest of any kind involved. It was just my own lack of—er—wit, that kept me from understanding what you were talking about."

"Ah," said Brian.

"Naturally, I couldn't ask for a better Companion than a gentleman like yourself."

"Quite."

"And I'm overjoyed to have you with me."

"Indeed."

Jim felt like someone knocking on the door of a house in which the owner was home but obstinately refusing to answer. A touch of annoyance tweaked at him; and on the heels of this came an idea at which he nearly smiled visibly. Ignorance of other people's customs could work both ways.

"Of course, if only I'd known your Social Security number right from the start," he said. "It would have been different."

Brian's eyes flickered. They continued to travel on side by side in silence for perhaps another full minute before the knight spoke again.

"Number, Sir James?"

"Why, yes," said Jim, raising his eyebrows. "Your Social Security number."

"What bloody number is that supposed to be?"

"Don't tell me," said Jim, "you don't have Social Security numbers here?"

"Blind me if I ever heard of any such thing!"

Jim clicked his tongue sympathetically.

"No wonder you thought it odd of me, not understanding the offer of your Companionship," he said. "Why, where I come from nothing can happen unless a gentleman's Social Security number is known. Naturally, I thought you were withholding yours for good reasons of your own. That's why it didn't dawn on me that you were offering me Companionship."

"But I haven't got one to withhold, dammit!" protested Sir Brian.

"Haven't got one?"

"By St. Giles, no!"

Jim clicked his tongue again.

"That's the trouble with living out in the provinces, here," Sir Brian said in an aggrieved tone. "They've probably been using these what-do-you-call-it numbers for a twelvemonth now at Court; and none of us out here have ever heard of them."

They went on a little farther in silence.

"*You've* got one, I suppose?" Brian said.

"Why—yes," Jim answered. Hastily, he delved into his memory. "469-69-9921."

"Damned fine figure."

"Well . . ." Jim decided he might as well pick up some credit while the opportunity existed. "I *am* Baron of Riveroak, after all."

"Oh, of course."

They rode on a little farther.

"I say," said Brian.

"Yes, Sir Brian?"

Brian cleared his throat.

"If I was to have a something-number of my own, what would you venture to say it might be?"

"Well, I don't know . . ."

"Well, well, I shouldn't ask it, I suppose. Puts me at a disadvantage, though." Brian turned a troubled face to Jim. "Here you tell me your number and I can't reciprocate."

"Think nothing of it," said Jim.

"I *do* think something of it, though."

"You shouldn't," Jim insisted. He was beginning to feel a little guilty in spite of himself. "I'm sure your number, if you had one, would be a very good one."

"No, no. Probably quite an ordinary figure. After all, what am I? Just an outlying knight bachelor, no chansons about me for the minstrels to sing, or anything like that."

"You underestimate yourself," said Jim, uneasily. The ploy was getting out of hand. "Of course, I wouldn't know what the official number would be; but in my country I'd guess you'd be at least a '"—he had to think rapidly to count the digits in his own Social Security number—"387-22-777."

The eyes Sir Brian turned on him were as round as dinner plates.

"Really? You think so, do you? All that?"

"At least that."

"Well, well. What was it again?"

Jim slowly repeated the number he had given Brian several times over until the knight had it by heart; and they went on cheerfully together, chatting like old friends. Like Companions, in fact, thought Jim.

Brian, having gotten over his stiffness of manner, turned out to be eager to talk. Specifically, his topic of conversation was the Lady Geronde, who was apparently not only the most beautiful of women, but a collection of all the other talents and virtues as well. Over and above Geronde, however, the knight was a repository of local gossip, both bloody and salacious. Jim had never considered himself to be someone easily shocked, but what he was now hearing was startling.

He was, in fact, learning fast. His mind had been translating the language and actions of Sir Brian into the fuzzy, quasi-Victorian image of a stage Englishman that most Americans carried around in that part of their mind reserved for stock characters. Now, a closer acquaintance with the knight was destroying that particular image rather thoroughly.

To begin with, Brian was entirely physical, pragmatic and human. "Earthy" might have been a better word. The taboo areas in his cosmos were restricted to those of religion and a handful of ideals and principles. Curiously, he seemed perfectly capable of highly idealizing something as an abstract idea, and at the same time ruthlessly being honest about it as a

81

specific reality—all without seeing any particular conflict between these attitudes. For example, Jim learned, to Brian his King was at once a majestic figure anointed by God, a ruler by divine right for whom Brian would die without question if the need arose, and at the same time a half-senile old man who was drunk half the time and could not be trusted with the more important decisions of his kingdom. The lady Geronde was somehow both a goddess on a pedestal, above and beyond the touch of gross males, and a thoroughly physical human female with whom Brian's hands were quite familiar.

Jim was still trying to fit this double view of the knight into a pattern with the other things, like intelligent dragons, talking watchbeetles and the existence of Dark Powers, which he had so far discovered in this world, when the daylight began to wane and Brian suggested they look about for a place to camp overnight.

They had left the fens well behind by this time, and had spent several hours striking at an angle northeast through the rather unpleasant wood Jim had flown over the day before and congratulated himself on not having to traverse at ground level. Happily, now, they had left it behind for a much less forbidding forest, still mainly populated by oaks and elms, but in the shape of larger specimens of these, which had killed off the more tangled undergrowth underneath them, so that the going was easier. They came at last to a small clearing by a brook, which in the last rays of the afternoon sun, filtering through the high branches of the trees, looked almost as inviting as Carolinus' property by the Tinkling Water.

"Should do us quite well, I'd think," Brian observed, cheerfully.

He dismounted, unsaddled his horse, rubbed it down with some handfuls of grass he pulled up, and left it tied on a long tether to crop its dinner from the clearing. For himself, Brian produced from his saddlebags something dark which was evidently smoked meat. For Jim, there was nothing; and, although his stomach twinged reproachfully at him, Jim could not really blame the knight for not offering to share the food. What had made a rather adequate meal for the man would have made a single, unsatisfyingly small gulp for the dragon. Tomorrow, Jim promised himself, he would find some excuse to leave Brian for a while and find a cow . . . or something.

He became aware that Brian was lighting a fire, something he viewed with only academic interest at first, out of his own newly discovered indifference to external temperatures. But, as the sun went lower behind the trees, its light reddened to the color of bright blood and deep shadows started forming between the surrounding tree trunks; and the fire, now blazing away heartily on the dry, fallen branches that Brian had accumulated, began to take on the appearance of the only mark of cheerfulness in the growing darkness.

"Getting chilly," observed Brian, hunching his shoulders and standing close above the fire.

He had divested himself of helmet, gloves and the plate armor from his legs, leaving only his upper body metal-covered. His hair, recovered from the pressure of the helmet, had expanded to show itself as quite a mane. It gleamed with ruddy highlights from the fire, as he stood facing the flames.

Jim drew close on the fire's other side. It would not have occurred to him to think of the night as growing chilly, but he was conscious of a sort of depression of the spirit which had come on him with the disappearance of the sun. The forest about them, which had seemed so friendly in the daylight, now began to acquire an ominous and threatening appearance as night closed in. Looking around, Jim could almost swear that the surrounding darkness was a physical entity trying to push inward upon them, only held back by the dancing light of the fire.

"Where are we?" he asked Brian.

"Lynham Woods," said Brian. He, too, looked about at the wall of night surrounding the circle of firelight. "Not such a bad place, ordinarily. But there's a difference about this night, wouldn't you say, Sir James? One gets the feeling there's something afoot out there in the dark, somewhere."

"Yes," Jim agreed, feeling a small, involuntary shudder inside him.

To his dragon-senses Brian's description was unpleasantly accurate—it did indeed feel exactly as if something was prowling out there in the woods, somewhere beyond the firelight, circling their camp and waiting for an opportunity to pounce.

"Stars," Brian commented, pointing upward.

Jim looked up between the treetops. Now that the sun was completely down, some stars were visible. No moon, but some stars. However, even as he watched, they began to disappear one by one, as if an invisible curtain was being drawn across the sky.

"Clouds," said Brian. "Well, there's one comfort. With a cloudy sky, it shouldn't get as cold here before morning as it might if the sky were clear. A clear sky and I'd have ventured to guess at a touch of frost before dawn. It's cool for this time of year."

The clouds to which Brian had referred had by this time covered all portions of the sky visible beyond the treetops. The clearing now seemed englobed in unrelenting lightlessness.

Slowly, the knight sat down by the fire and began to replace the cuisses and greaves he had earlier removed from his legs.

"What is it?" asked Jim. "What're you doing that for?"

"I don't like it," Brian said shortly. "There's something amiss this night. Whatever it is, it'll find me armed and ready for it."

He finished getting his body armor back on and went to get his helmet and lance from where he had placed them with his saddle and other gear. He drove the butt of the lance into the ground beside the fire, so that it stood point upward by his right hand, and put the helmet on, leaving the visor up.

"Let us keep facing each other with the fire

between us, Sir James," he said. "That way we can watch all about us, as far as the firelight shows."

"Right," Jim replied.

They stood facing each other. After a little while a sound began, very faint and faraway at first.

"A wind," Brian remarked.

It was indeed the sound of a wind. They could hear it far off, almost as if it was hunting among the bushes and the limbs of the trees. The sound of it rose, fell, and moved from quarter to quarter, but always off in the distance. Then, gradually, it began to come closer, as if it had been quartering the forest for them and was now closing in.

Still, in the clearing, not a breath of air stirred, except that drawn in by the updraft from the dancing flames of the fire. Brian threw more of the dried branches upon the blaze.

"My special thanks to St. Giles, whose day this is," muttered the knight, "and who moved me to gather wood enough to last until dawn."

The wind drew closer. They could hear the sound of its passage, now loud in the near-distance. It breathed closer and closer to them, leaving a sighing and groaning of branches where it passed. It was loud now, loud enough so that they had to raise their voices above its sound to speak to one another. Then, suddenly, it was on them.

It blew directly into the clearing with an abrupt force that threatened for a second to push them off their feet. The fire shot up a long trail of sparks into the darkness and its flames guttered nearly to extinction, so that the gloom all around suddenly flooded in on them, and they were peppered in the face by a shower of dried twigs and dead leaves.

Then, as quickly as it had come, the wind was gone. The fire flamed up again and the darkness was pushed back once more. Without warning, there was silence. The wind had gone.

Brian sighed softly within the open visor of his helmet.

"Stand to watch, Sir James," he said softly. "Now, it comes."

Jim stared at the knight.

"It comes—" he started to echo.

And then he heard it.

It was so small and distant at first, he thought it was only a singing in his eardrums. Then it grew ever so slightly in volume and he identified it for what it actually was: a continuous, high-pitched chittering—like the wind, now off at a distance, but gradually growing closer. He sensed something mindless about that chittering, something that made the skin crawl on the back of his dragon-neck, instinctively.

This body reaction stirred Jim almost more than the sound itself had done. What could there be out in woods like this, at night, of which even a dragon would be afraid? He opened his mouth to ask Brian what was making the noise; and found the question stuck in his throat. An almost superstitious fear checked him. If he asked Brian, and Brian told him, then whatever was moving in on them would become undeniably real. As long as he still did not know, it could be that it could all turn out to be an illusion, a bad dream from which he would awaken to a sunlit morning.

But as they stood, the chittering grew slowly louder and closer—and there was no awakening from a nightmare.

"Sir Brian," he said, at last. "What is it?"

The knight's eyes, within the firelit gloom of his visor, burned strangely on Jim.

"You don't know? Sandmirks, Sir James."

The moment Brian spoke the identifying word, something in the very blood and bones of Gorbash passed knowledge on to the mind of Jim—and he knew without further asking what they looked like, those hunters out in the night, circling ever closer and closer to this campfire and the two of them who waited here.

In his mind's eye Jim saw them, something of a

86

cross between a rat and a ferret in shape and the size of small dogs. Their eyes would shine red, reflecting the light of the flames when they came close enough, but their black, coarse-haired bodies would remain invisible in the darkness as they passed around and around the clearing, just beyond the reach of the firelight. And from their mouths would continue to come this same mindless chittering that was like the claws of spiders running up and down Jim's spine and into his brain.

"What they do here," said Brian, "this far from the sea, only the devil that helped them knows. Their proper runs are the cold salt beaches. Little shore animals and the poor castaways who have the ill luck to wash ashore at night are their proper prey. Here is an enemy against which my sword and your claws, Sir James, will be small help."

"If they come close enough—"

"They will not, while the minds are in our bodies. These are craven creatures, whose weapon is madness."

"Madness?" Jim echoed. The word had slid along all his nerves like an icy knife.

"What else did you think their noise meant?" Brian said. "The story is that they're possessed of the souls of other animals who have died insane, or in great torment, and so they are full of the stuff of madness, which they pour out on the night air to infect the minds of such as you and I. I know not how it is with you, Sir James, but Saint Giles has always been a good friend to me and he did not advise me to gather this huge pile of firewood for nothing. It's my counsel that we turn to that good saint, and to God with all his angels, for none else can aid us, here."

The knight drew his sword, rested it point down on the earth before him, and taking the hilt of it in both his hands, bowed his head above it in prayer. Jim stood still, watching the armored man, the fire and the surrounding darkness, hearing the steadily growing sound of the chittering.

He was not at all religious himself; and somehow,

in this particular moment, something in him rebelled at the thought of turning, or even pretending to turn, to religion for help. On the other hand, he could not help envying Brian for being able to find such a backup available and waiting.

For, whatever the truth was about the souls of animals who had died insane or in torment, there was no denying the fact that some quality in the chittering went clear through the conscious, logical, upper part of Jim's mind into the old, primitive levels behind it, and plucked the chords of atavistic fears he had not known he possessed. Deep within him, from the very first moment in which he recognized the chittering as something more than a singing in his ears, was the impulse to turn and run from it. To run and run, until either he could hear it no more, or his heart would burst from the effort of running.

In the end, that must be what all victims of the sandmirks did—run until they could run no more. And then, at last, with their prey exhausted and helpless, the black, fiery-eyed, humping shapes would close in, chittering, to kill and feed. While his conscious mind still worked, Jim recognized the fact that if he ran, he was lost. Like Brian he must stand here and fight back against the noise that was gnawing away at his sanity.

He could not bring himself to follow Brian's example; but there had to be other things he could do to set up a defense against the calling of the sandmirks. The multiplication tables?

He tried them. For a while, he was able to concentrate on them; and he congratulated himself on finding a weapon. But after he had run through all those that he knew readily and had started again on them, he found that the second time through they did not shut out the chittering as well as they had the first time. The third time he went through them, they were hardly any help at all, not much more than meaningless sounds muttered under the breath.

He searched his mind as best he could under the effect of the sandmirk voices—which were now clearly circling the camp at a distance of no more than fifty yards away or so—for something stronger than the multiplication tables with which to oppose them. In desperation, he began to recite the argument of his doctorate thesis on the changes in social custom deriving from the rise of the cities in France during the Hundred Years' War. Night after weary night, after all other work had been done, he had sat in the single light of his desk lamp, hammering out that thesis. If there was protective magic in anything he knew, it would be in that.

"*. . . Examination of the direct effects of the English military incursion into western France in the two decades immediately following the thirteen-fifties,*" he muttered, "*show a remarkable process of change at work unrecognized by the very people caught up in it. Particularly the port of Bordeaux . . .*"

Suddenly, to his joy, he realized it was working. All those midnight hours of effort he had put into the thesis had created a piece of mental machinery with a momentum that was too powerful for the chittering of the sandmirks to clog and stop. As long as he could keep the words of it running through his head, he could hold them off. It was as if the chittering was blocked now by a barrier that allowed only the harmless noise of it wash over the barrier's top. The thesis had been two hundred and twenty double-spaced pages of typescript when finished. He would not reach the end of his material too soon, as he had with the multiplication tables. He glanced across the fire at Brian, and found the other still praying. Neither one of them dared take time off to speak with each other, but Jim tried to signal with his eyes that he was holding his own and he thought that Brian understood and returned a like message.

The sandmirks were close now—just outside the circle of firelight; and the sound of their voices was so shrill and encompassing that Jim could hardly hear the sound of his own voice in his ears. Nonetheless, he and Brian were holding their own and the predators in the darkness would not dare attack while their prey still had the will and the strength to defend themselves. As Jim watched, Brian reached down to throw a couple more of the dead branches on the fire.

Flames spurted up on the new fuel; and for a second, straining his eyes, Jim thought he had a glimpse of shadowy shapes slipping back out of sight into the further darkness. He and Brian continued their watch, and their own private litanies.

The night wore on.

The fire blazed. The sandmirks continued to circle, never stopping for one moment their invitation to terror. Croaking, with voices gone hoarse from steady, long use, Jim and the knight faced each other above the fire. Sir Brian swayed a little with weariness; and Jim felt himself also growing light-headed with exhaustion. The dark continued unbroken around them. The raw, damp scent of dawn was in the air, but daybreak was yet some time off.

And now, for the first time since he had begun to recite his thesis, Jim felt the pressure of the sandmirk voices beginning to crumble away the barrier he had erected against them. His exhausted memory fumbled, lost its place on the remembered page it was quoting, and found it again. But in that second of weakness the effect of the chittering had gained ground. It pierced through the words Jim painfully uttered; and its power was growing steadily.

Jim became conscious that Brian had stopped speaking. Jim also stopped and they stared at each other across the fire while the sound of the chittering soared in volume all around them, lifting triumphantly into the night.

The knight reversed his sword, picking it up to hold blade upward in both hands.

"In God's name," said Brian, in such a torn and ragged voice that Jim could hardly understand him, "let's go to them, while we still have the strength to do so."

Jim nodded. In the final accounting, to charge

death was preferable to fleeing from it in sick fear. He stepped around the fire to stand beside Brian.

"Now!" said the knight in his husk of a voice, raising his sword overhead—

But before they could charge the almost invisible foe that encircled them, a scream almost worse than the chittering split the darkness to their right. At once, the sound that had driven them to the edge of madness ceased utterly, to be followed by the noise of many small bodies crashing away in flight through the woods.

Another scream sounded, this time straight ahead and farther out. A moment of waiting followed, during which the sounds of flight had all but died in the distance; and then came a third scream, farther off yet.

"By Saint Giles!" whispered the knight in the stillness. "Something's killing them . . ."

He had hardly finished before a fourth scream came, this time a long distance off. After that, utter silence.

Numbly, Brian moved to build up the fire. It crackled, blazed afresh and the shadows drew back a long distance. Jim glanced upward.

"Look," he said. "I think . . ."

Brian looked. An edge of cloud was pulling back from a few stars that were still visible; and the sky behind the stars was paling.

"Yes. Dawn," said Brian.

They stood watching as the sky turned toward light and the remaining stars faded to invisibility.

"But what was it that came to our rescue?" the knight asked.

Jim shook his head.

"I don't know," he said, hoarsely. "I can't guess what—"

He broke off.

Something had moved—a blacker black within the darkness of the still-deep shadows beyond the firelight. It moved again and came forward slowly, stepping into the light. A four-legged shape as large as a small pony, green-eyed, with long narrow muzzle, half-parted to show white, gleaming teeth and a tongue as red as the fire flames.

It was a wolf. A wolf double the size of the largest wolf Jim had ever seen in a zoo or on film. The green eyes went past the knight and the fire to burn savagely upon Jim.

"So it's you," a deep, harsh voice from the scimitar-armed jaws said. "Not that it makes all that difference. But I thought as much."

Chapter 9

The mind can take only so much before reaction sets in. With all Jim had been through since he had ended up in this world, and particularly after the ordeal he had just gone through as the prey of the sandmirks, he should not have been struck numb by the fact that now it was a wolf who could talk like a man. But he was.

He sat down on his haunches with a thump. If he had been in his regular human body, he probably would have collapsed on the ground. But the effect was the same. He struggled to find his voice while the monster wolf walked forward to the fire.

"Who—who're you?" he managed at last.

"What's the matter, Gorbash?" snarled the wolf. "Sandmirks got your memory? I've only known you for twenty years! Besides, there's few living who'd mistake Aragh for any other English wolf!"

"You're who— Aragh?" croaked Brian.

The wolf glanced at him.

"I am. And who are you, man?"

"Sir Brian Neville-Smythe."

"Never heard of you," growled the wolf.

"My house," said Sir Brian stiffly, "is a cadet branch of the Nevilles. Our land runs beyond Wyvenstock to the Lea River on the north."

"None of my people up there," grated Aragh. "What're you doing down here in my forest?"

"Passing through on our way to Malvern, Sir wolf."

"Call me Aragh when you talk to me, man."

"Then address me as Sir Brian, Sir wolf!"

Aragh's upper lip began to curl back from his gleaming teeth.

"Wait—" said Jim, hastily.

Aragh turned to him, lip uncurling slightly.

"This Sir Brian is with you, is he, Gorbash?"

"We're Companions. And actually I'm not really Gorbash. You see . . ." Jim tried hastily, with his weary throat, to explain the situation that had ended up bringing Brian and him to this place.

"Hmpf!" Aragh growled, when Jim had finished. "Pure nonsense, all of it. You always did get yourself mixed up seven different ways every time you tried something. However, if this Sir Brian's committed himself to fight alongside you, I suppose I can put up with him."

He turned to Brian.

"And you," he said. "I'll hold you responsible for taking good care of Gorbash. Soft-headed he is, but he's been a friend of mine for years—"

A light went on in the back of Jim's mind. This Aragh must be the wolf friend of Gorbash's which Smrgol had talked disapprovingly about, the one Gorbash had associated with while he was growing up.

"—and I don't want him chewed up by sandmirks, or anything else. D'you hear me?"

"I assure you—" Brian was beginning stiffly.

"Don't assure me. Just do it!" snapped Aragh.

"About those sandmirks," Jim put in hastily, once more in an effort to turn the Brian–Aragh conversation from possible disagreement, "they almost had us. Didn't that sound of theirs bother you?"

"Why should it?" said Aragh. "I'm an English wolf.

You don't catch me thinking of two things at once. Sandmirks belong on the seashore. They'll know next time what'll happen if I catch them here in my woods."

He snarled softly, as if to himself.

"You mean to say"— Brian took off his helmet and stared at the wolf in a sort of wonder—"you could hear that chittering and not be troubled by it?"

"How many times do I have to say it?" growled Aragh. "I'm an English wolf. I suppose if I sat around like some people and just listened, I might have noticed the noise they were making. But the second I heard them, I said to myself, 'That lot's got to go!' And that's all I had on my mind until they went."

He licked his lips with his long tongue.

"All except for four of them," he said. "They're no good for eating, of course. But they do scream well when you break their necks. I heard *those* noises they made, never fear!"

He sat down on his haunches in turn and sniffed at the fire.

"World's going to pot," he muttered. "Few of us left with any sense at all. Magicians, Dark Powers, all that nonsense. Break a few necks, tear a few throats out in the good old-fashioned way, and see how long these sandmirks and their sort'll go on acting up! See how much trouble the Dark Powers would be able to stir up after a few doses like that to their creatures!"

"Actually, how long *have* you known Sir James?" inquired Brian.

"Sir James? Sir James? He's Gorbash, far as I'm concerned," Aragh growled. "Gorbash he's always been. Gorbash he'll always be, in spite of any spell-and-body nonsense. I don't believe in people' being one person one day, then somebody else the next. You do what you want. As far as I'm concerned, he's Gorbash. Twenty years, to answer you. And didn't I say twenty years? Why?"

"Because, my good fellow—"

"I'm not your good fellow. I'm nobody's good fellow. I'm an English wolf; and you'll be wise not to forget it."

"Very well. Sir wolf—"

"That's a bit better."

"Since you've very little sympathy with the quest that Sir James and I are on, and since I see dawn is now breaking, it only remains to thank you for your assistance against the sandmirks—"

"Assistance!"

"Call it what you will. As I was saying"—Brian put his helmet back on, picked up his saddle and went to his horse—"it only remains to thank you, say adieu and resume our travel to Castle Malvern. Come, Sir James—"

"Wait a minute!" snarled Aragh. "Gorbash, what do you think you can do against those Dark Powers, anyway?"

"Well . . . whatever I have to," Jim answered.

"To be sure," growled the wolf. "And what if they send sandmirks against you again?"

"Well . . ."

"I thought so," said Aragh with bitter satisfaction. "Up to me, as usual. Give it up, Gorbash. Stop this madness of thinking you've a human mind in you and go back to being a plain, straightforward dragon again."

"I can't do that," said Jim. "I've got to rescue Angie—"

"Who?"

"His lady," put in Brian, stiffly. "He's explained how that other dragon, Bryagh, stole her off to the Loathly Tower."

"His lady? His LADY? What's the times coming to, a dragon mooning about over some female human and calling her his 'lady'? Gorbash, give up this nonsense and go home!"

"Sorry," said Jim through his teeth. "No."

Aragh snarled.

"Damned idiot!" He got to all four feet. "All right, I'll come along and make sure the sandmirks don't get you. But—only sandmirks, mind! I'm not going to be a party to the rest of this ridiculousness of yours!"

"Damme if I remember your being invited," said Brian.

"Don't need to be invited." Aragh's upper lip began to curl again as his head turned toward the knight. "I go where I wish, Sir knight, and I'd like to see any try to stop me. I'm an English—"

"Of course you are!" Jim broke in, "and there's no one we'd rather have with us than an English wolf. Is there, Brian?"

"Speak for yourself, Sir James."

"Well, there's no one I'd rather have with me, besides Sir James here," said Jim. "Sir Brian, you have to admit those sandmirks were more than we could handle ourselves."

"Hmph!" Brian looked as if he was being asked to agree to having a tooth pulled without as much as a drink by way of anesthetic. "Suppose so."

He suddenly swayed where he stood and the saddle dropped out of his hands to thump on the ground. He walked heavy-footedly over to the nearest tree and sat down with a clatter of metal, his back to the trunk.

"Sir James," he said hoarsely, "I must rest."

He leaned his head back against the tree trunk and closed his eyes. In a moment he was breathing heavily, with deep inhalations of air, just on the edge of snoring.

"Yes," said Jim, looking at him. "We both had a night with no rest. Maybe I should catch some sleep, too."

"Don't let me stop you," said Aragh. "I'm not the sort to need a nap every time I turn around; but come to think of it, I might just trail those sandmirks and make sure they kept going once they left here."

He glanced at the rising sun.

"I'll be back about midday."

He turned about and effectively disappeared. Jim had a glimpse of him slipping between two tree trunks and suddenly there was no sound or sign that the wolf had ever been there. Jim lay down on the grass himself, tucked his head under a wing, and closed his eyes . . .

But, unlike Brian, he did not find himself falling asleep.

He persisted in keeping his eyes closed and his head wing-tucked for perhaps twenty minutes before he gave up and sat up once more to look around him. Much to his own surprise, he was feeling quite well indeed.

He remembered now that the hoarseness of his own voice had disappeared while he was standing around engaged in the three-cornered conversation with Aragh and Brian. Evidently his fatigue had vanished at the same time. These things were remarkable; but apparently dragons simply had better recuperative powers than humans. He looked at Brian, who was now frankly snoring the snores of utter exhaustion and had slid down the tree trunk until he was very near to lying flat on the grass. The knight ought to be out of things at least until noon. Which left Jim with that much time to kill. He thought once more about something to eat.

He got to his feet. Now might be the very time to look around and see if anything was available. About to wander off, he checked himself. What if he lost his way in the wood and could not find the route back here? Perhaps he should mark the trees as he went—

He broke off his thoughts, mentally kicking himself for an idiot. Of course, on foot he could easily get lost. But who said he had to go on foot? Experimentally, he stretched his wings and found that all the stiffness and soreness was gone out of them. With an explosion of air, he leaped from the clearing and headed skyward. Behind him, Brian slid all the way down on to the grass and snored ever more loudly.

But within seconds the knight was forgotten below him. It was a sheer pleasure to be on the wing again. A few vigorous flaps took him above treetop level. He banked in a circle to take a look back down at the clearing and set up a memory of its appearance from the air, then mounted higher to relate it to its immediate surroundings. High up, he was happy to see that both it and the stream running through it were quite distinguishable from a distance.

Leaving Brian and the clearing to take care of themselves, he banked again and began to quarter above the wood, examining it.

From the air it looked more parklike than it had on the ground. The large trees were spaced evenly enough so that he could get a fair to good view of the earth between them. Unfortunately for his stomach, nothing was in sight that looked like food. He looked about for Aragh, but found no sight of the wolf, either.

There seemed to be little point to his soaring above the forest, except for the pleasure of doing so and the fact that he had time to spend. A finger of guilt touched his mind. He had hardly thought of Angie since he had met the knight. Was she really all right? Perhaps he should make some effort to go and find out for himself?

With these thoughts, he let himself go with the thermals, an uneasiness in him like the memory of the chittering the sandmirks had made that could make the skin on the back of his neck crawl in recollection. The only way to settle this uneasiness, he told himself now, was to go and make sure that Angie was all right. Carolinus' directions to stay away from the Loathly Tower until he had gathered the Companions who would aid him to overthrow the Dark Powers really did not make sense. He should decide, for himself, what to do—

He woke suddenly to the discovery that he was already at an altitude of at least several thousand feet and just rising into a tailwind blowing directly for the fens and the seashore—back the way he and Brian had come. Already, in fact, he was riding that air current in a long, soaring glide which would bring him eventually to ground at the point where the Great Causeway met the ocean. As he realized this, he heard echoing in his mind the memory of the chittering sandmirks. Overriding this was a knife-thin whisper calling him to the Loathly Tower.

"Now . . ." the whisper was saying. *"Go now . . . don't delay . . . go alone, now . . ."*

He checked himself with a chill of horror, and fell off sharply in a long, turning bank that would bring him down and back toward the woods where he had left Brian sleeping. Almost as soon as he had turned, the echoing memory and the whisper were gone, like Aragh a short while back, as if they had never been.

Had he actually heard them? Or had he merely imagined them?

He shook the questions from him with an effort of will. He had certainly not imagined that he had unconsciously lifted to an altitude and a wind that would have carried him directly to the Loathly Tower. It gave him an uneasy feeling to find himself so vulnerable to a call from that direction. He had not been so, yesterday, even when he was headed on foot toward the tower. Somehow, the sandmirks' chittering had opened up a channel through which the Dark Powers could call him to them. And if this were so, even though the ugly, small creatures had been driven off, the Dark Powers had won something by their attack.

Or—was it that simple? Aragh had certainly put in an appearance in the nick of time. Wasn't the coincidence of the sandmirks' arrival just a little too good to be true? What if the Dark Powers had never intended that the sandmirks should destroy him? What if, for their own purposes, what they wanted was not the death of Jim Eckert, but his coming to their tower?

That was another chill thought.

Jim found himself wishing he had Carolinus nearby to question. But something told Jim that if he should turn and fly to the Tinkling Water now—even assuming he could get there, find Carolinus in and manage to return to Brian by noon—the magician would not be pleased to see him. Carolinus had made quite a point of Jim's following the path that would lead to his gaining of Companions, before he did anything else.

Well, Jim thought, soaring low once more over the

Lynhan Woods back toward the clearing where Brian was sleeping, he had acquired two of the Companions so far, at least. Brian and Aragh. Now that he was turned resolutely away from the Loathly Tower once more, he found his momentary suspicion of Aragh had evaporated. Hadn't Aragh been a close friend of Gorbash for years? Not but what the wolf wasn't a grim enough character in his own right; but there was nothing secret, dark or hidden about that grimness. What he was, was all on the surface for anyone to see.

Jim checked himself as he soared over a small, dark object on the ground below. Turning back, he swept in and came down to land heavily beside it.

It was a dead sandmirk. Clearly one of the four Aragh had killed the night before.

Jim examined it. Here, after a fashion, was food; but he found that Gorbash's stomach recoiled from the thought. Why was not clear; but the reaction was undeniable. A tentative parting of Jim's jaws above the corpse brought a definite wave of nausea to the dragon-stomach. Apparently, Aragh had known what he was talking about earlier when he mentioned that sandmirks were no good for eating.

Jim left the carcass to some beetles and a few flies which were beginning to circle it, took to the air again and began his search for the clearing. It did not take him long to find, but the interval was enough for him to come to some conclusions about fueling this over-size body of his.

The touch of nausea had effectively cured his earlier appetite. Which made it pretty clear that it was only appetite, and not hunger, that he had been feeling. He and Secoh had divided the cow between them —in hindsight, Jim admitted that he had taken the lion's share of the meat—and even that large meal had not exactly filled up the stomach of Gorbash. In spite of this, he had really not been suffering for food, since. To be sure, he was ready to eat again at first opportunity, but he felt none of the interior hollow-ness and discomfort of real hunger. Apparently drag-ons were able to go for some time between meals, really stoking up only when fuel was available. The pattern of dragon feeding was obviously something like an enormous meal once a week or thereabouts. If so, he could probably go at least a few more days before really needing to eat. However, when he did, he had better do a good job of it . . .

By this time he had relocated the clearing and was gliding in to a landing on its grass. Brian, he saw, was still there, and still snoring.

A glance at the sun told Jim there were still at least three hours to go until noon, if not more than that. He walked to the stream, drank deeply, and flopped down on the grass. His outing had relaxed him. He felt limp and at peace with the world. He tucked his head under his wing once more without hardly thinking about it, and fell instantly asleep.

He woke to the voice of Brian, once more heartily rendering his musical promise of what the mere-dragons might expect from a Neville-Smythe.

Sitting up, Jim saw the knight sitting naked in the stream, happily splashing himself with what must be some fairly cold water and singing. His armor was laid about on the grass and his clothing was spread out and draped on sticks rammed into the turf, so that the various garments were spread to the sunlight. Jim got to his feet and walked over to examine the clothing. He assumed that Brian had washed it and that it was spread out like this to dry. But he found it already dry.

"Fleas, Sir James," called Brian cheerfully. "Fleas! Damme if they don't seem to love a gambeson under armor for breeding in more than any other cloth a gentleman might wear. Nothing like a good hot sun, or a good hot fire, to drive them out of the seams, eh?"

"What . . . ? Oh, yes. You're right," said Jim. "Nothing like it, as you say."

It had not occurred to Jim that body vermin might be as universal a problem on this medieval world as it had been in medieval times back on his own world. He took a second to be grateful for the fact that, evidently, his dragon hide was far too thick and tough to be bothered by the pesky creatures; then he glanced at the sun and saw that it was standing directly overhead.

"Aragh back yet?" he asked.

"He's not here," said Brian.

"Not here?" growled the voice of Aragh. He slid into sight from behind a tree that should have been too small to hide him. "I got back some time ago. Who says I'm not here?"

"No one, Sir wolf," Brian said, cheerfully, rising from the stream. Stripping the water off his body and limbs with his hands, he walked over to his clothes and began putting them on, without bothering with further self-drying. "We'll be ready to travel in a wink!"

It was slightly more than single wink's worth of time, but not too much more, before Brian had himself dressed and armored and his horse saddled. He swung himself up into the saddle.

"Shall we go?" he asked.

"Fine," said Jim.

Aragh melted into the woods and disappeared. Jim and Brian, side by side, followed after the wolf.

They found him sitting down, waiting for them two clearings farther on.

"I see," he growled. "One of these poke-along, take-forever-to-get-there trips. Is that what it's going to be? All right. I can dawdle along at a walk as well as the rest of you."

He fell in level with them and they paced forward together.

"I don't intend to trot my horse in the heat of the day, just to please you," said Brian.

"Why not? Trot's the only pace to move at," muttered Aragh. "All right. Suit yourself. Oh, not that way, Sir knight. This way."

"I know the route to Malvern Castle," Brian said, stiffly.

"You know *a* route," said Aragh. "I know the shortest one. You'll be a day and a half, heading in that direction. I can bring you there before sunset. Follow me—or not. Makes no difference to me."

He headed off to their right, tail swinging low behind him. Jim and Brian halted, looking at each other.

"But that way leads to the *lower* reaches of the Lyn River," Brian protested. "The closest ford's fifteen miles upstream."

"It's his woods, though," said Jim. "Maybe we ought to trust him."

"Sir James—" Brian began. "Oh, very well!"

He turned his horse's head in the direction Aragh had taken and together they moved after the wolf, catching up with him a little farther on.

They rode through the warm hours of the afternoon. The forest opened out even more, but never quite ceased being a forest. To begin with they did very little talking, Aragh and Brian growling "Sir knight" and "Sir wolf" at each other whenever Jim tried to draw them into any kind of conversation. But gradually the atmosphere thawed on the pleasant discovery by the two that they had at least one thing in common: a detestation of someone named Sir Hugh de Bois de Malencontri.

". . . sent his beaters through my woods!" snapped Aragh. "My woods! As if it was his private preserve. I broke up his hunting for him. Hamstrung half a dozen horses and—"

"I say, not the horses!"

"Why not?" Aragh said. "You humans in armor make yourselves safe by riding on somebody else's four legs. Catch an English *wolf* letting anybody laze about on his back!"

"A gentleman has a use for a good steed. Not necessary for game, though. Always dismount, myself, to go after a boar with a boarspear."

"Ah? Twenty or thirty of you at once, no doubt!"

"No such thing. I've gone into a thicket by myself, alone, several times!"

"Well, that's something," said Aragh, grudgingly. "No boar's a picnic. No brains, but no picnic either. Will charge anything. The only way to handle one is step aside and cut him up. Break a leg or two for him, if you can."

"Thanks, I prefer the boarspear. I take his charge. Crosspiece keeps him from getting at you. Then it's hang on until you can let go for a moment to get a falchion into his throat."

"Suit yourself," Aragh growled. "Anyway, de Bois' fine gentlemen didn't like being on their feet. I killed two, crippled eight, before the main party came up with crossbowmen."

"Well done!"

"Eh? All in the day's work. I missed de Bois himself, though. He knocked somebody else out of the saddle, took his horse and ran before I could follow. No matter," Aragh snarled lightly to himself. "I'll catch him one of these days."

"Unless I get to him first," said Brian. "By St. Giles! He had the affrontery to pay his court to the Demoiselle Geronde. Hah!"

"The de Chaney . . . ?"

"Exactly! My lady. I drew him aside at my lord the Duke's Christmas feast, nine months since. 'Lord Baron,' I said, 'a word in your ear. Keep your bastard's breath out of my lady's face or I may be forced to hang you by your own guts.' "

"He said?" growled Aragh.

"Oh, some nonsense about having his verderers skin me alive if he ever caught me near his lands. I laughed."

"And then?" put in Jim, fascinated.

"Oh, he laughed, too. It was my lord Duke's Christmas feast—peace on Earth, good will and all that—neither one of us wanted to make a public fuss. And that was how matters stood when we parted. I've been too busy with mere-dragons and now this quest of yours, Sir James, to get around to keeping my promise to him. But I really must, one of these days."

And so on . . . in the same vein.

About midafternoon, they came out abruptly through a screen of trees and bushes onto the banks of the River Lyn. Without pausing, Aragh stepped off into the water and proceeded to head across the stream, immersed almost to his backbone. Jim and Brian stopped.

"But there's no ford here, dammit!" said Brian.

"With weather the way it's been for the past month and this time of year," said Aragh over his shoulder, "there *is*—for this week and the next. But suit yourself."

In fact, the wolf was nearly to midstream now and his neck and head were still well above the surface of the water. Brian grunted and urged his horse down the bank. He began to ride across.

"I think I'll fly," Jim announced, looking at the river with disfavor.

He had not forgotten his swimming sessions in the fens. He leaped into the air, and with a few wingbeats passed over the heads of the others to land on the far bank and watch Aragh climb dripping back onto dry land. They waited together for Brian.

"Must say you knew what you were talking about," said the knight, grudgingly, to Aragh as he came ashore. "If this is Malvern Wood on this side, which it should be—"

"It is," said Aragh as they moved off together into the forest.

"—we should indeed see the walls of the castle there before nightfall," concluded Brian. "I must say, being on my lady's land is almost like a homecoming to me. If you'll notice, Sir James, how peaceful and pleasant things are here—"

A *thwock* resounded, and a three-foot arrow stood suddenly in the ground a few paces in front of them.

"Hold!" cried a high-pitched voice, the voice either of a woman or a young boy.

"What the hell?" demanded Brian, reining up and turning in the direction from which, judging by its angle in the turf, the arrow had come. "I'm going to crop myself some archer's ears—"

Thwack! sounded another arrow, materializing in the trunk of a tree a foot behind and an inch or two to the right of Brian's helmet.

"I'll take care of this," Aragh grunted, on a low note, and vanished.

"Hold where you are, Sir knight!" cried the voice again. "Unless you want me to put an arrow through that open visor of yours—or into one of your eyes, dragon! Don't move a muscle until I come to you."

Jim froze where he was. Brian, also, he saw, was prudently not moving.

They waited.

Chapter 10

It was a golden afternoon. In the Malvern Wood birds sang and a little breeze blew past Jim and Brian. Time went by and nothing else happened.

A deer walked across the open space between two trees about twenty yards from them, paused to look interestedly at the two unmoving figures and continued on, out of sight. A badger galumphed past, ignoring them completely in the tough, deliberate manner of its species.

Jim's feet were beginning to go to sleep, when he heard a droning sound in the air. A bumblebee buzzed into their vicinity, circled twice and then flew into the opening in the knight's visor. Jim waited interestedly, sleeping feet forgotten, for the explosion he was sure would come; but he had underestimated the self-control of Sir Brian. Neither sound nor movement emanated from the knight; although with his acute dragon hearing, Jim could now hear the bee buzzing hollowly around in the helmet and falling silent intermittently, which meant it must be landing on lip, nose or ear momentarily to assess the situation.

Eventually the bee flew out again.

"Sir Brian?" said Jim, questioningly, for he had actually begun to wonder if the knight was still conscious within his armor.

"Yes, Sir James?"

"Something's wrong. Whoever shot at us must have run off, right afterwards. Or something. We've been standing here twenty minutes. Why don't we go look?"

"Perhaps you're right."

The knight reached up, snapped his visor down and reined his horse behind the tree the arrow was stuck in. No further shots came in their direction. Jim followed him; and keeping some trees always as a screen between themselves and the point from which the arrow had probably been launched, they circled around to investigate.

The woods appeared as quiet and untenanted as they had been all day, for perhaps a hundred yards' distance. Slightly beyond, however, the two came upon a slim figure in brown hose and doublet, with a peaked hat over shoulder-length red hair, kneeling on the grass with a longbow and quiver of arrows laid to one side, massaging the furry neck of a large black shape.

The large black shape was Aragh's. He was lying on his stomach in the grass, his long muzzle stretched out on his forepaws and his eyes half-closed, growling softly to himself as the slim hands worked on his neck and scratched under his ears.

"What devil's spell is this?" roared Brian, pulling his horse to a halt as he and Jim came up.

"You," said the figure kneeling on the grass, glancing up at him, "guard your tongue, Sir knight! Do I look like the devil?"

Clearly she—for obviously the figure in the doublet and hose was no boy—did not look like any devil. The word "angel" might have fitted better, if it had not been for her rather steely gray eyes and the deep, practical tan of the skin on her face and uncovered hands and forearms. Aside from those two ordinary aspects, however, she appeared almost too good to have been cast from the ordinary human mold.

Even kneeling in the grass as she was, she was obviously almost as tall as Jim or Brian. Her legs were long, her waist tiny, her shoulders delicate but wide, and the curves of her body such as an artist of Jim's world might come up with for the illustration of some advertiser's commercial daydream. Her hair, a few shades darker than Brian's in the sunlight, was touched with highlights of honey-colored gold. She had a delicate curving jawline, a perfect mouth, a perfect nose and those same eyes which—except for the steeliness Jim had already remarked—had also to be considered perfect.

"No," admitted Brian. "But what're you doing to the wolf to make him growl like that?"

"He's not growling," she said fondly, stroking his neck. "He's purring."

Aragh opened his left eye and rolled it up to look at Brian and Jim.

"Mind your own business, Sir knight," he grated. "Up under the ears there, again, Danielle . . . Ah!"

He went back to his growling.

"I thought you were going to take care of things, Sir wolf!" said Brian, gruffly. "Do you know we stood there for—"

"The knight's a Neville-Smythe," snarled Aragh to the girl, lifting his head from his paws. "The dragon's an old friend of mine named Gorbash—thinks he's a knight, too, right at the moment. Sir James of something. Can't remember the Christian name of the Neville-Smythe."

"Sir Brian," said Brian, taking off his helm. "And the good knight with me, who's been ensorceled into a dragon's body, is Sir James, Baron of Riveroak, from a land across the sea."

The girl's face lit up with interest. She scrambled to her feet.

"Enchanted?" she asked, approaching Jim and looking closely into his muzzle. "Are you sure? I don't see human eyes within the beast eyes, as they say you should. Can you tell people what you were,

Sir James? What was it like being enchanted? Did it hurt?"

"No," said Jim. "Just, all of a sudden, I was a dragon."

"And before that you were a baron?"

"Well . . ." Jim hesitated.

"I thought so!" she said, triumphantly. "Part of the spell keeps you from telling who you really were. I mean, undoubtedly you were the Baron of Riveroak, but you were probably a lot more than that. A hero of some kind, probably."

"Well, no," said Jim.

"How would you know? This is exciting. Oh, my name's Danielle. I'm the daughter of Giles o' the Wold; except that I'm on my own, now."

"Giles o' the Wold?" Brian echoed. "He's that outlaw, isn't he?"

"He is now!" she flashed, turning on him. "He was a gentleman of rank once, though his true name I will tell to none."

Aragh growled.

"No offense," said Brian with surprising mildness. "I thought Giles o' the Wold, though, was of the King's Forest, up beyond Brantley Moor?"

"So he is," she said. "And there he and his men are, still. But, as I say, I now live apart from him."

"Ah," said Brian.

"Ah, yourself!" she said. "Why should I spend my days with a bunch of men either old enough to be my father, and women just as old, or clod-pated young bumpkins who turn red and stammer when they speak to me? My father's daughter deserves better than that!"

"Well, well," said Brian.

"And again, well!" She looked from Brian to Jim and her voice softened. "I feel no need to crave pardon, Sir James, but it's only fair to say I'd not have shot at you if I'd known you and this knight to be friends of Aragh."

"That's all right," said Jim.

"Quite all right," echoed Brian. "However, if

you're through tickling the wolf, my lady o' the Wold, perhaps we three should be moving on. We want to get to Malvern Castle before the gate's locked for the night."

He reined his horse about in the direction they had all been heading originally and began to ride off. Jim, after a moment's hesitation, moved after him. A second later they were joined not only by Aragh, but by Danielle, her bow and quiver slung upon her shoulder.

"You're going to Malvern Castle?" she asked. "Why?"

"I must ask permission of my lady Geronde de Chaney to companion Sir James here in the rescue of his lady."

"His lady?" She turned on Jim. "You've got a lady? Who is she?"

"Angela . . . uh . . . de Farrel, of Trailercourt."

"Odd names you have overseas," commented Brian. "What does she look like?" demanded Danielle.

Jim hesitated.

"She is fair," Brian put in, "according to Sir James."

"I'm fair," said Danielle. "Is she as fair as I am?"

"Well . . ." Jim stumbled. "Yes and no. I mean, you're different types . . ."

"Different types? What does that mean?"

"It's a little hard to explain," said Jim. "Let me think about it. I'll think of a better way to explain it after I've had a chance to mull it over."

"All right. You mull," said Danielle. "But I want to know. Meanwhile, I think I'll come along with the rest of you to Malvern Castle."

Brian opened his mouth. For a second he looked as if he would say something. But then he closed his mouth again.

They moved along together, Danielle refusing an offer from Brian to mount her behind him on his horse. She could, she stated, outrun the heavy white charger any day in the week. Certainly she could outwalk him.

Jim was more than a little baffled by Danielle. He had been prepared to take on in the way of Compan-

110

ions any who could be useful to him. When Brian had cropped up, he had wrestled a bit with the idea of the knight simply declaring himself in. Once he had accepted that idea, however, Aragh's joining them had seemed almost natural. But this girl—to be one of his Companions, to face the Loathly Tower and the Dark Powers and rescue Angie? In no way could he envision her being useful. Granted, she was good with a bow and arrow . . .

He lost himself in the mental puzzle of trying to reconcile all the unbelievable elements of this place he and Angie had fallen into. The dragons, the magician, the sandmirks (if he had seen them on film in a late, late movie he would have sneered at them), Aragh, and now this russet-haired goddess with a bow and arrow who talked like—he did not know what she talked like. Except that he was becoming more and more wary of finding himself in a conversation with her. She had a directness which literally scared him silly. What gave her the idea that she could ask any question she felt like?

Of course, he did not have to answer. But not answering simply made him look as if he were dodging something. The nub of the problem was that Jim had been very strictly trained not to ask embarrassing questions; and apparently Danielle had no inhibitions at all in that area.

The next time she asks me something I don't want to answer, he told himself, I'll simply tell her it's none of her business—

"Ridiculous!" he heard Brian saying to Aragh, "I tell you. From this angle we have to come in behind the castle, at the Little Lyn Stream, where the curtain wall is up on a rock and there's no way in, even if someone on the wall recognizes me."

"We come in facing the gate, I tell you!" snarled Aragh.

"Back!"

"Gate—"

"Look," said Jim hastily, waking once more to his

111

role as peacemaker between these two. "Let me ask somebody local. All right?"

Peace at any price.

He turned aside from their line of march through the apparently unending wood, and searched about for a source of directions. It certainly could not be too hard to find someone. Granted, there seemed to be no other humans about. But in this world, everything seemed capable of speech—dragons, watchbeetles, wolves . . . An exception might be the flora. So far he had seen no evidence that trees, flowers or bushes could speak. But if he could only find an animal or insect . . .

However, annoyingly, just at the moment, there was nothing in sight. He wandered on, looking for anyone at all: a mouse, a bird . . . Suddenly he almost tripped over a badger, in appearance a twin to the one he had seen galumphing by while he and Brian were holding their positions at the command of Danielle.

"Hey, wait!" he cried.

It did not seem disposed to wait. Jim flipped himself into the air on his wings and thumped again to earth, this time facing the badger.

He had it backed up against a bush. It bared its teeth in true badger fashion. Badgers, Jim remembered a zoologist saying once at a rather drunken faculty party, would tangle with anybody. This one was obviously not about to spoil the general reputation of its kind, in spite of the fact that Jim-Gorbash outweighed it something like a hundred to one.

"Take it easy," said Jim. "I just want some information. We're headed toward Castle Malvern. Will this way bring us up behind it, or to its front?"

The badger hunched its shoulders and hissed at him.

"No, really," Jim persisted. "I'm just asking."

The badger snarled and made a lunge for Jim's left forefoot.

When he snatched the foot back, the badger turned with a speed that was surprising in a creature of its apparent clumsiness, slipped around the bush and disappeared. Jim was left staring at nothing.

He turned away to find Brian, Danielle and Aragh behind him, all in a row, staring at him.

"I just wanted to get some directions from someone who knew . . ." he began; but his voice died in his throat at the sight of their stares. They were looking at him as if he had taken leave of his senses.

"Gorbash," said Aragh, at last, "were you trying to talk to that badger?"

"Why, yes," said Jim. "I just wanted to ask someone who knew the local area whether we would come out behind Castle Malvern, or in front of it."

"But you were talking to a *badger!*" said Danielle. Brian cleared his throat.

"Sir James," he said, "did you think you recognized this particular badger as someone you knew who had also been ensorceled? Or is it that in your country badgers can talk?"

"Well, no—I mean, I didn't recognize this badger; and no, in my country badgers can't talk," said Jim. "But I thought . . ."

His voice failed. He had been about to cite as evidence his experience that dragons, watchbeetles and wolves could talk; but faced with those stares, he got the abrupt but certain feeling he had just managed to make a fool of himself.

"Mixed up in the head, that's what he is!" Aragh said, gruffly. "Not his fault!"

"Well," said Jim, defensively. "I talk, and I'm a dragon."

"Don't dragons talk where you come from, Sir James?" asked Danielle.

"We don't have dragons where I come from."

"Then what gave you the idea they didn't talk?" demanded Aragh. "Been overworking your brains, Gorbash, that's the trouble. Try not to think for a while."

"We have wolves where I come from"—Jim turned on him—"and they don't talk."

"Wolves don't talk? Gorbash, you're addled. How many wolves do you know?"

"I don't exactly know any. But I've seen them in ... I mean, on ..."

Jim realized immediately that the words "zoos" and "films" would mean as little to the three in front of him as "Social Security number" had meant to the knight, earlier. In whatever language he was speaking now, they would be nothing but meaningless noises.

"How about watchbeetles?" he demanded desperately. "When I talked to Carolinus, he poured some water on the ground and a watchbeetle came to the surface and spoke."

"Come, come, Sir James," said Brian. "Magic, of course. It had to be magic. Watchbeetles can't talk, any more than badgers can."

"Oh, well," said Jim feebly. He gave up. "Never mind. As Aragh says, maybe I've been thinking too much. Let's forget it and get going again."

They took up their route once more, and a sudden shower caught them unexpectedly. For a moment, as the raindrops pelted down hard about them, Jim looked around for shelter—then recognized that the three with him were completely ignoring the wetting. Hard on this came his own recognition that his own armored hide was scarcely conscious of the moisture; and he decided to ignore it also. After a bit, the rain ceased and the sun tried to come out.

It was now in a quarter of the western sky which caused Jim to guess at a time of about 5 p.m.—an hour Brian and Danielle would probably refer to as midway between none and compline, from the canonical hours commonly in use in the Catholic Middle Ages. Momentarily, Jim ran back over his memory to fix those hours in his mind. The earliest was "matins," at midnight. Then came "lauds," at first daylight—call it plus or minus 5 a.m., depending on the season of the year. Then "prime," at sunrise—call that 6 a.m. Then "terce," midmorning—say, 9 a.m. "Sext," at noon. "None" at midafternoon—3 p.m. "Vespers" at sunset—5 p.m. or later . . . Finally, "compline," before retiring; which would probably be no later than an hour or so after sunset, particularly if you were a monk and had to look forward to getting up at midnight.

He had reached this point in delving his memory, when Aragh abruptly put his nose up into the air.

"I smell smoke," he said.

Jim sniffed the breeze which was blowing from them, not toward them. His dragon's sense of smell was not so much inferior to the wolf's but that he could smell smoke himself, now that his attention had been called to it. If they could smell it when the wind was carrying the odor away from them, then whatever was burning must be merely a short distance in front of them.

Aragh broke into a trot, and Brian spurred his horse to keep up. Jim increased his pace and Danielle ran easily alongside him. They went a short distance, emerged from among the trees and stopped, to find themselves in a clearing, at one end of a double row of huts made of mud and wattle, with straw-thatched roofs. Several of these were still smoking. The short rain had fallen here, too, and the bare earth between and around the huts was darkened and, in trampled spots, muddied by the water. The trees and the thatches still dripped moisture and the air was soft and damp. On it, here, the smell of smoke was strong. It hung still, for the breeze had now stopped.

The village—if that was what it was—was silent, with no one to be seen moving about it. Except for the few huts that had caught fire—only to have their flames apparently put out by the shower—there was nothing at all happening. The only people were four or five who had evidently fallen asleep about the street or in the doorway of some hut or other. About a dozen feet in front of Jim, as he pushed past Brian and Aragh for a better look, was a half-grown girl in a robe of coarse brown cloth, lying on her side with her back to them and her black hair spread on the mud.

Jim stared. Had the people here been having some sort of celebration, at which they became so intoxicated that they did not stir to put out the fires which drunken accident had started on their meager dwellings? He took one step more toward the girl to wake her up and ask her—and at that moment some twelve or fifteen men on horseback, with steel caps, half-armor and drawn swords, rode out from between the last huts at the far end of the village and turned to face Jim and the others.

The scene before Jim seemed to jump abruptly, like a faulty movie film, from one frame to the next. All at once, he saw the village with a difference: the people lying about were not merely sleeping, they were dead —killed—and their slayers were at the other end of the village street. He took a third step forward, looked at the dead girl before him, and from this fresh angle saw her arms stretched out before her without hands. They had been cut off at the wrist.

The smell of smoke now seemed to fill his brain. He launched himself into the air, swooping forward and down upon the mounted men. He saw their swords up, catching the watery sunlight as he drove into them, but he felt no blows. Three of the horses went down under the impact of his body and he tossed two of their falling riders aside with his clawed forepaws, cutting the third man—the one most directly in front of him —almost in half with one snap of his jaws. On the ground now, Jim reared up, striking out with claws, teeth and wings at once.

The action around him was a blur. He saw an arrow sprout suddenly, half out of the metal breastplate of a rider; and some gleaming metal drove into the fray on his right. The point of Brian's lance carried one rider clear off his horse and into another rider, who also flew from his saddle. Then the lance was dropped, and Brian's sword was cutting right and left; while under him the clumsy white charger—abruptly transformed—reared, screaming, lashing with its front hooves and savaging with its teeth, to beat to the ground the lighter horses about it.

At Jim's left a rider suddenly vanished from his saddle; and for one insane moment it was Aragh riding the mount instead, his jaws grinning as he launched himself from the leather under him into another of the opposing riders—

All at once, it was over. Two or three of the mounted men-at-arms, and as many riderless horses, were dashing off. Aragh, on the ground now, was tearing out the throats of any who still lived. Jim checked himself, snorting heavily through his nostrils, and looked around.

Neither Aragh nor Brian seemed to have been touched. Danielle, Jim was glad to see, was still several houses down the street, approaching them at a walk, bow still in hand and an arrow ready but not strung. She had stood back, it seemed, sensibly, and used her weapon as it ought to be used—from a distance.

Jim looked down at his own forearms and body. He was covered with blood, some of which was probably his own; but he felt nothing. Within, he was conscious of two conflicting emotions struggling for ascendancy. The dragon in him was savagely disappointed that there were no more enemies to kill; the man felt as if he badly wanted to be sick.

Chapter 11

"Hold still!" said Danielle. "How can I wash you off if you keep moving?"

He wanted to tell her that it was the dragon-adrenaline in him that was still making him twitchy. But he did not know how to explain this in terms she would understand. What had triggered him off had been a purely human horror at seeing the dead girl without hands, but after that he had been pure dragon.

117

Or had he? An impulse made him stop and question this. Perhaps not. Maybe he was in some ways as savage as Aragh, or Brian or those men he had killed.

"That's all right," said Danielle, having gotten him cleaned up. She was a competent, but not necessarily sympathetic, nurse. "You're cut up more than a little; but nothing important. Three or four of the cuts could use some oil and bandages. But if you keep them clean, they should all heal well, despite the lack. Don't roll in the dirt, Sir James."

"Roll? Why would I want to roll—" Jim was beginning, when Brian, who had been busy taking off his helm and gauntlets after retrieving his lance and checking it for damage, interrupted.

"It's plain to see," he said, "there's been no less than an attack on Malvern Castle. That lot of swine would not be foraying in such a manner unless the Malvern force at least were shut within walls and unable to sally. We'd best go carefully to get a look at the castle before we let the countryside know of our numbers and whereabouts."

"Catch me approaching any castle any other way." Aragh was standing nearby. Though his words were in character for the wolf, the tone was unusually mild. "And what if the castle is no longer in the hands of your lady? Shall we turn back?"

"Not far," Brian answered, tightly. His jaw muscles were lumped and the bones of his face seemed to stand out sharply under the skin. "If the castle is taken, I have a lady either to rescue or avenge—and that takes precedence over my desire to help Sir James. If unfriends indeed hold the castle, we must find another place for ourselves this night. There's an inn not too far off. But first, let's go see how matters stand with the castle."

"I can go and get back with no one seeing me," said the wolf. "Better the rest of you wait here."

"Those who got away might come back with help, if we stay here," put in Jim.

"Not with night coming on," said Brian. "Still, it won't be long until dark for us, as well. Perhaps it's best if you do scout the castle alone, Sir wolf. I and the others will head for the inn, to see if that's open to our using, or has been misused like this village. But wait—you don't know where the inn is."

"Tell me," said Aragh. "Though, given a little time, I could find it easily enough myself."

"Due west of the castle is a small hill with a crown of beech trees against the sky. If you look south from that hill's top, you'll see a place where the trees darken in a hollow, about two arrow-flights distant. You won't be able to see the inn, itself; but under those trees you'll find both it and the stream that runs by it."

"Soon," said Aragh, and was gone.

Jim, Danielle and Brian headed off through the wood, Brian leading.

"All this is familiar land to me," he explained. "As a boy I was a page here for three years, to learn my manners from Sir Orrin. My lady and I have walked or ridden over every foot of this ground, since."

The sun was setting now, and long shadows stretched out from the trees across the grass. They were not forbidding shadows, however, as they had been in Lynham forest, the night before. The evening hush lay on everything and, with half the sky overhead painted pink, for a moment the world about them seemed a different one from that holding the village they had just left.

But the moment passed. The light continued to fade and they came at last to a spot where Brian stopped abruptly, holding up his right hand to halt Jim and Danielle.

"The inn's just beyond these trees," he told them. "But walk and talk softly. Sound carries in this place, particularly when there's no wind."

They moved forward quietly together and gazed out from the shadows of the trees which the knight had indicated. They saw an open glade perhaps four hundred yards across at its narrowest. The stream Brian had spoken of to Aragh was ditched to flow completely around a long, stout building of logs, built in the center of the glade on a grassy mound of earth that seemed artificially raised within the circle of land. At the far end of the building—actually an extension of it—stood a sort of half-open shed in which two horses could be seen tethered, their heads in some sort of wall trough, feeding.

"The inn door's open, and the shutters are folded back from the windows," muttered Brian. "So they're not in a state of siege. On the other hand, it can hardly be a trap with men waiting for us inside, seeing there are only those two horses in the stable. Nor would these two feed so quietly if other horses had been taken off into the woods nearby to trick us. Those in the stable would be eager to get loose and join their stablemates. Nonetheless, we'd best wait for Aragh. Indeed I believed that, swiftly as he travels, he'd be here before us."

They waited. After only a few minutes, there was a movement behind, and Aragh was once more with them.

"Your fear's justified, Sir knight," he said. "The castle is barred and guarded. Also, I smelled blood spilled on the ground before the main gate, and the armed men on the walls talk of their lord, Sir Hugh."

"De Bois!" The name seemed to stick deep in Brian's throat.

"What other Sir Hugh could it be?" Aragh's red jaws laughed in the last of the light. "Rejoice, Sir knight! We'll both have our chance at him, shortly."

"Rejoice? With my lady no doubt in his hands, as well as her castle?"

"Perhaps she escaped," put in Jim.

"She's a de Chaney, and holds the castle for her father, who may be dead in heathen lands. She'd defend the castle to the death or her own capture." Brian's teeth clicked together. "And I won't believe in her death until I've had certain proof of it. Therefore, she's captured."

"Have it your way, Sir knight," said Aragh.

"I most surely shall, Sir wolf. And now, we need to

scout this inn more closely to make sure it holds no trap for us."

Aragh's jaws laughed again.

"Did you think I'd come to meet you here without first taking a look at that box down there? I came up close behind it, before coming to you here, and listened. There's an innkeeper, his family and two men servants. Also one guest. And that's all!"

"Ah," said Brian. "Then we go in."

He started off and the rest of them caught up with him, walking openly across the glade in the last of the light; but a slight frown grew on the knight's face as they got closer to the ditch that separated them from the open front door.

"It's not like Master Dick Innkeeper not to be out of doors by this time to see who we are and what intentions we have," he said.

Nonetheless, he kept walking forward. His armored feet rang hollowly on the rough-hewn planks of the bridge crossing the ditch before the inn's door. He stepped onto the artificial island on which the inn was built, mounted its slight slope and walked into the gloom within, where what looked like a single torch had been lighted against the darkness. The others followed him in and found him stopped dead still, a pace inside the building.

He was staring at a lanky figure seated in a rough chair with his hose-clad legs propped up on the table before him. In one hand, the seated figure held the longest bow Jim had ever seen; and the other held an arrow loosely fitted to the string.

"And perhaps you'd better tell me who you are, now," the figure said in a soft tenor voice with an odd, musical lilt to it. "I can put an arrow through each of you before one of you could take a step, you should all know. But you do be seeming a strange pack of travelers to be together on the road, and if you have something I should be hearing, I'm prepared to listen, look you."

Chapter 12

"I'm Sir Brian Neville-Smythe!" said Brian, harshly. "And you might think twice about whether you could put arrows through us all before one of us could reach you. I think I might just reach you, myself!"

"Ah no, Sir knight," said the man with the bow. "Do not be thinking of that armor of yours as something to make you different from the rest. At this distance the lady's doublet and your steel coat are the same as nothing to my arrows. The dragon a blind man could not miss, look you; and as for the wolf—"

He broke off suddenly, and laughed noiselessly for a second.

"It is a wise wolf, then," he said, "and a sly one as well. I did not even see him go."

"Master bowman," said Aragh's voice from out of sight beyond the open doorway. "You'll have to leave that inn, someday, and travel in the woods. When that day comes you'll be breathing without a throat before you can close your fingers on a bowstring, some moment when you least expect it, if either Gorbash or Danielle o' the Wold is harmed."

"Danielle o' the Wold?" The bowman peered at Danielle. "That would be this lady, now, whose face I cannot see any more than I can see the faces of you others, for the glare of the sunset light behind you. Would you be of some relation to a Giles o' the Wold, lady?"

"My father," said Danielle.

"Indeed! He is a man, then, and an archer—if report be true—whom I am most wishing to meet." The bowman raised his voice. "Rest you easy, Sir wolf. The lady will not be harmed by me, now; neither at this moment nor any other."

"Why do you want to meet my father?" Danielle asked, sharply.

"Why, to be talking to him about bowmanship," said the man at the table. "I am Dafydd ap Hywel, look you, a man of the longbow, the same which was first made and used in Wales, and which has since falsely come to be called an English weapon. So I am traveling about to teach these English archers that it is none of them can come near to matching a Welshman like myself, whether at mark or at rover, or at length of flight, or anything at all they wish to try with bow, string and shaft—and this because I am blood of the true bowmen, which they are not."

"Giles o' the Wold can outshoot you twice over, any day!" said Danielle, fiercely.

"I do not think he will, indeed," Dafydd said, gently, peering at her. "But I do have a great wish to see your face, lady—" He lifted his voice. "Inn-keeper!" he called. "More torches, here! And you have more guests also, look you!"

A faint sound came of voices and footfalls farther back in the building; and then light spilled through the doorway in the shape of a square-bodied, middling-tall man of about forty, holding a burning torch in one hand and carrying three unlit in his other fist.

"Sir knight—lady—dragon . . ." he said, a bit breathlessly, and began to stick the unlit torches in wall sockets around the room and light them.

As the new flames flared up, Jim could see that Brian's face was hard.

"How is this, Dick Innkeeper?" he said. "Do you treat all old friends this way—hiding in the back of your inn until some other guest summons you forth?"

"Sir Brian, I— Forgive me—" Dick Innkeeper was obviously not used to apologizing; and the words came with difficulty. "But my roof is over my head and my family alive only because of this guest. You may not

123

know it, messire, but Malvern Castle has been taken by Sir Hugh de Bois de Malencontri—"

"I know it," Brian interrupted. "But you seem to have been spared."

"Spared, we have been," said the innkeeper, turning from setting the torch from which he had been lighting the others into the last wall socket. The red light showed all their faces clearly now. "But only because of this bowman. It was two days since that he stopped here for the night; and early yesterday we heard horses outside and both went to the door to see fifteen or twenty men-at-arms riding out of the wood to my door."

" 'I don't like this,' I said to him, as we stood in the doorway together.

" 'Do you not, my host?' he answered; and, without saying anything further to me, stepped out of doors and called to them to come no nearer."

"It was no great thing," said Dafydd, from the table, on which his feet were still cocked, although he had now laid aside his bow and arrow. "They were a quarter of the way clear of the wood, and not an archer or crossbowman among them."

"Even so," said Brian, staring interestedly at him. "Dick spoke of fifteen or twenty, and all mounted. Not likely they'd stop at your word."

"Never they did," the innkeeper explained. "Whereupon he slew five of them in the time it takes me to draw a single breath. The others fled. When I went out to gather the bodies afterwards, every arrow was through the same place on each dead man's chest armor."

Brian whistled.

"My lady Danielle," he said, "it strikes me your father may have something to do in outshooting this man of the Welsh bow, after all. I take it, Dick, those fellows of Sir Hugh's haven't been back?"

"They may come if they wish," said Dafydd, mildly. "I am not a man of great dispute, but I have said they shall not come in here, and they shall not."

"Not likely," said Brian. "Sir Hugh's not fool

enough to waste any more men than he has already, even to take an inn as valuable as this one."

It was unfortunate—also involuntary—but at the word "valuable" Jim felt again that sensation that had kindled in him back at the dragon cave, when the word "gold" had been mentioned. Unfortunately, avarice seemed to be a built-in dragonly vice. He forced the reaction out of his mind. The innkeeper was still talking.

". . . But what would you wish in food and drink, Sir Brian?" he was saying. "I've meats both fresh and salted, bread and fruits of the season . . . ale, beer and even French wines . . ."

Jim felt a new sensation kindle in him.

"And what can I give the dragon?" The innkeeper had turned to Jim. "I've no cattle, swine, or even goats. Perhaps, if the good beast—"

"Dick," said Brian, severely, "this gentleman is Sir James Eckert, Baron of Riveroak in a land beyond the seas. He's been ensorceled into this dragon shape you now see him in."

"Oh! Forgive me, Sir James!" Dick Innkeeper wrung his hands. Jim stared at him, fascinated, having never seen it done before. "How can I make amends for my stupidity? Twenty-three years keeper of this inn, and never before have I failed to know a gentleman when he stepped through my door. I—"

"That's all right," Jim said, awkwardly. "It's a natural mistake."

"No, no, Sir James!" said Dick, shaking his head. "You're kind; but one who keeps an inn doesn't make mistakes, natural or otherwise, or he doesn't stay long in business. But what, then, can I bring you to eat, Sir James? Will you dine on what I can supply the others? I know not what food is preferred in lands beyond the seas. True, my cellar is stocked with great variety—"

"Why don't I just take a look down there," said Jim. "You did mention . . . wine?"

"Indeed. Wine of Bordeaux, of Auvergne, of—"

"I think I'd like a little wine."

It was a massive understatement. The moment the

innkeeper had mentioned the word "wine," Jim had experienced a glow inside him that very nearly equaled the feeling he had had at the mention of gold. In addition to their taste for treasure, it appeared, dragons had a fondness for wine.

"And I'll find something down in your cellar to eat," he said. "Don't bother about me."

"Then perhaps you'd come with me, Sir James," Dick offered, turning toward an interior doorway. "I think you can get through here all right? As for the entrance to the cellar, since we need to pass casks through it, it should be wide enough and the staircase stout enough to bear you . . ."

Talking, he led Jim through the doorway, down a passage that was narrow but adequate for Jim to pass, and into a large room that was obviously a kitchen. In the kitchen wall to their right a wide door stood open, with steps leading downward beyond it. Jim followed the innkeeper into the cellar.

The cellar, in fact, turned out to be worthy of the innkeeper's evident pride in it. Apparently it ran a full length of the inn building and was a storehouse of everything from what might be found in a medieval attic to what might be found in a medieval castle storehouse. Clothing, furniture, sacks of grain, bottles full and empty, casks of drinkables . . .

"Ah," said Jim.

. . . And toward the far end a forest of hooks in the heavy wood beams overhead supported heavy planks of smoked meats, including a small wilderness of good-sized hams.

"Yes," said Jim, stopping by the hams, "this should do me nicely. Where was that wine you were talking about?"

"All along the far wall, Sir James," said Dick, bustling about. "In the bottles—but perhaps you'd want to taste the wine I've got in casks, of which there's a greater assortment . . ."

He was rummaging on a dark shelf—the cellar was unlit except for the single torch he had carried down. Now, he came up with a large container of darkened

126

leather, with a wooden handle fixed to it by metal straps. It looked as if it might hold perhaps three-quarters of a modern American gallon. He handed this to Jim.

"Why don't you try the various wines—the wines are at this end of the row, beer and ale at the other—while I take some meat and drink up to Sir Brian and the others? I'll be back shortly, to carry up what you choose."

"Don't bother," said Jim, craftily. "Actually, the furniture up there doesn't suit this dragon-body of mine too well. It's embarrassing trying to eat with other humans in their natural bodies. Why don't I just eat and drink down here?"

"Whatever you wish, Sir James."

Dick went off, considerately leaving the torch he had brought down in a holder near the wine casks.

Jim rubbed his forepaws together, looking around him . . .

Chapter 13

Jim woke, under the vague impression that a conversation was going on somewhere in his vicinity. A pair of voices, both male, seemed to be talking in attempted hushed tones; but which, under the stress of emotion on the part of one voice or another, broke out occasionally to sound louder than its owner intended. Waking up a little more, but without opening his eyes, Jim identified one voice as Brian's, the other as that of the innkeeper.

Jim listened idly, only half paying attention to what he heard. He felt far too comfortable to concern himself about anything. For the first time since he had found himself in this body, his stomach was comfortably upholstered. He felt no further inclination to add to its contents, no matter what might be available within arm's reach. And the wine had been all that a dragon could have expected. Nor were there any noticeable aftereffects. Perhaps dragons did not get hangovers . . . ?

He was gradually drifting back to full consciousness as he lay there. His eyelids were bright with what must be additional torchlight—he remembered that the torch Dick had originally left had guttered out sometime before he was through eating and drinking; but his dragon-body was quite at home in the dark, and also by that time he knew the location of everything in the cellar which interested him. The two voices were now completely understandable, so that he found himself following the conversation in spite of himself, and despite the fact that the two were obviously trying not to disturb him.

". . . But Sir Brian," the innkeeper was saying, forlornly, "hospitality is one thing; but—"

"The bowman may have saved you from that small pack of rascals," Brian answered, sternly, "but if Sir Hugh's to be driven off and you and your family live once more in full safety, it'll be Sir James here, as well as myself, who'll provide you with that peace. How will you answer my lady, once she's been put back in possession of her castle, when she hears that you begrudged one of her rescuers a little food and drink?"

"A little!" Jim could imagine Dick wringing his hands again. "Forty-six of the choicest hams! A quarter of a tun of Bordeaux and perhaps two dozen bottles of other wines! Three such meals by Sir James, Sir Brian, and you'll see me a ruined man!"

"Lower your voice!" Brian snapped. "Want to wake the good knight with your complaining and crying? For shame, Master innkeeper! I've been with Sir James since two days ago and he's not eaten until now. It may well be he won't need to eat again until the castle's recovered. But, in any case, I've told you I'd see you paid for any costs he puts you to."

"I know, Sir Brian. But an innkeeper can't merely put your pledge instead of food before hungry guests, with the explanation that his cellar's empty. It takes time to gather such a store of foodstuffs as I have—*had*—downstairs here. As it is, ham alone is going to be a rare dish under my roof until Eastermass of next year—"

"Hush, I say! Come away!" hissed the knight sternly.

The torchlight and the sound of footsteps withdrew together.

Jim opened his eyes in utter darkness. The strong jaws of his conscience began to nibble at him. This strange world with its talking creatures, its magic and its Dark Powers, had somehow put that part of him to sleep. Now it awoke, a giant with its strength redoubled. However fairy-tale his existence appeared to be here, this was in fact a world where people were born in the ordinary fashion, suffered and died—were killed, too, like that poor child in the village with her hands cut off. He remembered how, back in his own world, he had wished to change modern times for a medieval period when problems were more solid and real. Now, here he was, surrounded with solid and real problems even if the rules were a little different—and far from appreciating that solidity and reality, he was acting as if it were some kind of dream in which he had no responsibility.

The innkeeper had a point. He had more than a point—he had a serious problem that was the result of Jim's simply helping himself to whatever and how much of the man's stock-in-trade had tickled Jim's appetite. The ripoff was no less than it would have been if Jim had walked into a supermarket back in his own world and made off with a hundred and twenty-six full-sized hams and twenty cases of wine.

And the fact that Brian had made himself responsible for the cost of the gargantuan meal made it no better. To begin with, Jim had no idea that he and the knight had become close enough friends so that one might be expected to undertake such an obligation for the other. Guiltily, Jim had to admit that if the situation were reversed, he, with his own world's twentieth-century attitudes toward someone he had only known for a couple of days, would have felt that the other had gotten himself into the situation and that it was up to the fellow to get out of it on his own . . .

An inspiration broke suddenly upon Jim like the light of a torch abruptly kindled in a pitch-black cellar. Some of Gorbash's memories seemed still to linger in this body Jim was using. Perhaps the memory of where Gorbash kept his hoard was still there also, if only he could evoke it. If he could discover where the hoard was, he could pay back Dick Innkeeper himself, and rid his conscience of its uneasy sense of obligation to the knight.

Feeling much better, now that he had thought of this, Jim roused himself and, with a dragon's sureness in the dark, strode back along through the cellar and up its stairs into the kitchen. No one was there but a stout woman of about the innkeeper's age, who bobbed him a curtsey when he appeared.

"Uh . . . hello," said Jim.

"Good morning, Sir James," replied the woman.

Jim went down the passageway and into the tavern room. He felt shamefaced about the idea of encountering the innkeeper or Sir Brian, but the room when he stepped into it was empty. Once more the front door was open—a natural response to the need for some circulation of air, Jim realized, since the windows of the inn, even unshuttered, were mere slits—designed more for defense than for light and ventilation. He stepped outside and heard the voices of Brian and the innkeeper again, but from a distance. They were down at the stable end of the building, concerned with Brian's white warhorse, which had also been slightly cut up in the fight at the village.

Talk of the horse's cuts reminded Jim of his own. He had hardly been conscious of them yesterday. Today, however, he felt them—not seriously, but in the same way half a dozen small razor cuts might feel on his face after he had done a clumsy job of shaving.

His Gorbash-body felt a sudden impulse to lick them; and he discovered that his supple neck and long tongue had no trouble reaching any of the wounds.

With the cuts all cleaned by his tongue, the discomfort from the wounds fell to a point where he could ignore them. He sat up and looked around, to discover Aragh sitting on his haunches not ten feet from him, watching.

"Good morning," said Jim.

"It's good enough," said Aragh. "Spent the whole night inside that place, did you?"

"Well, yes," answered Jim.

"Suit yourself," Aragh said, grimly. "You'll never catch me going into one of those boxes."

"You didn't come in at all?"

"Of course not," growled the wolf. "That sort of thing's for humans. Something soft about all humans, Gorbash, even if they can hold their own like that knight and the bowman. I don't mean just soft in the body, I mean soft in the mind. Takes ten years for one of them to be able to take care of itself, and they never get over that. They remember being petted and fed and looked after; and later on, when they get the chance, they try to set up things so they get petted and cared for some more. When they get old and feeble, that's all they're good for—more petting and caring. Not for me, Gorbash! The first warning I'll get that I'm growing feeble is going to be when somebody who oughtn't to be able to, tears my throat out!"

Jim winced slightly. This assessment of human nature, coming on top of his guilt about last night's indulgence, struck a more tender spot than it might have done otherwise. Then he thought of something.

"You liked having Danielle scratch under your ears, yesterday," he said.

"*She* did it. I didn't *ask* her to," Aragh replied, gruffly. "Hah! Wait'll she catches up with you!"

"Catches up with me?"

Aragh's jaws parted in one of his noiseless wolf-laughs.

"I know her. You and your nonsense about having a human lady, Gorbash! Now, you've got two!"

"Two?" said Jim. "I think you're imagining things."

"I am? Go see for yourself. She's just off there in the trees with that bowman."

Jim looked away in the direction Aragh's muzzle was pointing.

"Maybe I will," he said.

"Good luck!" Aragh yawned and lay down in the sun, jaws on forepaws, eyes closed.

Jim went off toward the area Aragh had indicated in the surrounding woods. Stepping into the shade of the first big trees, he saw no one. Then his dragon-ears caught a murmur of voices that would have been inaudible to his human ones, coming from a short distance farther off. Feeling like an eavesdropper, he moved quietly toward them, and halted when the speakers came into view.

They were standing in a small opening among the trees. The grass under their feet, the sunlight upon them and the tall elms all around them framed a picture that was almost too perfect to believe. Danielle, in her hose and doublet, looked as if she had just stepped out of a book of legends; and Dafydd, who stood with her, was hardly less imposing.

The bowman wore his bow and quiverful of long arrows—Jim got the idea that these two items were never more than an arm's length from him, even while he slept. Danielle, however, had left her own bow and arrows someplace else. She wore no weapon except the knife at her belt; although this, with its six-inch sheath outlining a near-equal length of blade, was certainly nothing to ignore.

". . . After all," she was saying, "you're just a common bowman."

"Not common, lady," Dafydd replied softly. "Even *you* ought to recognize that, look you."

He stood over her. Danielle was tall, but Dafydd was a good deal taller. Jim had not really appreciated the Welshman's height, on seeing him seated in the inn. Grottwold might have been as tall; but beyond the overall inches, any similarity between the two men ended. Dafydd was as straight and supple as his own bow and his shoulders were as wide as the inn's front door. His face was of the sort usually described as "chiseled"—straight nose, square jaw, level eyes, but all without the heavy boning of someone like Brian. His voice was soft and musical; and he had been entirely right about himself as a bowman—or anything else. He was not at all common.

Jim, watching, found himself completely caught up in wonder at Danielle's attitude. How, he wondered, could she prefer someone like himself—that is, if Aragh was telling the truth—to this medieval superman? For the moment, he had forgotten entirely that he was in a dragon's body, not in his ordinary human form.

"You know what I mean!" said Danielle. "Anyway, I've had enough of bowmen to last me for a lifetime. Besides, why should I care about you, bowman or not?"

"Because I find you beautiful, lady," Dafydd answered, "and I remember nothing in all my life that I found beautiful that I did not want it; and, wanting, never ceased from striving for, until I gained it."

"Is that so? I'm not some bauble to hang on your baldrick, Sir bowman! As it happens, I'll say who gains me!"

"Indeed, you shall. But shall no one else while I live—as you may now know from my telling you of it."

"Hmph!" Danielle did not exactly toss her head, but Jim got the strong impression that for two cents, or its medieval equivalent, she would have. "I'm going to marry a prince, when I marry. What can you do against a prince?"

"Against prince, king, emperor, God or Devil— the same thing I would do against any man or beast who came between me and the lady I wanted. One or the other of us would go down; and that is not likely to be myself."

"Oh, of course not!" sneered Danielle.

She turned and marched away from Dafydd. Jim woke suddenly to the fact that she was coming straight for him and that in a moment he would be discovered. There was hardly anything to do but pretend he had just arrived. He stepped forward, out of the trees.

"There you are, Sir James!" Danielle called, happily. "Did you have a good night's sleep? How are your wounds?"

"Wounds?" echoed Jim. She had certainly not dignified his cuts with the name of "wounds" when she had cleaned him up yesterday. "Oh, fine! Yes, I slept like a log!"

"Dear Sir James," she said, reaching him. "I've been waiting for you to wake up so that we can talk some more. There were things I wanted to know, you remember. Shall we take a walk, just the two of us?"

"Well . . . sure," said Jim. He had come into these woods with the firm intention of settling any foolish notions Danielle might have about him. Face to face with her, he felt his confidence evaporating. "Oh, good morning, Dafydd."

"Good morning, Sir James," said the bowman, pleasantly.

Danielle already held Jim by the forearm and was leading him off into the wood at an angle to the route he had taken on coming here.

"I'll talk to you later in the day," Jim called over his shoulder to Dafydd.

"Indeed now, we shall, Sir James."

In a moment the small clearing was out of sight. Danielle led the way through the trees for some distance, but soon slowed her pace.

"Have you remembered anything?" she asked.

"Remembered?" Jim echoed.

"Of who you were, besides being Baron of Riveroak."

"Well . . . who could I be?" Jim said. "I mean, just being Baron alone——"

"Come, Sir James," said Danielle, impatiently. "A

gentleman isn't just his rank. For that matter, he can have many ranks. Isn't our Lord Duke also Count of Piers, Steward of the East Marches and lots of other things? And as for our King in England, isn't he also King of Aquitaine, Duke of Brittany, Duke of Caraballa, Prince of Tours, a Prince of the Church, a Prince of the Two Sicilies, Count this, Count that . . . and so on, for half an hour? Baron of Riveroak is probably the *least* of your titles."

"What makes you think so?" asked Jim, feebly.

"Why, because you've been enchanted!" Danielle snapped. "Who'd bother enchanting a mere baron?"

Her manner softened. She reached up to pat him gently on the end of his muzzle. To Jim's surprise, the touch of her hand was a very pleasant thing. He wished she would do it again—and a small twinge of jealousy toward Aragh stirred within him.

"There! Never mind," she said. "It's the enchantment that keeps you from remembering. Are you sure it didn't hurt?"

"Not at all," said Jim.

She looked dubious.

"We used to do a lot of talking about magic in my father's band, in the wintertime. There wasn't much else to do from December until March, once we got snowed in, but sit around the fire and talk. Of course nobody knew—but everybody seemed to think there'd have to be this one, sudden, terrible flash of pain when you changed forms. You know, the same way it would be if you were getting your head cut off, just before your head rolled on the ground and you were really dead."

"It didn't happen that way with me," said Jim.

"You've probably forgotten it—just like you've forgotten being a prince."

"Being a prince?"

"Probably," Danielle answered thoughtfully. "Of course, you could have been a king or emperor; but somehow that doesn't seem to fit you like being a prince. What did you look like?"

"Well . . ." Jim coughed self-consciously. "I was

about as tall as Brian, say, and about the same weight. My hair was black and my eyes were green. I'm twenty-six—"

"Yes," said Danielle, decisively, "that's the right age for a prince. I was right."

"Danielle . . ." said Jim. He was beginning to get a little desperate. "I wasn't a prince. I happen to know I wasn't a prince. I can't tell you just how I know; but believe me. Take my word for it—I *know* I wasn't a prince!"

"There, there," said Danielle, "don't worry about it. It's undoubtedly just part of your ensorcelment."

"What is?"

"Thinking you know you weren't a prince. Undoubtedly, whoever ensorceled you didn't want you realizing who you really are. Let's not talk about it any more now, if it upsets you. Do you happen to know how you can end the enchantment?"

"You bet," said Jim, fervently. "If I can get Angela—my lady—back, I'll get out of this dragon-body in a hurry."

"Well, that's not hard, then. All you have to do is get your Companions together, go to the Loathly Tower, get this Lady Angela and send her back wherever she came from."

"How do you—?"

"I've been talking to Sir Brian," said Danielle. "How many more Companions do you have to get?"

"I don't know," Jim answered. "But you realize, once I get Angela free I'll be going back with her."

"Going back with her . . . ?"

"I love her."

"No, no," said Danielle. "You'll see, that's just another part of the enchantment. Once you're disenchanted, you'll see her as she really is; and realize you're not in love with her at all."

"As she really is?" Jim echoed, bewildered. "Now look, Danielle, I *know* how she really is. She . . . I . . . we've known each other very well for a year and a half, now."

"That's what the enchantment makes you think. It

came to me suddenly, last night. The reason you couldn't answer the question I asked you about whether she was as fair as I am was because, although you knew better, the enchantment was making you think she *was*. Nobody," Danielle insisted, "is as fair as I am. But I don't blame you for not being able to see that, while you're ensorceled this way."

"But—"

"Come, Sir James. You're going to have to face facts, eventually. Look me right in the eyes and tell me you really believe this Angela is as fair as I am."

Jim stopped, to keep from running into her. She had stepped around in front of him and was gazing directly into his eyes from less than a foot away.

He gulped. The absolute hell of it was, she was right. Much as he loved Angie, this suntanned figure of perfection would win any beauty contest between them in the moment of its announcement. But that was beside the point. It was Angie he wanted, not five feet eleven inches of—

"That's beside the point, Danielle," he made himself say. "It's the Lady Angela I'm concerned with; and I'm the one she's concerned with. Even if you could convince me things were different, I don't think you could convince her."

"Oh? Hmm," Danielle said, her fingers playing with the hilt of her knife. "Well, well. She and I can settle that little matter by ourselves when the time comes. But, Sir James, hadn't we better be heading back to the inn? The others will be wondering that you should keep me apart alone with you all this time."

"You're right," said Jim, and headed back with her.

It was not until he was a half-dozen steps along the way that he realized she had conned him again. Who was likely to wonder about his spending time with Danielle as long as he was still in the body of a dragon?

When they did arrive back at the inn, they found a table with benches—something like a picnic table —set up outside the front door. Brian and Dafydd were seated at it with leather drinking mugs and a bottle of wine before them. Aragh sat on his haunches at the foot of the table, his head well above the boards.

"Sir James!" Brian called, as Jim and Danielle emerged from the wood. "Come join us! We have plans to make for the retaking of my lady's castle."

Jim felt the pit of his stomach drop slightly. He had gathered earlier that Brian had definite intentions of evicting Sir Hugh de Bois de Malencontri and freeing his Geronde, but he had not bothered to think seriously about what the knight might do. Now, however, that they were down to the point of action, he recalled that the situation was somewhat unbalanced between their own numbers and those of the castle's probable occupiers. This discrepancy would not have bothered him so much if he had not gathered that Brian was the sort of individual who, having made up his mind to do something, was certain to do it.

He lumbered up and sat himself down at the open end of the table, opposite Aragh.

"Sir James," said Brian. "Oh, by-the-bye—would you like some wine?"

"Ye— No," said Jim, remembering his existing debt to the innkeeper.

"Very well. Sir James, I have some sorry news for us," Brian went on. "The good bowman here tells me that he sees no reason to join forces with us against Sir Hugh, his principles being—"

"'Let be who will leave me be,'" put in Dafydd. "Not that I do not wish you well, whatever. But it is not a quarrel of mine."

"Likewise," went on Brian, "Sir wolf here considers the matter of my lady and myself to be no quarrel of his; and he has reminded me that his promise to join us extended only insofar as we have to deal with sandmirks."

"Oh."

"Therefore," said Brian, cheerfully. "Clearly, it is to be you and I alone against Sir Hugh and his men. For that reason, let us put our heads together, for we will have need of what cleverness we can muster."

"Well, there you have it, Gorbash," said Aragh, with grim relish. "That's what you get for thinking you're human. Only humans would consider taking a castle full of enemies, when there were only two of them and the castle is built to keep out an army."

"It's certainly not sensible, Sir Brian!" put in Danielle, who was standing by Aragh, petting him behind the ears. "You have to admit that!"

"Sensible or not," Brian resumed, his jaw muscles bunching, "my lady is held and I will loose her. By myself, if need be. But I believe I can count on Sir James."

"It's not Sir James' duty to free your lady!" said Danielle. "His duty's to free himself from his enchantment by getting the Lady Angela out of the Loathly Tower. In fact, it's his duty *not* to risk his life—and that rescue—by trying anything as foolish as taking Malvern Castle, two-handed!"

"I constrain none," said Brian. His burning-blue gaze swung around to lock with Jim's. "Sir James, how say you? Are you with me in this matter, or do I proceed alone?"

Jim opened his mouth to make his apologetic excuses. Attacking the castle with Aragh and Dafydd to help put matters, perhaps, faintly within the realm of success. Without them, such an attack would be nothing less than suicidal. Better to make the situation plain to Brian right now, than to have to back out later.

But, oddly, the words seemed to stick in his throat and would not come out. Jim was under no circumstances the bravest man around—and he was no better a dragon than he was a man, as far as courage went. On the other hand, there was Angie . . . for whose rescue Carolinus assured him he would need Companions—and if he let Brian down now, it was not to be expected that Brian would still come along to the Loathly Tower to help him. Also, there was something about the knight's determination . . . and something, as well, about this crazy world he was now in: unbelievable as it seemed, there was something in him—in the human, not dragon, part of him—that wanted to try taking Malvern Castle, even if he and Brian must make that attempt alone.

"Well, Sir James . . . ?" said Brian.

"Count on me," Jim heard himself saying.

Brian nodded. Dafydd refilled his jack with wine, held it up to Jim and drank it off in silent toast.

"Oh, yes!" Danielle flashed, turning on the bowman. "And you were the one who would put yourself up against prince, or king or emperor, and were so sure it wouldn't be *you* who would go down!"

He looked at her in surprise.

"This is none of my concern, as I said," he answered. "How is it you're making a comparison between this and what I would do for you, in your own case?"

"Sir Brian needs help! Does Sir James hang back and say it's none of his concern? He does not! I wondered about your courage with all those fine speeches you've been making. I see I was right to wonder!"

Dafydd frowned.

"Ah," he said, "you mustn't go making talk like that. My courage is as good as any man's—and, in fact, I think better."

"Oh?"

He stared at her with a sort of slow wonder.

"You will be pushing me into this, now?" he said. "Indeed, I see you will."

He turned to Brian.

"What I said was no less than the truth," he told the knight. "It is nothing to me, one way or the other, about this Sir Hugh of yours. Nor am I some knight-errant, look you, to go rescuing maidens. That is for those of you who are liking such things. But for this particular maiden with us now, and no other, you may count on me, too, for what I can do to aid."

"Good man—!" Brian was beginning, when Aragh interrupted.

"You've got visitors, Sir knight. Turn and look."

Brian turned. They all turned.

Emerging from the trees opposite the inn were the

first of a number of men, all in steel caps, brown, green or russet hose, and leather jackets with metal plates fastened thickly upon them, wearing swords at their belts and with longbows and quivers of arrows slung from their shoulders.

"It's all right, Sir Brian," said Danielle. "It's just Giles o' the Wold, my father."

"Your father?" Brian turned back swiftly to dart a suspicious glance at her.

"Certainly!" Danielle explained. "I knew you'd need help, so I asked one of Dick Innkeeper's sons to ride secretly last night on one of his father's horses to summon him. I said to tell him you'd be glad to split whatever wealth was to be gained from Sir Hugh de Bois and his men in retaking the castle."

Chapter 14

Brian stared at her for a second longer, then turned back to look at the newcomers, who were already halfway across the open ground to the inn. Slowly he got to his feet. Dafydd rose also, casually, his hand on his quiver. Jim found himself getting to his feet as well, and Dick Innkeeper materialized in the inn door, stepping out to join them. Only Aragh stayed seated, his jaws laughing.

The man in the lead was a lean individual who looked to be in his fifties. The ends of hair seen escaping from under his steel cap were iron gray, and his short, curly, jutting beard was pepper-and-salt in color. Beyond his air of authority, he seemed little different from the men behind him, except that the weapon at his belt was not the short sword the others wore, but rather a longer, two-handed weapon like Sir Brian's.

He came up to the ditch girdling the inn, crossed its bridge and stopped before the knight.

"I'm Giles o' the Wold," he said. "And these are my free brothers and companions of the forest. I take it you're Sir Brian Neville-Smythe?"

"I am," Brian answered, stiffly. "Master outlaw, I wasn't the one who invited you here."

"I'm aware of that," said Giles. Above his beard, his face was tanned to almost the color of old leather and the skin had gone into small, shrewd wrinkles. "My daughter sent for me—"

He glanced past Brian for a moment.

"I'll talk to you later, girl," he said. "Now, Sir knight, what matters who sent for me? If you need assistance, here am I and my men, and the price of our aid's not so high as to be beyond reason. Shall we sit like reasonable men and discuss it, or should my lads and I turn around again and go?"

Brian hesitated a second—but only a second.

"Dick," he said, turning to the innkeeper. "Bring another jack for Giles o' the Wold; and see what his companions will have."

"Ale," answered Dick, in a somewhat grim voice, "is all I have in such quantity."

"Ale, then," said Brian, impatiently. "Bring it!"

He sat back down at the table. Giles took the other end of the bench that Dafydd had been sitting on.

Giles looked curiously at Aragh, and then at Jim.

"The wolf I know—by reputation, if nothing else," he said. "The dragon— My daughter's message said you were a knight under enchantment?"

"This is the good Sir James," Brian explained. "The bowman next to you is Dafydd ap— What's that family name of yours, Master archer?"

"Hywel," said Dafydd, pronouncing it with a lilt that Jim knew his own tongue certainly could not have managed. "I am in England to teach the English that

142

the longbow, as well as the true blood of they that best use it, are from Wales alone; and it is also that I am going to marry your daughter, Master Giles."

"He is not!" cried Danielle.

Giles' bearded face parted in a smile.

"If you ever get her permission," he said to Dafydd, "come talk to me about it. You might have to concern yourself not only with my feelings in the matter, but the intentions of some score or so younger members of my band."

"You've a clerkly way of talking, Master outlaw," said Brian as Dick came out with bottles and another jack for Giles, followed by his two men servants rolling a cask through the door into the yard.

"Use your caps," they could hear him directing the outlaws who came clustering around. "I've no store of jacks for such a number as this."

"I've been that, too," Giles answered Brian, carelessly. He took off his own steel cap and tossed it on the table, filled his jack from one of the bottles and drank deeply. His sparse hair stirred a bit in the light breeze that was blowing. "Now, Sir knights, Friend Welshman and Master wolf, I've heard some little about you all—"

His glance touched for a second on the unusual length of the longbow leaning against the table at Dafydd's side.

"—But to save time, perhaps it's best you tell me from the beginning all that bears on the matter here, including that about each of you."

They told him—Jim starting off, Brian taking up the story after he had met Jim, Aragh carrying the tale on from the defeat of the sandmirks, and Danielle, Dafydd and the innkeeper putting in their own reports. Giles drank and listened.

"Well, gentles and others," he said, when they were done. "Maybe I've brought my lads here on a fool's errand after all. My daughter's message gave me to believe you'd a chance to take this castle that only needed a few more stout fighters to secure. But a mixed bag you are—I mean no offense by that—and I know Malvern Castle, which is not a cattle shed to be taken by a rush and a few blows. My lads are fine bowmen, and swordsmen if need be, but no men-at-arms. My pardon to all, but how in hell did you think you might take half an acre of stone walls from perhaps fifty men in no less than half-armor and used to such defense?"

Brian scowled.

"I know Malvern Castle inside out," he said. "Fifty men scattered about it won't be more than two at a time in any one place. Here are three of us, at least —four if the wolf had joined us—who are each more than a match for any two of them in any place, at any time."

"I'll not deny that," said Giles. "But you'd need to be in the castle itself to match them. So, to take first things first, what magic had you planned to use to get into the castle?"

"Malvern will have food stored for siege," said Brian. "But that has to be dull stuff. There's better provender here. Sir Hugh tried to take this inn and failed—I don't doubt he knew there were choice wine and meats here. It was my thought that I could disguise myself as Dick Innkeeper, driving a wagonload of choice food as a peace offering to the new commander of Malvern. The wolf would ride along in the wagon as a dog of the inn, to snarl at any of the common sort that might be tempted to filch the dainties it carried before they reached Sir Hugh. Then, once within, and hopefully in the presence of Sir Hugh himself, he and I would kill the baron, and strive to reach my lady's quarters, where she will be held prisoner—"

"Why?" asked Giles.

"Why what, Master outlaw?"

"Why do you think the Lady Geronde will be locked in her own quarters?"

"Because," said Brian, with obviously hard-held patience, "Sir Hugh would waste no time in taking over the lord's chambers; and there'd be no place else

144

but my lady's room below the solar, to keep anyone like her prisoner in good health and safety. Strong men have been known to last little more than a few days in dungeons, of which Malvern has two, and none of the nicest. Anyplace else in the castle my lady could not be guarded from her own people, who might help her to escape, or to attempt such an escape that death would put her beyond her captors' power. Nor could she be safely guarded elsewhere from Sir Hugh's own men, some of whom at least—as you'd know, Master outlaw, having lived long enough to have a knowledge of men-at-arms—will be no more able than brute beasts to think of the consequences for what they do, when drink is in them."

"Granted," Giles acknowledged. "Go on, Sir Brian. You've slain Sir Hugh and guards and broken into the lady's room. Now what?"

"Now, the good Sir James, who has been on wing and waiting, sees our signal from the balcony of my lady's chamber. He swoops down and carries her away to safety and to rouse a force from the countryside, to retake the castle. Nothing is left but for the wolf and me to escape, ourselves—if God wills it."

"God?" snarled Aragh, abruptly. "Your god, knight, not mine! If anyone saves Aragh, it'll be me. When I was half grown and a full-grown sow bear broke my right foreleg, so that in no way could I run, was it the god of humans who saved me? No, it was I—Aragh! I stood, and fought and got my teeth through the fur and loose skin to the great vein in her throat, so that she died and I lived. That's the way it's always been for an English wolf—the way it will always be. Keep your god if you wish, Sir knight, but keep him to yourself!"

He paused, licked his jaws with one flick of his red tongue and yawned elaborately.

"But I forget," he said. "I'd already told you this business of your lady and the castle has nothing to do with me."

"So. Then what of your plan, Sir Brian?" said Giles. Brian scowled.

"Master outlaw, I'll remind you once more—it wasn't I who invited you here. Here, we're trying to decide what force is needed for a rescue, but how to do it with what we've got. If we lack the wolf, we lack him, that's all."

"How . . . ?" Giles began. "No, with all respect, Sir Brian, I think this trip of mine has been—"

"Wait a moment, Father!" said Danielle. "*I* was the one sent for you."

She turned and looked directly at Aragh. Aragh opened his jaws in silent laughter.

"This is Aragh!" he growled. "Did you think I was another lovesick bowman?"

"No . . ." Danielle replied, "I thought you were Aragh, my wolf-friend, who'd never betray me, any more than I'd betray Aragh. When I sent for my father and his men, it never crossed my mind that Aragh would abandon his friends, such as Sir James and myself. But, since he has—"

She turned back to the table.

"I may not be a match for any two men-at-arms, except with bow and from a safe distance," she said. "But I can be even more useful than a wolf for attracting attention away from Sir Brian, and with the help of surprise I could even aid in killing Sir Hugh and freeing Geronde. Once that's done, of course, I may not be so likely to fight my way to freedom, but I have an advantage over Aragh—like Sir Brian, I can leave my rescue to God."

"Girl—"

"Hush, Father! I'm my own mistress, now. So. Sir James—Sir Brian—count me with you in your attempt on the castle."

She looked back at Aragh.

"And you may sleep in the sun!" she snapped.

Aragh opened his jaws, licked them again and closed them. Then he did a thing that astonished Jim: he whined.

"No, you don't!" Danielle said, fiercely. "You had your chance. Now I'm going into that castle, and you're not going to have anything to do with it!"

Aragh's head dropped. It lowered and lowered until his nose almost touched the ground. He all but crept toward Danielle and pushed his head against her knees.

For a moment she merely glared at him. Then she sat down with a thump and put her arms around his furry neck and hugged his head to her.

"It's all right . . . it's all right," she said.

"I wouldn't have let Gorbash get hurt, either," growled Aragh, in muffled tones into the padding of her doublet. "I was just going to wait until time to go. What good am I if I can't kill for my friends?"

"Never mind." She rubbed behind his ears. "It's all set straight, now."

"I'll even get this knight out safely, afterwards."

"I know you will," said Danielle. "But maybe you won't have to."

She looked up from where she sat to her father.

"Now that Giles o' the Wold knows he'll have three strong allies inside the castle, maybe he can consider making use of himself and his men after all to take the castle?"

"Daughter," said Giles, "you stay clear of the whole affair."

"That's right," Aragh insisted, pulling his head out of her embrace. "*I* go. You don't, Danielle!"

"All right," she replied. "I won't go into the castle. Anything I can do outside, I'll do. Father . . . ?"

Giles refilled his jack and drank thoughtfully.

"My lads and I are no good unless we can get inside, too," he said. "If there was some way you could open the gate for us . . ."

"If it's to be a taking of the castle," said Brian, "I can then barricade my lady and myself in her quarters. Sir James, instead of carrying her off, can land somewhere within the walls and attract attention, during which the wolf can slip down, slay the guards and open the gate—"

He turned to Aragh.

"There's a rope hoist to the right side of the gate, within," he said, "by which one man may lift the bar. With your teeth in that rope, it should lift easily. Then throw your weight on the right-hand gate door—note, Master wolf, the *right*-hand door, not the left—and you should be able to swing it out enough for the archers to get in."

"Good enough, as far as it goes," said Giles. "But the gate won't stand unbarred for more than a moment, I think, even if it takes a dozen men together to cut down the wolf. And it'll take more than a moment or two for all of us, even at a dead run, to cross the open ground that I remember lies about Malvern Castle. Because it's from the nearest cover we must come, certainly. They'll have lookouts on the battlements against anyone creeping close, unseen."

"Shoot the lookouts first," Dafydd suggested.

The Welshman had been so silent that Jim had almost forgotten he was there. Now, they all looked at him.

"How, Master Dafydd?" Giles asked, ironically. "With head and shoulders only for target above the walls, and at a distance of close on half a mile? Clearly you've not seen Malvern Castle and the land it stands on."

"I can do it," said Dafydd.

Giles stared at the younger man for a long moment. Gradually he leaned forward, peering closely into Dafydd's calm face.

"By the Apostles," he said, softly. "I do think you mean that!"

"I know what it is that I can do," Dafydd said. "I would not say it, else."

"You do . . ." said Giles, and paused. "You do . . . and you'll never have to prove to me anything more about the bow and men of Wales. I know of no man living, or of any bowman in memory, able to make such a shoot and kill the men on watch. There'll be at least three, maybe four, of them on that front wall, or this Sir Hugh is no soldier; and you'll have to kill them all at near the same time, or the last one to fall will raise the alarm."

"I have said what I can do, look you," said Dafydd. "Let us pass on to other things."

Giles nodded.

"The thing at least seems possible," he agreed. He turned to Brian. "There'll be smaller details to keep us busy the rest of today and the evening. Twilight or dawn were the best times to surprise them; and dawn preferable, since it gives us as many hours of light after as we wish. So, we can take our time with the details. Meanwhile, let's agree on the pay for my lads and me. Sir Hugh's men will have some gear of weapons and armor which should come to us. In addition, it's only just that Malvern Castle should ransom itself —say, for a hundred marks of silver."

"If my lady chooses to reward you after she and hers are free," said Brian, "that's up to her. I've no authority or right to spend what belongs to the de Chaneys."

"There won't be any de Chaneys if Sir Orrin's indeed dead among the heathen, and the Lady Geronde isn't rescued—and you need us for that!"

"Sorry," said Brian.

"All right, then . . ." The sun wrinkles around the corners of Giles' eyes grew deeper. "Let us have Sir Hugh to ransom. He'll have family or friends who'll pay for his safe return."

"No," said Brian. "I've said he's to die. And he is. Not only I, but the wolf's vowed it. And Aragh's a part of this, as much as you and your men."

"Don't think to take his throat from my teeth, Master outlaw!" Aragh snarled.

"For my lads to risk their lives to gain only some metal and war tools is not enough," said Giles. "We're a band of free men, and they won't follow me at that price, even if I ask it."

He and Brian argued for some little time, without getting to a solution.

"See here, Master Giles," said Brian, at last. "I've

no hundred silver marks of my own to give you; but you'll have heard of me as one who pays his due. I'll give you my knight's word to speak of you and your men to my lady; and she's not the sort to let service go unrewarded. If, however, for some reason payment can't come from her, I'll myself undertake to pay you as I manage to gather that sum, or any part of it, until it's all accounted for. Damme, now, more than that I can't say!"

Giles shrugged.

"I'll talk to my lads."

He got up from the table and went to gather his men into a huddle at a distance large enough to give their discussion privacy.

"Don't worry, Sir Brian," said Danielle, quietly, to the knight, "they'll agree."

In fact, in about fifteen minutes Giles came back and announced agreement. Behind his back, Danielle smiled at the others sitting around the table.

"Let's get on to the details, then," Giles went on, sitting once more. "Sir Brian, you can hardly wear sword and armor when you drive the provision cart into the castle. On the other hand, you're not likely to be able to do much against men-at-arms, to say nothing of Sir Hugh himself, if you're naked. How to get your weapons and armor into the castle? Perhaps Sir James could carry them in a bundle and drop them to you—but then, there would be the time necessary for you to don them, and once Sir Hugh's men had seen a dragon deliver them to you—"

"Once inside the keep, with only one or two armed men for escort to Sir Hugh," said Brian, "the wolf and I can kill them quietly and make a few minutes in which I can dress and arm myself. As for my weapons and armor, these will be with me in the cart. They'll be hidden under the provisions, and the wolf may lie on top of all."

"And no one," snarled Aragh, "will rummage beneath me to find them—I promise you."

Giles nodded, slowly.

"Still . . ." he said to Brian, "even if you appear the

150

perfect innkeeper, or innkeeper's assistant, Sir Hugh and his men are bound to be wary, suspecting some attempt at rescue of your lady—"

"Ha!" said Dick, who had been standing in the doorway of his inn.

He turned about and vanished into the dark interior.

"What ails him?" said Giles, looking at the now-empty entrance to the building.

"As it happens," Brian said, "I'd thought myself about Sir Hugh suspecting me. I've got an answer to that worked out. To start with, I'll go to the castle this afternoon. Ride as close to the walls as I can safely, in armor, considering he'll have crossbows from the walls of Malvern Castle even if he failed to bring some with him; and challenge him to come out and settle the matter by single combat—"

"What silly sort of knight's trick is that?" broke in Giles. "By the scar on your face, you ought to know better than that, Sir Brian. Why should Sir Hugh come out to fight you, when he can simply stay safely in the castle and keep all he's got?"

"Exactly!" said Brian. "I count on him doing just that."

"But all you'll accomplish is letting him know you're outside Malvern Castle."

"Exactly. Then, when he sees the provision cart I'm driving closely pursued by a knight in armor on a white horse, he'll be all the more ready to swing wide the gates, let the cart in and believe the man driving it."

"And how's that to be arranged, unless you've two suits of armor and a twin to wear one of them? To say nothing of the fact—" Giles broke off, abruptly. "By the way, Sir Brian, does this Sir Hugh know you by sight?"

"He does," said Brian, grimly.

"Then what if he's on the wall when you drive up? Do you think rough clothes'll keep him from recognizing you?"

151

"Dick Innkeeper has a false beard among some stuff left here by several strolling players who could not pay their shot," said Brian. "With that to cover most of my face, I stand a chance; and beyond that—well, I have to take some risks."

"A beard?" Giles hesitated. "That's a thing I hadn't thought of. This innkeeper's a man of possessions. It might work."

"A man with a large cellar," said Brian. He paused and listened, cocking his head toward the doorway behind him. "And here, I think, comes the answer to your objection of a moment since . . ."

A thumping sound came from inside the inn. All turned to see a shape materialize in the doorway, filling it. It was a shining figure in full plate armor, with beaked helm and closed visor; and in one mailed fist it carried a mace.

Chapter 15

"By God!" Giles exclaimed, sitting back down on the bench, picking up his jack and drinking deeply from it. Like all the rest, except Brian, he had half risen to his feet at the sight of the figure in the doorway. "You don't want to startle an old bowman so, Master Innkeeper—if it is indeed you, in that suit. You might have had an arrow through you before you were recognized!"

"That was my own thought, also," said Dafydd.

"Your pardon, Sir James, lady, and my masters," boomed Dick's voice hollowly inside the helm. "As Sir Brian has just said, my cellar is large. And an inn acquires many things from its various guests over a pair of lifetimes—for my father kept it here, before me. But can I not pass for a knight, think you? Particularly on horseback and from a distance?"

"Hmm," said Giles, getting up again to examine the innkeeper more closely. "I'd counsel you not to wear that assortment of metal in actual battle, Master Innkeeper. Now that I look close, you've got parts of four different suits upon you, none of which fits as armor ought. Can you raise your right arm above your head?"

Dick tried. The arm creaked halfway to shoulder height and stopped with a clank.

"Yes," said Giles, "I thought so. Your couter on that arm is overlarge, and your pauldron too small for a man of your shoulder. But from a distance . . . from a distance, and sitting on a horse, you might pass."

"Good," Brian said, briskly. "Something to eat then, Dick, and I'll ride to the castle to present Sir Hugh with my challenge."

"I'll go along with you," Jim offered. "I'd like you to point out where you want me to land inside the walls."

"I'll go, too," said Giles, "along with six of my lads, who'll each lead five to eight other bows against some particular part of the castle, once we're inside. We all need to look Malvern over and make our plans."

"And I," said Dafydd, "will have a glance at those walls where the lookouts may be standing."

"We might as well make it a bloody picnic," grunted Brian. "Anybody else want to come along, eh? How about you, Sir wolf?"

"What for?" Aragh replied. "I'll go in with you and Gorbash; and stay with you, killing all I find, until it's over and I go out again. That takes no study or planning."

The meal was served, as Brian requested; and a little more than an hour later all those who had spoken about going stood in the cover of a thick clump of beech trees, looking out at the broad stretch of cleared ground around Malvern Castle. Brian, armored and with spear upright in hand, rode his white warhorse forward at a walk to within perhaps sixty or eighty yards of the castle gate. There he stopped, and shouted to the heads whom those in the woods could see showing above the merlons and crenels of the battlements.

"He makes a brave show," said one of the outlaws.

"It's a custom of knights to do so, Jack," replied Giles, dryly.

"You were not wrong indeed, Master Giles," said Dafydd. The Welsh bowman was shading his eyes with one hand, peering at the heads on the walls. "It is, in fact, close to half of one of your English miles. But at dawn the wind should fall, and with no strong cross-breeze I see no trouble with up to six of them. I will mark the nearest crenel to each steel cap I see, then first shoot one watchman and wait for the others to look out, which they will surely all do when they see their comrade struck dead, and no one in view in the open ground. I will have five other arrows stuck in the ground before me, and I will put those in the air so close together that the five looking out will die almost at once— Hold, the knight speaks!"

In fact, Brian had begun to issue his challenge. A headgear brighter than the others had appeared on the battlements and the individual wearing it had called out something. Brian was responding. The fact that he was facing away from those in the forest edge caused a good share of what he said to be lost, even to Jim's sharp dragon-ears. Those words that Jim heard, however, were nearly all obscenities. He had not realized Brian had such a command of colorful language.

"Now, Sir Hugh answers," said Giles, for Brian had fallen silent and the voice that had shouted earlier was making itself heard again—though none of its words were understandable to those at the forest's edge. "It'll be Sir Hugh, beyond a doubt, because of the high crest and visor of the helm that takes the light so. That's a headpiece for horseback."

"Master Giles," asked Dafydd, looking sideways at the outlaw, "is it that you ever wore such a helm and armor yourself, now?"

Giles glanced back for a second.

"If you ever do become one of the family," he said, "you can ask me that again. Otherwise, I don't hear such questions."

"Now come the bolts," commented the outlaw whom Giles had addressed as Jack. "Best he turn and ride now. There—he does so!"

Brian had turned his charger and was galloping away from the castle.

"Can the crossbows get through his armor with their bolts at that distance?" asked Jim, fascinated.

"No," said Giles. "But they can cripple his horse— and that's a beast worth twenty farms, if it's worth one. Ah, they've missed . . ."

A swarm of what looked like little black matchsticks against the blue of the sky was descending around Brian and his galloping steed. Jim was puzzled about how Giles could be sure the quarrels from the crossbows had all missed, when most of them seemed still to be in the air. A matter of the trained eye, he supposed. In fact, by the time he finished his thought the missiles had fallen either behind or to one side or the other of the running horse.

"And that's that!" said Jack, spitting on the ground. "Sir knight'll be in the woods with us here before they can rewind those engines for a second shot. Give me two of our better men and the horse would have been down within ten strides—and the knight, too, with any luck."

Dafydd, leaning on his great bow, looked aside and down at Jack. For a second it looked as if he would say something, but then he turned his attention back to the approaching Sir Brian.

"Good, Master Welshman," said Giles, softly. He had been watching the tall young man. "A slow tongue indicates a wise head."

Dafydd said nothing.

In the next moment Brian came riding into the shadows of the forest and pulled his snorting charger to a stop. He wheeled the animal around, pushing up his visor.

"Half thought they might make a sally after me," he said. "But I see not."

He swung down from the saddle with surprising lightness, considering the weight of metal he was carrying.

"You tempted those crossbows closer than I should have," said Giles.

"Blanchard of Tours, here," Giles answered, slapping the white horse affectionately on one sweaty shoulder, "is faster than most would guess."

He looked around at them.

"What do you think of what you saw?" he asked.

"Judging by the heads on that front wall," said Giles, "your Sir Hugh has at least the fifty men with him. But he's got no archers, or he would have used them against you right now; and his men with the crossbows were nothing admirable. Draw me a plan of the castle, now, while we have it out there in front of us; so I can gain some idea of where my lads should go, once they're inside."

Brian drew the dagger from his belt, bent stiffly at the waist and began to scratch on the ground.

"As you see," he said, "Malvern's more wide than deep. The top of the keep you can barely see from here. It's in the left corner of the rear wall, its upper part rising above the towers in the other three corners —which are watchtowers and granaries, only. The Lord of Malvern's chambers are just under what was the original top floor of the keep, back when the keep was the same height as the watchtowers. My lady's grandfather added two more floors and a new battlement floor above the keep, so as to give Sir Orrin and his new bride separate bed space, with a solar above them for good measure, and the new battlement floor above the solar, with supplies of heavy stones there to cast down and kettles for the heating of oil to pour on any who might try to scale the keep's outer walls."

His dagger scratched in the dirt.

"Below and before the keep, in Sir Orrin's time," he explained, "was added a great hall, mainly of wood —the original walls and towers of the castle are stone, as you see. This filled up much of the old courtyard. It is joined to the keep as high as the first floor and has served both as dining hall and as barracks for the large number of men Sir Orrin would gather about him from time to time when he went off to war. Stables of wood and outbuildings were also added inside the outer walls, so that there's much that can burn—but look that Sir Hugh's men don't try to set fires to cover their escape, once we're inside and they find themselves losing the fight. Of your men, Master outlaw, there should be a party to secure every tower, another party to hold the courtyard, and yet another strong party to invade the keep by way of the great hall. I, and possibly Sir James, will already be in the upper levels of the keep when you and your men come through the gate—if so we be still alive. Now, give me your questions . . ."

Giles, Dafydd, and even some of the other outlaws Giles had brought along proceeded to do so. Their queries had mainly to do with distances and angles within the castle.

Jim found his attention wandering. What he himself wanted, he thought, was to get a direct look at the inside of those walls—and there was no reason he should not be able to do so. Flying high enough, and in a direct line, on a pass that took him by but not directly over the castle, he should be able to use his telescopic vision to get a pretty fair view of everything inside. At a sufficient distance, he might not even be noticed by Sir Hugh's men; or, if he was, they might merely take him for a large bird.

Even if they identified him as a dragon, a dragon who was simply passing by and apparently paying no attention to them should hardly be cause for alarm or speculation. At the same time, it probably would not hurt to make his overflight just at twilight, when at the end of the day and their evening meal, the watchers on the castle walls would be least likely to be alarmed by something passing high overhead.

Accordingly, he waited until the questions of the others had been answered to Brian's best ability and they had all returned to the inn. Once there, however, he took Brian aside and explained what he planned to do.

"What I mainly want to be sure of," Jim said, "is where I ought to land, when I come in."

"My lady's main chamber has a balcony—but a small one," Brian pointed out. "The solar above has no balcony, but very large windows through which you might fly directly."

Jim felt doubt stir in him.

"I don't know that," he said. "I haven't had all that experience in flying."

"Then," said Brian, "there's only the battlement floor—the open top level of the keep. In fact, it might be the best place for you to land, since there'll be at least one guard on duty there, and possibly someone else belonging to Sir Hugh in the solar. So that if you can slay those and fight your way down to Geronde's floor, you'll have made all safe to the top of the keep; and in case of anything going amiss, you can carry her off from there by air, to safety."

Secretly Jim had a few doubts about his ability to carry the weight of an adult human, and still fly. True, his wings were capable of exerting tremendous lift for a short time. But he was fairly sure that he would not be able to soar with the added burden of a grown woman; and if he could not soar, how far could he fly by wing power alone? For safety, it should be at least to the edge of the surrounding wood, which Giles had pointed out was half a mile away. But there was no point in loading these doubts on Brian. The knight had enough uncertainties already to trouble him, although Jim had to admit that Brian showed little sign of being overwhelmed by them.

"I'll let you know what I see," Jim said.

But he did not. Half an hour later, he cruised past the castle at about twelve hundred feet altitude and his telescopic vision failed to catch one of the guards so much as looking up, let alone watching in his direction. Nor did he discover anything about the castle that was different from what Brian had said. He checked out the battlemented roof of the keep and saw only one man on guard there, as Brian had guessed. Things were working out almost too predictably to be interesting.

He circled back at a distance and landed at the inn just as darkness was closing in. To his surprise, most of the outlaws—except Giles and a few of his subsidiary leaders—were already asleep, the ale apparently having assisted them to slumber. Brian, with no more than a normal amount of wine in him, was also slumbering. So was Danielle. Aragh had gone off into the night woods and would probably not return until morning. Even Dick Innkeeper, with most of his family and employees, was asleep—except for one older woman who was supplying wine to Giles and ale to his outlaw lieutenants.

Disgruntled, Jim settled down in the main room of the inn, tucked his head under his wing, and prepared himself to spend a sleepless night . . .

It seemed he had only blinked and then again lifted his head from under his wing, however, to find activity all around him.

Dick, his family and the servants were bustling about. Danielle was bandaging Aragh's neck—the wolf had somehow managed to get himself hurt or wounded during the night. Giles was seated at a table, drawing plans of the castle on thin leather sheets, in quintuplicate for his lieutenants; and Dafydd, working in a concentration that hinted he would not welcome interruption, had set up a small pair of pan balances and was weighing half a dozen of his arrows, one at a time, then slightly but meticulously trimming their shafts and feathers. Brian, seated at a table a few feet away, was eating an enormous breakfast of bacon, bread and cold beef, with several more bottles of wine.

Outside, it was still dark. Far from being daybreak, it was not even first light. Jim guessed the hour to be about 4 a.m.

He looked enviously at Brian. Anybody who could have that kind of appetite before the sun was up, on a day when he might well expect to be killed—

"Ah, there, Sir James," said Brian, waving his jack. "Have some wine?"

Jim decided he deserved a drink, in spite of his debt to Dick Innkeeper.

"Yes," he said.

Brian uncorked a fresh bottle and passed it over. Jim took it in one claw grasp and put it to his jaws, swallowing its contents in a gulp.

"Thanks," he said.

"Dick!" roared Brian. "Wine for Sir James!"

Dick Innkeeper came up, wringing his hands.

"Sir knight, please," he said, "not another quarter tun of Bordeaux—"

"Nonsense!" said Brian. "Of course not! Just a few dozen bottles, or their equivalent. Just enough to wet the good knight's throat."

"Oh, in that case . . . of course, of course . . ."

Dick hurried out of the room. Jim heard him shouting for one of the menservants.

What appeared a few minutes later was not a few dozen bottles of the innkeeper's best, but a small cask holding no more than ten gallons or so of good, if second-rate, wine. But the cask was full and Jim, with a momentary wistful thought for the vintages he had sampled in the cellar, settled down to its contents philosophically. After all, not even a dragon could have the best of everything all the time.

He sat drinking with Brian and gradually absorbing the bustle going on around him. Everybody was very busy and very businesslike. He heard a great deal of sharpening of weapons, making of last-minute repairs in equipment, checking of maps, and directions and orders. Correspondingly, he noted almost a complete lack of the cheerful jokes and insults that had been a noticeable part of the give-and-take between the outlaws, in particular, the day before. Now, everybody was serious. Torches smoked and glared everywhere. People went back and forth at high speed, each one engaged in some task that did not brook interruption. Giles was neck-deep in lieutenants, and unapproachable. Aragh, bandaged, soon went out; and Danielle was now nowhere to be seen. Dick and his staff were like the captain and crew of a ship fighting a hurricane. Finally, even Brian gave up the wine bottles and suggested in a friendly voice that Jim get the hell out, take a walk or something, because it was time he was seeing to Blanchard and his weapons . . .

Jim took the advice and left the inn for the deep, chilly, pre-dawn darkness outside. He was feeling a distinct loneliness and awkwardness, like a stranger at a large family gathering; and this feeling was reinforced by a sort of gentle melancholy induced by the wine he had just drunk. He was not really lonely for his own world—strangely enough, with all its hard, medieval realities, he was discovering he liked it here— but for somebody to whom he could anchor. Preferably Angie; but, failing that, anyone who could give him a feeling of belonging, instead of one of being a sort of wandering soul adrift between worlds.

He looked around again for Aragh and remembered he had seen the wolf leave the inn immediately after Danielle had bandaged him. But neither his dragon-nose or ears gave him any evidence that the wolf was anywhere in the vicinity; and Jim had seen enough of Aragh to know that unless the other was plainly in evidence, his chances of finding him were close to non-existent.

Jim gave up and sat down by himself in the darkness. Behind him were the noise, the odors, and the light of the inn. Before him were the solid blackness of the trees and overhead a thickly overcast sky, through which the faint gleam of an obscured moon came milkily now and then, low in the western quarter of the heavens. The moon would be down, soon, and there would be no light at all.

He might well be dead at the end of this day that would soon be dawning. The thought brought with it no particular fear but an increase in the feeling of melancholy. If he could be cut, as he had been in the brawl at the village, he could be seriously wounded or killed. In which case he would die here, at some impossible remove from everything he had ever identified with. Nobody would even know of his death. Even Angie, assuming she survived the Loathly Tower and the Dark Powers which Carolinus had talked about, would probably never know what had happened to him. He might not even be missed . . .

He was sinking steadily deeper into a sort of luxurious self-pity, when he realized that he was no longer sitting on the ground. He was, instead, lying down on it, about to turn over on his back, spread his wings and roll back and forth on the rough, sandy soil. Echoing in his mind, just in time to stop him, came the remembered words of Danielle: "Don't roll in the dirt, Sir James!"

He had wondered at the time why she should think he would ever want to roll in the dirt. Now he understood. Thinking about his cuts had reminded his subconscious of them. The day after he had gotten them, they had smarted like small shaving cuts; but he had come to ignore them and they had passed out of mind. Now, however, he realized that they were healing; and, in the process of doing so, they had developed a new sensation: they itched.

A good scrub against the hard earth would be a satisfying way of scratching those itches. Of course, it would also not only reopen the cuts, but get dirt and infectious materials ground into them.

162

He sat up again. Of course, Danielle was right. The worst of it was, though, that now that he had recognized the itch feelings, they redoubled, as if fiendishly and consciously determined to drive him crazy. He forced his body onto all four of its legs. If Brian could remain motionless with a hornet buzzing around the inside of his helmet, he ought to be able to ignore a little itching.

On his feet again, he could now smell the coming day—not an odor he could identify precisely, but a generally damp, fresh variation in the night breeze that was blowing in his direction. His ears caught the faint sound of paws on ground, and suddenly Aragh was before him.

"They all awake in there?" growled the wolf, softly. "Time they were moving!"

"I'll tell them."

Jim turned toward the inn door; but just at that moment it opened, and Giles stuck his head out.

"Sir James?" he asked, quietly. "Have you seen the wolf?"

"He has," snapped Aragh. "I'm here. What are you whispering for, Sir outlaw?"

Giles pulled his head back in and shut the door without answering. He had not, in fact, been whispering. His voice had only been lowered—as had Aragh's a second before. Almost immediately, the door opened again and Giles with his lieutenants came out, followed by Danielle.

"Dick Innkeeper's gone to put his armor on, and harness the horses," she told her father. "His men have the cart already loaded. Sir Brian's still with him, over at the stables."

"All right. Jack, will you tell the knight that we're ready to move?" Giles asked. "The rest of you go assemble your lads."

Jack went down along the building toward the stables; the other lieutenants moved out into the darkness, to where the rank and file of the outlaws had set up camp.

Fifteen minutes later, they were on the march. Brian on Blanchard, Giles on one of the inn horses that gleamed a strange, pale grayish-white in the murkiness, and Jim on foot, led the march. Behind them came Dafydd and Danielle, followed by the wagon driven by Dick, then the general body of the outlaws. Aragh had disappeared into the darkness of the forest at their first movement, growling that he would meet them at the edge of the forest facing the castle.

The promise of daylight began to deliver itself as they moved. It was a good hour yet till sunrise when they left the inn; but as they wound their way among the trees, the taller trunks began to emerge from the darkness as the sky overhead lightened. As these two things happened, the light wind dropped, just as Dafydd had predicted, and the mist filling the lower levels of the forest gradually became visible; it was a landscape of white, black, and gray they moved through—a land fit for spirits and night demons. In the semi-gloom of the emerging day, the earth underfoot was a dark platform and the mist a ghostly blanket reaching twice a man's height up into the trees, so that to the right, left, and all about, things were hidden. Even the gradually brightening sky was swag-bellied with thick, cold clouds.

They moved with little talk, the mist, clouds and darkness acting like a smothering blanket upon any enthusiasm. The wagon, weapons and armor jingled. The hooves of the horses thudded on the earth. Their breath—and Jim's—smoked as white as the mist in the damp, cold air. Gradually the light became true daylight and the mist began to thin; and almost before Jim was ready for it, they reached the edge of the wood looking out on the plain where Malvern Castle stood. The last mist still trailed in streamers across the open ground, and the tops of the stone walls and towers rose from it like the upper parts of some castle half drowned by the sea. Suddenly, even as they halted and looked, the first rays of the rising sun slid through the treetops to the east and struck at a long slant into the mist, thinning it further.

Slowly, the plain began to become fully visible, everything on it sharply seen, down to the very stones at the base of the battlements.

Jim glanced up once more at the sky. The heavy cloud cover was beginning to be torn open in places by the upper winds, although the air was still calm at ground level. Enough of the clouds remained, and hung low, however, so that for the first time it occurred to him that he would not be able to fly high in approaching the castle. If he was to come in by air to the top of the keep during the next half-hour or so, he would have to fly at little more than a few hundred feet; and there would be no disguising to those on watch about the castle walls and towers that a dragon was coming—nor the destination to which that dragon was heading.

Chapter 16

"Right!" said Brian, loudly and cheerfully. "Everybody present? How about Sir wolf?"

"Worry about yourself, Sir knight," answered the voice of Aragh. "I've been here long enough to kill twenty sheep."

"All right," said Brian. "Make ready, then. Master Giles, you know your men and your bow work. I know my part. Do you take charge of your archers, including the Welshman. Sir James, Dick, wolf—to me here."

The expedition split into two groups.

Dafydd, a few yards off by himself, was carefully

unwrapping one by one the cloths in which he had individually cased the arrows on which Jim had seen him working at the inn. He handled the shafts delicately, planting six of them before him point-down in the earth and sliding the other two into his quiver. Dick descended from the horse he had ridden here; and now that Jim saw it clearly in the daylight, he noticed that the light-brown animal had been liberally powdered with flour or some other white substance to lighten it to something like Blanchard's color. Brian swung down from Blanchard now and began transferring to the smaller, whitened horse the breastplate and body armor his charger customarily wore.

"Like rider, like steed," he said. "You and your mare here will be a pair for unfit armor, Dick. The chaufrain's too wide for her head, the crinet too long for her neck. But she can carry them a short while without too much trouble. The petrel's also too wide for her chest, but that can hang loose. On the other hand, I can buckle the flanchards tight around forearms and shoulder and they'll carry almost as well as they do on Blanchard."

"It's still not going to hang well," said Danielle. "And that horse's coloring is poor. I don't see why you don't just let the innkeeper ride *your* horse."

Brian frowned.

"Wish me no bad luck, mistress," said Dick, cheerfully, out of the depths of his helmet. "I've stabled such horses before. I can ride most beasts; but I'd not throw leg over one like Blanchard for a hundred pounds of silver. Not only would he not endure for a moment anyone but his master on his back, but having thrown me, he'd hardly be content to stand. He'd turn on me with hooves and teeth, as he's been trained, until either he had me killed, or I managed to escape."

"Quite right," said Giles, turning from his own men. "The knight knows what he's about, Danielle. Try not to command everyone, for once. Horses such as Blanchard wouldn't be worth the duke's ransom they are, if they were the sort that could be found on any farm. I'd wager Sir Brian paid a heavy penny for this one."

"My full inheritance," grunted Brian, hard at work fastening the second horse's straps. "The armor's my father's; but all else that came to me went to buy Blanchard. Never made a sounder move. He'll face lance, battle-axe, mace or sword, and defend me if I'm down against any man or beast that lives. I can ride him with knees alone and both hands busy with shield and weapon. And damned few other warhorses can match him for weight or strength."

He glanced at the innkeeper.

"No offense to you, friend Dick," he said. "But even if Blanchard'd carry you, I'd not let him. He's my horse alone."

"No fear, Sir Brian. I'm happier on Bess here, in any case." Dick hesitated. "But will you not at least wear a chain shirt under your cloth one?"

"Chain shirt alone won't do, anyway, if I run into Sir Hugh in full armor," said Brian. "He's a whoreson, but he knows how to fight. And if one of his men should think to search me early and find the mail, the alarm'll be sounded ahead of time. No, best to take the chance and dress later."

"You don't make the most likely innkeeper, either," Danielle remarked.

That much, Jim thought, was true. Sir James was clad in tight leather breeches with belt and sheath knife that had originally belonged to Dick's son, a loose gray shirt and a clumsy, thick, dark cloak. As clothes, nothing was wrong with them. They would have looked all right on someone like Dick, himself—assuming that the breeches could have been gotten to fasten around the innkeeper's relatively thick waist. But the trouble with them on Brian was the way he wore them. Jim's earliest impression of the knight had been of piercing blue eyes, the erect carriage that comes from living in the saddle and bearing armor, and an aggressively jutting chin. All these were still very visible, in spite of the humbleness of the garments that now clothed him.

"I've the beard, here," said Dick, producing it from among the load in the wagon. "It's not an exact match for your hair, Sir Brian; but then it's not unknown for a man with brown hair your color to have a beard touching on the red. These threads go over your head under your own hair to fasten in on . . . and if you then comb your own hair forward to mingle with it in front, as the player showed me . . . Let me assist you, Sir Brian . . ."

Together, they got the beard on. It did, indeed, go a long way to disguise the knight, giving him an unkempt, raffish look above which the blue eyes looked merely villainous.

"You might try slouching a bit," said Danielle.

"Like this?" asked Brian.

He tried, without any great success.

"I'm not a damned jack-o-motley, you know!" he fumed at them all, finally. "Leave be! I'll either coney-catch Sir Hugh and his men, or not, as God wills!"

He got up on the seat of the wagon, and picked up the reins of the two horses harnessed to it.

"Ready?" he demanded.

"Ready, Sir Brian," said Dick, who was already mounted on the whitened and armored Bess.

"Give me a good lead, now, so that they don't see you having to hold Bess back from catching me."

"Yes, Sir Brian."

"And you, Giles, don't forget to leave a party on the gate. If Sir Hugh's first warning is to look out his chamber window and see fighting within the walls, he'll stop to arm and armor himself before all else. Once he shows up, full-accoutered, make sure those in the gate party stand back and try only to keep him from a horse, until I myself——"

"Or I," interrupted Aragh.

Brian glanced at him, impatiently.

"Sir wolf," he said, "what might you do with a man in full armor?"

Aragh snarled softly, leaping up to settle himself in the wagon.

"Sir knight," he said, "someday you may see."

"At any rate," Brian went on, turning back to Giles, "hold the gate and keep Sir Hugh from horse!"

"Fear not, Sir Brian," said Giles. "I've some little knowledge of such things."

"Doubtless. But saying it makes all certain." Brian flipped the reins he held, starting his wagon horses forward. "Now—for God and my lady!"

He drove out of the woods.

Out on the small plain surrounding the castle, the last of the mist had now disappeared and the gray stone walls were warmed by the clear yellow light of early day. Brian whipped the wagon horses into a trot, and then into a clumsy gallop along the tracks leading toward the castle gate.

"Not yet, Master Innkeeper! Not yet . . . *Now!*" snapped Giles; and Dick kicked Bess into movement, clanking out from the screen of trees at what was already a gallop.

Giles glanced at Jim.

"Yes," said Jim, "I'd better get started."

He badly wanted to stay and see whether the gate would be opened for Brian and Aragh, and whether Dick would be able to turn and get back safely. But he must take off in the opposite direction to approach the castle from an angle and altitude where he would not immediately be spotted.

He turned, accordingly, and ran back some distance in the wood before leaping into the air and mounting to just above treetop level. Looking back over his shoulder, he saw he was now far enough from the castle so that the trees hid him from the viewers on the battlements, and commenced to fly in a wide circle toward the back of Malvern.

Shortly, he caught his first thermal. Circling up on this, he found himself just under the cloudbank, which was unbroken here but showed openings toward the north and west. On impulse, he decided to fly up through the clouds and see if it was possible to get above them.

It turned out to be so; although he had to climb nearly twelve hundred feet to achieve it. Once above the clouds, he headed directly toward the castle, looking for a gap in the white masses below him through which he could orient himself. Locating one, he soared toward it and looked through at an angle that gave him a view of both the plain and Malvern. No wagon or armored figure on horseback was in sight, but there was a patch of sunlight on the ground to the west of the castle, indicating another rift in the clouds somewhere above it.

He lifted his head, searched for this other rift from above and found it, not far off. He soared to it, saw the castle at a sharper angle below and identified the roof of the keep. He was about three-quarters of a mile from it and about a thousand feet above. He went into a dive, not through the rift, but through the clouds just beyond it, directly above the castle.

For a long moment he was wrapped about and blinded by cloud mist. Then suddenly he was back in open air again and the castle was right under him. Half folding his wings, he dropped like a stone from a catapult, arcing to its target. At the last moment he pulled up and, with a thunderclap of cupped air, slammed down on the top of the keep.

Only one guard met him. The man gaped, turned and disappeared down the stone stairway leading to the floor of the solar, below. Jim plunged after him, gained the solar and ducked in time to avoid a spear flung through the air. Instinctively, he struck out with a wing, and that powerful member literally picked up the man-at-arms and slammed him against a wall, to drop and lie still.

The dragon-blood of Jim—or Gorbash; under these conditions it was impossible to identify whose blood it was—was up and boiling!

He heard the sound of steel clashing on steel below

him and plunged down the next flight of stairs to catch a momentary glimpse of a tall, slim girl in white holding a short pike and facing out an open doorway. He brushed past her as she cried something he could not understand and tried to stick him with the pike. But by that time, he was through the door and into a short corridor where Brian, wearing only a helmet and with the rest of his armor in a pile at his feet, was holding off three men-at-arms with his sword.

Jim slammed into the three and they went down.

"Thanks!" gasped Brian. "Hold the lower stairs, will you, Sir James? And aid the wolf, if need be. He's either opened the gate by this time, or they have him dead. Bring word as to which—if you can."

Snorting, long red tongue flickering out between parted jaws, and wings half raised, Jim hurled himself down the last flights of steps. At the bottom he discovered a large, dim hall to his right, somewhat divided by curtains, beyond which came the sounds of fighting and the shouts of men. To his left was a doorway to open sunlight. He went through.

To his right now, around a curving wall of weathered logs, he saw the space of an interior courtyard and the castle gates, one of which was swung partway inward and open. Two fights were going on in the courtyard. One was over by some open sheds containing horses, where five of Giles' men were engaged with swords against about the same number of Sir Hugh's men-at-arms. Just inside the gate, a shouting semi-circle of nearly a dozen more men-at-arms had Aragh against the battlement, none of them apparently too eager to be the first to close with him, but all trying by sword feints and gestures to hold his attention long enough for someone else to get in a blow.

"ARAGH!" thundered Jim, using his full dragon-voice.

He plunged at the semi-circle, which disintegrated as he hit it. Immediately, he was fighting four men,

Aragh was killing three others, and the rest were flee-ing.

"Where's Giles?" Jim shouted at the wolf as he finished off three of his own four opponents and saw the other turn and run.

"Inside the hall," Aragh panted, "when last I saw him."

"Sir Hugh?"

"No sign of him."

"He's not in the keep!" Jim said. "I just came from there. Brian's getting into his armor. I'll check the rest of the castle."

He leaped into the air and with one pump of his wings put himself atop the wall. To right and left he saw the bodies of several men-at-arms down and motionless, a single arrow through the chest of each. The battlements were abandoned except by the dead.

Jim wondered where Dafydd was. Still back in the forest? Or had he come in and joined Giles' men, who were fighting in the hall or otherwise?

At that moment, an entrance on the far side of the keep suddenly disgorged men-at-arms carrying the same sort of short pikes that the girl had bran-dished. They bore down on the fairly even battle that was going on near the stables between some of their comrades and the outlaws.

The dragon-fury was now completely in possession of Jim. He leaped from the wall at this new body of the enemy. None of them had been looking up and he cannoned into them without warning. Suddenly he was in the midst of battle, hissing, roaring, fighting with teeth, claws and wings all at once, balanced on his hind legs like some gigantic bird of prey.

They melted about him. It was like battling straw men armed with candy-cane weapons. The pikes broke at his touch; he flung the men who carried them about like dolls. A savage feeling of power flamed up in him. Out of the corner of one eye he saw Aragh again surrounded by a fresh group of Sir Hugh's re-tainers and thought of going to the wolf's aid as soon as he had finished matters where he was. What was it Aragh had said about seeing that Gorbash got back safely? But Jim needed nobody's help. Who could stand against a dragon? No one. He was invincible, and when this was over he would remind them all of that—wolf, outlaws, knight . . . Then, abruptly, the men-at-arms who had been attacking him began to shout and yell triumphantly.

"Gorbash!" howled Aragh. *"Gorbash!"*

Was the wolf calling for help? Jim looked and saw Aragh hard-pressed, but in no way badly wounded or in trouble.

"The hall, Gorbash!" cried Aragh.

Jim looked, between the pikeheads that came flashing at him suddenly with renewed vigor. The main doors of the hall were opening; and slowly, as he watched, a ponderous figure all in mirror-bright armor, already mounted with long lance in one gauntleted hand, rode out through the opening.

The armored figure did not appear to be in a hurry. It rode out into the center of the courtyard, turned its head in the direction of the wolf, looked toward Jim, then put its horse into a leisurely trot and rode —not at either one, but out of the castle gate.

Howls of reproach and anger replaced the shouts of triumph of the men-at-arms. They retreated from Jim and Aragh. Some dropped weapons and tried to run. Aragh was immediately upon those who ran from him, bringing them down from behind; but Jim ignored the men-at-arms falling away from him.

"You clean up here, Aragh!" he roared at the wolf. The feeling of unmatchable power was blazing in him now, and he could not wait to close with the mounted figure he had just seen. "I'll go get him!"

"No! Stay! Hold, Sir James—!"

It was another fully armored figure, shouting, bursting out of the same exit from the keep that Jim had used. Brian, fully dressed and weaponed at last, ran heavily toward the stables, where horses still neighed

173

and pulled at their tethers, upset by the excitement around them.

"Too late!" Jim thundered, joyously. "I spoke for him first!"

He took to his wings, lifting up and over the wall. Outside, the armored figure on the horse was already three-quarters of the way to the forest edge.

"Surrender, Sir Hugh!" shouted Jim at full volume. "I'll get you, anyway!"

He had expected the escaping knight, particularly after showing he was the kind to leave his men to die while he saved himself, to do nothing but put his heavy roan into a panic-stricken gallop at the sound of a dragon-voice and the sight of dragon-wings swooping after him. To Jim's surprise, however, Sir Hugh pulled his steed to a stop, turned and lowered his lance to attack position. Then he broke the horse into a run, charging directly for Jim.

Jim almost laughed. The man had lost his head. Either that, or else he had faced the fact that defeat and death were inescapable and had decided to go down fighting. At the same time, it was odd; and Jim had a sudden, reasonless memory flash of Smrgol, demanding of the other dragons in the cave: "How many of you here would like to face just a single george in his shell, with his horn aimed at you?"

Then he and Sir Hugh came together with a crash, an unbelievable impact that in one blinding, pain-shot moment blotted out sight, thought, memory and all else . . .

Chapter 17

"My boy . . ." said Smrgol's voice, brokenly. "My boy . . ."

It had seemed a very long time now that Jim had been conscious of shapes moving around him, of alternate periods of light and darkness, of voices that came and went . . . voices familiar and voices strange. But he had paid little attention to them, lost as he was on a sea of pain which sucked him down, now and again, into dark waters of unconsciousness, then let him return partway to reality. The pain had become the whole world to him lately. It filled his mind completely. It dissolved his body in sensation. No one part of him suffered; it was his total being. And this situation had continued and continued . . .

But now, with his identification of Smrgol's voice, the waters of the pain-ocean receded a little. The reduction in discomfort made him feel almost comfortable—almost luxurious. What pain remained was like an old disability, grown into a companion over the years, something that would be missed if it were suddenly to disappear altogether. He tried to focus his eyes on the large, shadowy shape near him.

"Smrgol . . . ?" he asked.

The voice that came from his throat was a ghost-voice, a wraith of that dragon-resonance with which he had become familiar since he had first awakened on this different world in Gorbash's body.

"He spoke to me!" It was Smrgol. "Praise to the Fires! He'll live! Wolf, call the others! Tell them he's going to live, after all. Tell them to come, quickly!"

175

"I'll go," snarled the voice of Aragh. "But I said he would. Didn't I say he would?"

"Yes, yes . . ." Smrgol's voice was throaty. "But I'm an old dragon; and I've seen so many go down before those horns of the georges . . . Gorbash, how do you feel? Can you talk . . . ?"

"A little . . ." Jim whispered. "What happened?"

"You were an idiot, boy, that's what happened!" Smrgol was trying to sound stern and was not succeeding very well. "What gave you the wild idea you could take on a shelled george—one on a horse at that—single-handed?"

"I mean," husked Jim, "what happened to me?"

"You got a horn—a lance, they call it—through you, that's what happened. Anyone but a dragon would've been dead by the time he hit the ground. Anyone but one of our branch of the family would've died within the hour. As it is, it's been eight days now with you teetering on the edge; but now that you're back enough to answer me, it'll be all right. You'll live. A dragon that's not killed outright survives—that's the way we are, boy!"

"Survives . . ." echoed Jim. The word had a strange sound in his ears.

"Of course! As I say, that's the way we are. Three more days and you'll be on your feet. A couple of days after that and you'll be the same as ever!"

"No," said Jim, "not the same . . ."

"What're you talking about? Nonsense! I say you'll be as good as ever, and you will! Don't argue with me, now. I say you will!"

The old dragon went on talking, but Jim found his mind slipping back into dark waters once more. He would not argue with Smrgol. There was no point to it. But that did not mean he was allowing the old dragon to convince him. There was a change in him now; and he would never be the same again.

That recognition of a change stayed with him in the days that followed. As Smrgol predicted, he mended rapidly; and as he mended he began to respond to the visitors coming to see him. From them he slowly pieced together what had happened to him since that second in which he and Sir Hugh had crashed together outside the castle walls.

He understood now why the dragons, magnificent animals as they were, were still correct in fearing an armored knight, particularly one on horseback and armed with a lance. Over a ton of horse, man and metal—moving at speed of better than ten miles an hour with all that mass concentrated on the sharp point of a sixteen-foot shaft—gave awesome penetrating power. In Jim's case the lance had missed his heart and both lungs, or even Gorbash's constitution could not have saved him. The point of the weapon had entered high on his chest where the massive pectoral muscle of the left wing was not thick, and gone clear through him to emerge beside the left scapular with about eight inches of point and shaft. In addition, the back twelve feet of the lance had broken off, leaving a short stub of thicker shaft protruding from the entry point in his chest.

At first, the others had thought him dead. Certainly Hugh de Bois had thought so; for, without waiting to make sure, he had climbed back on his horse—which had gone down in the collision—and ridden off before he could be chased and caught by Brian on one of the castle horses.

The others had gathered around Jim on the plain, where he lay unmoving; and it had been Aragh who had first established that he still breathed, if only barely. They had not dared move him, as he was clearly on the very precipice edge of extinction. So they had built a makeshift hut of poles and branches over him where he lay, covered him with cloths and built a fire within the shelter to keep him warm while the wolf went for S. Carolinus.

Carolinus had come, accompanied by Smrgol, to whom he had somehow gotten word. At the magician's direction, the old dragon had used his strength to do what the others had seen no way of doing, even if they had been willing to risk it. Smrgol had carefully drawn out the broken shaft.

With the wound cleared, Jim had bled heavily for a while, but eventually the bleeding had stopped; and Carolinus had announced that since Jim had survived so far, nothing more was to be done for him. The magician had made ready to leave.

"But there must be something we can do!" Danielle insisted.

"Wait," snapped Carolinus, "and hope."

He left.

They built the hut into a more permanent structure. Smrgol and Aragh took turns sitting with him, occasionally with Danielle, Brian, or one of the other humans for company; and they waited. Finally the day had now come on which he answered Smrgol.

Now, all were coming around to talk to him and convey their satisfaction that he had survived. Each of them had an individual way of doing this: Smrgol lectured him. Aragh growled sourly at him. Danielle insisted that he had been stupid, but thought at the same time that it was rather princely of him to hurl himself to almost-certain death; she was briskly unsympathetic, but very gentle in changing his bandages, which she would not allow anyone else to touch. Giles was curious as to the style of fighting Sir James had known in his proper body, and came close to hinting that Jim must have had some secret ploy up his sleeve or he would not have risked making a frontal attack on Sir Hugh in the first place. Dafydd came and sat and worked at his fletcher's craft of arrow-making, and said nothing.

Geronde de Chaney (who had been the girl in white, with the pike, in the keep) came by and promised him revenge. She wore a bandage herself on her right cheek.

It appeared that Sir Hugh had originally ridden up with a half-dozen followers and obtained entrance to the castle by saying he had word of her father's death. Once inside, the men with him had overpowered the gate guards and let in the rest of his retainers. With the castle in his hands, he had admitted he knew nothing about her father; but since he intended to have Malvern, he told her he expected her to marry him immediately. When she refused, he had threatened to disfigure her in stages by slashing first her right cheek, then three days later her left, then three days after that by cutting off her nose, then by putting out her eyes one at a time until she gave in. She had defied him and now would carry the scar on one cheek for the rest of her life. She was a frail, rather ethereal-looking maiden with ash-blond hair and detailed plans for cooking Sir Hugh over a slow fire as soon as she could make him her prisoner.

Brian brought wine and sat and drank with Jim, telling his bad jokes and endless stories, some of which were apparently true—according to Aragh or Smrgol—but all of which were incredible.

Dick Innkeeper sent the last of his hams to tickle Jim's appetite.

Actually, Jim found that for the first time in his dragon-body appetite was missing. The wine was pleasant on his throat; but even that did not tempt him except in what, for a dragon, were very small quantities.

Nevertheless, he mended. He took to sitting outside in the sun, and the clear, bright light of early autumn warmed his body even if it did not touch the inner coldness that had come to swell in him. The truth was that Death, in the shape of Sir Hugh's lance, had come too close. The broken spear was out of his body now and most of the pain was gone, but there was still a low-level general interior ache that stayed with him and nourished a bleakness of spirit. The color had gone out of things, the uniqueness and value out of the people about him. Even the thought of Angie dwindled in importance. His mind held only one overriding thought: he would never attack an armored knight head-on again. He would, in fact, never attack anything again but in the easiest and surest way. Only survival was important; and it did not matter how survival was accomplished, just so that it was . . .

Perhaps, the thought came to him much later, the others might have noticed this change in him and would have worked to reverse it, if it had not happened that, just at that time, as soon as he was well enough to participate, he was drawn into their discussion about what should be done next.

". . . The decision," said Brian firmly at length, "must rest with you, Sir James. Geronde, he lent us his aid to get you free from Sir Hugh, and I'm in his debt for that. If he wishes to go first to the rescue of his lady—and Lord how can I object to that, seeing he's helped me to recover mine—I must go. You know that, milady."

"Of course I do," Geronde said, quickly.

They were all—except Smrgol, who had flown back on business of his own to the dragon cave—sitting at the high table of the castle hall after dinner and Jim was slaking an appetite for wine that had greatly recovered. Geronde was seated on the other side of Brian from Jim, and she leaned around the knight now to look directly into the dragon's eyes.

"I'm as much in debt to Sir James as you are, Brian," she said, "and bound like you to honor his decision. But, Sir James, I only want you to consider the advantages of moving against Hugh de Bois at just this time."

"Advantages for you, perhaps," Aragh growled at her. The wolf was always uncomfortable inside any building, and this made him even more bad-tempered than he was ordinarily. "I've no use for a castle. Nor should you, Gorbash!"

"But you wish an end to Sir Hugh as much as we," Geronde said to him. "You should want to go after him now, just as we do."

"I'll kill him when I find him; I won't hunt him. I hunt for food—not, like you humans, for anything cold or warm, wet or dry, that takes your fancy," snarled Aragh. "And Gorbash is like me, not like you."

"Gorbash may well be like you," Geronde retorted. "Sir James is not. And Sir James will be back in his own proper body one of these days. When that day comes, he may have need for a castle. Under law, I cannot acquire Sir Hugh's land and castle as long as there's doubt whether my father lives or not; and Malvern Castle and lands will go to Sir Brian as my husband, on our marriage, in any case. Meanwhile, once Sir Hugh is taken care of, we'll need a reliable neighbor; and the Bois de Malencontri is not an ill estate, even for a"—she glanced briefly down the length of the high table at Danielle—"person who may be of considerable degree."

"I say again, castles and lands are nothing to me," snarled Aragh. "What good are cold stone and dry earth? And I also say again they should be nothing to you, Gorbash. If Smrgol were here, he'd tell you that, too. In any case, I've been with you to guard your back and stand with you against the Dark Powers, not to help you gain human toys. You start lusting after things like that, Gorbash, and we go different ways!"

He rose to all four feet, turned and trotted from the hall, the castle people moving out of his way as he came close to them.

"Indeed," Dafydd agreed, when the wolf was gone, "and he could be right at that. Defending yourself is one thing, going to seek the killing is quite another, no matter how good the reason, look you."

"Don't listen to them, Sir James," said Danielle. "You don't need them, anyway. If you don't take that castle, somebody else will. Isn't that right, Father?"

"Since there's pay in it, count on me and my lads," Giles said to Lady Geronde. He turned to Danielle. "But it's business—business only—that takes us there. Beyond that, leave me out of this."

"I've promised you and your band half of the wealth Castle Malencontri contains," Geronde assured him. "You know it should be worth your while. Sir Hugh has been robbing his lesser neighbors for years."

"And I've agreed," said Giles. "It's not me you need consent from. It's Sir James."

Jim started to shrug before he remembered his dragon-body was not equipped to do so. Carolinus had told him that Angie would not be in discomfort while she was waiting for him to rescue her. A few more days, he thought now, out of his new inner bleakness—even an added week or two—should make little difference. Besides, just in case Carolinus couldn't get the two of them sent back to where they belonged, a castle and lands would not be a bad thing for them to own. The need for food and shelter—good food and comfortable shelter—was as much a reality here in this world as pain itself. And realities were not to be ignored.

"Why not?" he said. "All right, I'm in favor of moving on Hugh de Bois de Malencontri and his property now."

The moment he said it, a strange sort of ripple seemed to run through the air in the hall, something like the momentary shimmer of a heat wave, and the bleak feeling inside him expanded into a sensation of hollowness as if he and Gorbash's body together were only a shell enclosing nothing at all. Jim blinked, half inclined to think his eyes were playing tricks on him because of the wine or the smoky atmosphere of the candle-lit room. But the impression was gone in the same instant it had seemed to exist; so that he found himself unsure he had really felt anything in the first place.

He looked around at the others, but they seemed to have noticed nothing, except for Dafydd, who was looking at him penetratingly.

"Good," said Geronde. "It's settled, then."

"I do not think it is good," Dafydd put in. "In my family, from father to son and mother to daughter for many generations now, there have been eyes to see warnings. And a moment past the candle flames here all bent, though there was no wind in the hall. I do not think this going after Sir Hugh now is good at all."

"Aragh frightened you, that's all," said Danielle.

"I am not frightened. But, no more than the wolf, am I a knight to be holding or taking of castles."

"I'll make you a knight," Danielle told him. "If I make you a knight, will that do away with your doubts?"

"For shame, Danielle!" said Giles. His face had darkened. "Knighthood is no jest."

Dafydd got to his feet.

"You are making sport of me," he said. "But since you will do this thing, I'll do it also, because I love you. For now, I will go out into the clean air and the clean woods by myself."

He, too, left the hall.

"Here, here!" said Brian, cheerfully. "Let's have an end to doom-saying for a bit. Fill your cups! We've agreed now. To the soon taking of Sir Hugh and his castle!"

"And Sir Hugh himself, one day closer to the fire," added Geronde.

They drank.

Early the next day they set off, without Aragh but with Giles' outlaws reinforced by some forty men drawn from Malvern Castle and the other de Chaney estates. Geronde herself had been fiercely eager to come with them; but her sense of duty to the castle and lands of her father was capable of overriding even her thirst for vengeance. So, she had agreed to stay behind. They saw her standing on the castle wall, looking after them, until the trees of the forest blocked her from view.

The morning was overcast as it had been on that day when they had retaken Malvern Castle from Sir Hugh. This day, however, the clouds did not clear. Instead they thickened, and soon a light, steady drizzle began.

Their way led at first through alternate woods and open spaces, but as the morning wore on the tree cover became general, the ground low-lying and wet. They were moving into an area of small lakes and bogs, and the wagon track they were following soon became miry and slippery. Their party straggled, and separated into groups spread out over half a mile.

But more than their pattern of travel seemed affected by the grayness of the day: the damp dullness of the atmosphere seemed to produce a sullenness of temper. Those on foot, like the outlaws and the forty men from the Castle Malvern lands, trudged along head-down against the falling water, their bowstrings cased, their weapons hooded. The outlaws' previous custom of rough jokes and friendly insults had vanished. When they spoke it was sourly, expressing their dissatisfaction with the weather, the route, and the probable cost—in deaths and wounds—of reducing the castle they were going to assault. Old arguments were dredged up between individuals and tempers grew short.

Even the leaders of the expedition seemed affected by the general change in attitude. Giles was grim, Danielle sharp-tongued and Dafydd completely uncommunicative. It was as if the whole party was reacting to a feeling that something was wrong.

Jim took refuge, at last, at the head of the column with the single exception to this general malaise: Brian on Blanchard was his invariable self. There was something cheerfully spartan and unyielding about the knight. His personal world appeared to have had all its essential questions and uncertainties settled long ago. The sun might shine, snow might fall, wine might flow or blood be spilled—but all these were surface variations, to be ignored ordinarily as beneath notice. Brian gave the impression that he would joke with his torturers as they were stretching him on the rack.

Jim told him about the way the others were acting, particularly the leaders.

"Shouldn't worry about it," said Brian.

"But it's important to keep everybody working together, isn't it? For example, what if Giles suddenly decided to pull out with all his band? We'd be left with the forty men from Malvern, half of whom don't look as if they know anything about fighting."

"I don't think Giles would do that," said the knight. "He knows there's wealth to be got for him and his

184

lads in Sir Hugh's stronghold. Also, he's agreed to go —and was a gentleman once, pretty clearly, though he won't admit it now."

"Well, even if Giles personally can be counted on," Jim added, "there could be trouble with Danielle and Dafydd that might end up involving her father. Dafydd's been saying less with every mile, and Danielle won't let up on him. Actually, she shouldn't be along on this, anyway, except that nobody seems to have had the guts to tell her she couldn't come."

"Master Welshman wouldn't have come without her."

"True," Jim admitted. "But you have to concede she's no warrior—"

"Are you sure about that?" asked Brian. "Ever seen her shoot?"

"Just that time her arrows came at us. And in the looted village. All right, she can handle a bow—"

"Not just *a* bow," the knight said. "She draws a longbow with a hundred-pound pull, like half the archers in her father's band."

Jim blinked. Years ago in college, he had taken a passing interest in bow-hunting. Practicing at targets, he had begun with a forty-pound bow and graduated to a sixty-pound one. Sixty pounds had felt, to him, like the practical limit—and he did not consider himself weak.

"How do you know?" he asked.

"Saw her shooting after you were lanced, at the taking of Malvern Castle while some fighting was still going on."

"She was at the castle?" Jim asked, startled. "I thought she stayed in the woods. But how could you tell, just seeing her shoot?"

Brian looked sideways at him with curiosity as they moved forward together.

"It's a strange land you must come from overseas, James," he said. "By watching the arrow as it leaves her bow, of course."

"Watching her arrow?"

"See how much it lifts as it leaves the string," Brian explained. "When I saw her, she was still aiming under her mark at ten rods' distance. Pull no more than an eighty-pound bow myself. Of course, I'm no archer. But Mistress Danielle is no weakling."

Jim trudged on alongside Blanchard and the mounted knight for a long moment of silence, absorbing this.

"If she pulls a hundred-pound bow, what does Dafydd pull?"

"Lord, who knows? A hundred-and-fifty? Two-hundred? Even more than that? The Welshman doesn't fit any ordinary suit of clothes. You've seen he's his own bowyer and fletcher—and a rare craftsman at both. I wager there's not an archer in Giles' band—assuming he could draw it when he got it—who'd not give ten years' earnings for that bow of Master Dafydd's. With the longbow, the secret's all in the taper towards the ends of the bowstave, you know. Even allowing for the man's strength, it's not just a case of cutting himself a heavier, longer bow that lets him shoot the flights he does, and that accurately. There's a cunning and an art built into his weapon that goes beyond the skill of the ordinary bowyer. You heard Giles when Master Dafydd first undertook to slay the guards on the castle walls from the edge of the woods. And, of course, the same holds true for the arrows the Welshman makes. Any of these outlaw lads'd no doubt trade half the teeth in his head for a quiverful of those."

"I see," said Jim.

The information sank into the back of his mind and lay there leadenly. Once upon a time, he realized, before his encounter with Sir Hugh, he would have found this kind of information fascinating. Now, it only left him vaguely resentful—against Dafydd for possessing such knowledge and skill, and toward Brian for the condescension he thought he heard in the knight's voice when explaining it to him.

He said nothing more; and Brian, after making a

few further remarks aimed at continuing the conversation, gave up and turned Blanchard about to trot back down the track and check on the rest of the expedition. Left alone, Jim plodded on, scarcely noticing where he was going. He realized he was traveling by himself now, but that suited his present mood. He had no wish for company—particularly for the company of these medieval characters, both beast and human.

In fact, now that he glanced about, himself, he could see neither people nor horses, nor anything of the wagon track they had been following. Undoubtedly the track had taken one of its reasonless curves—like a footpath, it had evidently developed along the route of easiest travel. There was no construction to it as a road at all, with the result that it often went widely out of its way to avoid a patch of bushes which a man with an ax could have cleared in an hour or two of work. It had probably detoured; and he, tied up in his thoughts, had unconsciously taken the direct route, straight ahead—in which case, he would be running into it again shortly, when it curved back to its base line of direction.

Meanwhile, as Jim was telling himself, the isolation was not unwelcome. He had had it with strange worlds, talking creatures, blood, battle, superhumans and supernatural forces—all of these in the context of a primitive technology and elemental society.

When you got down to it, he thought, there was a limit to how much living you could do with animals. Smrgol and Aragh, as well as the other dragons, were animals in spite of the fact that they could talk. For that matter, the humans he had met were no better —human animals, operating by custom, instinct or emotion, but never by civilized thought. For all her beauty, Danielle was hardly more than a fur-clad female out of the Stone Age. Similarly, for all his craft and skill, Dafydd could have stepped right out of a Cro-Magnon hunting party. Giles was a clever old criminal, no more; and Brian was a pain-indifferent killing machine who thought with his muscles. As for Geronde—she was a pure savage in her happy anticipation of the torture she would inflict on her enemy once she had captured him.

What had made him think—back in the cleanliness and comfort of the twentieth-century world he belonged to—that he would ever find it attractive, let alone pleasant, to live with people like these? Their redeeming qualities were nil. Any obligation or affection he might think he was developing toward them was nothing but the product of a false romanticism.

He broke off at this point in his thoughts to realize that he had been traveling for some time and had not yet come upon the wagon track or seen any sign of the rest of the party. Possibly the wagon track had run out. Possibly they had turned off on some other route. Possibly, even, they had decided to halt for the day—because the rain was now coming down quite heavily. Well, in any case, they could take care of themselves; and he could rejoin them tomorrow. He felt no need of their company; and with his dragon's insensitiveness to temperature and weather, it made little difference to him that the day had grown wet and chilly.

In fact, now that he thought of it, it suited his own mood to have the day drawing to a prematurely gray close and the skies pouring down upon the dripping trees and sodden earth that surrounded him.

Nevertheless, he looked about, picked out a grove of trees and walked over to it. It was a simple matter to pull up some of the larger saplings by the roots and lean their tops together, teepee-fashion, to produce a makeshift shelter. The interlaced tops, still thick with leaves, did provide him some protection against the falling rain.

Jim curled up inside the shelter with a good deal of satisfaction. The day was gathering into gloom, now. He had no idea where the others were, he could not find them if he wanted to, and that was as it should be.

They could not find him either—and *that* was as it should be . . .

He was preparing to tuck his head under a wing, when a sound registered on him that he had been hearing faintly but which had been growing slowly in volume for some time. For a second his mind refused to identify it; and then recognition came, clear and unmistakable.

Sandmirks—approaching.

Chapter 18

Jim was out of the shelter before he realized he had moved—and was ready to run. What checked him was the same instinct he felt at the time he had encountered sandmirks before: the wordless understanding that to try to run from them was the beginning of the end. It was a knowledge that came from the deepest levels of Gorbash's brain.

He stood where he was, in the increasing darkness, his jaws parted, his tongue flickering in and out between them. His breath was snarled in his throat. If he had any idea in which direction Brian and the others could be found, there might be some sense in running. If he could reach them, there was perhaps safety in numbers. Just why there should be, he was not quite sure; but the impression persisted, instinctively. Furthermore, he knew that sandmirks vastly preferred to attack a helpless and outnumbered victim. Maybe a large group of humans or animals together could resist the fear the sandmirks tried to breed in the minds of those they wanted to destroy and devour. If the victims could resist, then they might be able to attack the sandmirks in turn. The sandmirks, as he had seen, were not likely to stand against those who had no fear of them—witness, the speed with which they had fled when Aragh had driven them off.

But which way should he go to find the expedition against Sir Hugh? As he had considered earlier, they might have diverged from the path or halted for the night, some time since. They might even have turned back. If he began to run and it turned out he was headed in the wrong direction, he would be running into the sandmirks' jaws.

One thing was certain: he had no Aragh to come to his rescue here. Even if the wolf had hung around Malvern long enough to see whether Jim would, indeed, go along on the expedition, he would have had his worst fears confirmed long since; and he would have taken off in a direction back to his own woods. He would be miles beyond hearing the voices that were closing in on Jim now.

Fear and rage, combined, flared like living flames inside Jim. The breath snarled once more in his throat. His head darted left and right, reflexively, like the head of a driven animal hearing the sounds of the beaters closing in on it from all sides. There had to be some way out. Some way . . .

But there was none.

The frantic, instinctive darting of his head slowed and then stopped. The rage in him died. Now he was only afraid, and the fear filled him completely. At last, he faced the fact that he was right to be afraid: there was something wrong with him if he was not. It was death he heard coming—his death.

He stood in the rainy darkness, hearing the chittering of the sandmirks growing closer. They were only minutes away from surrounding him now. He had no place to flee to; and it would be too late to flee once they had arrived. His mind reached the furthest possible limit of despair and went beyond, into a kind of limitless, colorless clarity.

He saw himself clearly now. He had wandered off,

rehearsing in his mind all the things he could find wrong with Brian and the others. But the arguments against them that he had summoned up were only a smoke screen for what was wrong with himself. It was not Brian, Smrgol, Aragh and the others who were so much less than he, but he who was so much less than they. If it had not been for the accident that had landed him in the powerful flesh he now wore, he would be nothing. In his own body he would not have been able to qualify as the least member of Giles' band. Could he pull a hundred-pound longbow, let alone hit anything with an arrow from it? Could he, clad in the best armor in the world and mounted on the best warhorse, delude himself that he could last as an opponent of Brian's or Sir Hugh's for two minutes?

He knew better now. It was very ego-pampering to cannon into men-at-arms whom he outweighed five to one and send them flying. It was very comfortable to tell people living in a rigidly stratified society that he had been a baron, and let them surmise that he had perhaps been a prince. But what had happened when a real lance actually went through him? All at once the fun had gone out of the game. He was ready to pick up his marbles and go home.

Now, alone, with the sandmirks closing in on him, and facing himself at last, he saw that this was no soft world he and Angie had landed in. It was a hard one; and all those he had met here—Smrgol, Brian, Aragh, Giles, Dafydd, Danielle, even Secoh and Dick Innkeeper—were battle-scarred survivors of it. They were survivors because they had the courage required to survive. That courage he had resented in them when he had flown onto the lance point of Hugh de Bois and discovered that he could be killed, just like anyone else. The discovery had woken him to a realization of how little of their sort of courage he had ever been called on—in his own world—to show.

Now it no longer mattered whether he could be courageous or not, because he was going to die, anyway. The sandmirks were just beyond the trees that ringed him; and the panic born of their chittering was beginning to eat at his brain. They would be certain of him this time. He had not even a campfire to keep them at a distance. Cleverly, once again, they had come on a rainy, cloud-thick night when a dragon could not take to the air for fear of flying blindly into a tree or cliff; and when he, like any ordinary earth-bound animal, could only attempt to escape on foot. The only difference now from the time before was that he had at last come to terms with himself—a single, small triumph, the one thing that made him different from a simple dragon-victim.

The breath checked in his lungs. For a moment even the sandmirk voices were forgotten. He had, at least, a final choice. He would die either way, but he could still choose how. What was it he had said to Carolinus, back when they first met? ". . . But I'm not a dragon"?

Nor was he. Gorbash might have no choice in this situation, but he was Jim Eckert, who had. He could go down, he could die, still trying to reach the Loathly Tower and rescue Angie—by himself, if necessary—not as a helpless meal for sandmirks.

It might be death to fly, but he preferred that death to staying here. He gaped his jaws and roared at the sandmirks. He crouched and sprang upward into the rain and the darkness; and the sound of the chittering faded quickly to silence and was lost, far below and behind.

Pumping his wings, he reached for altitude. It was a forlorn hope to think that the cloud cover would be low enough for him to mount above it. And, even if it was, and he did, above those clouds and rain on a night like this one where would he find thermals to soar on? A good wind could save him—but weather like this did not go with strong, steady winds above a layer of rainclouds. If he could not soar, sooner or later he would become wing-weary and start to lose altitude. After that the crash to earth would be inevitable.

But for now, his strength was still with him. He beat upward through the downpour. Darkness surrounded him—before, behind, above, below. He felt as if he were hanging still in a wet and lightless void, exerting all his strength but going nowhere. No pause came in the rain, no rift in the darkness overhead to show a patch of starlit sky.

Judging by the altitude he had gained previously in a first few minutes of upward flying, he thought he should easily be above five thousand feet by this time. He tried to remember what he knew about rain-clouds. Most precipitation, he vaguely remembered learning once, fell from nimbostratus, altostratus or cumulonimbus clouds. Cumulonimbus were low-lying, but the other two were in a middle range—up to twenty thousand feet or so. Clearly, he could not fly above twenty thousand feet. His lungs were the lungs of any animal adapted to a planetary surface. He would run out of oxygen at that altitude—even if the cold of the higher air did not freeze him.

A faint but steady wind pushed the rain along at his present altitude; and instinctively he had been heading into it to gain lift. He took a chance now and stiffened out his wings in soaring position while he caught his breath. He had no visible evidence that he was losing altitude, but he could feel the pressure of the air on the underside of his wings; and this sensation sent clear signals to his dragon-brain that he was now on a shallow glide back toward the ground. He dared not prolong the glide. He might be losing altitude faster than he thought.

He began to use his wings again, and his pressure points signaled that he was once more gaining altitude, though at a slow rate. His mind, working at a steady white heat from the moment he had decided to leave the sandmirks on the ground behind, now tossed something at him out of the very back of his reading experience: a passage from a very old book dealing with somebody lost underwater who no longer knew even which way was up to the surface. He had thought, when he had read that passage, that what was needed in such a situation was some sort of diver's personal sonar. That memory triggered off in his mind the recollection that not only was his dragon-voice of unusual proportions but his eyesight and hearing were unhumanly sensitive. Bats could fly blind at night, or even—as experimenters had discovered—when the animals had been physically blinded, because of their echo-sounding—their sonar. What if he could do something like that?

Jim opened his mouth, gathered the full force of his lungs, and sent a wordless cry booming out into the falling rain and darkness around him.

He listened . . .

He was not sure whether he had heard anything echoing back at him.

He boomed again. And listened . . . and listened . . . straining his ears.

This time, he thought he heard an echo of some sort.

Once more he boomed, and once more he listened. This time, clearly, an echo returned. Something was below him and off to his right.

Lowering his head toward the ground below, he boomed again.

His dragon-hearing was evidently quick to learn. This time he was able to make out, not only a general echo, but some differences in the areas from which the echoes came. Far to his right, the response was soft, close to his right it was sharp, and far to his left it became soft again. If these were any indication, they should signal a hard surface almost directly underneath him.

He checked on that thought. It was not so likely that the echoes indicated hard surface, as that they did a reflective one. This could mean that right under him was an area of open land, while to right and left were areas where tree growth interfered with echo response.

He stopped experimenting and resumed flying,

while he thought this out. The real problem, he told himself, was to discover if he could determine the distances between himself and the source of the echoes. A sort of glee ran through him. It was not that, even now, he had any real belief in his ability to save himself—win an overall victory against the sandmirks. He was merely doing something about his situation.

He flew for a while, again deliberately trying to gain altitude—enough so that he would be able to tell by what he heard whether there was any real difference between the echoes he had caught at a lower altitude. He once again stiffened his wings into soaring position and sent his pulse of sound winging into the rain-drenched darkness.

The echoes came back—and for the first time hope leaped up within Jim. For what he was hearing was essentially the same distribution of strong echoes and weak—indications of high reflective surfaces adjoining softly reflective ones—in the same directions in which he had found them before, but with a very clear weakening of the echoes—an obvious indication that the echoes' strength might be usable as indexes to his height.

He was now caught up in what he was doing. A fever of optimism burned inside him. The odds were still large against his being able to learn anything in time to let him land safely; but the odds had been astronomical against him before.

He continued alternately to fly, soar, experiment with changes in altitude. His life-and-death situation helped him learn: his ability to interpret what he was hearing was growing by leaps and bounds. Not merely was his hearing becoming more sensitive, but also more selective; so that he was able to distinguish not merely two types of surfaces below him, but perhaps half a dozen—including a thin streak of sharp, almost metallic echo which might indicate a stream or river.

Also, little by little, his skill in using the information from the echoes was increasing. Gradually building in his mind, like the negative of a photograph, was an image of the area below. He could now ignore two sounds which—had he considered them earlier —might have kept him from trying the experiment: the noise of the falling rain, hissing around him, and the steady sound of it beating on the earth below. His dragon-hearing apparently was capable of control by conscious intent.

For a moment it crossed Jim's mind that dragons might have more in common with bats than was generally thought. Certainly their wings were like enormous bat wings. If he was able to do what he was now doing, possibly any dragon could; and it was surprising that most dragons believed nighttime to be a time when they could not fly unless by a bright moon.

Of course, he remembered, dragons obviously had a different orientation to darkness than humans did. He remembered how he had felt in the dragon caves— he had not had so much as a touch of claustrophobia. As a dragon, he did not mind being underground, or enclosed in darkness. Similarly, in the cellar of Dick Innkeeper, the fact that the torch had gone out while he was eating had left him completely undisturbed. Darkness as such, and the inability to see, held no terrors for him. It struck him now that the real reason for other dragons' fear of flying at night, when they could not see, was that for them aboveground was considered a strange and possibly dangerous place; and the lack of light to fly by was a good excuse not to go there. Gorbash, Jim remembered, was thought of as an almost unnatural dragon for spending so much time aboveground. Now, Gorbash's abnormal attitude, complemented by Jim's normal human attitude that the surface was a good place on which to be, opened up a whole new dimension in dragon night travel.

Meanwhile, although he was gaining more and more control over his situation, Jim had no way of judging his altitude. It did no good to know that he was getting closer and closer to the ground, if he had no way of guessing when getting close changed abruptly to being there!

It occurred to him that he had only one solution: he could fly down toward the stronger echoes, coming as close to their source as he dared, and hope that when he got very near there would be enough light—even on this dark night—for him to pull up at the last moment. The attempt would be a bit like playing Russian roulette; but what other choice had he?

Putting himself into the shallowest of glide paths, he began to descend. As he did, inspiration came to him for a second time. He remembered the streak of particularly sharp echoes and his own guess that it might represent a river or creek, with a highly sound-reflective surface. He altered his path slightly toward that particular echo. If he was fated to crash-land, he would have more hope if he came down on water than on earth or into a grove of sharp-branched trees.

He continued his descent, sending out pulses of sound as he went. The echoes came back, more and more sharply, more and more swiftly. Straining his eyes, he peered ahead; but all he could see was blackness. Closer he came, and closer—and still he could see absolutely nothing.

Abruptly, he pulled up; and as he did so his tail, hanging down behind him, splashed through water. A split second later he was climbing again, and cursing his own stupidity.

Of course, dammit! Voice, ears—he had completely forgotten nose. Suddenly he had *smelled* water! His dragon-olfactory sense might be no match for Aragh's superb physical instrument, but it was a great deal more sensitive than a human's. He checked his climbing instinctively and went again into a shallow glide, once more aimed toward the water echo below. But this time he paid attention to the odors reaching his nose.

Conscious awareness, he found himself thinking, was a wonderful thing. What he now identified through his nostrils should have been apparent to him on the way down before, but because he had not been expecting to use his sense of smell to orient himself, he had paid no attention. Now, deliberately sniffing, he smelled not only water, but grass, pine needles, leaves and the damp earth itself.

Coming down over what he now knew was water, he smelled soil to right and left of it. He had been right: it was a small river, perhaps fifty yards wide. He descended until his tail touched water, and then rose a little and drifted toward the smell of earth on the right. He glided at an angle toward it, and—

Oops! He pulled up just in time as he smelled a stand of elm trees rising thirty feet into the air above the right bank, directly in his path. Beyond them was a scent of grass and earth. He glided down again above the bank's edge beyond the trees, veered just off it over the water, once more—

And pancaked into the liquid below.

Jim made a tremendous splash. But the water by the bank turned out to be only shoulder-deep on him —perhaps the height of a man. He stood in the stream for a moment, the cool liquid streaming slowly around him, savoring the simple feeling of being safely on the surface of the earth again.

After a few moments, the rapid beating of his heart slowed and he turned and climbed out of the water onto the bank, his head dizzy with success.

It occurred to him, tantalizingly, that he might even have succeeded in coming down safely on the bank itself. Then he rejected the thought. Landing on something solid was more than a bit risky. It would be wiser to wait until he had practiced these new night-time skills some more.

His headiness began to fade. It was a great thing to be alive and to have escaped the sandmirks, but he was still without Companions or a plan of action.

He was no strong staff for Angie to lean her hopes

of rescue on, he thought now, in guilty reaction; but he was all she had. Briefly, he thought of waiting until morning and then taking wing to see if he could find Brian and the rest. Then he remembered how he had already promised to help them take Hugh de Bois' castle first. His change of heart would probably be excuse enough for the troupe to consider itself free of any obligation to help him with Angie. Even if they didn't, he now realized how far he was from understanding his strange new friends. All of them, even the humans, thought and acted according to standards entirely different from his. It was a sobering example of how one could speak the same language as someone else without being on the same mental wavelength at all.

He needed to get straightened out on the way his medieval friends thought and felt, before he made any more mistakes about them and this world; and the obvious person to help him was Carolinus.

He lifted his head. It had almost stopped raining while he was coming in for a landing and during these heavy thoughts. In fact, the clouds seemed to be thinning a trifle. He thought he saw a milky gleam behind one patch of them that could be the moonlight struggling to get through.

If the moon came out—or even if it didn't, he thought, now—he ought to be able, once airborne, to locate the Tinkling Water again. His wing muscles, which had been tiring while he tried to interpret the echoes he heard from the ground, now felt rested once more—another instance of the amazing dragon-strength and endurance. It was too bad dragons could not be studied by competent physiologists, zoologists and doctors of veterinary medicine to find out how they managed to have such physical gifts.

Jim took off with a bound into the now-rainless air—and a little afterward, as he soared in a direction he could only hope was toward Carolinus' cottage, the moon came out to reveal the silver-black landscape about nine hundred feet below him. Five minutes later the sky was all but clear and he was in a long glide toward the woods holding the Tinkling Water, which he could see now, less than two miles ahead of him. He had only been off in his heading by about five compass points.

Chapter 19

Among patches of white moonlight and India-ink shadows, Jim landed with a thump on the gravel path leading to Carolinus' front door. Far off in the woods some sleepy bird clucked loudly enough to be overheard by Jim's dragon-ears. Otherwise, there was complete silence.

Jim hesitated. No light at all showed from the windows of the house; and now that he was here, he was feeling a reluctance to awaken the magician.

As he stood indecisively, a conviction began to creep over him that the building was not merely shut up for the night, but was deserted. In the little clearing, an air of abandonment and emptiness hung on the air itself.

"So, there he is!" growled a voice.

Jim spun around.

"Aragh!" he shouted.

The wolf was approaching from the shadows at the edge of the clearing. Jim was so glad to see him, he could have hugged him. Behind the lean, gleaming-eyed shape strode a larger, familiar dragon-figure.

"Smrgol!" said Jim.

He had not realized until this moment how he had come to feel for these two, and for Brian and the others. It became clear to him that the space between contrasting life forms in this world was not so great as in the world he had left. Life and death were next-door neighbors; similarly, love and hate were as close as two doorways at the end of a corridor, and if you did not learn to hate someone within a short space of time, you learned to love.

"What are you two doing here?" he asked.

"Waiting for you," Aragh snarled.

"Waiting for me? But how did you know I was coming here?"

"The Mage did," said Smrgol. "He called me here yesterday by a cliff sparrow who brought me his message. *'Dragon,'* he said, when I got here, *'James Eckert, whom you know as Gorbash, and I each have long journeys to make—alone. If I make mine, I'll find you all together, later on. If James makes his, he'll come looking for me, here. Wait for him, and tell him what I just told you. Also, tell him that the hour is close and the battle is greater than I thought. More than one plane is involved—can you say that word, dragon?'*

"'Plane,' I said. And then: *'What does it mean, Mage?'*

"'Very good,' he said. 'And never mind what it means. James will understand. More than one plane is involved, and if we can fight together to save the sickness here from spreading out over all, so much the better our chances. But if we can't fight together, still it behooves each of us to fight on as he can, alone; for if our opposition succeeds, there'll be nothing left for any of us . . . Have you got all that, dragon?'*

"'I can recite all the legends from the First Dragon on—' I was starting to tell him, but he cut me short.

"'And never mind legends either, right now, if you please, Smrgol,' he said. 'Also tell that wolf—'*

"'Aragh?' I asked. 'Is he coming here, too?'

"'Naturally. He'll be wanting to know what's got into James. Now stop interrupting!' he said. 'Tell the wolf to go find the knight, the bowman, the outlaw *and his daughter, and tell them all that they're needed for the last battle. Also, there's no use in their going on to Malencontri. Sir Hugh and his men have already turned aside to answer the call of the Dark Powers in the Loathly Tower, whose minions they now are. Even if Sir Brian and the others should take Castle Malencontri now, it'd be worthless to them. For if the Dark Powers win, Sir Hugh will gain it back with one stroke of his sword on its gate and a single crossbow bolt over its walls. Tell them that they'll see me before the Loathly Tower, if I return from my journey. Likewise, they'll see James there if he returns safely from his. And so farewell.' "*

" 'And so farewell'?" Jim echoed. "Was that part of the message?"

"I don't know. But they were his last words," said Smrgol. "Then he disappeared—you know, the way magicians do."

"What was your journey, Gorbash?" asked Aragh.

Jim opened his mouth and closed it again. It would not be easy—or comfortable—to explain to these two about his recent inner pilgrimage into self-examination and self-discovery, which Carolinus by some magical means seemed to have anticipated.

"Someday, maybe," he said, "I might be able to tell you. But not right now."

"Oh, one of those journeys," Aragh growled, leaving Jim uncomfortably uncertain as to how much the wolf actually knew or understood. "All right, you're here. Let's get to this Loathly Tower, then, and settle matters!" His teeth clashed together on the last word.

"Gorbash and I will go," said Smrgol. "You forget, wolf, you've a message to the knight and his company. In fact, you were probably supposed to go right away, when I told you."

"I'm at nobody's orders," said Aragh. "I wanted to stay to see Gorbash safely back from this journey of his, and I did."

"You'd better go now," Smrgol insisted.

"Ha!" snapped Aragh. "I will, then. But, save a

couple of those Dark Powers for me, Gorbash. I'll catch up with you."

The shadows seemed to close about him; and he was gone.

"Not a bad sort—for a wolf," said Smrgol, glancing back into the darkness, for a second. "Touchy, though. But then, they all are. Now, Gorbash, as soon as it's dawn, we'd better be pressing on to the Tower. So what you'd better do is get some rest after your long journey the Mage talked about—"

"Rest?" said Jim. "I don't need rest!"

And in fact, even as the words popped out of his jaws, he realized that they were correct. He felt fine.

"Perhaps you don't think you need rest, my boy," Smrgol was saying severely. "But a dragon of any experience knows that to be in good fighting trim he needs sleep and food—"

"Food?" Jim asked, suddenly alerted. "Have you got something to eat?"

"No," Smrgol replied. "And all the more reason you should plan on getting five or six solid hours of slumber—"

"I couldn't sleep."

"Couldn't sleep . . . ? A dragon who can't sleep? Enough of these wild stories, Gorbash. Any dragon, and particularly one of our family—can always eat, drink or sleep—"

"Why not take off right away?" Jim asked.

"Fly at night?"

"There's a bright moon," Jim said. "You just saw me fly in here."

"And very reckless it was. Youngsters like you always like to take chances. They get away with something nine hundred and ninety-nine times out of a thousand. Then, one day, their luck turns sour and they wish they'd listened. But by then it's too late. What if while you were in the air the sky'd clouded up before you realized it, and suddenly you found you couldn't see the ground?"

Jim opened his jaws to tell the older dragon what he

had discovered about flying in utter darkness and rain, then decided to leave well enough alone.

"Come come," said Smrgol, gruffly. "No more of this nonsense. We both need sleep."

Something about Smrgol's insistence touched the new sensitivity of Jim's emotional perceptions. He looked at Smrgol as closely as he could without seeming to openly study the older dragon. There was something different about the large body he saw, something hard to pin down but undeniably different from the last time he had seen Gorbash's grand-uncle. Suddenly it struck him what it was.

Smrgol's left eyelid was half closed. It drooped down over the long, narrow eye. Smrgol's left wing also drooped, slightly but visibly; and as he stood on all fours the older dragon seemed to be resting most of his weight on his right two legs. Jim had seen physical signs like these before—if not in dragons. His grandfather had shown similar marks of physical distortion on one side of his body following his first stroke, three years ago.

But dragons didn't get— Jim checked the thought. Apparently they did, if they were old enough or otherwise vulnerable. In any case, whether they did or not was unimportant here. What mattered was that Smrgol was now crippled; and whether he understood the exact nature of what had happened to him or not, he was in no condition to fly right now.

"All right," said Jim. "I guess I can wait until morning."

Smrgol would be no better in the morning, but a few hours would give Jim some time to puzzle out a way of handling the situation. He tucked his head under one wing and pretended to go to sleep. His ears caught what he thought might be a faint sigh of relief, and when he peered out from under his appendage a few minutes later, Smrgol also had his head tucked in and was beginning to snore lightly.

Jim fell asleep while he was still pondering what should be done, but woke with the answer already formed in his mind.

"Smrgol," he said, once they were both awake in the dawn of a new day, "I've been thinking—"

"Good boy!"

"Er—yes," Jim said. "And what came to mind was this. I should probably fly to the Loathly Tower as quickly as I can. If Carolinus is right about Sir Hugh and his men being headed there, then the Dark Powers are probably gathering all their forces. Who knows what they're likely to come up with? Thousands of sandmirks—or anything! Meanwhile, why don't *you* go secretly on foot back to the dragon caves, so that no one will know you're planning to gather the other dragons, get them together—"

Smrgol coughed self-consciously.

"My boy," he said. "I meant to say something to you about that. As a matter of fact . . . well, the others aren't coming."

"Not coming?"

"They voted against it. I did what I could, but . . ." Smrgol let his voice trail off.

Jim did not press him. He could imagine why the other dragons had voted against it, if Smrgol had already had his stroke when he tried to talk them into coming. An overage and crippled leader was not one to inspire followers with a thirst for combat. Besides, Jim had acquired enough knowledge of dragons by now, both through his Gorbash-body and -brain and from association with Smrgol and the others, to know that they were basically conservative. *Let's sit tight, and maybe it'll all blow over,* would be basic dragon philosophy.

"Well, that's even better!" said Jim, quickly. "That means you'll be free to walk towards the fens while I fly there, and act as liaison with any of our side that you run into on the ground."

" 'Liaison'?" Smrgol said, suspiciously. "Is that a word you got from Carolinus or that knight?"

"No . . . Well, maybe. At any rate, it means—"

"I know what it means," said Smrgol, sadly. "It's just that it's such a george type of word for you to be using, my boy. Well, well, you really need me to go towards the fens on foot?"

"I think it'd be wise," Jim answered. "That lets me head right for the tower, and leaves you to take care of . . . well, everything else."

"That's true." Smrgol's glance darted for a second to his left side. "Perhaps I ought to do just that . . ."

"Good!" said Jim. "All right then, I'll be taking off right away."

"Good luck, Gorbash!"

"Good luck to you, too, Grand-uncle!"

Smrgol's eyes lit up happily at the last word.

"Well, well, Nephew—don't just stand there. You said you were leaving. Get on with it!"

"Right!" answered Jim; and leaped into the air.

The new morning was as free of rain and clouds as the previous day had been full of them. A stiff wind was blowing toward the fens. At about six hundred feet, Jim spread his wings into soaring position and rode the airstream like an eagle. He had hardly been in the air five minutes, however, before the wind inexplicably changed direction a full hundred and eighty degrees and began to blow inland from the fens, against him.

He tried shifting to various altitudes in an effort to find at least one where this contrary wind did not blow; but it seemed to be everywhere. Battling it for some time, he made very slow process. If this kept up, he might as well have joined Smrgol at making his way to the fens on the ground. In fact, if things didn't improve—

The wind quit abruptly. Suddenly, there was no breeze at all. Caught unprepared, Jim lost nearly five hundred feet of altitude before he could adjust himself to the new conditions and start hunting for thermals.

"What next?" he asked himself.

But there was no next. The air stayed dead calm, and he continued, working his way from thermal to thermal, mounting on one and gliding forward to catch another and climb again. It was faster than walking, but still not the swiftest way of traveling.

By the time he reached the fens, it was midmorning. He made out the line of the Great Causeway and began to work his way out above it at a height of merely a couple of hundred feet.

The land end of the Great Causeway was thickly enough covered with trees and bushes to look similar to the forest land behind the moors and above the fens. The vegetation stood with leaves and branches motionless under the clear autumn sun, as Jim alternately soared and flew above it. Nothing could be seen on the ground, under or between the trees, that Jim could make out. No human or animal figure—not even a bird or cloud of insects—showed itself below. The emptiness of the scene was at once both forbidding and reassuring. Jim found himself being lulled into nearly forgetting why he had come here. Reasonlessly, there came into his head a fragment of a poem he had tried to write in his undergraduate days, before he had sensibly decided to be a teacher:

> *An hour, an hour . . . another hour . . .*
> *Without a difference I can see,*
> *Like faceless children on a wall*
> *That stretches to eternity . . .*

"Jim Eckert! Jim Eckert!"

A tiny voice, calling from far off, roused him from his thoughts. He looked around but could see nothing.

"Jim Eckert! Jim Eckert!"

A shiver went down his back and spread out to chill his whole body as it came again, more loudly; and now he pinpointed its location as somewhere on the causeway up ahead.

"Jim Eckert! Jim Eckert!"

It was full-strength now, a dragon's voice, but not the voice of a dragon with the volume of a Smrgol or Bryagh.

Jim stared ahead, raking the causeway with his

207

sharp vision. Finally he caught sight of something gray that moved slightly, far up in a patch of tall grass surrounded by trees and bushes. He swooped toward it.

As he approached, he saw what he had already almost guessed to be the source of the calling. It was Secoh, down on the ground, his wings spread out over the grass on either side of him, like some captured bird cruelly stretched on display. The mere-dragon was lifting his head, almost hopelessly, from time to time to call.

Jim was almost above the mere-dragon now. Secoh had plainly not yet seen him approaching—not surprising, considering that Secoh was facing in the wrong direction. Jim thought swiftly. The calling of his real name was eerie; and there was something more than that—something unnatural about the odd position in which Secoh was extended—that made even the thought of answering the mere-dragon an uneasy one.

Jim hesitated; and as he hesitated, the momentum of his glide carried him beyond Secoh and the mere-dragon caught sight of him.

"Jim Eckert! Jim Eckert!" Secoh cried. "Don't go! Come back and listen to me, first! I've got something to tell you. Please come back! Oh, help me! Help, your worship! I'm just a mere-dragon . . ."

Jim glided on, closing his ears to the cries fading behind him; but there was a war going on within him. Somehow Secoh had learned to call him by his right name. That meant the mere-dragon had either really discovered something, or else the Dark Powers were using him as an intermediary. Could the Dark Powers be ready to negotiate Angie's release?

He kept a firm grip on the hope that sprung up in him at that last thought. Negotiation was a possibility . . . and if, on the other hand, Secoh had only discovered something useful, Jim would be foolish not to take advantage of it. Also, although Jim sternly throttled down the idea that emotion had any strong influence over whatever decision he might make, he was touched by the note of despair in Secoh's voice and the mere-dragon's desperate appeal for help.

Grimly, Jim banked into a turn, beat his wings for more altitude and started to glide back.

Secoh was in the same spot, his position unchanged. He set up a chorus of glad cries as he saw Jim once more coming toward him.

"Oh, thank you, your highness! Thank you, thank you . . ." he babbled as Jim slid in to land on the grass beside him.

"Never mind all the thanking!" snapped Jim. "What's this you've got to tell me—"

He broke off, for he had just noticed the reason for Secoh's unnatural, spread-eagled position. Cleverly hidden in the grass were pegs driven into the earth, to which Secoh's wingtops and toes had been cinched tight by leather cords.

"Hold, dragon!" cried a voice.

Jim looked up. A figure in bright armor, which he had last seen coming at him on horseback, lance in hand, stepped out from the cover of trees on his right; and all around Jim, shoulder to shoulder, a solid ring of crossbowmen had appeared, their weapons aimed and cocked, the quarrels pointed at Jim's chest.

Secoh wailed.

"Forgive me, your greatness!" he cried. "Forgive me! I couldn't help it. I'm just a mere-dragon and they caught me. The Dark Ones told them that if they made me call you by that name, you'd come and they could catch you. They promised to let me go if I could get you to come. I'm just a mere-dragon and nobody cares about me. I had to look after myself. I had to, don't you see? I *had* to . . . !"

Chapter 20

The figure in armor walked intrepidly forward until he stood less than three feet from Jim's jaws. He put his visor up and Jim saw a square, cheerfully brutal countenance with a large nose and pale, cold, gray eyes.

"I'm Sir Hugh de Bois de Malencontri, dragon," he said.

"I know you," Jim answered.

"Damme if I see why you're any different than any other dragon," said Sir Hugh. "Still, who's to argue if it makes Them happy. Tie him up, lads. He's too heavy for the horses, but we'll make a sledge and drag him on it to the tower."

"Please, Sir knight, your lordship, will you untie me now?" Secoh called. "You've got him. Will you just cut these tight thongs and let me go—"

Sir Hugh looked over to Secoh and laughed. Then he turned back, considering Jim.

"Sir knight! Sir knight!" Secoh quivered all through his body. "You promised! You promised you'd let me go if I got him to come. You wouldn't go back on your knightly words, would you, your Royalty?"

Sir Hugh looked at the mere-dragon again and burst into a roar of bass-throated laughter.

"Hark at him! Hark to the dragon! Knightly honor, he says! Knightly honor to a *dragon?*"

His laughter cut off abruptly.

"Why, dragon," he said to Secoh, "I want your head for my wall! What sort of jack-fool would I be to turn you loose?"

He turned away; and as he did so a deadly shower came down from the clear sky—a ran of clothyard shafts whistling upon them. Half a dozen of the crossbowmen fell. The rest, some with arrows in them, broke for the cover of the trees. Four shafts fell around Sir Hugh, and one long arrow drove through the top edge of his left pauldon to ring loudly on the breastplate below, but without penetrating the second thickness of armor.

Sir Hugh swore, snapped down his visor and also ran heavily for the trees. A second flight of arrows descended in a large circle among those same trees, but it was impossible for Jim to tell what damage they had done. He heard the sounds of feet running away, of a man in armor mounting and galloping off. Then silence. He and Secoh were unhurt, but alone except for the dead and dying crossbowmen on the ground about them.

A whimper from Secoh brought Jim's attention back to the mere-dragon. He stepped over and drove the claws of one forepaw into each of the pegs holding Secoh down, in turn, and pulled them out. They came up easily to his muscles. Secoh immediately sat up and began biting through the leather thongs that had held the pegs to his toes.

"Why didn't you pull the pegs out yourself?" Jim asked Secoh. "It's not easy, stretched out like that, I know, but any dragon—"

"They had all those bows and swords and things," said Secoh. "I'm not as brave as you are, your magnanimity. I couldn't help being afraid; and I thought maybe if I did what they wanted, they'd let me go."

He stopped biting through the thongs and cowered.

"Of course, I understand how your worship would feel. I shouldn't have called you down to land here—"

"Forget it," said Jim gruffly.

Secoh took him at his word and went back to biting through leather.

Jim made a small tour around the fallen crossbowmen. But there was nothing to be done for any of them. Those who were down were either already dead or within minutes of dying; none of them yet retained enough consciousness to realize that someone was standing over them. Jim turned away just in time to see Secoh preparing to take off.

"Wait a minute!" he snapped.

"Wait? Oh, of course—wait. I understand, your highness!" Secoh yelped. "You thought I was about to fly away. But I was just stretching the cramp out of my wings—"

"You aren't going anywhere," Jim said, "so settle down and answer a few questions. Who told you to call me Jim Eckert?"

"I already said!" protested Secoh. "The george— the knight—told me; and the Dark Ones told him."

"Hmm. And how did they catch you in the first place?"

Secoh looked unhappy.

"They—they put out a fine piece of meat," he said. "Half a large boar . . . lovely, fat meat, too."

A tear trickled down from the eye on the side of his head nearest Jim.

"Such lovely, fat meat!" Secoh repeated. "And then they didn't even let me have a bit of it. Not a bite! They just aimed their crossbows at me and tied me up."

"Did they say why?" Jim asked. "Did they give any reason for gue sing I'd be along, so you could call me down in the first place?"

"Oh, yes, your worship. They talked about it a lot. The knight said you'd come at just this time, and after they caught you the six men he named must take you without delay to the tower; and he with the rest would catch up with them on the way."

"Catch up?" Jim frowned.

"Yes, your importance." Secoh's eyes looked suddenly a good deal shrewder than Jim had ever seen them before. "This knight was going to stay behind to lay a trap for the other george—your friend. And that was something he wasn't supposed to do: the

212

Dark Ones had sent him out just to get you, and come right back. But he really has a terrible anger against your friend, you know, the one who goes around chasing us mere-dragons all the time. So this knight was going to catch your friend in spite of what the Dark Ones wanted—"

Secoh stopped to shiver.

"That's what's so terrible about them, these georges," he went on. "Nobody can make them do what they're told, not even the Dark Ones. They don't care for anything, just as long as they can go riding around in their hard shells and sticking their sharp horns into poor mere-dragons like me, or anyone they want to. Imagine somebody else going ahead and doing just what he wanted after the Dark Ones had given him orders!"

"I wonder where they all went when they ran off from here though?" Jim wondered.

"The knight that was here and those crossbowmen?" Secoh nodded his head back toward the mainland end of the Great Causeway. "There's a swamp off to the left there where you'd drown in a minute if you couldn't fly, your highness. But the Dark Ones showed that knight a way through it. He and his men have gone out there, and they'll be circling around to get back on the causeway behind your friends who shot all the arrows in here, just now. I know, because that's the way this knight told his men they'd surprise and take your friends after you'd been dragged off to the tower."

"That means they've cut us off from the mainland—" Jim was beginning, when he became aware that he had been listening to the sound of approaching horses' hooves for some seconds; and a moment later Brian rode into the clearing.

"James!" cried the knight, joyously. "There you are! I've been feeling seven sorts of rascal for trying to talk you into that assault on Malencontri. After you disappeared yesterday, I got to pondering and it struck me that we'd probably been counseling you against your duty; and you'd determined to go it alone, after all. Said as much to Giles, Dafydd, and Danielle; and blind me if they hadn't all been thinking along the same lines themselves. First the wolf, then you, gone. Bad omens, those, for a group of Companions, eh? So we'd already turned toward the fens here, when the wolf caught up with us last night— Hullo! Is that one of our local dragons you've got here?"

"Secoh, your mightiness!" yelped the mere-dragon, hastily. "Just Secoh, that's all. I know you well, your georgeship, and admired you from afar, many times. Such speed, such dash—"

"Really?"

"Such kindness, such gentleness, such—"

"Oh, not all that, actually—"

"I said to myself, a knight like that'd never hurt a poor mere-dragon like me."

"Well, of course," said Brian, "I would have, you know. Chopped your head off if I could have caught you, just as I would any other dragon. But I take it you're on our side now, from seeing you here with James."

"Your . . . ? Oh, yes sir, yes. I'm on *your* side."

"Thought so. Struck me you had the look of a fighter about you the moment I noticed you there. Lean, hard-muscled, deadly—not like most of the other local dragons I've seen."

"Oh yes, your knighthood. Lean—"

Secoh, who had half spread his wings as if he was about to try leaving once more, broke off, checking himself in midmotion to stare at the knight. Brian, however, had turned back to speak to Jim.

"Others'll be here in a minute—" he had begun.

"Wrong," said a sour voice. "I've been here since before you rode in. But I was busy tracking our enemies. They went off into a swamp by the causeway. I could have tracked them there, too, but decided to come back and see how Gorbash was. Are you all right, Gorbash?"

"Fine, Aragh," said Jim, for the wolf had stepped into the clearing as he was talking.

Aragh looked at Secoh and grinned evilly.

" 'Hard-muscled' and 'deadly'?" he said.

"Never mind all that now, Sir wolf," said Brian. "Important thing is we're all together again, and the next step calls for a bit of planning. As soon as— Ah, here they are, now."

Dafydd, Giles and Danielle, together with the rest of the outlaws, had in fact been coming into the clearing from the moment Aragh had appeared. The outlaws were already moving around the fallen forms of the crossbowmen, retrieving their arrows. Dafydd paused in the center of the clearing and looked about.

"Carried my shaft off, he must have," the bowman said to Jim. "Was he wounded, then?"

"That was your arrow that hit Hugh de Bois? I should have known it," said Jim. "It went through part of his armor but not through the rest."

"It was a blind loose," said Dafydd, "with a dropping shaft because of the trees between us. Yet I am not happy hearing that I put point in him but did him no harm."

"Peace!" Danielle said to him. "With the intercession of Saint Sebastian, you couldn't have done more from that distance on such a shot. Why do you keep pretending you can do the impossible?"

"I am not pretending, whatever. As for 'impossible,' there is no such a thing as an impossible, but only a thing the doing of which has not yet been learned."

"Never mind that now, I say," Brian interrupted. "We're back together with Sir James and there's a decision to be made. Sir Hugh and his crossbowmen, having escaped us here, have taken refuge in a swamp. Should we follow them, post a force to hold them from returning, or press on to the tower, leaving them behind us? For myself, I would not willingly leave enemies free to follow upon my rear guard."

"And they aren't just in the swamp," said Secoh loudly and unexpectedly. "By this time they're back on the causeway."

Everyone turned to look at the mere-dragon; who

wavered and seemed on the verge of cringing under so much attention, but ended by straightening his spine and staring back at them.

"What's this?" said Giles.

"Hugh de Bois and his men are fighting under the orders of the Dark Powers in the tower," said Jim. "Secoh here tells me the Dark Ones told Hugh how to get through the swamp safely and back on the causeway. That means they're on firm ground somewhere between us and the mainland."

"No argument, then," said Brian. "The Tower before and those crossbowmen behind are no situation to wish for. Let's turn and go back to meet them."

"I don't know . . ." said Jim. There was an uneasiness in the pit of his stomach. "The rest of you go meet them, if you think that's best. I've got to get on to the Loathly Tower. Somehow, I've got the feeling time's running out."

"Ha?" said Brian, and became suddenly thoughtful. "That was the feeling that came on me when I found you gone yesterday. In some sort, I've got it with me even now. Perhaps best you and I together go on toward the tower, James, and to whatever awaits us there. The rest can hold here and deal with Sir Hugh and his men if they try to pass."

"I'm going with Gorbash," said Aragh.

"And I, too," said Dafydd, unexpectedly. He met the eyes of Danielle. "Do not look at me so. I said the taking of castles was not my work—nor was it, at all. But when, in Castle Malvern, the flames all bent and there was no wind, a coldness came into me. That coldness is still there, and my mind is that it will never leave me until I seek out and help to slay its source."

"Why, you *are* a knight," said Danielle.

"Mock me not," said the Welshman.

"Mock? I'm not mocking you. In fact, I'm going with you."

"No!" Dafydd looked over her head at Giles. "Make her stay."

Giles grunted.

"You make her stay," said the older man.

Danielle put her hand on the knife at her belt.

"No one makes me stay—or go—or anything else," she said. "In this hap, I'm going."

"Giles," Brian put in, ignoring her, "can you hold Sir Hugh and his men, alone?"

"I'm not quite alone . . ." Giles said, dryly. "I have my lads here. And the Malvern Castle stalwarts! Sir Hugh and his troop will pass into Heaven before they pass us by."

"Then let's go on, in God's name!"

Brian remounted his horse and started down the causeway. Jim fell in beside the large white charger.

". . . Any more objections?" Danielle was challenging Dafydd.

"No," the bowman answered, sadly. "Indeed, a part of the cold feeling was that you would be with me when the final time came. As the shadows point, the day will wend. Let us go, then."

The two of them fell in behind Jim and Brian, and their voices dropped to confidential tones, not so low but that Jim could not have used his dragon-ears to overhear what they were telling each other, but low enough so that he could give them the privacy of ignoring them. Aragh came trotting up on the other side of him from Blanchard.

"Why so glum, Sir knight, and Gorbash?" he said. "It's a fine day for slaying."

"In the matter of this tower and those within it," said Brian, shortly, "we go against something that touches our souls."

"The more fool you, for having such useless, clogging things," Aragh growled.

"Sir wolf," said Brian, grimly, "you understand nothing of this, and I'm in no mind to instruct you."

They continued to travel in silence. The air stayed windless and the day seemed hardly to alter with the ordinary movement of time. Gradually the horizon, where land met sea, began to be visible as a gray-blue line ahead of them, still some miles distant. Jim looked up at the sky, puzzled.

"What time is it, do you think?" he asked the knight.

"Shortly before prime, I should say," responded Brian. "Why?"

"Prime . . .?" Jim had to pause to remember that prime was noon. "Look how dark it's getting!"

Brian glanced around and also raised his gaze skyward before looking back down to Jim. To the west, above them, although the sun still floated in an apparently cloudless sky, a sort of darkness of the air itself seemed to dull the colors of heavens and landscape. Brian looked sharply to his front.

"Hullo!" he said. "See ahead, there!"

He pointed. Jim looked. Before them the causeway now held only an occasional tree or clump of bushes intermixed with the tall fenland grass. Somewhere up there—it was impossible for the eye to measure exactly how distant—the grass was being pressed down along what seemed to be a sharp line extending across the causeway and out into the fen on either side. Beyond that line everything looked coldly gray, as if seen under a chill and winter sky.

"It's moving this way," said Aragh.

It was.

It took a moment or two of watching for Jim to make it out, but by watching the grass bend and rise again it was possible to discover that the line, whatever it might be, was creeping slowly forward. It was as if some heavy, invisible fluid slowly and heavily flooded outward along the causeway, overwhelming the meres and islands of the fens. Jim felt a slow chill mounting his spine as he watched.

Instinctively, Jim and the knight came to a halt as they watched; and Aragh, seeing them stop, also halted. He sat down now and grinned at them.

"Look up, and west," he said.

They looked. For a second Jim's hopes bounded upward at seeing what he thought was a dragon shape about four hundred feet above the causeway, soaring in their direction. But then a difference gradually registered upon him. This was no dragon, or anything near the size of a dragon, although it was too large to be any soaring bird. It looked to be half again the wing-spread of an eagle, but it had an odd, heavy-headed silhouette that gave it a vulturous look. Jim squinted hard into the sky, but the strange darkness of the air baffled him in his efforts to make out the flying shape's detail.

It was coming straight for them, gliding. All at once, as the flying shape grew closer, Jim began to resolve the features of that odd, bulky head. He soon saw it clearly—and his vision blurred, refusing to accept what his mind recorded. It was a huge, dun bird—all but the head. Its head was the head of a woman, her pale face staring forward and down at Brian and himself, her lips parted, showing pointed white teeth.

"Harpy!" said Brian beside him, on a slow intake of breath.

It came on.

Surely, thought Jim, it would veer aside at the last moment; but it continued to swoop directly toward the two. Now he saw why his eyes had refused to focus on that white face. It was not merely that it was human and female. More terrible than that, it was completely mad. The frozen features of insanity rode above the pinions of the huge, winged creature swooping toward them—

Abruptly it was on them, driving at Jim's throat; and everything seemed to happen in a single moment.

A dark shape shot into the air toward the harpy just before it reached him. Long jaws clicked on emptiness where a fraction of a second before the white face had been, and the harpy screamed hideously, yerking aside into Brian, half tumbling the knight from Blanchard's back before it's long wings caught on the air and beat upward once more to safety.

On the ground, Aragh was snarling softly to himself. Brian pulled his body upright again in the saddle. The harpy, its strike missed, was now winging away from them through the air, back toward the tower.

"It's well for you the wolf turned it away," said Brian, somberly. "Its bite is poison. I own that hell-face had me spellbound and frozen."

"Let it try again," said Aragh, viciously. "I don't miss twice."

A voice broke in on them, wailing from out over the still fenwater to their left.

"No! No! Turn back, your worships! Turn back! It's no use. It's death for you all, up there!"

They turned their heads.

"Why, dammit!" Brian exclaimed. "Its' that mere-dragon of yours."

"No," said Aragh, testing the air with his nose. "Another. Different scent."

A mere-dragon, looking enough like Secoh to be a twin, was perched precariously on a small tussock of half-drowned soil and marsh grass about forty feet out from the causeway.

"Oh, please!" it cried, stretching out its wings and fanning them to maintain its balance on the tussock. "You won't be able to do any good; and we'll all suffer for it. They're woken up now in the tower, and you'll just make Them angry if you go there!"

"Them?" called Jim. "You mean the Dark Powers?"

"Them—Them!" wailed the mere-dragon, despairingly. "Them that built and live in the Loathly Tower, that sent the blight on us five hundred years ago. Can't you feel Them, waiting for you there? Can't you smell Them? They that never die, they who hate us all. They who draw to Them all terrible, evil things . . ."

"Come here," said Jim. "Come onto the causeway here. I want to talk to you."

"No . . . no!" whined the mere-dragon. He threw a terrified glance at the line approaching over the grass and water. "I have to fly—get away!" He flapped his wings, rising slowly into the air. "They've broken loose again and now we're all lost—lost—!"

A breeze out of the chill wintriness beyond the moving line seemed to catch the mere-dragon and whirl him away into the sky. He went, flying heavily, back toward the mainland, crying in a thin, despairing voice.

"Lost . . . lost . . . lost . . . !"

"There, now," said Brian. "What was I telling you about mere-dragons? How can a gentleman gain honor or worship by slaying a beast like that—"

In midsentence, the words died on his tongue. While they had been talking to the mere-dragon, the line had come upon them; and as Brian spoke, it passed beneath them. The cold winter colors beyond it enclosed them, and the knight and Jim looked at each other with faces gone ash-colored and pinched.

"In manus tuas, Domine," said the knight, softly, and crossed himself.

All about and around them, the serest gray of winter light lay on all things. The waters of the fens stretched thick, oily and still between the patches of dull-green grass. A small, cold breeze wandered through the tops of the bullrushes, making them rattle together with dry and distant sounds, like old bones cast out into some forgotten churchyard. The trees stood helpless and quiet, their leaves now dried and faded like people aged before their time; while all about, a heaviness—as of hope gone dead—pressed down on all living things.

"Sir James," said the knight in an odd, formal tone and with words Jim had never before heard him use, "wit thee well that we have in this hour set our hands to no small task. Wherefore, I pray thee that, should it be thou alone who return and I am slain, thou shalt not leave my lady nor those who are of my kindred live on in ignorance of mine end."

"I—I'll be most honored to inform them—" Jim answered, awkwardly, from a dry throat.

"I thank thee for thy most gentle courtesy," said Brian, "and will do in like event for thee, so soon as I may find ship to take me beyond the western seas."

"Just—tell Angie. My lady, Angela, I mean," said Jim. "You needn't worry about anybody else."

He had a sudden mental picture of the strange, brave, honest character beside him actually leaving home and family to head out over nearly three thousand miles of unknown ocean in obedience to a promise given a near-stranger. The image made him wince inside, in its comparison to the picture he had of himself.

"I shall do so," said Brian—and at once reverted to his ordinary self, swinging down out of his saddle onto the ground. "Blanchard won't go another inch, damn him! I'll have to lead him—"

He broke off, looking back past Jim.

"Where'd the bowman and Mistress Danielle go?" he asked.

Jim turned. Brian was correct. As far as the eye could see, there was no sign of the two who, they had assumed, were following them.

"Aragh?" Jim asked. "Where did they go?"

"They fell behind, sometime since," said the wolf. "Perhaps they changed their minds about coming with us. They're back there somewhere. If it weren't for the trees and bushes, you might still see them."

A moment's silence followed.

"Then, let's on without them," said Brian.

He tugged at the bridle of Blanchard. The white horse reluctantly took one step, then another. They moved off. Jim and Aragh fell into step alongside.

As they traveled onward, the dreariness all around and pressing down upon them had the effect of stifling conversation. Even existing seemed to be an effort under its influence, and each movement of their bodies required a conscious exertion of will; their arms and legs were like lead weights swung heavily and reluctantly into each slow, necessary step. But the effect of their silence was worse, for it left them isolated, each set off alone in the dark pool of his own thoughts. They moved as if in some pale dream, speaking now and then for a moment, then falling silent.

As they progressed, the causeway narrowed. From forty yards across, it dwindled until it became as many feet. The trees, too, shortened and became more stunted—more twisted and gnarled—and under their feet the thinning grass revealed a different soil, an earth lacking in the rich blackness of the fenland toward the main shore. Here it was sandy, with a sterile, flinty hardness. It crunched under their weight and under the hooves of Blanchard, and was at once unyielding and treacherous.

The white warhorse checked himself suddenly. He tossed his head and tried to back up instead of going forward.

"What the hell!" exploded Brian, tugging on the reins. "What devil's into him now—"

"Listen," said Jim, who had also stopped.

For a moment, Jim could almost make himself believe he had imagined what he had just heard. But then it sounded again and began to grow in volume. It was just ahead of them and getting closer. It was the chittering of sandmirks.

The volume soared upward. Clearly, the sandmirks were not just in front of them, but all around. The dark predators had simply not all given voice, to start with; but now they were in full chorus. Jim felt the sound they made reaching through, once more, to the old primitive areas of his midbrain. He looked at Brian and saw the knight's face beneath the open visor of his helmet; it looked drained of blood, its skin fallen in to the bones like the face of a man ten days dead. The chittering was rising to a crescendo and Jim felt the ability to think slipping from him.

Beside him, Aragh laughed his silent laugh.

The wolf threw back his head, opened his long jaws, and howled—a long howl that cut like a razor slash across the sound of the sandmirks. It was not merely lupine night music from some moonlit hilltop that Aragh uttered, but a call that began on a low note and climbed in tone and volume to a pitch greater than all the chittering; then it fell again, dropping . . . dropping into nothingness. It was a hunting howl.

When it ceased, there was silence. Only silence. Aragh laughed again.

"Shall we go on?" he said.

Brian stirred like someone coming out of a dream, and tugged on the reins. Blanchard stepped forward. Jim, too, moved; and they once more took up their journey.

The sandmirks did not begin their chittering again. But as the knight, the dragon and the wolf moved on, Jim could hear innumerable small ripplings in the water and rustlings behind the trees, bushes and bullrushes that surrounded them—a noise that paralleled their path and kept up with them, as if a small army of heavy-bodied rats was providing them with escort. He did his best to put that sound from his mind. An instinctive terror was inspired by the noise of those feet and bodies alone; and he had other terrors to watch for.

But the watching was becoming more difficult.

"Getting darker, isn't it?" Jim said, finally. "And misty."

They had gone perhaps a mile and a half since they had crossed the line. And the sky had, indeed, been blackening. It was not a natural darkness, but a sort of thickening of the air, a premature night that seemed to be coming over them. With it came low clouds above their heads, and banks of mist, moving at water level off to either side of the causeway.

Abruptly, Blanchard balked again. They stopped. But around them the noise of the sandmirks began to mount toward a frenzy of invisible movement. There was something triumphant about their mad activity. Unexpectedly, ahead and off the causeway to the right, rang out a single, heavy splash, like the sound of something large heaving itself out of water onto land. Aragh's nose lifted abruptly, and he growled, deep in his throat.

"Now," he said.

"Now what? What comes?" Brian demanded.

"My meat," snarled Aragh. "Stand clear!"

Stiff-legged, he walked a few paces forward from them and stood, tail hanging in a low arc, head a little down, jaws slightly open, waiting. His eyes burned red in the dimness.

Now Jim's nose caught the scent of whatever it was Aragh had smelled. The odor was oddly familiar—and then he realized it was the same scent he had been picking up from the sandmirks, who had kept company with them. Only, this was stronger and far more rank. Now, too, his ears picked up the sound of something heavy-bodied approaching them from down the causeway—the sort of creature that would go through bushes rather than around them.

Brian drew his sword. Aragh did not turn his head, but his ears flicked at the sound of metal sliding against metal.

"My meat, I said," he repeated. "Stand back! Go when I say."

Jim found his every muscle tensed, his eyes almost aching with the effort to see through the gloom to what was coming. Then, all at once it was visible, moving toward them: a great, black, four-legged shape, its close body hair still gleaming slickly from the waters it had just left. It made no effort to hide, but came on until it was less than three times its own body length from Aragh. Then it reared up and from its throat came a sick-sounding chuckle that was a deep-toned version of the same chittering the three intruders here had heard earlier.

"Apostles guard us!" Brian muttered. "Is *that* a sandmirk . . . ?"

A sandmirk it was, but many times the size of the smaller creatures that had now three times awakened an ancient fear in Jim. This individual was at least as large as an adult grizzly bear; in fact, very nearly the size of one of the great Kodiak Island brown bears. Aragh, standing forward to challenge it, seemed in comparison to have shrunken from pony-size to the dimensions of a small dog.

But the wolf showed no signs of backing off. From

his throat came the steady, slow rumble of a growl, unvarying and continuing. For a long moment the monster sandmirk stood swaying a little on its hind legs, chuckling its bass chitter. Then it moved forward, yet upright—and suddenly the fight had begun.

It was a flurry of action, too fast for human or dragon eye to follow in detail. For all its size, the great sandmirk could move its body and legs with vision-blurring speed. Only, Aragh was faster. He was in, out, around, up and down on the towering black figure, so swiftly and continuously that Jim's eyes gave up trying to follow his actions.

As suddenly as they had come together, the two parted. Aragh stood back, head low, sounding his steady growl while the huge sandmirk panted, swaying on its heavy hind legs, its black coat marked here and there with lines of red.

Aragh's growling now broke off, though his tense watching of his opponent did not relax an inch.

"Go!" he said, without turning his head. "The others won't follow you as long as I hold their mother in play. And they won't mob me to help her, because they know that the first five to reach me will die; and none of them want to be among those."

Jim hesitated. Brian spoke for both of them.

"Sir wolf," he said, "we can't leave you to face these odds alone—"

But before the last words were out of his mouth, battle had been joined again. Once more, the movement was too fast to follow; but this time it lasted longer—until a sudden, ugly, breaking sound rang out and Aragh leaped back to stand on three legs, his left foreleg dangling.

"Go!" he snarled, furiously. "I told you—go!"

"But your leg—" Jim began.

"Did I ask your help?" Aragh's voice was thick with rage. "Did I ever ask help? When the she-bear caught me when I was a cub, alone and with three legs I killed her. I'll kill this Mother of sandmirks, again with three legs and alone! *Go!*"

The monster now wore a bright pattern of red, bleeding slashes all over her body. But though she panted hoarsely, she did not seem weakened, or slowed. Nevertheless, Aragh's decision to fight alone was plainly not to be altered; and to throw away the wolf's deliberate sacrifice of himself was unthinkable. Certainly, if he was killed, it would only be a matter of time before the sandmirks would finish the other two.

Brian looked at Jim.

"Let's go," said Jim.

The knight nodded. He tugged on the reins of Blanchard and led the horse forward. They moved off, as the wolf and the giant sandmirk matriarch closed in combat again behind them.

The sounds of fighting behind them soon died in the distance. The darkness and the mist enclosed them. But Aragh had been right about one thing: none of the smaller sandmirks followed them. They plodded on; and for a long time neither of them spoke. Then Brian turned his head to Jim.

"A very worthy wolf," he said, slowly.

"If that big sandmirk kills him—" Jim began, and heard the sentence die in his mouth.

He had been about to promise revenge upon the killer, and then it had come to him that he could do nothing. If the huge black creature should kill Aragh, there was no way he could find her again; and if he found her, there was no way he could destroy her before she and her legion of children killed him. He was not an English wolf, to ignore the effect of the chittering voices.

It was bitter for Jim to face the fact that he was helpless to strike back against a cruel wrong. Intolerable. He had reached his present age never having cause to doubt that injustice must eventually be brought to book, and that any unfairness of life must, in the end, be balanced. Now he had to accept the debt of Aragh's possible self-sacrifice, knowing it might be something he could never pay back. Marching slowly along under the eerie and unnatural darkness that held the fenlands, he forgot for the moment where he was, and what might become of him, in the internal struggle of finding some way to live with that debt.

It was hard to let go of cherished illusions; but he had no choice. Gradually, as he faced that fact, his convulsive grip on the belief that life *must* be fair, or else it could not be endured, relaxed; and he saw one more shackle upon the strength of his individual spirit fall away and sink into the waters of oblivion.

"Getting darker, isn't it?" Brian's voice roused him from his thoughts.

Jim looked around. They had gone perhaps a mile and a half since leaving Aragh and the sandmirks behind; and indeed the air had further thickened, even as the mists were closing in solidly on either sides of the causeway.

"Much more of this," Jim said, "and we won't be able to go on."

It was by now all but impossible to see any distance farther than the water's edge on either hand or for more than a dozen yards in front of them. They drew the cold viscousness of the air into their lungs, and it seemed to settle and pool there, stifling them. Walking had become even more of a labor as their wills sagged under the sense of depression which pressed without letup upon them. Nor was this all; for with the additional darkening had come a blanketing of sound. The noise of their footsteps and hoof-treads on the sandy soil was all but lost to their ears; and even their voices seemed to sound distant, thin and faraway.

"Brian?" called Jim, groping through the gloom.

"Here, James . . ." The dim outline of the armored knight moved toward Jim and blundered against him, as they both came to a halt.

"I can't see to go any farther," Jim said.

"Nor I," Brian admitted. "We shall have to stay where we are, I suppose."

"Yes . . ."

They stood facing each other, but no longer able to make out the features of each other's faces; they were lost in an impenetrable darkness. And this darkness became even blacker, until any last intimation of light was gone and the obscurity was total. Jim felt chill, hard, iron fingers grip his left shoulder.

"Let us hold together," said Brian. "Then, whatever comes on us, must come on us at the same time."

"Yes," Jim agreed.

They stood in silence and in lightlessness, waiting for they did not know what; and soon the blackness about them pressed further in on them, now that it had isolated them, and was nibbling at the very edges of their minds. Out of the nothingness came no material thing; but from within Jim crept up, one by one, like blind white slugs from some bottomless pit, all his inner fears and weaknesses, all the things of which he had ever been ashamed and striven to forget, all the maggots of his soul . . .

He opened his mouth to speak to Brian—to say something, anything, to break the black spell upon him. But he found that already a poison had been at work within him. He no longer trusted the knight: for he knew that evil must be in Brian because of the evil he had rediscovered in himself. Slowly, stealthily, he began to withdraw from under the other's touch . . .

"Look!" Brian's voice came suddenly to him, distant and strange, sounding like the voice of someone who has gone a long way off. "Look back the way we came!"

Jim turned. How he knew the proper direction to look, in that nothingness, he was never able to tell. But he turned; and he saw, faraway—so very far away that it was like the glimmer of a star seen across uncounted light-years of space—a tiny, distant point of light.

"What is it?" he gasped.

"Don't know," replied the distorted, toy-like voice

of the knight. "But it's coming this way. Look at it grow!"

Slowly, very very slowly, the far-off light waxed and advanced. It was like a keyhole into daylight, enlarging as it came closer. The minutes ticked off, measured second by second in the beating of Jim's heart. Finally, the light stretched tall, lengthening as it came on like a knife slit cut through a cloth of darkness.

"What is it?" cried Jim, again.

"I don't know . . ." the knight repeated.

But both of them felt the goodness of it, as it came. It was life and courage again; it was a power against the power of dark helplessness that had threatened to overwhelm them. They felt their strength returning as it came on, brightening; and Blanchard stirred beside them, stamping his hooves on the hard sand and whinnying.

"This way!" called Jim.

"This way!" shouted Brian.

The light shot up suddenly in height, reaching for the heavens, as if activated by the sound of their voices. Like a great rod it advanced, upright, toward them, now broadening as it approached. The darkness was rolling back and lifting. The black was graying once more into a thick twilight, then the twilight thinning and dispersing. The scuffing sound of feet nearing them came to their ears, they heard a sound of slow breathing, and all at once—

It was daylight again.

And Carolinus stood before them dressed in his robes, a high-pointed hat on his head, holding erect before him—as if it was blade and buckler, spear and armor, all in one—a tall, carven staff of wood.

"By the Powers!" he said, gazing at them. "I got to you in time!"

Jim and the knight looked at each other like men snatched back from the brink of a cliff. Blanchard tossed his bridled head and stamped his feet again, as if to reassure himself that he was once more upon the solid earth of a world he knew.

230

"Mage," said Brian, "my thanks!"

"The fabric of Chance and History was stretched this time in your favor," said Carolinus. "Otherwise, I could never have reached you in time. Look!"

He lifted the staff and drove it point-down into the sand at his feet. It went in, and stood upright like the denuded trunk of a tree. He gestured at the horizon and they looked around.

The darkness was gone. The fens lay revealed, far and wide, stretching back the way they had come and, up ahead, going perhaps another half-mile to where they met the thin dark line of the sea. The causeway had also risen in altitude; until now, where they stood, they were perhaps twenty feet above the level of the surrounding landscape. Far ahead to the west, the sky was on fire with sunset. It lighted all the fens, the meres and the causeway with a red glow which lay bloodily on earth and grass and stunted trees; and it pooled just ahead, around a low hill, at a rise of a hundred feet or more above the seashore where, touched but uncolored by that same dying light there loomed over all, amongst great, tumbled boulders, the ruined, dark and shattered shell of a tower as black as jet.

Chapter 21

This much and little more they saw in the brief minute or so that the light lasted, for the sun was on the very lip of the sea horizon and went down as they watched. Night—true night, this time—came in from the east in one swift stride.

Carolinus had been bending over something on the ground beside his staff. A little flame now leaped up beneath his hands; and going a little off to one side, he brought back some dry branches fallen from one of the causeway's dwarfed trees. He threw these on the flame, and a fire blazed up, lighting and warming them.

"We're still within the circle of strength of the Loathly Tower," said the magician. "Stay within ten paces of the wand if you care to be sure of your own safety!"

Tucking up his robe, he sat down cross-legged before the fire.

"Lie down, Sir knight," he said, "and you, too, my enchanted friend. When that sun comes up again, you'll find you'll need all the rest you've been able to get."

Brian obeyed willingly enough, but Jim sank reluctantly to the ground by the fire.

"What about Angie?" he asked. "We haven't seen any sign of Bryagh. Do you suppose—?"

"Your damsel's in the tower," Carolinus interrupted him.

"In there?" Jim started up. "I've got to—"

"Sit down! She's perfectly safe and comfortable, I

promise you," said Carolinus, testily. "The forces in strife here don't center around her—not for the present, at least."

He winced, and reached into his robes to produce a flask and a small cup made of cloudy glass. He poured white liquid from the flask into the cup and sipped it.

"What the devil?" said Brian, staring.

"How do you know?" Jim demanded of the magician. "How can you tell—?"

"By the Powers!" snapped Carolinus. "I'm a Master of the Arts. How do I know? Forsooth!"

"Pardon me," said Brian, his blue eyes staring. "Is that *milk* you're drinking, Mage?"

"A bit of a sympathetic magic, Sir knight, for an ulcer-demon that's been plaguing me lately."

"Tell me how!" Jim asked again.

"I should think there'd be danger of it giving you a flux," said Brian, frowning. "Children, now . . ."

"I will not tell you!" exploded Carolinus. "Did I spend sixty years to get my degree, only to be demanded an account of my methods at every turn? If I say Saturn is in the ascendant, Saturn *is* in the ascendant. And if I say the maiden is perfectly safe and comfortable, then the maiden is perfectly safe and comfortable. By the Powers!"

He snorted indignantly to himself.

"Listen to me, my young friend," he went on to Jim, draining his cup and tucking it with the flask back out of sight in his robes, "you may have a little kitchen knowledge of Art and Science, but don't let that give you delusions of understanding. You're here for a purpose, which comes into operation after sunrise tomorrow—just like this knight."

"I, too, Mage?" inquired Brian.

"Do you think you just happened to run into our mutual friend, here?" Carolinus asked. "You laymen always think of Chance as a random operative factor. Nonsense! The operations of Chance follow the most rigid rules in the universe. Chance is invariably determined by the point of greatest stress between the other Prime Operators, such as History and Nature—particularly History and Nature, I might say, since as any fool knows, their particular strife makes changes in the pattern almost hourly. Otherwise, the universe would become so orderly we'd all die of sheer boredom. Listen to me, then—"

He pointed a long, bony forefinger at Jim.

"Nature is always at work to establish a balance of factors, which the operation of History is as unfailingly and continuously at work to disturb. The rub to all this lies in the fact that the new balance may always be established at more than one point, and it is in the determination of exactly which point that Chance—as a compensating element—enters the equation. This truth is the basis on which all magic, as a product of Art and Science, is constructed. *Now* do you understand the situation we have here?"

"No," said Jim.

"Oh, go to sleep!" cried Carolinus, throwing up his arms in exasperation.

Jim blinked . . .

. . . And it was morning.

He sat up in amazement and found himself yawning. On the other side of the staff—or wand, as Carolinus had called it—Brian was also sitting up with a look of surprise. Carolinus was already on his feet.

"What happened?" asked Jim.

"I sent you to sleep. What d'you think happened?" retorted Carolinus. He produced his flask and cup, poured himself some milk and drank it down, making a face. "I'm beginning to hate this stuff," he grumbled, putting the utensils back out of sight again. "Still, there's no doubt it's working. Come now!"

He turned snappishly on Jim and Brian.

"On your feet! The sun's been up for an hour and a half and our forces are strongest when the sun is in the ascendant—which means, we have our best chance of conquering before midday."

"Why didn't you wake us up earlier, then?" asked Jim, getting to his feet as Brian also rose.

"Because we had to wait for them to catch up with us."

"Them? What them?" asked Jim. "Who's going to catch up with us?"

"If I *knew* who, exactly," said Carolinus, gnawing on his beard, "I'd have *said* who. All I know is that the situation this morning implies that four more will join our party— Oh, so they're the ones!"

He was staring over Jim's shoulder. Jim turned and saw the approaching forms of Dafydd and Danielle, followed by two dragon shapes a little farther down the causeway.

"Well. well—Master Bowman!" said Brian, heartily. as Dafydd came up. And Mistress Danielle! Good morning!"

"A morrow it is, but whether good or not, I'd not wish to guess," said Dafydd. He looked around. "Where is the wolf, Sir knight?"

A cloud crossed Brian's face.

"You haven't seen him?" Jim asked. "You must have passed him. Some ordinary-sized sandmirks and one particularly large one caught us, and he stayed behind to fight the large one. You must have passed the place where we left them fighting."

"Left them?" cried Danielle.

"It was the wolf demanded it," said Brian, grimly. "We wouldn't have left, otherwise—as I think you might know, mistress!"

"We saw neither him, nor any sign of sandmirks or battle," said Dafydd.

Jim stood silent. It was like absorbing a hard blow to the stomach to hear this, for all that he thought he had faced the fact the day before that he might never see Aragh alive again.

"Just because he asked you," Danielle said, fiercely, "you didn't have to leave him alone to face—"

"Danielle," Carolinus interrupted. She turned to face him.

"Mage!" she said. "You here? But you were a hundred years old even when I was little. You shouldn't be here!"

"I am where I must be," said Carolinus. "As was your wolf; as are Sir James and Sir Brian. Accuse them not. It was the task of Aragh to stay and fight alone, so that these two could come to this place at this time. That's all, and there's no more to be said!"

His old eyes were steady on her. Her own became unhappy, and she turned away from him.

"I'll go look for him . . ." said Jim, half to himself. "As soon as this is all over, I'll go and find him."

"Perhaps," said Carolinus, dryly. He looked past Jim once more. "Good morrow, dragons!"

"Secoh!" Brian exclaimed. "And—who's this?"

"Smrgol, george!" huffed the older dragon. He was approaching with a pronounced limp and with his left wing draped on the back of the mere-dragon. His left eyelid was now drooped almost shut. "Give me a minute to catch my wind! Not as young as I used to be; but I'll be all right in a moment. Look here who I've brought with me!"

"I—I wasn't too keen on coming," stammered Secoh to Jim. "But as your wor— I mean, as you know, your grand-uncle can be pretty persuasive."

"That's right," boomed Smrgol, evidently having recovered the larger share of his breath in the moment of pause while the mere-dragon spoke. "Don't you go calling anybody 'your worship.' Never heard of such stuff!"

Then he turned to Jim, himself.

"And letting a george go in where he didn't dare go, himself! 'Boy,' I said to him, 'don't give me this nonsense about being only a mere-dragon! Mere's got nothing to do with what kind of dragon you are. What kind of world would it be if we all went around talking like that?'"

Smrgol tried to mimic someone talking in a high

voice, but succeeded in lifting his tones only into the middle-bass level.

"'Oh, I'm just a plowland-and-pasture dragon. You'll have to excuse me.—I'm just a halfway-up-the-hill dragon. . . .' 'BOY!' I said to him, 'you're a DRAGON! Get that straight, once and for all time! And a dragon ACTS like a dragon, or he doesn't act at all!'"

"Hear, hear!" said Brian.

"Did you hear that, boy?" Smrgol demanded of the smaller dragon. "Even the george understands *that* fact of life!"

He turned to Brian.

"Don't believe I've met you, george."

"Brian Neville-Smythe," said Brian, "knight bachelor."

"Smrgol. Dragon," said Gorbash's grand-uncle. He ran an approving eye over Neville-Smythe's armor and weapons. "Good harness! Wager you carry your shield somewhat high when fighting on foot."

"Matter of fact, I do. But how did you know?"

"Shiny place there on your rerebrace where the elbow cop's been rubbing back against it. Good shield tactics against another george, but I wouldn't advise you to try it on me. I'd have my tail between your legs and you off your feet in a second."

"Is that a fact?" said Brian, plainly impressed. "Remarkably sporting of you to tell me so! I'll remember that. But aren't you making it rather hard on the next dragon I fight, if it isn't you?"

"Well, I'll tell you," rumbled Smrgol, clearing his throat. "Pardon me—I've been thinking, for some time, that maybe you georges and us dragons could stop fighting and get together. We're really a lot alike in many ways—"

"If you don't mind, Smrgol," cut in Carolinus sourly. "We're not exactly oversupplied with time to chat. It'll be noon in—"

He was interrupted, in his turn, by a cry from Danielle. The rest turned to see her running down the causeway. Limping slowly toward them on three legs was the figure of Aragh.

Danielle reached him and dropped on her knees beside the wolf, hugging him. Sticking out a long tongue, he tried to lick her left ear, which was the closest part of her he could reach, held as he was. After a moment, however, he pulled from her grasp and walked on up to the rest of them, in spite of her efforts to make him lie down and let her examine the broken leg. Only when he had joined the group did he lie down and give in to her.

". . . You ought to know better than to walk on this!" she was saying.

"I didn't walk on it," said Aragh. His jaws grinned evilly at them all. "I walked off it."

"You know what I'm saying!" Danielle flashed. "You know better than to travel on it."

"What else could I do?" he snarled. "I killed the Mother, but the kits are all around us. They want your meat after those in the tower get through with you. They want lots of meat to start feeding up a new mother. None of you can handle them but me. With me beside you here, they'll stay their distance."

"We thought you dead," said Brian, somberly.

"Dead, Sir knight?" Aragh glared at him. "Never count an English wolf dead until you see his bones well bleached by the sun."

"Enough chitchat!" Carolinus snapped. "Time moves, and both Chance and History change. As I was saying, it'll be noon in— When will it be noon, you?"

"Four hours, thirty-seven minutes, twelve seconds, at the second gong," replied the invisible voice Jim had heard before. There was a momentary pause; and then a mellow, chimed note sounded on the air. "Chime, I mean," the voice corrected itself.

Carolinus muttered something under his breath. Then he addressed them all.

"Come on, now," he ordered. "Stay together. And stay behind me!"

He pulled the staff from the ground; and they all moved off in the direction of the tower, Brian now back in Blanchard's saddle since the horse seemed to have ceased his objections to going forward.

With their first steps, however, the day which had dawned as bright, clear and ordinary as any day anywhere, began to cloud and darken and its air to thicken as it had the day before. Swiftly, this time, the mist closed in on the sea side and on the waters to either side of the causeway. The clouds became a solid bank, lowering until they touched the top of the tower, to hang literally no more than a hundred feet over the challengers' heads. The dreary, drab chillness of the day before settled down on the group and added its weight once more to Jim's spirits.

He looked around him.

Surprisingly, none of this strangely assorted bag of individuals who were his Companions appeared to show any sign of being affected by the fresh demonstration of the power of whatever lived in the Loathly Tower. Aragh was limping along on three legs, grumpily assuring Danielle he would lie down, and stay lying down, in a moment so that she could set and splint the broken leg. Carolinus, leading them all, looked as if he was merely out for a brisk walk and his wand was no more than a staff to help him along. Dafydd was carefully untying the cords binding what looked like a plastic tube that had encased the string of his bow against the overnight dampness. After a second's puzzling, Jim suddenly realized that it must be a length of animal gut—probably pig or sheep—which had been carefully cleaned, dried and put to that purpose.

Smrgol marched along quite stoutly, his bad wing and some of his weight bearing on the mere-dragon beside him. On the other side of the old dragon rode Brian, and the two of them were now in earnest conversation.

". . . About this business of people and dragons getting together," said Brian. "It sounds interesting—

must say that. But hardly practical, d'you think? We'd be bound to run into a lot of rock-hard prejudice against, on both sides."

"Got to make a start sometime, george," said Smrgol. "There's times when it'd pay to work together —like now, for instance. Not that you're not right, of course. For example, you'll notice I couldn't get any more of the dragons from our cave to join me here."

"Ah, yes," said Brian, nodding.

"Not that they're fearful, you understand, george. I don't think that for a minute. But when you live for a couple of hundred years—with luck, that is—you hardly feel like risking everything on the first chance that comes along. I'm not excusing it, you understand; it's just the way we are. Knight-erranting may make sense for you georges. Dragon-erranting would make no sense, at all, to us."

"Well, then, where's the hope?"

"The hope's in us—you and me, george—and of course Gorbash here, the Mage, young Secoh alongside me here, that bowman and the female george with him, the wolf, mage and all. If we can pull this off— defeat the Dark Powers, that is, and win a victory— it'll be a tale to tell for five hundred years. Now, I don't know about you georges, but we dragons love tales. That's what we do in the caves, you know, for months on end, lie around telling each other tales."

"Months? Really?" said Brian. "I'd hardly think— months?"

"Months, george! Give a dragon a few pieces of gold and jewels to play with, a good cask of wine to drink and a good story to listen to—and he's happy. Why, if I could count the times I told the story of how I slew the ogre of Gormely Keep, all those years ago— Oh, of course the younger dragons all groan and moan when I mention it; but they curl up, fill their flagons and listen all the same, for all they've heard it time and again."

"Hmm," murmured Brian. "Now that I think of it, we humans do a bit of sitting around and listening to old stories ourselves. Particularly in winter, you know, when it's hard to get about and there's not much to do if you could. By St. Denis, I cut my teeth on some of those old tales—they were one of the things that made me want to be a knight."

"Exactly!" said Smrgol. "Exactly the same with us dragons! Every dragon hearing the tale of how we defeat the Dark Powers here at the tower will want to go out himself and team up with some georges and maybe a wolf or some such, and have a like adventure of his own. From that, it's only a step to working together . . ."

"Tell me something," Jim said to Carolinus, abandoning the knight–dragon conversation to catch up with the magician and walk a half-pace behind him, "what's the price that has to be paid for the magic you used to drive away the darkness yesterday?"

"It's already paid," replied Carolinus. "The first to invoke magic incurs the debit. Counter-magic only balances the ledger. Not so with this—"

He lifted the staff and shook it slightly in the air before Jim's eyes.

"I had to go a long way to get this," he explained. "And I had to mortgage a lifetime of credit with the Auditing Department to make the journey. If we should lose here, I'm destroyed as a mage. But then, if we lose, we're all destroyed, anyway."

"I see," said Jim, soberly. He thought for a minute. "What is it, exactly, that lives in the Loathly Tower?"

"What *lives* there just now, I don't know yet—any more than you do. What *is* there—neither alive nor dead, but just in presence on that spot—is the manifestation of Evil, itself. There's nothing we or anyone else can do to get rid of that. You can't destroy Evil, any more than the creatures of Evil can destroy Good. All you can do is contain one or the other, if you're strong enough, and render it momentarily ineffective in your own situation."

"Then how can we do anything about the Dark Powers . . . ?"

"We can't—as I just said. But we can destroy the creatures, the tools by which Evil is currently working its will. Just as its creatures, for its purpose, will be trying to destroy us."

Jim felt a cold lump in his throat. He swallowed.

"You must have some idea," he said, "of what kind of creatures they'll be, the ones who'll be trying to destroy us."

"We already know who some of them are," Carolinus answered. "Sir Hugh and his men, for example. Also, the sandmirks. In addition—"

He stopped speaking and walking as abruptly as if he were an automaton that had been turned off. Jim checked himself, too, staring at the tower. From the windows just below its ruined battlements, figures had come boiling out—several dozen at least of great-winged, heavy-headed shapes that dipped and swung in the air about the top of the tower, screaming.

For a second they swarmed there, like a cloud of giant gnats. Then one of them swooped down toward the Companions—

And plummeted from the air like a body flung from the top of a cliff, a slim shaft impaling its body. It struck heavily, dead upon the causeway at Jim's feet, its woman's face frozen in a silent, maniacal scream.

Jim turned to see Dafydd standing with a fresh arrow already drawn to his bow. The screaming had cut off, completely and suddenly. Jim looked up and saw that the tower had no longer any swarm about it.

"Indeed, it will be no trouble if they are all of that size and swiftness," said Dafydd, coming forward to reclaim his arrow from the slain harpy. "A child could not miss at such a distance!"

"Don't mislead yourself, Master Bowman," said Carolinus over his shoulder as he began to walk forward once more. "It won't be anything like that easy with the others—"

He had turned his head west again as he spoke, and once more he broke off, stopping sharply. He stared down at a patch of grass in which, apparently, something lay hidden. Above the long beard his old face grew bony and grim. Jim stepped forward to see what had caused the magician's reaction.

With a shuddering wave of nausea, he twisted his head away again, just as the others came up to look. Lying in the grass before them was what had once been a man in armor.

Jim heard Brian's deep intake of breath as he sat on Blanchard.

"A most foul death," said the knight, softly, "most foul . . . most foul . . ."

Getting down from Blanchard, the knight went down on his armored knees beside the dead body in the grass, joining his steel gauntlets in prayer. The dragons were silent. Dafydd and Danielle stood with Aragh, none of them saying anything.

Only Carolinus, among the humans, bent his fierce old eyes on the scene before them with something besides horror. The magician poked with his staff at a wide trail of slime that led around and over the body and back in the direction of the tower. It was the sort of trail a garden slug leaves; only, to leave such a trail the slug would have had to be two feet wide where it touched the ground.

"A worm . . ." said Carolinus to himself. "But it was no worm that killed this man so. Worms are mindless. Something with great strength and patience plucked and crushed, in that slow fashion—"

He stared at Smrgol suddenly; and Smrgol bobbed his massive head in an oddly embarrassed gesture.

"I didn't say it, Mage," the old dragon protested.

"It'll be best none of us says it until we're sure," retorted the magician. "Come along!"

Brian rose from beside the corpse; made a small, helpless gesture over it, as if he wished to straighten out the limbs but saw the utter futility of bringing anything like decent order to what remained; and climbed back on Blanchard. The group went on up the causeway to perhaps a hundred yards from the tower; and here Carolinus stopped, driving his wand once more into the earth so that it stood upright.

Aragh dropped, panting, into a lying position and Danielle, getting to her knees beside him, began to set and splint his leg, using some dry, fallen limbs from a stunted tree nearby and a sleeve of her doublet cut into strips.

"Now," said Carolinus; and the word tolled on Jim's ear like the sound of a bell.

The mist had closed in on them. Whiteness was on all sides and close overhead. Only the tiny plain where they stood below the tumbled boulders of the tower hill, the boulders themselves and the tower were clear of it. Or was it quite clear? Tendrils of mist drifted above it below the clouds, and something about the air and the light filtering through the clouds themselves baffled the eyes and made it hard to focus on any one thing.

"As long as my wand and I stand," said Carolinus, "no power of theirs can completely take from us light, breath or strength of will. But stay within the space the wand keeps clear, or it and I may not be able to protect you. Let our enemies come to us here."

"Where are they?" asked Jim, glancing around.

"Patience," said Carolinus, sardonically, "they'll come soon enough; and not in such form as you may expect."

Jim looked around himself at the causeway's end: the boulders and the tower. No breeze stirred from out of the mist. The air was heavy and still. No, it was not exactly still; it seemed to shiver faintly, with a quivering unnaturalness, like that of an atmosphere dancing to heat waves. Only, here it was all dim, wintry and chill. As Jim noted this trembling of the air, there came to his ears—from where, he did not know—a high-pitched, dizzy singing like that which sometimes accompanies delirium or high fever.

When he looked again at the tower, it seemed to him that the appearance of the structure itself was distorted by these happenings. Although it had seemed only an ancient, ruined shell of a building, between one heartbeat and the next it had appeared to change.

Almost, but not quite, he thought he caught glimpses of it unbroken and alive, thronged about with half-seen figures. His heart thudded more strongly; and the causeway and the tower upon it seemed to shake with every contraction of his chest, seemed to go in and out of focus, in and out, in and out . . .

Then he saw Angie.

He knew he was too far from the tower to see her as clearly as he now saw her. At this distance, in this light, her face should have been hard to make out. But he saw her both from a distance and as if from close up, with a sharp and perfect clarity. She stood in the slight shadow of a ruined doorway opening on a balcony halfway up the side of the tower. Her blouse stirred to the slow movement of her breath. Her calm blue eyes stared closely into him. Her lips were half parted.

"Angie!" he cried.

He had not realized how much he had missed her. He had not understood how much he had wanted her. He took a step forward and found his way blocked by something as unyielding as an iron bar set in posts of concrete. He looked down. It was only the length of the wand, held in the old arm of Carolinus, but it was a barrier beyond his strength to pass.

"Where?" Carolinus demanded.

"There! On the balcony of the tower, there! See?" Jim pointed; and the others lifted their heads to peer where he indicated. "In the doorway! Can't you see? Up on the side of the tower, in the doorway!"

"Not a thing!" said Brian, gruffly, dropping the hand with which he had been shading his eyes.

"Maybe," said the mere-dragon, doubtfully. "Maybe . . . back in the shadows, there. I'm not sure, really . . ."

"Jim," said Angie.

"There!" cried Jim. "You hear her?"

He pushed the restraining staff once again. But it was no use.

"I can hear you, Angie!" he shouted.

"You don't have to raise your voice," she answered, softly. "I can hear you, too. Jim, it's all right. It's just all those others that don't belong here. If you come up by yourself and get me, I can leave, and we can go home and everything will be fine."

"I can't!" cried Jim, almost sobbing, for Carolinus' staff would still not let him pass. "They won't let me go!"

"They've got no right to keep you, Jim. Ask the Mage what right he has to keep you, and he'll have to let you go. Ask him, and then come up here by yourself to get me."

Jim turned, raging, on Carolinus.

"What right—?" he began.

"STOP!" Carolinus' voice went off like a cannon exploding in Jim's ears.

It dizzied, deafened and half blinded him, so that vision and hearing were blocked as if by thick, soft barriers. His unnaturally keen vision and hearing of Angie were gone, but he could still make himself think he saw her—as a shadow-in-shadow in the doorway behind a balcony on the tower.

"Why?" Jim turned on Carolinus in fury.

The magician did not back off an inch. His dark eyes glittered above his white beard.

"By the Powers!" he shouted, and *his* words came very clearly to Jim's ears. "Will you walk blindly into the very first trap They set for you?"

"What trap?" Jim demanded. "I was just talking to Angie—!"

The sentence broke off on his lips as Carolinus swung his staff to point. About the base of the tower, between it and the boulders on the slope, had just arisen the wicked head of a dragon as large as Jim himself.

Smrgol's thunderous bellow split the strangely singing air.

"Bryagh! Traitor! Thief—inchworm! Come down here!"

The distant dragon opened his mouth. His booming answer rolled down to them.

"Tell us about Gormely Keep, old bag of bones!" he thundered. "Ancient mud puppy, fat lizard, scare us with words!"

"Why, you—" Smrgol lurched forward.

"Hold!" shouted Carolinus; and Smrgol reared high, checking himself, his heavy foreclaws digging deep into the sandy soil as his body came down.

"True . . ." he rumbled, his eyes hot.

"Old iguana! Go sleep in the sun!" Bryagh taunted.

But the older dragon now turned away, without answering, to the magician.

"What's hidden, Mage?" he asked.

"We'll see."

Carolinus' voice was tight. He raised his staff and brought it down endwise, three times, on the earth. With each impact the whole causeway seemed to shake.

Up among the rocks, one particularly large boulder tottered and rolled out of the way. Jim's breath shuddered in his throat and he heard Brian, behind him, grunt hoarsely. Secoh cried out on a thin, sharp note.

In the space that the dislodged boulder had revealed, a huge, slug-like head lifted from the ground. It raised up even higher as they watched, yellow-brown in the harsh sunlight, its two sets of horns searching as its upper body waved from side to side, revealing a light external shell, a platelet with the merest hint of a spire. Its horns twitched and the eyes on the end of the primary pair aimed themselves at the group below. Slowly, it began to creep down the slope toward them, leaving a glistening trail on boulders and sand behind it.

"The Worm," said Carolinus, softly.

". . . that can be killed," growled Smrgol, thoughtfully. "Though not easily. Blast it, I wish it were Bryagh alone!"

"Nor is it those two alone." Carolinus struck at the ground three times again.

"Come forth!" he cried, his old voice piping high on the quivering air. "By the Powers! Come forth!"

And then they saw it.

From behind the great barricade of enormous rocks near the top of the tower hill, there slowly raised a bald and glistening dome of hairless gray skin. Gradually, this revealed two perfectly round blue eyes, below which was exposed no proper nose but, instead, two air slits side by side, as if the whole of the bare, enormous skull was covered with a simple sheet of thick skin. As it rose still farther, this unnatural head—as big around as a beach ball—showed its wide and idiotically grinning mouth, entirely lipless and with two jagged but matching rows of pointed teeth.

With a clumsy, studied motion, the whole creature rose to its feet and stood among the boulders. It was man-like in shape, but was clearly nothing ever spawned by the human race. A good twelve feet in height it stood, a rough patchwork of untanned hides studded with bones, bits of metal and clusters of tiny color points that could have been gems and made a kilt around its thick waist.

But this was not the extent of its difference from the race of man. It had, to begin with, no neck at all. Its unnatural hairless, near-featureless head was balanced like an apple atop perfectly square shoulders of gray, coarse-looking skin. Its torso was one straight trunk, from which arms and legs sprouted with disproportionate thickness and roundness, like sections of pipe. Its knees were hidden by its kilt and its lower legs by the rocks; but the elbows of its oversize arms had unnatural hinges to them, while the lower arms were almost as large as the upper and near-wristless, and the hands themselves awkward, thick-fingered parodies of the human extremities, with only three digits, one of which was a single-jointed, opposed thumb.

The right hand held a club, bound with rusty metal, that surely not even such a monster should have been able to lift. Yet one thick, crook-fingered hand hefted it lightly, as deftly as Carolinus had carried his staff.

The monster opened its mouth.

"He!" it went. *"He! He!"*

The sound was chilling. It was an incredibly bass titter, if such a thing can be imagined. And though the tone was about that of the low note of a three-valve tuba, it clearly came from the creature's upper throat and head. Nor was there any real humor in it. Having sounded its voice, the monster fell silent, watching the advance of the great slug with its round, light blue eyes.

Jim found his dragon jaws open, panting like a dog after a long run. Beside him, Smrgol stirred slowly.

"Yes," he rumbled sadly, almost as if to himself, "what I was afraid of. An ogre."

In the silence that followed, Sir Brian got down from Blanchard and began to tighten the girths of his saddle.

"So, so, Blanchard," he crooned, softly. But the large white horse was trembling so violently it could not stand still. Brian shook his head, and his hands fell from the girths. "I must fight on foot, it seems," he said.

The rest were watching Carolinus. The magician leaned on his staff, looking very old indeed, the lines looking even deeper in the ancient skin of his face. He had been watching the ogre, but now he turned back to Jim and the other two dragons.

"I'd hoped all along," he said, "that it needn't come to this. However"—he waved his hand at the approaching worm, the now-silent Bryagh and the watching ogre—"as you see, the world goes never the way we want it, but must be haltered and led."

He winced, produced his flask and cup, and took a drink of milk. Putting the utensils back again, he turned to Dafydd.

249

"Master Bowman," he said, almost formally. "The harpies are again in the tower, but when the others attack they'll be out again. See how the clouds overhead now sag down from the tower's height."

He pointed upward. It was true: the cloud cover now bellied down like the worn-out ceiling of some ancient room. The thick, eye-baffling vapor hung less than thirty feet above their heads.

"The harpies will come diving swiftly out of that cover," said the magician, "giving you all but no time whatsoever to shoot before they're on you. Do you think you can hit them with those arrows of yours under such conditions?"

Dafydd cocked an eye upward.

"If the clouds come no lower——" he began.

"They cannot," said Carolinus. "The power of my staff holds them at no closer than this."

"Then," Dafydd replied, "provided they come no faster than the one I shot a short while ago, I have a fair chance, look you. I do not say that one may not get through, for I am but a man, after all—though there have been those who thought I was something more, with bow and arrow. But it is a fair chance I can put a shaft through each of them before it can do us harm."

"Good!" said Carolinus. "More than a fair chance, none of us can ask for. Don't forget that their bite is poisonous, however, even when the harpy itself is dead."

He turned back to Brian.

"I'd suggest, Sir Brian," he said, "particularly since you're to be on foot, that you take the worm. You'll be most useful that way. I know you'd prefer that renegade dragon, but the worm is the greater danger to the others who have no armor."

"Difficult to slay, I imagine?" queried the knight, stopping from adjusting the armstrap on the inner face of his shield to squint up the slope at the approaching slug shape.

"Its vital organs are hidden deep inside it," Car-

250

olinus explained, "and, being mindless, it will fight on long after being mortally wounded. Cut off those eye stalks and blind it first, if you can."

"What—" Jim began, then found his voice hampered by the dry throat. He had to swallow before he could continue. "What am I supposed to do?"

"Why fight the ogre, boy! Fight the ogre!" roared Smrgol; and the inhuman giant up on the slope, hearing him, shifted his round-eyed gaze from the worm to fasten it on the old dragon. "And I'll take on that louse of a Bryagh. The george here'll chop up the worm, the Bowman'll deal with the harpies, the Mage'll hold back the evil influences, the wolf keep off the sandmirks—and that'll be that!"

Jim opened his mouth to cure Gorbash's granduncle of what seemed a bad case of false optimism—then suddenly realized that it was nothing of the kind. Smrgol was deliberately trying to pass the matter off lightly in order to put heart in Jim. This, when the old dragon was himself half dead and certainly no match for the powerful young Bryagh.

Suddenly Jim felt as if his heart had turned over in his chest. He looked around him at the others. If the old and crippled Smrgol was no match for Bryagh, was Brian any more a match for that obscene worm now only about thirty yards off? Was it a fair match, Aragh on three legs, for all the wolf's indifference to their chittering, against the horde of small sandmirks that remained alive? And Dafydd, miracle archer that he was, how could he hope to shoot down without error harpies that could appear practically on top of him without warning? Finally, was it fair to expect the old magician by himself to hold down all the impalpable evil in this place while the battles were going on?

Jim himself had a good reason for being here: Angie. But the others were here primarily because of him, involved by him in a fight where the odds would all be against them. Guilt moved deep inside Jim and weakened his legs. He turned to the knight.

"Brian," he said. "You and the others don't need to do this—"

251

"Lord, yes!" replied the knight, busy with his equipment. "Worms, ogres—one fights them when one runs into them, you know."

He considered his spear and put it aside.

"No, not as long as I'm to be on foot," he murmured to himself.

"Smrgol," Jim said, turning to the dragon, "don't you see? Bryagh's a lot younger than you. And you're not well—"

"Er . . ." Secoh muttered, hastily, and broke down in what seemed to be embarrassment and confusion.

"Speak up, boy!" rumbled Smrgol.

"Well . . ." stammered the mere-dragon, "it's just —wh-what I mean is, I couldn't bring myself to fight that worm or that ogre. I really couldn't. I just sort of go to pieces when I think of one of them getting close to me. But I could, well, fight another dragon. It wouldn't be quite so bad—not so frightening, I mean —if that dragon up there were to break my neck . . ."

He broke down and stammered incoherently.

"I know I'm sounding silly . . ."

"Nonsense! Good lad!" bellowed Smrgol. "Glad to have you! I can't quite get into the air myself at the moment—still a bit stiff. But if you could fly over and work that sea lizard down this way, where I can get a grip on him, we'll stretch him out for the buzzards."

He dealt the mere-dragon a tremendous thwack with his tail by way of congratulations, almost knocking the other off his feet.

Jim turned back to Carolinus.

"There's no retreat," said the magician, before Jim could speak. "This is a game of chess where, if one piece withdraws, all on his side fall. Hold back the creatures, all of you, and I'll hold back the forces; for the creatures will finish me if you go down and the forces finish you if they get me."

"Now, look here, Gorbash!" Smrgol shouted in Jim's ear. "That worm's almost down here. Let me tell you something about how to fight ogres, based on experience. You listening, boy?"

"Yes," said Jim, numbly.

"I know you've heard the other dragons calling me an old windbag when I wasn't around. But I *have* conquered an ogre—the only one of our race to do it in the last eight hundred years. They haven't. So pay attention, if you want to win your own fight."

Jim nodded.

"All right," he said.

"Now, the first thing to know"—Smrgol glanced at the oncoming worm and lowered his voice confidentially—"is about the bones in an ogre."

"Never mind the details," said Jim. "What do I *do?*"

"In a minute, in a minute . . ." Smrgol answered. "Don't get excited, boy. An excited dragon is a losing dragon. Now, about the bones in an ogre. The thing to remember is that they're big—matter of fact, in the arms and legs they're mainly bone. So there's no use trying to bite clear through. What you want to do is get the muscle—that's tough enough, as it is—and hamstring. That's point one."

He paused to look significantly at Jim. Jim managed with an effort to keep his mouth shut and be patient.

"Now, point two," Smrgol went on. "Also connected with bones. Notice the elbows on that ogre. They aren't like a george's elbows. They're what you might call double-jointed. Why? Simply because, with the big bones they've got to have and the muscle on them, they'd never be able to bend a bone more than halfway up before the bottom part'd bump the top, if they had a george-type joint. Now, the point of all this is that when that ogre swings his club, he can only swing it in one way with that elbow. That's up and down. If he wants to swing it side to side, he's got to use his shoulder. Consequently, if you can catch him with his club down and to one side of his body, you've got an advantage; it takes him two moves to get it back up and in line again—instead of one, like a george does."

"Yes, yes . . ." said Jim, watching the advance of the worm.

"Don't get impatient, boy! Keep cool! Now, his knees don't have that double joint, so if you can knock him off his feet you've got a real advantage. But don't try that unless you're sure you can do it; because once he gets his arms around you, you're a goner. The only way to fight him is in and out—fast. Wait for his swing, dodge it, dive in while his arm is down, tear him up, get back out again. Got it?"

"Got it," said Jim, numbly.

"Good! Whatever you do, remember, don't let him get his grip on you. And don't pay any attention to what's happening to the rest of us, no matter what you think you hear or see out of the corner of your eyes. It's everyone for himself, once things start. Concentrate on your own foe. And, boy . . ."

"Yes?" Jim answered.

"Keep your head!" The old dragon's voice was almost pleading. "Whatever you do, don't let your dragon-instinct get in there and run away with you. That's why the georges have been winning against us all these years, the way they have. Just remember you're faster than that ogre and that your brain'll win for you if you stay clear, keep your head and don't rush. I tell you, boy—"

He was interrupted by a sudden cry of joy from Brian, who had been rummaging around in the panniers behind Blanchard's saddle.

"I say," shouted Brian, running up to Jim with surprising lightness and agility, considering the weight of his armor. "The most marvelous stroke of luck! Look what I just found!"

He waved a wispy length of white cloth at Jim.

"What?" Jim demanded, his heart leaping.

"Geronde's favor! And just in time, too. Be a good fellow, will you," Brian went on, turning to Carolinus, "and tie it about my vambrace, here on the shield arm . . . Thank you, Mage."

Carolinus looked grim, but nonetheless tucked his wand into the crook of one arm and with his freed hands fastened the cloth around the armor of Brian's left forearm. Brian turned about, drove his spear into the ground and tethered Blanchard's bridle to it. Then, catching up his shield position, he turned back and drew his sword with his other hand. The bright blade gleamed even in the dull light. He leaned forward to throw the weight of his armor before him; and ran at the worm, which was now hardly more than a dozen feet away.

"A Neville-Smythe! A Neville-Smythe! Geronde!" he shouted as they came together.

Jim heard but did not witness the impact of their collison. For just then everything began to happen at once. Up on the hill, Bryagh screamed suddenly in fury and launched himself down the slope and into the air, wings spread like some great bomber gliding in for a crash landing. Behind Jim was the frenzied flapping of leathery wings as Secoh took to the air to meet him—but this was drowned by a sudden, short, deep-chested and grunting cry, like a wordless shout. Lifting his club, the ogre had stepped clear of the boulders, coming straight down the hill with heavy, ground-covering strides.

"Good luck, boy!" said Smrgol in Jim's ear. "And Gorbash—"

Something in the other's voice made Jim turn his head to look at him. The ferocious mouth-pit and enormous fangs were close to him, but behind them Jim read an unusual expression of affection and concern in the dark dragon-eyes.

"Remember," Smrgol said, almost softly, "that you are a descendant of Ortosh and Agtval, and of Gleingul who slew the sea serpent on the tide banks of the Gray Sands. And be, therefore, valiant. But remember, too, you are my only living kin and the last of our line—and be careful!"

The old dragon's voice stumbled and choked. It seemed to struggle for a fraction of a second before it went on.

"And—er—good luck to you, too—er—James!"

Then Smrgol's head was jerked away as he swung

about to face Secoh and Bryagh, who came crashing to earth entangled together, almost on top of him. Jim, turning back toward the tower, had only time to take to the air himself before the rushing ogre was upon him.

He had lifted on his wings without thinking, out of his dragon-instinct when attacked. He was aware of the ogre before him, halting now, its enormous gray feet digging deep into the ground. The rusty-banded club flashed before Jim's eyes and he felt a heavy blow high on his chest that swept him backward through the air.

He flailed with his wings to regain balance. The oversize idiot face was grinning only a couple of yards from him. The club swept up for another blow. Panicked, Jim scrambled aside in midair, retreating, and saw the ogre sway forward a step. Again the club lashed out—quick! How could something so big and clumsy looking be so quick with its hands? Jim felt himself smashed out of the air down to the ground, and a lance of bright pain shot through his right shoulder. For a second a thick-skinned forearm loomed over him and his teeth met in it without thought.

He was shaken like a rat by a terrier, and flung clear. His wings beat for the safety of altitude and he found himself about sixteen feet off the ground, staring down at the ogre, who grunted and shifted the club to strike upward. Jim cupped air with his wings, flung himself backward and avoided the blow. The club whistled through the unfeeling air; and, sweeping forward, Jim ripped with his teeth at one great shoulder before beating clear. The ogre turned to face him, still grinning. But now blood welled and trickled down where Jim's teeth had torn, high on the shoulder.

Abruptly, Jim realized something.

His panic was gone. He was no longer afraid. He hung in the air, just out of the ogre's reach, poised to take advantage of any opening; and a heat of energy, a sharpness of perception was coursing all through him. He was discovering that, with fights—as with a great many similar things—it was only the beforehand part that was bad. Once battle was joined, several million years of instinct took over and there was no time or thought for anything but confronting the enemy.

So it was, now.

The ogre moved in on him again and that was his last intellectualization of the fight; for everything else was lost in the moment-to-moment efforts to avoid being killed and, if possible, to kill, himself.

It was a long, blurred time—about which, later, he had no clear memory. The sun marched up the long arc of the heavens and crossed the midday point and headed down again. On the torn, sandy soil of the causeway he and the ogre turned and feinted, smashed and struck at each other. Sometimes he was in the air, sometimes on the ground. Once he had the monster down on one knee, but could not press his advantage. At another time they had fought halfway up the slope to the tower and the ogre had pinned him in a cleft between two huge boulders. The club was hefted for the final blow that would smash Jim's skull. Then he had somehow wriggled free, between the very legs of his opponent; and the battle was on again.

Now and then, throughout the fight, he would catch brief kaleidoscopic glimpses of the combats being waged about him: Brian, wrapped about by the blind body of the worm, its eye stalks now hacked away, and the knight striving in silence to draw free his sword and sword arm, which were pinned to his body by the worm's encircling form. Or there would roll briefly into Jim's vision a tangled, roaring tumble of flailing, leathery wings and serpentine bodies that was Smrgol, Bryagh, and the mere-dragon. Once or twice he had a momentary view of Carolinus, still standing erect, his staff upright in his hand, his long white beard flowing forward over his gown, like some old seer in the hour of Armageddon. Then the gross body of the ogre would blot out his vision and he would forget all but what was before him.

The day faded. A mist pressed inward from the sea and fled in little wisps and tatters across the battlefield. Jim's body ached and his wings felt leaden. But the ever-grinning ogre and his sweeping club seemed neither to weaken nor to slow. Jim drew back in the air for a moment, to catch his breath; and in that second he heard a voice cry out.

"Time is short!" it called, in cracked tones. "We are running out of time! The day is nearly gone!"

It was the voice of Carolinus.

Jim had never heard it raised before with such a desperate accent. Even as he identified it, he realized that it had sounded clearly to his ears—and that for some time now, upon the causeway, except for the ogre and himself there was silence.

He had been driven back down from the slope to the area from which he had started. To one side of him, the snapped ends of Blanchard's bridle dangled limply from the earth-thrust spear to which Brian had tethered the horse before advancing against the worm. A little off from the spearshaft—from which the terrified horse had evidently broken free—stood Carolinus, leaning heavily on his staff, his old face shrunken, almost mummified in appearance, as if life had been all but drained from it.

Jim turned back to see the ogre nearly upon him once more. The heavy club swung high, dark and enormous in the dying day. Jim felt in his limbs and wings a weakness that would not let him dodge in time; and with all his strength, he gathered himself and sprang instead up under the sweep of the monster's weapon and inside the grasp of those cannon-barrel-thick arms.

The club glanced off Jim's spine and he felt the ogre's arms go around him, the double triad of bone-thick fingers searching for his neck. He was caught, but his rush had knocked the ogre off its feet.

Together they rolled over and over, on the sandy earth, the ogre gnawing with his jagged teeth at Jim's chest and striving to break the spine or twist the neck, while Jim's tail lashed futilely about.

As they rolled against the standing spear and snapped it in half, the ogre found his neck hold and commenced to twist Jim's neck as if it was a chicken's being wrung in slow motion.

A wild despair flooded through Jim. He had been cautioned by Smrgol never to let the ogre get his arms around him. He had disregarded that advice and now was lost, the battle was lost. Stay away, Smrgol had warned, use your brains . . .

But the wild hope of a long chance sprang suddenly to life in him. His head was twisted back over his shoulder and he could see only the darkening mist above him; but he stopped fighting the ogre and groped about with both forepaws. For a moment of eternity, he located nothing—and then something hard nudged his right foreclaw, a glint of bright metal flashed before his eyes. He gripped what he had touched, clamping down on it as firmly as his clumsy claws would allow—

And, with every ounce of strength that was left to him, he drove the broken half of the snapped spear deep into the middle of the ogre, who now sprawled above him.

The great body bucked and shuddered. A wild scream burst from the idiot mouth beside Jim's ear. The ogre let go, staggered back and up, and tottered to its feet, towering above Jim as the stone edifice itself towered above them both.

Again, the ogre screamed, stumbling about like a drunken man, fumbling at the broken end of the spear that was sticking out of him. Jerking at the shaft, he screamed again; and lowering his unnatural head, bit at it like a wounded animal. It splintered in his teeth. He then screamed a final time and fell to his knees. Slowly, like a bad actor in an old-fashioned movie, he rolled over on his side and drew up his legs like someone with a cramp. An ultimate scream was drowned in the bubbling in his throat; black blood trickled from his mouth. He lay still.

Unsteadily, Jim crawled to his feet and looked about him.

The mists were, oddly, drawing back from the causeway and the thin light of late afternoon stretched long across the bouldered slope, the tower above it and the small plain below. In the rusty light, Jim saw that the worm was dead, literally hacked in two. Aragh lay, grinning, a splint on his broken leg. Brian, in bloody, dented armor, leaned wearily on a twisted sword not more than a few feet from Carolinus. Dafydd was down, his shirt half torn off, the shape of a harpy sprawled motionless across his chest. Danielle stood above him, an arrow still notched to her own bow. As Jim watched her, she slowly lowered her weapon, cast it aside and dropped down beside the Welshman.

A little further off, Secoh raised a bloody neck and head above the motionless, locked-together bodies of Smrgol and Bryagh. The mere-dragon stared dazedly at Jim. Jim moved painfully, over to him.

Looking down at the two immense dragons, he saw that Smrgol lay with his jaws locked in Bryagh's throat. The neck of the younger dragon was broken.

"Smrgol . . ." Jim croaked.

"No . . ." gasped Secoh. "No good! He's gone . . . I led the other one to him. He got his grip—and then he never let go . . ." The mere-dragon burst into sobs and lowered his head.

"They all fought well," creaked a strange, harsh voice.

Jim turned and saw the knight standing at his shoulder. Brian's face was as white as sea foam below the now-helmetless tousled brown hair. The flesh of his features seemed fallen in to the bones, like the face of an old man. He swayed as he stood.

"We have won," said Carolinus. "At a price!"

He turned to Danielle. Jim and the knight turned

with him. She was still beside Dafydd; but she had pulled the harpy from Dafydd's upper body, and the shreds of his shirt. Brian's helm, now filled with water from beside the causeway, was with her and she was gently sponging a red tear that ran from near the joining of Dafydd's neck and left shoulder to his middle ribs.

Jim, the magician and the knight walked together to stand over the two of them. With his shirt off, Dafydd's upper body looked twice as large as it had, clothed. It was a sculptor's find of a chest: the shoulders lay back, square and incredibly broad of bone, and powerful muscle lay in cables across the bowman's lean torso from the pectorals to the abdominals, as if molded by an anatomist building a display model. But the body was limp now, and still.

"Indeed," said Dafydd to Danielle, so faintly that, had it not been for the utter stillness now all about them, the three watchers would not have understood him, "you are wishing the impossible. As the Mage said, their bite is death, and I feel that death now in me."

"No," said Danielle, sponging away at the ragged slash the harpy's teeth had made in him.

"But it is so," Dafydd insisted, "though I wish it were not so, for that I love you. But to every bowman comes death, in time. I have always known this, and am content."

"You are no longer merely a bowman." Danielle's voice was steady and composed. "I made you a knight and you are a knight; and as a knight, it's ungentlemanly of you to take leave without my permission. And I do not wish you to go. I will not let you go!"

With a strength that startled Jim, for all that Brian had told him about how she pulled a hundred-pound warbow, Danielle lifted his upper body easily in her arms, laid his head against her shoulder and held him to her.

"I have you," she said; and though her eyes were perfectly dry and her voice quite calm, almost businesslike, the sound of it wrung Jim's very guts, "and I'll never give you to anything else—even to death —unless you want to leave me. You have to tell me you want to leave me, or else you can't die."

Dafydd smiled faintly.

"Indeed . . ." he said; and in that moment after, in which he said nothing, Jim was ready to believe that the single, faintly breathed word had been his last.

But the bowman spoke again.

"Then it's true, that you really wish me to live. If so then death must come get me against my will, which I do not think it or any other thing can do, since never have I been forced against my will nor shall be now, look you."

He closed his eyes, turned his head a little to rest against her breast and said nothing more. But his chest continued slowly to rise and fall steadily.

"He'll live," Carolinus said to Danielle. "He asked no price for coming here, and not even the Auditing Department can ask a price of him, now that he's helped win this day."

The girl did not answer the magician, but bowed her head above Dafydd's slowly moving chest and sat holding him as if she would sit there forever, if necessary. Jim, Brian and the magician turned back to Aragh, and to Secoh, who had conquered the explosion of his grief and now sat quietly above the body of Smrgol.

"We have won," said Carolinus. "Not again in our lifetimes will this place gather strength enough to break out against the world."

He turned to Jim.

"And now, James," he said. You wanted to go home. The way is open."

"Good," said Jim.

"Home?" asked Brian. "Now?"

"Now," said Carolinus. "He has wished from the beginning to return to his own place, Sir knight. Fear not, the dragon who's the original owner of this body James has been wearing will remember all that's happened here and be your friend."

262

"Fear?" Brian somehow managed to dig up a spark of energy to spend on hauteur. "I fear no dragon, dammit! It's just that . . . I shall miss you, James!"

Staring at Brian, Jim saw the knight's eyes unexpectedly brimming with tears. He had forgotten learning, in his studies of the European Middle Ages, that people cried then as naturally as they laughed; his own self-conscious twentieth-century self felt acute embarrassment at the sight.

"Well, you know . . ." he muttered.

"Well, well, James," said Brian, wiping his eyes on a trailing end of Geronde de Chaney's favor. "What must, must! In any case, in respect to the old boy here"—he nodded at the dead Smrgol—"I'm going to see what can be done about this dragon–human alliance business, so I'll be seeing a fair amount of whoever owns this body you've been in, and it'll be somewhat like having you around, in any case."

"He was great!" burst out Secoh, staring at the body of the old dragon at his feet. "He made me strong— for the first time in my life. Anything he wanted, I'd do it!"

"You come along with me, then, to vouch for the dragon end of things," said Brian. "Well, James. I suppose it's good-bye, then—"

"Angie!" cried Jim, suddenly remembering. "Oh— excuse me, Brian. But I just remembered. I've got to go get her out of the tower."

He spun around.

"Wait!" said Carolinus.

The magician turned to face the edifice itself; and raised his wand.

"Deliver!" he cried. "You are vanquished. Deliver!"

They waited.

Nothing happened.

Chapter 22

Carolinus struck his wand once more, end-wise, upon the hard sand.

"Deliver!" he cried.

Once more they waited. The slow seconds stretched out into minutes.

"By the Powers!" Suddenly, strength seemed to have flowed back into S. Carolinus. His voice was once more full and he looked to have grown six inches. "Are we to be flouted? *Auditing Department!*"

Something happened then that Jim was never to forget. The memorability of it lay not in what happened, but in the quality of the event. Without warning, the whole earth spoke—the sea spoke—the sky spoke! And they all spoke with the same, single, bass voice that had responded from thin air to Carolinus before, when Jim was present. This time, however, nothing was apologetic or humorous about the voice.

"DELIVER!" it said.

Almost in the same second, something dark came swiftly out of the blackness of the arched, ground-level entrance to the tower. Drifting down the slope toward them, it seemed to float; but it arrived more quickly than its leisurely velocity indicated. It was a mattress of intertwined fir boughs, the needles still fresh and green upon them; and on that mattress Angie lay, her eyes closed.

The mattress reached them and settled to the ground at Jim's feet.

"Angie!" he exclaimed, bending over her.

For a moment a deep fear had stirred in him; but

then he saw that she was breathing steadily and calmly, as if only sleeping. In fact, as he watched, she opened her eyes and looked up at him.

"Jim!" she said.

Scrambling to her feet, she threw her arms around his scaly neck and hung on to him. Jim's heart did a flip-flop in his chest. His conscience ripped him like a bandsaw for not having thought of her more during the past days, for not having managed to come for her sooner.

"Angie . . ." he murmured tenderly—and then something struck him. "Angie, how did you know it was me, and not some other dragon?"

She let go and looked up at him, laughing.

"Know it was you!" she exclaimed. "How could I miss, after all this time in your head—"

She broke off suddenly and stared down at herself.

"Oh, I'm back in my own body, again! That's better. That's much better!"

"Head? Body?" Jim's mind wobbled between two incredible questions; and finally chose the one that sounded the more ominous. "Angie, whose body were you in?"

"Yours, of course," she said. "That is, I was in your mind, which was in your body—or Gorbash's body, to be exact. At least, I *was*—unless I'm dreaming now. No, there they all are, just the way they should be: Brian, Dafydd, Danielle and the rest."

"But how could you be in my mind?" demanded Jim.

"The Dark Powers, or whatever they call themselves, put me there," said Angie. "I didn't catch on, at first. Right after Bryagh brought me here, I got sleepy and lay down on those fir branches. The next thing I knew, I was in your head—seeing everything that was going on. I could tell what you were thinking, and I could almost talk to you. At first I thought some accident had happened; or maybe Grottwold had been trying to bring us back and got us mixed up together this time. Then I caught on."

"Caught on?"

"The Dark Powers had put me there."

"The Dark Powers?" Jim asked.

"Of course," said Angie, calmly. "They were hoping I'd want to be rescued so badly that I'd keep trying to push you to come to the Loathly Tower here, alone. When I was about half asleep, I thought I heard some voice or other talking to Bryagh about ways of getting you to come after me without Companions to help you."

"How did they know?" Jim frowned.

"I don't know, but they did," said Angie. "So, when I remembered that, it wasn't hard to guess who'd put me in your mind, and why. As I say, I couldn't really *talk* to you, but I could make you feel the way I was feeling, if I sort of pushed hard enough, mentally. Remember when Brian told you he had to get Geronde's permission to be a Companion of yours and you would both have to go to Castle Malvern, first? You remember how you suddenly felt guilty about turning your back on the tower, with me there? Well, that was me in your mind. I'd just woken up there, and didn't realize why. Then it hit me that you might be in pretty terrible danger going on to the tower alone, if Carolinus had insisted you get some Companions before trying it; and I remembered what I'd heard when I was falling asleep. I put two and two together, and stopped wishing you'd come to rescue me. The moment I did that, I could tell that you began to feel better about going with Brian to Castle Malvern."

She ceased talking. Jim stared at her, too full of questions to sort out what he wanted to ask first. Now that he had a moment to notice, he realized that apparently Angie had grown in translating to this other world. He had thought of Danielle as tall, but now he saw that Angie was equally so. Not that she looked any the worse for the increase in size. To the contrary—

Carolinus clicked his tongue.

"Two minds in one body!" he said, shaking his

266

head. "Highly irregular! Highly! Even for the Dark Powers, that's taking a chance. Could be done, of course; but—"

"But wait!" Jim had found his voice. "Angie, you said Gorbash was in my mind, too? How could he be?"

"I don't know how, but he was," Angie said. "He was there already when I got there. I couldn't communicate with him, though. You had him sort of locked up."

Jim winced internally. Now that Angie had identified Gorbash as the other mind in the back of Jim's, he could feel the original owner of the dragon body strongly. Gorbash had evidently returned to his own head back during that moment in the dragon caves, when Jim—alone with Angie—had been as good as knocked out by some invisible force. Now Jim could feel Gorbash clearly—wanting control of his own body again.

"Three!" Carolinus was saying, staring at Jim.

"What do you mean, 'locked up'?" Jim asked Angie, feeling a twinge of conscience toward the dragon.

"I don't know how else to describe it," said Angie. "You've been sort of holding his mind down with yours —that's the best explanation I can give you. I didn't *see* any of this, you understand, I could just feel what was going on. He couldn't do a thing unless you got emotionally wound up about something and forgot him for a moment."

"Three!" Carolinus repeated. "Three minds in one skull! Now that really is going over the line, Dark Powers or not! Auditing Department, are you copying all this—"

"Not their fault," said the voice out of thin air.

"Not . . . ?"

"Not the fault of the Dark Powers that Gorbash was there," explained the Auditing Department. "They did put the Angie-mind in with the James-mind, but the responsibility for the presence of the Gorbash-mind lies outside our departmental area."

"Ah. Complicated matter?" asked Carolinus.

"Decidedly. Wheels within wheels. So if you'll start to straighten things out as soon as possible—"

"Count on me," said the magician. He turned back to Jim and Angie. "All right, now. What do you want? Am I to send you both back?"

"That's right," said Jim. "Let's go."

"Very well," said Carolinus. He looked at Angie. "And *you* wish to return?"

She looked at Jim for a moment before answering.

"I want whatever Jim wants . . ." she said.

Jim stared at her, bewildered.

"What sort of an answer is that?" he asked. "What do you mean?"

"I mean what I say," Angie said, with a hint of stubbornness in her voice. "I want what you want —that's all."

"Well, I want to go back, of course. I just said so." She looked away from him.

"Very well," Carolinus agreed. "If you'll both move over here by me—"

"Wait!" said Jim. "Wait just a minute!"

He turned to face Angie.

"What's all this?" he demanded. "Of course we're going to go back—just as quick as we can. What else can we do? There's no choice about this!"

"Of course there's a choice," said Carolinus, irritably.

Jim looked at the magician. The old man appeared tired and cross.

"I say, of course there's a choice!" repeated Carolinus. "You've now got sufficient credit with the Auditing Department for a return. You can spend it all going back; or stay and keep some of it to help build your life here. It's up to you. Make up your mind, that's all!"

"Stay, James," said Brian, quickly. "Malencontri can be yours—yours and the Lady Angela's, just as we promised earlier. Together, our two estates and families will be too strong for any enemies."

Aragh growled, a wordless sound. When Jim looked over at him, the wolf glanced away.

Jim turned back at Angie. He was feeling completely mixed up.

"Come on," said Angie, putting her hand on his massive dragon-shoulder. "Let's go and talk for a second."

She led him toward the side of the causeway. By the edge of the water, they stopped and Jim heard the lapping of tiny waves against the edge. He looked down into her face.

"Did you really know everything I did?" he asked.

She nodded.

"Everything you did and thought!"

"Hmm." Jim remembered a stray thought or two he had had about Danielle.

"That's why I believe you ought to think about this."

"But what do *you* think?" he insisted.

"I said what I think. I want whatever you want. But what do *you* want?"

"Well, of course I want to get back to civilization. I'd think we'd both want that."

Again she said nothing. It was very irritating. It was as if she forced his words to hang in the air in front of his nose, staring back at him.

"Hmm!" he growled to himself.

It was ridiculous, he thought, to suppose that he could want anything other than to go back. His job was waiting for him at Riveroak, and sooner or later they would be finding someplace to live—admittedly, nothing palatial—but it would be at least a one-room and kitchenette. And later on, when they both had teaching positions, they could move up to something better. Meanwhile, back there they had all the blessings of civilization—doctors, dentists, accountants to figure out their bills, time off every summer to do what they liked . . .

Moreover, all their friends were back there: Danny

Cerdak; and, well, Grottwold . . . Here, there were only a bunch of strange characters they had met only the week before last: Brian, and Aragh, Carolinus, Danielle, Dafydd and the dragons and so forth . . .

"To hell with it!" said Jim.

He turned around to take his decision back to Carolinus, with Angie trotting along beside him. No one was looking at them now, however. All were facing the approaching figures of Giles o' the Wold and the men with him. The little army was a sorry looking lot, and many bore evidence of wounds, but they were smiling through their weariness as they began to report the final rout of Sir Hugh's men, now fleeing back in the direction of Castle Malencontri.

"And Sir Hugh?" Brian asked.

"Alive, worse the luck," Giles told him. "Though he was reeling a bit in the saddle, the last I saw of him. One of my men got a shaft through his armor, and he'd be losing blood. Less than half his men go back with him."

"Then we can take Malencontri before he can recoup his losses," Brian exclaimed. Then he frowned uncertainly and turned his face toward Jim. "That is, we could, if we had reason . . ."

"I'm staying here," Jim told the knight gruffly.

"Hurrah!" shouted Brian, throwing his helmet into the air and catching it, as if he was twelve years old.

"Very well!" Carolinus said, testily. "If that's your decision. You realize that if you spend your credit with the Accounting Department to get your own body back here, you won't have enough left over to change your mind and return whence you came? You'll have enough to get you started here, but not enough to get moved back, after all."

"I understand. Of course, I understand that."

"All right, then. Stand back, all the rest of you! We're going to be having two bodies where one is now. All right, then"—Carolinus lifted his staff and thumped its end down on the earth—"there you are!"

270

And there he was.

Jim blinked. He found himself looking directly into the dangerously toothed jaws of a dragon-muzzle less than six inches from his nose; and clutching a pillow to his body, which was now dressed only in what seemed to be a white hospital gown.

"Just who do you think you are?" demanded the dragon-jaws.

Jim took a couple of steps backward, partially to keep himself from being deafened and partially to get a better look at what was confronting him.

"Gorbash?" he said.

"Don't try pretending you don't know me!" said the dragon, which Jim was now seeing entire.

It—Gorbash—was a very large and fierce-looking animal. Larger and fiercer than Jim had realized, from his experience inside the body.

"Of—of course I know you," Jim gasped.

"You certainly do! And I know *you*. I ought to. Who do you think you are, taking over somebody else's body, doing what you want with it and treating the dragon who really owns it as if he just appeared in it yesterday? All the time using it the way you choose to. Mishandling it, taking risks with it! Would anybody believe what this george did with my body in just the first few days after he had it?"

Gorbash turned appealingly to the others standing around.

"Shut me up completely. Wouldn't let me twitch a muscle—in my own body, mind you! Then, before I could think, he went headfirst off a cliff and started flailing around with my wings so much that I could barely get them beating properly in time to keep us from smashing on the rocks. Then, he nearly got the Mage here to turn us into a beetle. Next, he overflew and got my muscles stiff. Then, instead of resting up, he swims—mind you, *swims*—across all sorts of water in the fens. Never a thought about our toes and vicious sea turtles or giant sea lampreys come into the tidewater. And that's only the beginning. Then—"

"I—I didn't end up in your body on purpose," protested Jim.

"But you certainly acted like you owned it from the minute you got there! And don't interrupt!" Gorbash roared, resuming his appeal to the audience. "And that was just the beginning. He nearly got us eaten by sandmirks, *did* get us nearly killed by the horn of that other george, and never a bite to eat or a drop to drink . . . er, except for that time at the inn. But that hardly counts!"

"Oh, it doesn't, doesn't it!" cried Secoh. "I heard about that feast of yours at the inn. All the lovely meat without hardly any bones you could stuff into you! All the rich, rich wine! It wouldn't be James who wanted to drink that cellar dry, and you know it as well as I do—"

"WHAT? *Shut up, mere-dragon!*" boomed Gorbash.

Secoh gave a sudden bounce that landed him nose to nose with Gorbash, who reared back instinctively.

"I will not shut up!" roared Secoh. "I don't have to shut up! I'm as good as any other dragon, mere-born or not."

"Mere-dragon, I'm warning you . . ." Gorbash began ominously, beginning to hunch his shoulders and gape his jaws.

"You don't scare me!" cried Secoh. "Not anymore, you don't. It was your own grand-uncle taught me I didn't have to bow down to anyone. Death before dishonor! I've just fought a dragon as big as you were—to the death! Well, anyway, I helped your uncle fight him. *He* didn't scare me and *you* don't scare me. *You* haven't done anything—all you did was get carried along by what James wanted to do with your body. But you'll go around preening yourself for the next hundred years, talking about how you were in a fight with an ogre! All right, you go ahead, but don't try to push me around. I'll tear your wings off!"

And Secoh snarled into the very teeth of the bigger dragon.

Gorbash bobbed his head and looked uncertain.

"Yes, and another thing!" said Secoh. "You ought to be ashamed of yourself! If your grand-uncle was alive, *he'd* certainly tell you so. *He* was a real dragon! You're just one of those fat cave lizards. Here, James made you famous and all you can do is complain . . ."

"Ha!" said Gorbash—but he said it without quite the force he had in his words a moment before. He looked away from Secoh toward the others. "I don't have to worry about what some mere-dragon thinks. The rest of you were around and saw how it was with this george taking over my body—"

"And a good thing he did!" Danielle interrupted, sharply. "You don't sound like anyone I'd trust to face an ogre."

"I—"

"Gorbash," said Aragh, grimly, "you never had much in the way of brains . . ."

"But I—"

"Nor will I stand by and hear Sir James maligned," Brian announced. The knight's face was set and dark. "Another word from you, dragon, about this good knight and gallant gentleman and I'll find yet one more use for my sword this day, bent as it is from the worm."

"I'll help!" said Secoh.

"Enough!" snapped Carolinus. "Dragons, knights— you'd think there was nothing in the world but fighting, ready as you all are to do it at the drop of a leaf. Enough of this now! Gorbash, another word from you and you can be a beetle, after all!"

Gorbash collapsed abruptly. He thumped down on his haunches and began making choking noises.

"You don't have to cry!" said Danielle, slightly less sharply. "Just don't go around making foolish statements like that."

"But you don't know!" mourned Gorbash, in his sub-bass voice. "None of you know! None of you understand what its been like. One minute, I'm counting my diam—cleaning my scales. And the next, I'm in some tiny magician's room aboveground, and this george—I don't know if he was the Mage there or not—bending over me. Naturally, I get up and start to tear him apart, but all I have is a sort of george-body, no claws at all, no teeth to speak of . . . And a lot of other georges come in and they try to hold me, but I get away and run out of this large castle I'm in and some georges dressed all in blue, with clubs, corner me; and one hits me over the head with his little club. That george's head I've got can't even stand a little hit like that; and the next thing I know I'm back in my own body, but this george called James is already there, and he keeps me crowded back into a corner so that I can't do a thing unless he's so busy he almost forgets about me. I can't even do anything when he's asleep, because when he goes to sleep the body goes to sleep and I have to go to sleep, too. That time in the inn when we drank a little wine is the only time I got loose at all, and if I hadn't been so hungry and thirsty—"

"Gorbash," said Carolinus. "Enough."

"Enough? Oh, all right." Gorbash gulped and fell silent.

"Speaking of wine, Mage," said Brian, a little hoarsely, into the stillness. "Can you do something? It's been a day and a night since any of us ate. A day since we drank—and nothing but the water of the few fresh ponds of the meres for drinking, even now."

"Also, if nothing else," put in the clear voice of Danielle from where she still sat on the ground beside the bowman, "Dafydd needs shelter and warmth for the night; and he's in no condition to travel. Can't your Auditing Department do something for him, after all he did for *it?*"

"His credit lies in another area," Carolinus explained.

"Look," said Jim, "you said I'd have some credit left over with the Auditing Department even after getting my body back, if I decided to stay here. Let's use some of that to get food, drink and shelter for every-one."

"Well, perhaps . . ." Carolinus answered, gnawing his beard. "However, the Auditing Department doesn't keep a kitchen and a cellar stocked for entertainment. But I *can* use some of your credit, James, to move everyone to where food and drink are available."

"Go ahead," Jim suggested.

"All right, then"—Carolinus raised his staff and struck its end against the ground once more—"done!"

Jim stared around him. They were no longer on the fenland causeway by the Loathly Tower. They were back once more before the establishment of Dick Inn-keeper. The sunset was rosy behind the treetops to their west and a gentle twilight held everything. A mouth-watering smell of roasting beef came from the open doorway of the inn.

"Welcome, welcome, travelers!" called Dick, him-self, bustling out of the open door. "Welcome to my inn, whoever ye may—"

He broke off, his jaws dropping.

"Heaven help me!" he cried, turning to Brian. "Sir knight, Sir knight, not again! I can't afford it. I simply can't afford it, no matter how many times you're af-fianced to milady in the castle. I'm only a poor inn-keeper, and my cellar holds only so much. Here you are now with not one dragon but two, and at least one other—uh—" He stared doubtfully at Angie, and at Jim, still dressed in his hospital gown. "Gentleman and lady?" he wound up a questioning note; and added hastily, "Plus the Mage, of course. And all the rest . . ."

"Know you, Dick," said Brian, sternly, "that this other gentleman is Baron James Eckert of Riveroak, just lately freed from his ensorcelment into the body of the dragon, after slaying an ogre at the Loathly Tower and defeating the Dark Powers who threatened us all. This is his lady, the Lady Angela. Over there you see the dragon—Gorbash, by name—in which the ensorcelment took place. You can even see the scar of Sir Hugh's lance upon him. Beside him is a dragon of the meres and fens—Secoh, by name—who despite his smaller size has fought most valiantly this day—"

"No doubt, no doubt!" Dick was wringing his hands. "A worthy company, indeed. But Sir knight, *someone* must pay me this time. I . . . I must insist."

"Unfortunately, Dick," said Brian, "sensible as I am of your situation and the strain our party threatens to put upon it, I am not wealthy myself, as you know. Nonetheless, as I did previously, I will pledge—"

"But pledges do me no good, Sir knight—with all respect!" cried Dick. "Can I feed other travelers with the pledges, which is all I will have left after you and your friends have been accommodated? And if I cannot feed travelers, what will become of me and mine?"

"Carolinus," Jim offered, "I've still got some credit left, haven't I? Why don't we use that to pay Dick?"

"It's not that kind of credit," said Carolinus, grumpily. "For an instructor in the arts, your ignorance is appalling sometimes, James."

"Dick Innkeeper," said Danielle, and her voice had an edge to it that made all look at her, "whether or not you feed and house me, or these others—all but one—means nothing to me. But Dafydd needs warmth and sustenance; and I give you fair warning, if it becomes necessary for—"

"Not necessary," growled Aragh. "Though if it comes to that, there is an English wolf at your side. But we've no problem here. Gorbash can afford to pay for the best for all—and will!"

"I . . . ?" Gorbash grunted like a dragon just hit in the solar plexus by a particularly powerful ogre. "I? I've practically nothing, no hoard at all to speak of—"

"You lie!" cried Secoh. "You were next of kin to that great dragon, your grand-uncle. As next of kin, you've been told where his hoard lies; and since he was very old he was very rich from years of hoarding.

You have two hoards, let alone one; and you're a wealthy dragon!"

"But I—" Gorbash began.

"Gorbash," said Aragh, "I've been a friend when you had none other, except your grand-uncle. This day you've lost him. You owe a debt to James and these others who've made life safe for you and touched you with the mantle of their courage. The least—I say, the least—you can do to discharge a part of that debt is to cease whining about what little you'll pay here. If you can't do that, you're no friend of mine and I leave you alone in the world."

"Aragh—" began Gorbash, but the wolf turned his back. "Wait, Aragh! Of course I didn't mean . . . Of course, I'm happy to make a, well, a celebratory feast in honor of my grand-uncle who slew the ogre of Gormely Keep and today in his old age . . . Well, what more do I need to say? Innkeeper, your best for these people, and you shall be paid in gold before we leave."

In a daze, Jim found himself ushered into the inn just behind Danielle and Dafydd, who was carried gently to the best bed and tucked in to recover under Danielle's care. In another room, Jim struggled into a number of clothes brought up from the store in the inn's basement; and eventually emerged, richly clad, with Angie, onto the grounds outside, to find that tables and benches laden with the materials for a feast had been already set up.

While they had been inside, the sunset had died completely and now night was come. Great torches on tall standards blazed all about them and made a warm cave in the new night. Their fires crackled and sparked around the long table with benches on either side. The surface of the table was hidden under roasts and joints, fruits and cheese and other food of all kinds; while at the far end stood a massive hogshead of wine, already tapped, and before that, a row of drinking vessels both human- and dragon-sized.

"Well done!" said the hearty voice of Brian behind them, and Jim and Angie turned to see the knight emerge from the inn, his eyes fixed on the table. "Dick Innkeeper has sent to tell Geronde we're here. She'll be joining us in a bit. Dick's really done us up well, eh, James?"

Brian had also dressed. He was out of his armor and wearing a scarlet robe Jim had never seen before. Jim suspected the knight of also benefiting from the inn's store of clothing. In the robe, belted around his narrow waist by a broad tapestry-like gold cloth holding a dagger in a gold sheath skeined with ivory threads, Sir Brian Neville-Smythe was a noble figure. The sight of him reminded Jim of his own inadequacies.

"Brian . . ." he began, awkwardly, "I should tell you something. You see, I really don't know a great deal about using a sword and shield, or a lance, or a great many things like that. I'm not sure how much use I'll be as a friend—now that I'm staying. I'm not even in training for the sort of thing you take for granted. It's not as if I still had Gorbash's dragon body, with all its muscles . . ."

Brian smiled.

"Well now, James," he said, "indeed, it will be a pleasure for me to train you myself in the noble use of arms and all else that becomes a gentleman of your rank. As for muscle, it would be strange if one of your size and thews could not make a good man of deeds."

"Size . . . ?" Even as Jim echoed the words, he realized he had been aware of what Brian was talking about for some time; in fact, ever since his mind had returned to his own body.

He had not paid real attention to it until this moment. He had seen how Angie had grown in translating to this world. But as he compared himself now to Brian, he faced the fact that beside him the knight looked no larger than a half-grown youth.

Understanding woke inside him.

He had forgotten one thing—or, in fact, a number of things: the suits of medieval armor he had seen in museums, the plans for medieval boats, buildings and furniture . . . In the European Middle Ages the average size of men and women was much smaller than it had become by the twentieth century, his own time. Jim had been merely middling tall in his own time and place. Here, he was a giant.

He opened his mouth to explain this, but before he could speak he felt Angie squeeze his arm. Behind Brian, others were coming out of the inn. Danielle, and Giles o' the Wold, closely followed by Carolinus, and two sons of Dick Innkeeper, who carried wooden platters and goblets. The heavy shapes of Gorbash and Secoh had also loomed up in the torchlight out of the darkness beyond the open terrace and now Aragh slipped up, too, to join them. There was a clean, fresh splint on the wolf's broken leg.

"The innkeeper says all is ready," he growled.

"God be thanked!" commented Giles. The leathery face of the outlaw leader was bent into new creases by a rare smile. "For, I vow, we were all close to failing there for lack of proper meat and drink."

"Amen!" said Brian, limping a little as he led the way toward the benches and the tables. "Take seats, friends, and let us all be joyous, for we're given pains enough in life so that we should not lack will to make good use of pleasure such as this, when it is truly earned."

DEL REY SCIENCE FICTION CLASSICS

FROM BALLANTINE BOOKS

CHILDHOOD'S END, Arthur C. Clarke	27603	1.95
FAHRENHEIT 451, Ray Bradbury	27431	1.95
HAVE SPACESUIT, WILL TRAVEL, Robert A. Heinlein	26071	1.75
IMPERIAL EARTH, Arthur C. Clarke	25352	1.95
MORE THAN HUMAN, Theodore Sturgeon	24389	1.50
RENDEZVOUS WITH RAMA, Arthur C. Clarke	27344	1.95
RINGWORLD, Larry Niven	27550	1.95
A SCANNER DARKLY, Philip K. Dick	26064	1.95
SPLINTER OF THE MIND'S EYE, Alan Dean Foster	26062	1.95
STAND ON ZANZIBAR, John Brunner	25486	1.95
STAR WARS, George Lucas	26079	1.95
STARMAN JONES, Robert A. Heinlein	27595	1.75
TUNNEL IN THE SKY, Robert A. Heinlein	26065	1.50
UNDER PRESSURE, Frank Herbert	27540	1.75